NATASCHA BIROVLJEV

SHADOW WOLF OF THE ROCKY MOUNTAINS

novel

TRANSLATED FROM GERMAN BY LEANNE LOCKWOOD CVETAN

Website: natascha-birovljev.com
Contact: autorin@natascha-birovljev.com

Based on: "Die Schattenwölfin der Rocky Mountains" by Natascha Birovljev
First published in Germany by NovaMD (nicht BOD), first edition 2021

Translation: Leanne Cvetan
Editor: Rachel Reynolds, e-Mail: rehildebrandt@gmail.com
Cover design: Kristin Pang · kristinpang.com
Layout and E-Book: BÜCHERMACHEREI · buechermacherei.de
Cover images: photomaster / shutterstock.com (wolf), Raphael Mathon-Goupil / shutterstock.com (mountains), Pakhnyushchy / shutterstock.com (clouds), KuLouKu / shutterstock.com (lights)

Imprint: North Raven Books

ISBN-Print 978-1-7782567-7-6
ISBN-EBook 978-1-7782567-8-3

Prologue

Two Wolves

The indigenous woman silently went to the fire, taking the enamel coffeepot, blackened with soot, off the flames. She poured the coffee into cups and handed them to the listeners who had accepted her invitation to gather around the campfire. Before returning to the blanket she had laid out next to the fire, she lovingly stroked her son's black hair.

The trees around them cast eerie shadows. The fire crackled, its orange flames surging toward the sky. She looked over to the indigenous man standing near the edge of the forest, wearing his traditional suede leather garb. He nodded to her, and she returned his greeting. She waited patiently until everyone had made themselves comfortable and the attention of her mostly white audience silently fell to her.

"The light and the dark," she began. "They are like the two wolves that live in our hearts."

"What does that mean?" her son asked with sparkling eyes.

The woman threw him a stern glance; he ought to know by now that impatience ruins a story and upsets the spirits, as they were also listening. But her son had asked her already so many times before to tell this legend, and his spirited enthusiasm made her smile. She held up a pouch from around her neck that had been concealed by her jacket and with the tips of her two fingers, took out a pinch of dried sage and sweetgrass. With a flick of her wrist, the herbs flew up and scattered over the fire. This was meant to appease the spirits one more time. She inhaled the fragrant smoke, looked around at the others, and began telling them the ancient legend of the two wolves:

"In each and every one of us there lives two wolves. One with light fur and one with dark fur. The light wolf embodies everything that we hold as good. Joy, peace, love, hope, friendliness, goodness, empathy, generosity, truth, and all that is light within us. In the shadow wolf lives anger, jealousy, sadness, arrogance, self-pity, and other negative feelings. Every one of us experiences the struggle for dominance between the two wolves, for both animals live inside the hearts of each one of us."

"And which wolf wins?" her son asked. This time, she nodded at him. It was an important question.

"The one you feed," she answered.

"Then I will only feed the light wolf."

Some of the other listeners nodded and exchanged a few words.

The storyteller raised her hand, and the murmuring stopped. She knew that most people were scared of the dark wolf. It lingered just outside their field of vision, avoiding all light.Only the very few possessed the courage to search the shadows for him. Others feared they might uncover something sinister if they got too close to the slumbering wolf.

"Remember, my son, if you only feed the light wolf, the dark wolf will always be there around every corner, waiting for you. For even without sustenance, he remains a part of you."

A young man laid more wood on the smoldering fire, poking at the embers until the light of the flames burned brightly again. Mindful that no one dwelled on the shadows of their lives with pleasure, the narrator continued: "The dark wolf will continue to strive for the attention he needs."

"But what can we do about it?" The question came from a girl sitting next to her son.

"We must acknowledge that along with our light side, we each carry facets of darkness around inside us. It does no good to suppress them or deny them. Only once we accept our dark side can we find our center, but finding this inner balance remains one of our greatest challenges."

The woman took a sip from her cup, taking in the sweetness of the maple syrup she had added to the bitter coffee, as she thoughtfully studied the faces around her. It was obvious that her listeners, residents of the local community, as well as from towns further out, were not heeding only to her words; they were beginning to form their own ideas. One man cleared his throat. With a nod, she invited him to speak.

"But if the shadow wolf is the embodiment of negativity, why should I give it attention?"

"The dark animal also has worthwhile qualities, such as patience, determination, and fearlessness. He is decisive and persevering. In him are the virtues that the light wolf does not possess. We need these for the times when the light wolf has no authority, for he too has his weaknesses. If you feed them both and look after them well, they will become a part of something much bigger inside of you and can nurture harmony. Once you have achieved that, you will no longer feel yourself being pulled in opposite directions, but will be able to hear your inner voice. It will guide you to the right path."

"That sounds ideal," a young woman said.

"And it is," the narrator concurred. "A person who lives with both their dark and their light wolf in harmony inside them has everything they need. But a person at war with themselves has nothing. Life can be happy or sad, beautiful or cruel—we create our own story. We experience love and hate, peace and loss. That is life."

Again, a murmur rippled through the audience. The First Nations woman allowed this unrest to continue for a few minutes, then she cleared her throat. Her voice was penetrating. "Keep this legend in your hearts, always be conscious of your shadows. They belong to you just as much as the light. Never underestimate this animal with its piercing gaze and disheveled fur. It is dark like the night. Welcome it into your midst."

The sound of a wolf howling rang out in the distance. The woman got to her feet and listened. From some other distant spot, a second wolf answered. Smiling, the narrator extended both her arms. Her son stood up and put his hand in hers; together they disappeared into the darkness of the trees.

(Loosely based on a Cherokee legend)

May

The smell of coffee made its way to Woodwind's nose. Dammit, he had wanted to be gone before Una got up. He yawned as he rubbed his eyes, threw back the comforter, and sat up on the edge of the bed. He loosened the leather band around his wrist and used it to tie back his black hair. Then he stood up, collected his clothes that were strewn across the wooden floor, and got dressed. He quietly left the bedroom and observed Una in the small kitchen. Dressed in only a T-shirt, the young woman stood at the window, gazing out at the gray May morning while sipping from her mug. Woodwind shot a glance at the front door, then sighed and crossed the hallway into the kitchen.

"I have to go," he said.

Una turned around. "At least stay for breakfast. Coffee's already done." She smiled, but her eyes didn't. She knew what he would answer.

"Thanks for the offer, but I'd better be on my way."

Her shoulders stiffened, and she briefly pursed her lips. "Will I see you this evening?"

"We really shouldn't." He stepped closer and cupped her cheek in his hand. She pressed her cheek into it briefly, but then shook it away.

"I'm sorry. You deserve a better man than I'm capable of being," he muttered. He didn't know how to respond to her abrupt sullenness.

A thin smile played on her lips. "You have nothing to apologize for. Neither of us wanted a permanent relationship. I'm just sad that our time together is over." Her hazel eyes now gazed softly at him. She leaned forward and kissed him. It was more of an airy graze than an actual kiss, and her touch communicated both hope and goodbye. He looked at her questioningly.

"Next week, my relative who owns this house will be returning from her trip abroad, and I'll be moving back in with my dad at the reserve. My little brother Nuka is back too. He needs me."

Woodwind nodded. Continuing his relationship with her under these conditions was indeed impossible for the time being. Ever since he'd moved onto the reserve a year ago, her father had had his eye on him. Bull was sure to give him and Una hell if he ever found out about their relationship. "Take care of yourself, Una. I really like you."

"I know. You take care too, flute maker," she said. "See you whenever."

Out in front of the small house, located a few miles outside the reserve, he got into his shabby old car and drove off. He was going to miss the intimacy that had sprung up between him and Una. Before he'd met her, he'd been with a multitude of other women, but none of them had enchanted him as much as Una. However, since he wasn't made for long-term relationships, Una's offer of a friends-with-benefits type of affair had hit the mark. Woodwind knew that she didn't intend on staying at the Sunchild Reserve, but she also never told him the reason why she'd dropped out of college and moved back home.

Twenty minutes later, he arrived at his own house on the Sunchild Reserve. He wanted to take a shower and then head off to the animal rescue center where he'd taken over as director a few months prior. His neighbor was once again busy tinkering on the truck parked in his driveway. The guy seemed to do nothing else the entire day but stand there with his head stuck under the hood, fixing this or that. Woodwind parked, got out, and gave the man a nod.

"So you've made another woman unhappy, eh?"

"What's it to you?"

"Monogamy doesn't seem to be your strong suit, does it? If you keep on like that, they're going to kick you off the reserve."

"Is it my fault if the other guys are too stupid to know how to keep a woman happy?" Woodwind retorted, tearing off a flier taped to the front of his mailbox before striding inside. His neighbor was right, and he knew it. There was a group of men on the reserve who weren't all that enthusiastic about him. They were jealous of his success with the ladies, and many of them distrusted him simply because he'd spent time in prison. He glanced at the flyer in his hand; it was an announcement for the upcoming community gathering. Participation was voluntary, but essentially, everyone who resided on the reserve was expected to attend at least one such meeting a month. So far, he'd managed to avoid going to any, which only prolonged his status as the new guy whom no one here really knew as of yet.

Apart from Chinook, the chief shaman of the Sunchild Reserve. He was the one who had advocated for Woodwind's acceptance into the community and had procured this house for him. The rent he paid to the reserve was next to nothing, and Woodwind made an effort to maintain a sort of friendly rapport with Chinook at least. Sighing, he balled up the paper and threw it in the garbage. He could only imagine all too well the way the other residents would spin some story about him if he showed his face at one of these meetings. No, thank you.

As he stood under the shower, he recalled his neighbor's words. Woodwind hadn't truly been in love with any of the women he'd fleetingly known, not even Una, but that was altogether his own fault. His capacity for love had vanished ten years ago when he lost his fiancé and their unborn child in a car accident. He had been in the driver's seat after having had too much to drink, and had crashed into a tree. He rubbed his skin dry with the towel until it hurt. All of that was behind him now, dammit. He had paid his debt to society and was trying to make a new home for himself here, a future. He didn't need to justify himself to anyone else.

They all need to mind their own business, he thought as he slipped on some fresh clothes and drove to the wildlife center.

"No, that board goes over there," Rosie called out to her brother, Jim, standing on the cabin's crooked porch.

Jim nodded and put in a few screws to attach the shelf to the timber wall. Rosie looked at it critically from a few different positions, then she waved him over.

"Do you think it's too low? I wanted to put flower pots on it."

Jim shrugged. "Looks good. I'm starving. Are you going to feed me before I go?"

"I'll give Hazel her food and then make us something to eat," she replied, grinning. Upon hearing her name, the dog came trotting over. Rosie affectionately ran her hand over the dog's long ears and led her into the house. After spooning the rest of what was left in the can into the dog's bowl, she set a pot of water on the gas stove. Her brother came in and took off his jacket and boots.

"Is spaghetti and meatballs okay for the best brother in the world?"

Jim made himself comfortable on the large leather couch. "Sounds delicious. So I'm your favorite brother, eh? Don't let Darryl and Bob hear that."

She smirked as she took a can of root beer out of the fridge and tossed it over to Jim. At twenty-four years old, Rosie was only three years younger than Jim, while her two other brothers were eight and ten years older than her. Both Darryl and Bob were married, had kids, and good paying jobs in the energy sector. Jim had two college degrees and worked as an environmental consultant for a nationwide Canadian sawmill. Their parents were proud of their sons. "Ambition and hard work will help you reach your goal. Make a plan for yourself and go after it," her mother always said, and Rosie's brothers had accomplished exactly that. Whenever she compared her life with those of her brothers, she felt like a leaf in the wind.

"It was really nice of Uncle Eric to let you take over the cabin," said Jim. "And once you've taken care of these few small repairs, you'll have a real cozy place here."

Rosie smiled as she prepared the sauce. Her uncle, who was in his mid-sixties, was a fur trader and was now married to Jeanne, the love of his life, since last summer. "We love each other," her uncle had said at first. "But that doesn't mean that we can stand being around each other every single day." But then a few weeks ago, the couple had thrown caution to the wind, and Eric had moved into Jeanne's little house at Willow Ranch. And he'd offered Rosie, who was living with him at the time, the chance to rent his cabin from him. For the first time in her life, she lived alone. It still felt a little strange, but it was good. She took a bag of meatballs out of the freezer and added them to the tomato sauce.

"Are you getting paid enough to cover your rent and food and all that?" Jim asked, pulling her out of her thoughts.

"I can manage." She placed two plates and glasses on the small dining table along with knives and forks.

Jim stood up and set the table. "Are you sure you won't get lonely out here? This cabin is pretty remote."

"I've got Hazel to keep me company."

A little while later, they sat down to eat. Rosie was glad to see Jim clean his plate. When he was finished, he looked at the clock. "I'd better get home. I've got a number of important business meetings with Japan next week. Video conferences at ungodly hours."

They got up and put their dishes in the sink.

Rosie and Hazel walked Jim to his truck.

"Thanks again for your help and for the wood."

"Don't mention it, Sis. I can come again next weekend to help you around the cabin."

"But only if it's no trouble. I can manage the majority of it on my own," she said.

"I know. But you won't be able to lift up those heavy wooden beams by yourself and screw them in." He grinned at her.

She smiled back. "Yeah, you're right. Then I'll see you next week." She gave him a hug and watched his truck drive away until the rear lights disappeared around the curve. A slight feeling of loneliness washed over her, and she wrapped her arms around herself. Hazel had gone into the paddock and was sniffing around the hayrack. Rosie strolled over to her. "Would be nice to have horses here again, wouldn't it?" She ran her hand over the fence. Even though she was surrounded by horses all day long working over at Willow Ranch, it wasn't the same thing. When she and Calvin had been dating, she had worked at his father's riding stables and had observed how they trained the ranch horses.

Most people underestimated just how much a horse needed to be able to do in order to actually be of use to a rancher. There was only one outfit in all of Alberta that offered a professional training certification program to a select number young people every year. As far as Rosie knew, only two women had successfully completed the training at Gordsteen's thus far. Calvin considered paying for such training to be nothing more than a waste of money. He himself took part in rodeo events, and had always encouraged her to try to make a name for herself by competing in barrel racing competitions. "When I see you fly around those three-ton barrels in your rodeo outfit, I can't get enough of you," he had often crooned. Unfortunately, she wasn't the only cowgirl he had said that to.

When their relationship had ended, she had also given up rodeo riding without many regrets. Her heart lay more with ranch horses, and she'd loved to be certified by Gordsteen's.

The stars were starting to appear in the sky as Rosie and Hazel returned to the house. She wanted to make a list of her income and expenses, just to have a better idea. If she was frugal, maybe she could fulfill her dream of applying to Gordsteen's. And if everything went smoothly, even bring a few horses here. With a smile on her face, she got busy with her calculations, but her good mood quickly faded. Without additional sources of income, her dream wasn't going to come true anytime soon.

Cody turned down the radio as he exited the highway onto the gravel road. In another fifteen minutes, he'd arrive at his parents' dairy farm. The last time he'd been here was for his older brother's funeral a few months ago. Cody sighed and ran his fingers through his hair. Scott. He never would've thought that he would take his own life. The letter he had left behind consisted of only two words. *I'm sorry*. Cody wasn't sure if he wanted to know the reason why he had done it, though the question nagged at him constantly. He felt like he would never understand his brother's actions. Just as he would never understand why his father couldn't give him a hug at the funeral. The older man had simply offered to shake Cody's hand, his eyes somber and full of grief.

Cody swallowed. The memories connected to the funeral as well as the neighbors urging him to take over Scott's position at the farm and later inherit it were unbearable. That would mean he'd have to stay and help his parents manage the farm with its one hundred and fifty cows. Cody could still almost feel the countless hands clapping him on the back, each one like the blow of a hammer, nailing him to this place. He could hardly wait to leave the farm again. With the excuse that he was needed at the Willow Ranch, he had left as the last funeral guests were departing.

And now, he was on his way back because his father had broken his leg and his mother had pleaded with him to come.

Luckily, his boss and the owner of Willow Ranch, Lee, had given him two days off. He didn't need any more than that, Cody had assured him. There was no way he had planned to stay any longer. He had plans to ask the neighbor to help out until his father had recovered and was back to work. As the entrance to the farm came into view, he smoothed back his hair and put on his cowboy hat that was lying on the passenger seat. *Tippet Dairy Farm est. 1906*, the sign over the driveway read. The farm had been in their family for more than a hundred years, and for Scott, it had always been clear that he would be the one to take it over some day. But now he was dead. What had happened? What had sent him over the edge? Cody squelched these thoughts once he caught sight of his mother coming out of the house. She must've heard his truck pulling up. She had probably been watching the driveway from the kitchen window ever since he'd told her an hour ago that he was just about to leave Willow Ranch. He parked and got out.

"Hi, Mom."

"Hello, Honey." She threw her arms around him, and it felt more like she was clinging to him than hugging him. She smelled of freshly baked bread and rosemary. "Thank God you're here."

His mother had always been a full-figured, perennially cheerful woman. However, from her eyes and her now sunken features, he could see she was weighed down by a weary despondency.

"How's Dad?" He followed her into the house with his bag thrown over his shoulder.

"It was a complicated fracture, but they're releasing him tomorrow. The doctors have ordered strict bed rest. He's got a full leg cast for three weeks, and then they'll put him in a walking cast."

Cody pulled off his boots in the hallway. "I can only stay for two days," he declared as he followed his mother into the kitchen. He poured himself a cup of coffee from the thermal carafe on the table.

"But your dad needs you here now. Surely you can take vacation time. Lee Myers seems like a real nice boss and would certainly understand given the circumstances."

"It's just not possible," he interrupted her, pouring creamer into his coffee. "I'll have a talk with the neighbors. Maybe they can come and help out in the meantime. Otherwise, you'll just have to hire someone."

His mother set a plate of cookies on the table and sat down across from him. "We can't afford to pay someone full-time."

Cody raised one eyebrow. He had always assumed that the farm was doing well financially. At least during his sporadic telephone conversations with Scott, he had never mentioned any money problems, though it had been years since he'd spoken with his father about any business concerning the farm. "I'm sure we can come up with a solution," he replied evasively.

His mother placed her hand on top of his. "Honey, I know that you and your father don't always see eye to eye. But now that Scott ... I mean, now that he's not here ..." Her words were choked by a sob, and she quickly wiped away the tears that were filling her eyes.

"Oh, Mom. You know that I'm the last person in the world that Dad would want to have on the farm. Besides, I don't know the first thing about dairy farming. I'm a cowboy. Horses are what I know."

"You grew up here. It's in your blood."

Dad doesn't think that, he thought, but remained silent. There was no point in explaining to her that it was more than just a difference of opinion between them. He needed to find someone who could help give his parents a hand. There was no way he was going to give up his job at Willow Ranch.

Woodwind concluded his inspection round of the wildlife center, strolling along the narrow pathway between the enclosures. All of the rescue center's residents had been taken care of. With Maja and the group of volunteers, he had an excellent team on his side. He heard a car engine and glanced up. Was that someone bringing in a new animal in need of help?

Woodwind returned to the main building through the back door, passing through the small kitchen which doubled as the feeding station near the building's entrance. A black Labrador ran toward him, panting and wagging his tail like mad.

"Hi, Mr. Mud, you old stinker. Where's your mom?" He rubbed the dog's head and saw his brother Lonefeather coming in the door with his girlfriend Lyla and another woman he didn't know. She was carrying a young child in her arms. Woodwind thought she looked to be in her mid-forties

"Hey, big brother. You busy?" Lonefeather asked.

"Not at all. I was just about to take a break. Have you guys got time for a cup of coffee?"

"Yeah, sure. This is my aunt Ayita and her son Wynono, by the way," Lyla said.

"Hi, nice to meet you," said Ayita with a deep, velvety voice as she extended her hand to him. It was warm and slightly rough, and her handshake firm. Her dark eyes studied his face much like the fingers of a blind person.

"Woodwind Jones," he said, blinking and turned his attention to the little boy. He was playing with his mother's long braid and eying him critically.

"Hello, Wynono, how old are you," he asked with a smile.

"He's three," Ayita said quickly as she set down the fidgety toddler.

Wynono walked over to the dog and wrapped his fingers around its collar, and the two of them set off to explore the building together. Mud, who knew the wildlife center like the back of his paw, seemed to be showing the little boy all his favorite places. Woodwind grinned. "The two of them seem to be an inseparable team."

"Wynono and Mud were already inseparable when I was in the Yukon last year," Lyla explained.

"My son has missed his four-legged babysitter very much. They seem to understand each other despite their lack of words."

Ayita sounded sad, and Woodwind's mind immediately flew to the thought that Wynono might be deaf. He also seemed rather small for his age, but what did he know about kids? Besides, it wasn't any of his business. Lonefeather came up next to Woodwind. "Let's go make some coffee." He playfully punched him in the side.

"And we'll go find Wynono and Mud, and meet you out on the porch. This May is turning out to be so beautiful." Lyla smiled and took her aunt with her.

In the small kitchen, Woodwind dumped a few tablespoons of coffee grounds into the filter, while Lonefeather retrieved some mugs from the cabinet.

"How are you doing?" Lonefeather asked.

"Just swell. Are you worried about me, little brother?"

Lonefeather held his gaze, waiting to hear the truth that Woodwind seemed reluctant to provide. "You seem a little low. When was the last time you did anything fun? Or played your flute?"

Woodwind shrugged, but then recalled the last time he had played it. Una had asked him to play her a song, but when he did, the melody sounded empty and meaningless. He stifled the memory. "The rescue center is keeping me busy."

"And how's it going at the reserve?" Lonefeather pressed.

Woodwind raised one eyebrow. "Why?"

"Oh, Chinook and I just had the impression that you didn't really feel at home there."

Woodwind poured water into the machine and turned it on. Then he stood with his back leaning against the cabinet and crossed his arms over his chest. "And why does the all-knowing shaman speak to you about it and not me?"

Lonefeather shrugged. "Chinook said he barely sees you, even though he's invited you a number of times to come by. And you aren't taking part in the monthly meetings at the community center either, are you?"

Lonefeather took the full coffeepot and filled the four cups. "You also haven't given them the opportunity to get to know you at all in the past few months."

Woodwind pulled out a tray and set the mugs on it along with milk and sugar. But before he picked it up, Lonefeather placed his hand on his shoulder.

"Brother, I'm not trying to tell you how to live your life. But if you want to continue living at the reserve, you're going to have to put in more effort into the community there."

"Maybe living there isn't for me." Woodwind could see from Lonefeather's expression that he didn't buy that. In all honesty, he didn't believe it himself either. He lifted the tray. "I got a lot on my plate, but I'll see if I can make time to go to the meeting on Sunday."

Lonefeather smiled and nodded. "Do that. Even a grizzly needs community."

"Oh, bear brother, you always think you know everything."

Woodwind turned and headed for the porch. Lonefeather followed him with the tray. Lyla and Ayita were sitting on the plastic chairs there, and he handed them each a mug. Wynono and Mud had made themselves comfortable underneath a nearby apple tree. The boy kept tearing off handfuls of grass and sprinkling them over the dog's fur. The Lab merely twitched one of his ears sleepily.

"Lyla told me that you took over the wildlife rescue center from her," Ayita said. "It must be nice to have such a worthwhile calling."

"Yes, I am very grateful to her for trusting me with it. I love working with the animals."

"And he's doing an amazing job," Lyla threw in. "Anyway, I'm more than happy that you took over the lead here, Woodwind. That gives me and Lonefeather time to implement our plans for the shop." She smiled at her partner.

"You two make a great team." Woodwind took a sip of coffee. "The shop can only be a success. Will you also be selling your handiwork there, Lonefeather?"

"No, I plan to continue making my dreamcatchers only by request for those who can't overcome their fears and grief."

"Sounds like a good decision, brother. Your magic is something sacred and can't be offset with any amount of money."

"Alongside my drawings, we also plan to sell Native artwork in the shop and earn a small commission on it. That will give unknown artists the chance to display their work."

Woodwind saw the joyful anticipation in Lyla's eyes at this new chapter in their lives and was happy for the couple. He turned to Ayita, who was pensively watching her son. Wynono was cuddled up against the snoozing dog and looked like he was just about to drop off himself.

"You've got a really quiet boy there. Is he always so content?" he asked, thinking of all the boisterous kids on the reserve whose mothers or older siblings were constantly out tracking them down.

Ayita studied him for a moment, then let out a sigh. "He's hardly slept the past few nights at Lyla and Lonefeather's cottage."

"When did you two arrive?"

"A week ago." She placed her mug on the table and stood up. "May I use the restroom?"

"Of course. It's the door just next to the kitchen."

She nodded and disappeared into the building.

"How long is she planning to stay?" Woodwind asked.

Lyla shrugged. "No idea. To be honest, I also don't know why she suddenly decided to come back after twenty-five years of being away."

"She's looking for something," Lonefeather said.

"Aren't we all?" Woodwind avoided his brother's inquisitive look and turned to Lyla instead. "Do you know why she moved up north back then? The Sunchild Reserve was her home."

"No, she won't talk about it." Lyla's eyes darted to Wynono, who had now gotten to his feet. "Honestly, my biggest concern is about him. When I met him last year, he was a lively child. But since he's been here, he hasn't said one single word."

"Maybe that's just the effects of the long trip and the new surroundings," Woodwind surmised.

"Maybe," she relented and cleared her throat. "Say, do you think you could look after Ayita and her son a little? I don't want to push her off, but Lonefeather and I just have so much to do. And the cottage is a little claustrophobic with the four of us there all day long."

"But she'll want to visit people at the reserve, won't she?" The thought of having Ayita and her son hanging around unsettled him in a way he couldn't explain.

"My aunt thinks she isn't welcome at the reserve. Only Chinook knows that she's back."

Woodwind wasn't surprised to hear what all the shaman was in on. Presumably, he knew Ayita would be coming before she even decided to make the trip. "I spend most of my time here at the center," he said. "I don't know if this is such a great place for a little kid."

"But you live on the reserve and can help Ayita feel at home there again. Take her with you to the meeting on Sunday."

Woodwind threw his brother a look of annoyance. "Ah, so that was what all that talk in the kitchen was about, was it?"

Lonefeather raised his hands. "No, Chinook and I really did talk about you."

Woodwind grunted. "I can take care of myself."

At that very moment, Ayita came back and walked over to Wynono who was dancing around Mud as he slept. She reached her hand out to her son, but the boy ignored her. She turned around. "Could we go around and have a look at the cages?" she asked.

"We should go," Lyla answered. "But maybe Woodwind has some time in the next few days to give you a tour." She winked at him, and he gave her a crooked smile in return. He wasn't about to make any promises.

"We'll see," he replied evasively, then accompanied his visitors to Lyla's car.

Rosie said goodbye to the mares on Willow Ranch. In only a few days, the first of the six of them should be giving birth; the rest of them were due to deliver within the next four weeks. She had taken over full care of the mares last spring. Before that, Lee's sister Lyla had cared for them. Rosie loved her job, even though she didn't particularly want to be doing it for the rest of her life. The conversation with her mother on the phone last night had given her much to think about.

"You need to have a plan, sweetie. You can't continue to spend your life this way; it's not sustainable. Look at your brothers. They've made their dreams come true, and have good careers and families."

"But, Mom, I don't want a career. And I have plenty of time to think about having kids. Plus, Jim—"

"Jim has been in a relationship with Martin for many years," her mother interrupted her. "I know you still think about that two-timer, Calvin, but you need to forget about him. Come up with a new plan, stick with it, and make it come true. And then, you can look for a husband."

Rosie didn't bother trying to convince her mother that she wasn't actually still pining after Calvin Dunn. However, she did feel a little lost in the world since she didn't have a plan for herself. Where had her ambition gone? What did she want to achieve in life at this point? Consumed with these questions, she bolted the doors to the barn. Lee and Naira, the owners of Willow Ranch, were coming her way, holding hands.

"Going out for a walk?" Rosie asked.

"Yeah, it's such a beautiful evening. Hopefully, we'll get lucky, and winter will finally be moving on soon," Naira answered.

Lee nodded. "We haven't had such a warm May in a long time. How are the little mothers getting along?"

"Every one of them is healthy and round." Rosie smiled. "They're all set for the night, and I'm just on my way home."

"Head on out. We'll see you in the morning." Lee nodded to her.

"Enjoy your evening," Naira added, and the couple continued walking toward the pastures.

Rosie watched them go; they were such a happy couple. Although Rosie knew that they'd faced a few hurdles over the past year, Lee and Naira's love had been strong enough to bring them back together. Naira was still living in her cottage, but Rosie was convinced that it was only a matter of time before she moved permanently to Willow Ranch. With their program for indigenous youth as well as the small bed and breakfast they ran, the couple had a common goal to work towards at the ranch, and Rosie envied them for their cohesiveness. What did it feel like to have a partner who actually supported you? Hazel appeared at her side and nudged her hand with her snout. Rosie smiled as she stroked the dog's head. "You're right, Hazel Mae, you and I aren't going anywhere. I can always count on you."

As she turned into her driveway twenty minutes later, Rosie wondered whose truck it was parked in front of her cabin. Hazel sat up, alert, and growled under her breath. "Well, girl, who do you think has come for a visit?"

The driver-side truck door opened, and a man got out. Doug? She pulled into her spot in front of the cabin's small porch. She hadn't seen him in over a year, when he had helped her string the Christmas lights around the outside of Eric's cabin. After that, he had disappeared on a special training exercise as a so-called smokejumper to Australia. She got out and returned his broad smile.

"Hey, girl, how you been?"

"Hello, Doug. What a surprise to see you! Have you been in Australia all this time?"

He ran his hands through his sandy blond hair. "No, my troop was only there for four weeks, then we were dispatched to California and a few other assignments after that. Basically, wherever they needed to send in groups of parachuting firefighters to any inaccessible areas. But I'm home now for a while and since we never exchanged phone numbers, I thought I'd just swing by and see how you were doing. You don't mind, do you?"

His boyish smile put a smirk on Rosie's face, and she shook her head. "Nah, no problem. Want to come in for a beer?"

"I'd love to." He followed her inside the cabin and looked around. "You live here alone now?"

She pulled two beer bottles from the refrigerator and handed him one. "Yeah, how did you guess that so fast?"

"From what you told me about your uncle back then, I suspect he wouldn't be a fan of that colorful rug or the scented candles, or uh ... this lamp shade." He was standing near the large paper shade hanging from the ceiling above the coffee table. The paper was printed with horses, and Rosie could tell from the look on his face that he thought it rather kitschy.

"I like it," she said off-handedly and sat down on the narrow armchair, while Doug settled on the couch.

Rosie took a long swig of her beer. "How long will you be home this time?"

"I don't have any assignments planned for the foreseeable future. Are you still working at Willow Ranch?"

She nodded, and Doug began telling her about his dangerous work and how much he loved fighting fires. Most of it sounded like something out of a Hollywood movie, and Rosie suspected he may have slightly exaggerated in a few spots. Nevertheless, he had a warm, soothing voice, and she was astounded to hear of all the different countries his work as a smokejumper had taken him. All of a sudden, her stomach rumbled so loudly that it made him hesitate.

"Sorry." She smiled apologetically, placing a hand over her stomach.

"No worries. After all, I did ambush you just as you came home from work. I should be going anyway. Do you have plans for the weekend?"

"I was going to paint the front deck if the weather's nice."

Doug set his beer bottle on the coffee table and stood up. "Okay, if you don't mind, I'd like to stop by again."

Rosie also got up and accompanied him to the door. "Sure. I even have two paint brushes."

"Great, then I'll see you soon." He grinned, took a step closer, and drew her into his arms for a hug.

She only came up as high as his chest, but she reveled in the feeling of security she found in his arms and briefly nestled into him. He kissed her on the cheek. "Good night, Rosie."

"Thanks for dropping by," she replied as she closed the door behind him.

The next few days flew by. The first of the foals was born at Willow Ranch, and Rosie spent two nights with the mares. During the birthing season, she spent more time at work than she did at home. Since the next birth wasn't due for a few more days, Lee had given her the weekend off. "If anything happens, I'll call you. Now you go and have a couple of nice days. I know you're in the middle of renovating," he'd said as he sent her out of the stables.

Since the temperature was nice enough outside, Rosie had started painting the deck on Saturday. Over and over again, she caught herself listening for the sound of a motor and hoping to see Doug's truck come up the drive. "You're such a dork," she told herself and was indeed disappointed that he still hadn't shown up by the end of the afternoon.

With a sigh, she wrapped her paintbrush in plastic wrap, washed her hands, and drove into town. Jim would be coming over tomorrow, and she had promised to put something on the grill for dinner. At the meat counter, she decided to buy three steaks. Maybe Doug would show up on Sunday, and if he did, she wanted to be sure there was enough food in the house.

Late Sunday afternoon, Jim arrived with another load of wood, and he surprised Rosie with a dog house for Hazel.

"It wouldn't hurt your couch potato of a dog to sleep outside sometimes during the summer," he said, petting the bloodhound on the head. "Since she doesn't need to be tied up like the rest of her species, she can at least keep the coyotes and bears away."

Rosie laughed and thanked him. She had rescued Hazel a few years ago from an animal trap. The poor thing had been half starved and had practically never strayed from Rosie's side ever since. Bloodhounds were known for needing to be leashed or fenced in, because their sense of smell was so strong that they couldn't help but wander away. But not Hazel Mae.

"Then I'd say, let's get started." Rosie put on her working gloves and started unloading the wood off the truck. After that, they replaced some of the rotten boards on the tool shed. And later, Jim got to work on the wooden base for the dog house while Rosie painted the porch.

Two hours later, she pulled off her gloves and wiped the sweat from her brow. The sun had smiled on them with another unusually warm day. "I'll get us something to drink. Do you want beer or water?" Rosie asked.

"Water'd be great." Jim stretched out his back.

Just as she finished filling up two bottles of water, her phone rang. The display said that it was her ex-boyfriend, Calvin Dunn, on the line. What did he want?

"Hello?" She answered.

"Hey, Rose, how are you?"

It annoyed her that he called her by the nickname he had used for her when they were still together.

"Everything's great. What are you calling about?"

"Maybe I just want to know if you're doing all right."

She rolled her eyes, but was unsettled by the warm feeling his familiar voice had sparked in her. They had been together for four years, and Rosie had believed that he was the one, up until a year and a half ago when her house of cards had collapsed and she had been left with no man, a job, and no place to live. She quickly suppressed these thoughts. "I'm in the middle of painting the porch. What do you want?"

"I need to find somewhere to rehome Lori. You remember, the American Paint, right?"

Rosie smiled. "Of course." Lori had been her favorite mare during the time she had worked and lived with Calvin at his father's riding stables.

Before she could ask, he continued. "I had her sired by Dragon. I know you don't know him," Calvin chuckled, "but it doesn't matter. I—"

"You bred Lori again? But she's sixteen!" she interrupted him.

"She's in good health, and this will be her last foal."

"Why can't she stay in the riding stables? There's enough room there."

"Well, uh, Dad wants to rent out the stables for folks to board their horses there. He claims that riding and training horses bring in more money than studding does. Besides, there's constant coming and going in the riding stables now that he has added on to it. Lori needs a quiet place to foal."

And so you thought of me, Rosie wondered. It didn't make any sense to her why he was asking her for help.

"I can ask around," she said, putting him off.

"Don't you live with your uncle anymore? He's got a small stall and a pasture if I remember correctly."

"Yes, but ..." She'd completely forgotten that she and Calvin had visited her uncle Eric at the cabin a few times.

"Once the foal is old enough, I could leave Lori with you. I remember how fond you were of her."

The front door to the cabin opened, and Jim stepped inside. "I am dying of thirst," he said. "What's taking you so long?"

She pointed at the phone and turned her attention back to the conversation. "Um, okay. I'll think about it."

"I have to know by next week," Calvin told her, and they ended the call.

Jim stood at the sink and drank from one of the water bottles. "Who was that?" he asked.

Rosie avoided answering; Jim didn't like her ex, mainly because Calvin hadn't treated her well and had also cheated on her. And then there was the fact her ex had made some disparaging remarks about gay people shortly before they broke up.

"Oh, just an old friend asking for a favor," she said hastily.

Jim looked at her skeptically. "An old friend, eh?"

"That's right," she mumbled, taking the other bottle of water and walking outside to the porch. Jim followed and stood next to her.

"Do you think the stall needs much fixing up?" she asked.

"Why? You looking to get a horse?"

"I might be."

The sound of a motor reached them as a green truck approached the cabin.

"You expecting company?"

"Um, that's Doug Fry. We know each other from, um, well ..." She was annoyed that she felt the need to justify herself to her brother. "I met him last year," she said and walked over to Doug, who was getting out of his truck.

He gave her a quick hug and looked at Jim. "I see you've found someone else to help you instead."

She was taken aback by his slightly accusatory tone.

"This is my brother Jim. He's helping me with the renovations."

Doug smiled, reached for her her shoulders, and pulled her close. "Ah, I see. No problem. Sorry I couldn't come yesterday. I had to help out a friend."

"That's all right," she replied, swallowing back her disappointment that he had only just now showed up. At the same time, Doug hadn't actually promised to help her. "Do you want to stay for dinner?"

"Sure, that'd be great," he answered with a grin.

She introduced the two men properly and then got started preparing the grill. She watched from the kitchen window as the two of them chatted. She could read from Jim's face that he didn't quite know what to think of this guy standing before him in his trendy ripped jeans, sneakers, and baseball cap. Typical Jim. No man was ever good enough for his little sister. Jim had always kept an eye on her. Her other brothers had also been protective of her, although they had gladly taught her how to change a tire, how to repair various things around the house, and how various machines work.

"Even as a girl, you still should be able to do things for yourself," Jim had said, before quickly adding, "just don't stay solo too long. A pretty girl like you needs a man by her side, if for nothing else than to keep all the scumbags from lurking around."

When Rosie was sixteen, her brothers had tried to set her up with guys they thought would be a good match for her. Most of that had completely backfired. And then a year later, Rosie had met Calvin. At first, he had treated her like a princess. And much to her parents' dismay, she gave up her plans of becoming an elementary school teacher and had moved in with him. Their relationship had ended bitterly, and she had struggled with grief for a long time afterwards. However, she had been left with her love of horses and had been overjoyed when her uncle Eric had offered her the job at Willow Ranch.

"The grill is ready for the steaks," Jim called out, pulling her out of her thoughts.

"I'll bring the meat right out," Rosie answered back.

Half an hour later, they were sitting at the table together, eating. Doug kept shooting her looks, to which she responded with a smile.

"I won't be able to help you out anymore for a while," said Jim. "The sawmill has got a massive order to fill, and I'll have to work over the weekends."

"That's all right. I can do the rest by myself."

"What do you mean by yourself?" Doug interjected. "Now, I might not be a farm boy, but I have muscles enough to complete any task." He winked at her.

Rosie noticed the skeptical look Jim gave him. "Don't look like that, big brother. You know me, I can help myself."

Jim rolled his eyes. Before he could say anything else, she stood up and cleared the table. "There are only a few little things left to be done," she said. "And for the rest, I don't have the money right now anyway."

"Do you aren't going to fix up the stall?" Jim asked.

Rosie set the plates in the sink. "I haven't decided yet," she admitted. "Hopefully, there isn't all that much to do there." Her phone beeped, but before she could grab it, Doug picked it up.

"A text from Calvin. Who's he?" he asked, gazing at the display.

"Rosie's idiot of an ex," Jim answered. "With whom she hopefully has nothing more to do. Was that your old friend from earlier?"

"That's my business." She snatched her phone back and folded her arms across her chest.

"Why did he call you?" Jim pressed.

"He's looking to rehome Lori. She's pregnant."

"Is Calvin looking to sell her?"

"No, I don't think so," Rosie stalled. "I still have to think about it, so just chill."

Jim now also stood up. "I just hope you'll stay away from him. I have to go. Thanks for dinner."

He hugged her and shook Doug's hand. "It was nice to meet you. Maybe we'll see each other again sometime soon."

"I'm sure we will. And don't you worry, I'll keep an eye on your little sister for you."

"Just watch you don't get burned," Jim replied as he left the house.

Doug went over to Rosie and tried to put his arms around her.

She pushed him away. "I don't need a man to look after me," she hissed.

He threw up his hands in concession. "Whoa there, slow down. I didn't mean it like that. I was only looking to pacify your over-protective brother."

"It's fine," she relented. "Jim just wants me to be happy."

"Don't you see, that's exactly what I want too." Doug reached out his hand. Rosie took it and let him pull her in for a hug.

Cody saddled Jazz, the Palomino gelding he had brought with him to Willow Ranch a year ago. Lee had asked him to inspect the fence around the western pasture. Last summer, Cody's job had been to take care of the pack horses that carried the equipment for the ranch guests into the mountains. Lee and Naira had altered the plan for this year. They would still be housing overnight guests who wanted to experience the great outdoors, but their main focus now lay on indigenous youth who would be staying at Willow Ranch and learning more about their traditions. For him, it was all the same thing, work-wise. He would continue to oversee the horses and accompany the summertime jaunts into the mountains.

Cody mounted Jazz and rode to the gate. He was able to open it easily from the back of his horse before heading to the western pasture. Despite his love for being in the saddle, he often felt awkward around other people and never knew what to talk about. But in the company of horses, he was at his best and understood them intuitively.

Jazz broke into a gallop, and Cody held on until they reached the fence. Reducing their speed, rider and horse strolled along the barbed wire, searching for spots that needed fixing. He was startled by the abrupt sound of his phone ringing. "That dumb thing," he cursed, pulling it out of the inside pocket of his jacket. "Hello, Cody Tippet here."

"Hi, it's your mom. Am I disturbing you?"

"It's okay. What's up?"

"Mr. McKnight said he has too much to do next week at his own place, and can't come help us milk the cows anymore or clean out the stalls."

"Did you ask the Vandermeers? They said they might be able to loan out one of their hands. Kurt knows the farm and all that needs to be done. I'm sure he'd help out."

"I did, but they want us to take over paying his salary to cover his work."

"Okay, and?"

"We can't afford that."

Cody tugged on the reins and brought Jazz to a halt.

"Honey, are you still there?"

"Yes. Listen, Mom. I'll see if I can get some time off again and come up with a solution, okay?"

"Then you'll come on Sunday?"

"I have to speak to Lee first, and I'll let you know." He hung up and took a deep breath. Dammit. He hated having to ask for days off again.

After he returned to the ranch, he tried distracting himself with work. By the late afternoon, his arms were sore from cleaning out the stables, and he was starving. The refrigerator in his trailer contained nothing except one yogurt, a jar of pickles, and two cans of soda. Great. Since he didn't feel like cooking something, he decided to shower and drive into town to Mary's diner.

The bells hanging above the door jingled when he entered the small restaurant an hour later. Only two tables were occupied. The diner made most of its money during the lunchtime hours and was only open until six-thirty in the evening. He saw a familiar figure sitting at the counter. He walked over to the young Native man and gave him a light slap on the back.

"Hey, Rabbit, how's it going?"

The man jumped and turned his head.

"Did you have to scare me like that?"

"Sorry, I didn't know you were so deep in thought. What's the trouble?"

Mary joined the two of them and glanced at Cody. "What can I bring you?"

"The daily special and a glass of water."

She nodded. "You want to order anything else, Ray?"

"Just give me some more coffee."

"Coming right up." The diner's owner returned with a jug of water in her hand and filled up one of the glasses on the table before turning around and disappearing through the swinging doors into the kitchen.

"Do you prefer to be called Ray or Rabbit?" Cody asked.

"It depends on who's talking to me. Not a lot of people know my native name, and that's okay. My real name is Ray Bull."

Cody took a sip of his water and recalled his first encounter with the young man, who was only a few years younger than him. He had met Rabbit last summer while accompanying an equestrian group from Willow Ranch into the mountains. The young man had been wandering on a pilgrimage together with a friend of his.

Mary set his plate in front of him, and Cody took a bite of the grilled ham and cheese sandwich. Out of the corner of his eye he watched Rabbit sip his coffee with a shuttered expression on his face. When he had first met him, Cody had thought the name Rabbit didn't suit his pal. With his wiry, almost haggard stature, he reminded Cody more of a young wild horse after a hard winter. But after their first meeting, something of a friendship had emerged between the two, and Cody soon came to understand why he was called Rabbit. His voice was soft and his demeanor initially reserved. Add to that his large dark brown eyes framed by jet black lashes, which had a certain alertness about them. Once Cody had shoved the last bite of his sandwich into his mouth, he turned to his silent friend. "Well, spit it out, what's bothering you?"

"My brother Nuka is back."

"Did he run away from his foster family?"

"No. After he and a pair of his buddies were charged with petty theft and graffiti tagging, they pretty much threw him out."

Cody took a drink of water. "Can they do that? Nuka is only fourteen."

Rabbit shrugged. "No idea. As far as I know he would have landed in a home if my father hadn't taken him back in."

Following the death of his wife five years ago, Jeremy Bull had given his nine-year-old son Nuka up to a foster family. Rabbit, who was sixteen at the time, had remained living in the house with his father at the reserve. To Jeremy, love meant running a tight ship.

"How are Nuka and your dad getting along?"

Rabbit groaned and shook his head. "They have one fight after the other. I've considered moving back in with my dad so I could keep an eye on Nuka, but he doesn't want anything to do with me. He hates me because he was pushed off on someone else while I was allowed to stay at home."

"That's a crappy situation," Cody mumbled.

"You can say that again. At least our older sister will be moving back in. I think Una might be able to get through to Nuka. She's eleven years older than he is and has Mom's patience." He took his last swallow of coffee and pushed the cup away. "I'm afraid that if no one has an eye on my little brother, sooner or later he's going to do something really stupid."

Mary cleared away the dishes. Cody paid for his dinner and for Rabbit's coffee. "Why don't you have a talk with my boss, Lee," he suggested. "Perhaps he'll have an idea how he can help both you and Nuka. This year at Willow Ranch, they're planning to host summer camps for indigenous youth."

"My dad would lose it if I went around telling people our family problems."

"You don't have to say anything about that," Cody said, but he could see from Rabbit's pursed lips that he wasn't open to the idea. "Then at least talk to Woodwind. He might have some advice."

"I thought about speaking to one of the elders, but most of them would turn right around and run to my father."

"Aren't the elders supposed to be the oldest members of the Council?" Cody asked, not really knowing too much about the societal regulations inside the reserve.

"Not necessarily. A person is not automatically an elder just because of their age. It has to do with their level of experience, their knowledge, their wisdom, and the things they do to enrich the community; that all plays a decisive role. To be an elder means that you've earned the community's respect and esteem."

"And what about the shamans? Are they automatically elders?"

"For the most part, yes. Did you know that the term shaman has its roots in Sanskrit and Chinese Buddhism? Nowadays, the term is used to describe native spirituality, but it's not actually the same thing."

"No, I didn't know that." Cody was impressed by Rabbit's knowledge.

"There isn't a straightforward translation for *wicasa wakan* in English. But we also use the word shaman or medicine man or woman." He waved off this last comment. "Sorry, I'm getting off-topic. Let's just say, an elder is not on the same level as a spiritual leader. This role is reserved for the shamans who are our holy men and women. Elders, whether young or old, are advisors in the forms of teachers, counselors, or masters of ceremony."

"You learn something new every day," said Cody, who was grateful to his buddy for not disparaging him for his ignorance, but for always being willing to explain things.

"Yeah, well, my dad will never be granted the title of elder, even if he lives to be a hundred." Rabbit's lips curled into a crooked smile. "I have no idea how he thinks he's going to be elected chief."

"Can he only be one or the other?"

Rabbit stood up. "No, but my father has always had his own ways to get what he wants."

"The chief is like the mayor of the reserve, right?"

Rabbit nodded. "The chief is the more secular, political leader of the reserve. Along with the Council who elects him, he represents the concerns of our people. My dad can do what he wants for all I care; Nuka is more important to me." He pulled on his jacket, then paused. "Sorry, I never even asked how you're doing. We haven't seen each other since your brother's funeral."

"I'm back to the daily grind," Cody replied. His friend had enough to contend with; he didn't want to make things worse for him by telling him about the conflict with his own father.

"So, all is well in the cowboy world?"

"Yep, everything's grand."

They left the diner together. Out on the sidewalk, they said their goodbyes with a handshake and a brief embrace.

"Take care, cowboy. See you later."

"Let's meet next time for a beer and some pool," Cody answered. "And have a talk with Woodwind."

Rabbit gracefully tossed his braid over his shoulder, nodded, and strode across the street to his rusty car. Cody went to his truck and headed back to Willow Ranch.

Woodwind made the rounds at the wild animal rescue center and was satisfied that all the animals were set for the night. Then he locked the main entrance and drove home to the reserve. Chinook had invited him over for dinner, and he wondered whether his invitation had anything to do with Ayita. His curiosity had driven him to accept. He parked his car in front of his own house, grabbed the strips of beech bark that he had collected for the elder, and walked the few yards to Chinook's bungalow. Lonefeather had advised him not to show up empty-handed when he had mentioned the invitation. "The shaman makes a salve for himself using birch skins. He says it's the only thing that helps relieve his painful joints."

He stepped into the house, which smelled like freshly baked bread and roasted meat.

"Woodwind, is that you?" The voice came from the living room.

Woodwind pulled off his shoes and entered the living room.

Chinook was sitting in his rocking chair, smiling.

"I thought I heard something. Come, sit down next to me."

"I brought you some beech bark strips." Woodwind raised up the plastic bag.

"Wonderful, thank you. Would you like a beer? There are two bottles in the refrigerator."

Woodwind stood up. "Would you like one too?"

"No, I'm going to stick with my tea."

Soft music was playing in the kitchen, and Woodwind saw a young woman cooking. "Hello," he said as he caught sight of her.

She turned around. "Oh, hi, flute player."

"Una, what are you doing here? I didn't recognize you with that colorful scarf around your head."

"I often cook for Chinook and the other elders. I've mentioned that to you before."

He grinned apologetically. "How's it going at home with your little brother and your father?"

Una sighed. "Rough. The two of them fight about every little thing. And I am swamped with all the paperwork that I have to do for my dad's council member work." She shrugged. "I swear he thinks I'm his secretary as well as his housekeeper." She turned back to the pots.

Woodwind drew closer and briefly laid his arm around her. "If there's anything I can do, just let me know."

With a tired smile, she escaped his embrace. "Stop that. My dad helped me out of a sticky financial situation, and now I just want to be there for him and Nuka."

"But for how long? You have your own life."

Una went over to one of the cabinets, pulled out two plates, and set them on the counter. "My dreams will just have to wait. I don't intend on owing anyone anything." She gently pushed him to the side so that she could drain the boiled potatoes.

He pulled away from the hot steam and didn't know what

more he should say. It pained him to see Una so dejected. Nevertheless, he understood her attitude about not wanting to be in anyone else's debt. But if his impression of Bull was right, he would do everything he could to keep his daughter at the reserve. Una had once told Woodwind that it was only because of her mother that she had been able to begin a bachelor's degree in culinary arts. Her father had thrown a fit when his daughter had moved out and wanted to become a cook. He refused to accept that going to college meant much more to her than just learning how to cook, and he had cut off all contact with her up until her mother's sudden death. She had never told him what had happened since then.

"The food needs about another fifteen minutes," she muttered, dragging him out of his thoughts. A slight smile appeared on her lips and tugged at his heart.

He forced himself to smile back. "It smells divine, I'm sure it'll be worth the wait. I was just coming in to get myself a beer." He took a bottle out of the refrigerator, then stood around unsure of what to do next.

"I really enjoyed our time together, you know that, right?" she said, without a trace of reproach in her voice.

"Yeah, of course. Listen, Una, I—"

She raised her hand, and he fell silent. "It is what it is," she said. "Now that I'm living at my dad's, we can't see each other anymore. At least for the time being."

He nodded. "Okay. But if you ever need help, I'm there for you."

"I know that. There will be better days to come, and I'm just happy that I can be there for Nuka. He has so much anger inside of him."

"Is he making trouble around the reserve as well?"

"He's running around with some gang who are up to no good." Una grabbed one of the spices from the shelf and sprinkled some of it into the pot. "Rabbit and I have been trying to keep an eye on him."

Woodwind nodded. Neither of the sons had a good relationship with their father, but it was probably best not to get involved. "I'll leave you to finish cooking," he then said.

"Okay. I'll bring it in as soon as it's finished."

Thirty minutes later, Woodwind and Chinook were sitting at the small dining table, enjoying their dinner. Una had left, and Woodwind was eager to hear what the shaman had to say and why he wanted to speak to him. The old man chewed slowly, enjoying every bite, seeming to have all the time in the world. Once his plate was empty, he leaned back in his chair and looked at Woodwind through his milky gray eyes.

"You've met Lyla's aunt, or so I've heard."

"Ayita, yes. Lyla stopped by the wildlife center with her and her son."

"And what's your impression of her?"

Woodwind raised one eyebrow. Didn't Chinook know Ayita better than he did? Why was he so interested in Woodwind's thoughts about Lyla's aunt? He took a drink of water and tried to find the right words.

"She seems lost," he finally said.

"You ought to make some time for her and Wynono."

"Lyla asked me the same thing. Did she speak to you about it?"

Chinook slowly shook his head. "I had hoped Ayita would come to me, but she isn't ready yet."

"What happened back then?"

"That's her story. Perhaps you can help her rediscover her roots."

"And how am I supposed to do that?"

Chinook tilted his head. "First you must learn how to breathe again." The smile that appeared made the wrinkles on his face dance.

"I would've thought I'd figured out how to breathe by now," Woodwind joked and earned himself a look of reproach.

"I'm speaking of the sacred breath ceremony that you should be doing. Ideally early mornings, right after you wake up." Chinook struggled a little to get out of his chair, shuffled to one of the narrow bookshelves, and pulled out a thin booklet. He flipped through the pages until he found the one he wanted and handed it to Woodwind. "Here, follow these instructions."

Woodwind realized that it was a notebook that someone with beautiful penmanship had filled up page after page with the ceremonies and rituals of his people.

"Is that your handwriting?" Woodwind asked, but the shaman shook his head.

"These entries are much older than even I am." He chuckled. "Yes, such a thing exists."

"Okay, I'll do the ceremony, and then?"

"Then you teach Ayita how to do it."

Chinook said it so matter-of-factly that he didn't dare make any objection, despite the thousands of excuses that were running through his head as to why he wasn't the right person to help her.

"You'll be fine. I am happy that Ayita has begun her return home. Also for her son."

Before Woodwind could ask what Chinook meant by *begun*, the shaman settled down on his rocking chair and yawned. "I'm tired. Will you please put the dishes in the kitchen? Una will come in the morning to do the washing up."

"I can do that quickly." He cleared the table.

When Woodwind returned a few minutes later to say goodbye to Chinook, he found the other man asleep in his rocking chair. Woodwind quietly left the house and walked the short distance home. There were around a thousand tribal people who lived at the reserve. The exact number couldn't be determined since many of the members lived in other towns and cities and only came back occasionally for short stints, much like Una. Most of the streets were only partially paved and were riddled with potholes, which reminded Woodwind of the reserve he lived on while growing up. They both had the same identical, pre-fabricated, houses where all the tribal members lived, most of which were in dire need of fixing up. Every house had a small patch of grass out front, which was typically covered with children's toys, broken bicycles, and overgrown weeds.

Woodwind went up the narrow, worn path to his front door and had to admit that, like so many others here, he too had barely spent any time maintaining his house or yard. He sat down on his old, black leather couch in his sparsely furnished living room, opened the book the shaman had given him, and began reading:

We are all connected to the Creator and the Earth. Ceremonial rituals are our emotional connection to this truth. This breathing ritual will connect you with your core and allow you to come into harmony with your feelings.

He gave up and closed the book. It was exactly these feelings that had gotten him in trouble in the past; he wasn't about to open himself up to them. Woodwind stood up and set the book on the shelf, his hand lingering on it briefly. He wasn't the right person for this task. He trusted Chinook's wisdom, but even a shaman could make mistakes. He tapped his finger on the leather book cover. He also didn't want to completely disappoint the elders. "Okay, this ritual isn't for me," he mumbled and turned away from the shelf on the wall. "But I will try to make an effort with Ayita." Woodwind thought this sounded like an acceptable compromise.

Rosie ran her hand over the mare's bulging stomach. "Not much longer for you," she said softly. Calvin's request echoed in her mind. Should she call him and ask what exactly he had in mind? Her salary as a horse handler barely covered her cost of living, and she didn't know how she would be able to also cover the cost of horse feed. Since she hadn't been able to sleep the night before, she had read the pedigree papers for the stallion that had impregnated Lori. He seemed to be a well sought-after sire.

Distracted by her apprehension, she gave the broodmares an extra portion of their specially formulated supplemental feed, stroked the three foals that had been born last week, and left the stable. She caught sight of Nick, Lee's former business partner, outside in the yard, as he left the main house and headed for his truck. "Hey, Nick. How are your stallions?" she asked, and he stopped in his tracks.

"Oh, hi. Things are going great at the Tanner Ranch. How are the foals doing?"

"We've got three more on the way. Listen, do you know a stallion named Dragon?"

"Of course. What kind of a breeder would I be if I didn't know him? How do you know him?"

Since Nick had no partiality regarding her decision, she decided to tell him of the offer.

"Wow, I could almost envy your ex. A foal from Dragon, nice! You ought to make sure that you take home a portion of its selling price," he replied, taking off his cowboy hat and running his hand through his blond hair.

"Would you mind telling me why?" Rosie found herself closely watching the man's attractive features. His rugged, three-day stubble looked good on him. When she had met him about a year ago, he had come across as an obnoxious jerk, intent on getting his way. Now that he and Lee were no longer co-owners of Willow Ranch, Nick seemed to be a lot more relaxed. He had taken over Lee's breeding stallions, and Rob Tanner had made him manager of the neighboring Tanner Ranch where the stallions, and also Nick, now lived.

"If you keep looking at me like that, I'm going to start to think something," he teased.

Rosie tucked a strand of hair behind her ear as her lips spread to form a crooked smile. "And what makes Dragon's offspring so valuable?"

"Primarily the fact that this is the last year that he will be bred. He's getting to be too old. Many of the mares he was paired with didn't get pregnant."

"Isn't there any frozen semen from him?"

He shook his head. "His owner doesn't want that. The few offspring that Dragon did sire have gone on to be very successful in a number of rodeo disciplines. Are you also familiar with the mare's lineage?"

Rosie told Nick what she knew, and he was impressed.

"Wow, you sure did read up on all this. I didn't know that you were so interested in horse breeding."

She gave him a wink and put her hands on her hips. "You wouldn't have expected all that from a blonde like me, eh?"

"That's not true. Just because you look so damn good doesn't mean you've got nothing upstairs. I've never been a fan of such prejudices against women."

"So, you think I look good, do I?" She teased and socked him lightly in the side. "May I draw any conclusions from that?"

He laughed, and she joined in before turning serious again. "To be honest with you, I'm a little bit worried about Lori. She's already sixteen years old and has spent her entire life at Calvin's father's stable. I find it a terrible idea to rehome her while she's pregnant."

"New surroundings, especially leaving her in the care of someone she doesn't know, can certainly be stressful," said Nick. "Lori knows you already though, and she would certainly be in capable hands with you." He smiled and looked at his watch. "Shoot, I have to go. Sorry. As I said, if you can swing it, you should take her. Maybe you might even get the chance to buy her foal."

She sighed. "Thanks, Nick. You've been a great help. I will strongly consider it."

He raised his finger to the brim of his cowboy hat and walked over to his truck. *Shit*, Rosie thought as she started to estimate how much she had in savings, then she gave up. She would call Calvin.

June

Woodwind sat in his office at the wildlife rescue center and double-checked the feed orders for the coming weeks. They currently had a total of thirty animals; a number of them were young orphaned mammals, along with numerous injured birds of prey and waterfowl. Maja was a master with the paperwork. She had been a great help to Lyla and was an expert in every aspect regarding the center's operation and procedures. Her knowledge of how to care for the animals, her gentle way, and her unrelenting enthusiasm for her work made the young First Nations woman irreplaceable to him. He decided that he would give her a raise starting next month.

"Woodwind, could you come here for a minute? We have a new addition." Maja's voice echoed through the building's main corridor. He closed his laptop and hurried to the front entrance to where a truck belonging to a game warden stood outside. The tailgate was down, and there was a large cage in the cargo area containing something wrapped in a blanket.

"What have you brought us?" Woodwind slowly approached the open cage.

"A wolf pup. I reckon she must be about three months old, but she's barely hanging on."

Woodwind cautiously pulled back the edge of the blanket and uncovered a snout. The pup didn't move. He extracted the bundle from the cage. "Who found her?"

"Some hiker discovered her along the trail and contacted us.

The little one is starving and hasn't had anything to eat for a good long time."

Woodwind asked Maja to call the veterinarian and patted the emancipated figure. The pup's breathing was shallow and barely perceptible. "She must've been born around the end of March, which is early. Wolf pups are normally born in mid or late April."

The game warden nodded. "I was also surprised, but it does happen. We looked around for other littermates, but we didn't find any."

"Dr. Langley will be here as soon as he can," Maja said, tucking her phone in her pocket. "He said we should keep her warm and that an electric blanket would be best."

"Good luck with her. I need to get going." The game warden ran his finger over the wolf pup's snout as she lay in Woodwind's arms. "Take care, sweetheart," he mumbled and walked away.

With the pup secure in his arms, Woodwind went back into the rescue center. Maja warmed up an electric blanket and wrapped the pup inside it. Then Woodwind carefully laid her in the old dog bed that Lyla's dog had once used and sat down on the floor next to her. "What made your mother abandon you?" he wondered out loud.

The wolf pup raised her head slightly before closing her eyes again. Had her mother been trying to escape an attacker? Where were her littermates? A wolf mother typically bore a litter of four to six pups. And what about the rest of the pack that normally looked after the pups? The arrival of the veterinarian pulled him out of his thoughts.

Dr. Langley confirmed the approximation of the pup's age. "Yes, she is about ten or eleven weeks old. I don't see any injuries, just extreme malnourishment."

"Should she still be nursing?" Maja asked.

Dr. Langley shook his head. "Wolf pups are usually weaned between seven and eight weeks, and start taking on solid food at that point." The vet prepared an IV. "For right now, the most important thing is that she gets the nourishment she needs to regain strength."

"The game warden didn't find any other pups. That's a bit unusual, isn't it?" Woodwind took a step next to the vet.

"A wolf mother giving birth to only one pup would be very rare, that's correct. I'm more concerned as to why this little pup was left behind. A wolfpack takes care of its offspring like an extended family. It must've been a very dramatic incident to have forced the pack to leave the pup behind."

"I had the same idea, but I doubt we'll ever get an answer. What do you think her chances are?" Woodwind asked.

Dr. Langley applied the infusion needle and taped it in place around the pup's smooth-shaven front leg. "Right now, I would give her about a thirty percent chance of survival."

Woodwind let out a gasp of surprise. "What can we do?"

"Unfortunately, not much." The vet packed his things together. "She needs to have an IV for the next four to five days. Keep her warm, and cross your fingers."

The wolf pup survived the following days, which according to the vet was a miracle. Woodwind had moved her into a corner of his office, where he set up a movable, three-foot tall metal barrier around the dog bed. The pup showed no intention of wanting to leave this set-up, appeared apathetic, and refused all offers of meat and food apart from gruel. Woodwind sighed as he removed the bowl of cut-up chicken from the wolf pup's enclosure.

"But you have to promise me you'll eat something later tonight, okay?"

He heard voices coming from the main entrance and turned around. Ayita and her son stepped inside, and he went to greet them.

"Hello, what a surprise! Isn't Lyla with you?"

"She just dropped off Wynono and me. It's not easy running errands with him in tow, and Lyla thought that we—"

"I get it, no worries." Woodwind smiled. The apprehensive look on her face made something inside him soften, and he noticed that he was genuinely happy to see the little boy again.

"Great, thanks. What animals do you currently have here?"

He told them about the various animals they had at the station at the moment. "Our latest little orphan just came in a few days ago." He led them into his office and pointed to the wolf pup. She was lying on the dog bed and seemed to be sleeping.

"A wolf," Ayita whispered, awestruck.

Wynono appeared just as fascinated. He stood there on his chubby little legs next to his mother and then started toward the metal gate. Ayita held out her hand to hold him back, but the toddler ignored her. Woodwind watched in astonishment as the pup opened her eyes and lifted her head. Her eyes lingered on the boy, and her ears were perked. For the first time, the little she-wolf seemed alert and interested. The animal's amber eyes watched Wynono attentively. The little boy sat down in front of the gate.

"It's a female, right?" Ayita asked quietly.

Woodwind nodded. "She's about three months old and was half starved when she was found. Unfortunately, I haven't been able to convince her to eat much." He pointed to the bowl with the pieces of chicken.

"Want to try it again?" Ayita asked.

He shrugged. "Sure, why not?"

Before he could set down the bowl in front of the pup, Ayita asked him to wait a moment. She pulled a banana out of her bag, peeled it, and handed it to her son. Then she nodded at Woodwind, and he placed the bowl in front of the pup. He watched, stunned, as the pup studied Wynono as he ate his fruit, then slowly stood up and took a piece of chicken. Ayita tugged Woodwind's sleeve, and together, they backed away.

"What happened to her?"

He told her how the pup had been discovered and what the vet had said. "Now, she's at least had something to eat," he added, relieved.

"Yes, she has. Have you already given her name?"

"No. Any suggestions?"

Ayita studied the wolf pup for a long moment. "The markings on her head are quite unusual. Do you see those two white stripes running along either side of the bridge of her nose? And the pale black line that goes all the way to the tip of her nose?" She used her finger and traced what she meant over her own nose.

Woodwind smiled in agreement. The pup's grayish brown fur had specks of caramel brown; she would grow into a beautiful wolf.

"Kachina would be a good name for her," said Ayita suddenly. "It means 'dancing spirit,' and the name brings good luck."

"Kachina," Woodwind mumbled. "Yes, I like that." He looked at Ayita, who was watching her son. "Lyla told me that Wynono hasn't spoken for a long time," he continued softly.

Ayita turned toward him, gazed at him for a moment, and then slowly nodded. "I don't know what to do. None of the experts we went to for advice in the Yukon could help us." She ran her hand down her long, black braid. "Really, I'm just as lost as my son is," she said softly, her eyes fixed on the wolf pup.

"I think it's good that you came here with him." The words simply slipped out of him. And along with them came the feeling that he wanted to help Ayita and her son. It was like a call to arms, a mission he needed to fulfill. "I would like it if we could spend more time together."

She smiled and tilted her head. "We don't want to be a burden. You already have so much to do here, and time is precious."

He met her gaze, and her dark eyes seemed livelier all of a sudden. "Time is precious when you use it wisely," he replied.

Ayita laid her hand on his arm and took a deep breath. He recalled the breathing ritual that Chinook had suggested. Perhaps he just might find the right time and the courage for it with this woman's encouragement? This thought felt so fragile that he very carefully pushed it to the back of his mind. Don't overdo it. He suggested they go outside for a short walk, and she agreed. As they walked along the narrow paths between the enclosures, they didn't say very much to one another. They were both concerned about the little wolf. But Woodwind could see from Ayita's face that, like him, she didn't find the silence awkward. A smile kept flitting across her face, and time seemed to fly by until Lyla returned to pick up her aunt and her son.

Cody and Lee each sat on one of the hay bales in the barn at Willow Ranch. They had just finished moving them to make room for this year's hay. Cody wiped his sweat from his face with his sleeve and accepted the bottle of water that his boss held out to him.

"How is it going with your parents? Have they been able to arrange for someone to help them?" Lee asked.

"No, unfortunately not. That's also why I wanted to ask if I could take another weekend off."

"At the moment, that's not a problem. But as soon as we get started with the first group of teens, I won't be able to spare you."

"I know that. And my place is here. I'll figure something out. It's just so damn tough because my parents always relied on Scott for everything. His suicide hit them hard."

Lee placed his hand on his shoulder. "And how are you handling Scott's death? Have you had time to work through it?"

"I'm getting along," he answered quickly. "I just wish I knew of someone who could help out on the farm with the cows. I hate leaving you and Naira here hanging."

"You're not. Maybe it would be good if you took a week or a little longer to go to the farm. We don't really need you here until July."

Cody wanted to say no. He couldn't imagine spending more than a few days in the same house with his father. However, he knew that he owed it to Scott to at least ensure that everything on the farm ran smoothly until his father recovered. "Okay, thanks, Lee."

"No problem. Isn't that young lady from Germany also supposed to come in July? The one you got along with so well last year?"

Cody could feel his face getting red, and he hastily got to his feet. "Uh, yeah. Emma will be coming with a friend of hers. They've rented a guest house from Mary, not too far from Rosie's cabin."

"Oh, I had no idea that Mary rented out guest houses on top of running her diner."

"Apparently, it belonged to an old woman for many years who had to move into an assisted living center. Emma was very happy to get it. Her enthusiasm is really contagious."

Lee also stood up and gave Cody a friendly jab in the side.

"I'm happy for you. And I also think it's a good idea that you are taking care of the family farm. Not too many of us can look back at a more than a century of history."

Cody followed Lee out into the barn yard and continued on his way home. He had planned to drive to his parents early in the morning. Lee's words resounded in his ears as he packed his clothes. It had always been clear that Scott would one day inherit the farm. He was the older brother, and their father had always included him in the daily operations at the farm from a very early age. "But you're not here anymore, Scott," Cody mumbled, stuffing a pair of jeans into his overnight bag. "Why? Dammit, big brother, why did you do that?"

Rosie sat on the paddock fence next to her cabin, pulled her cell phone out of her pocket and eventually pressed the call button. She held her breath until a man's voice sounded in her ear.

"Calvin, hi, it's Rosie."

"Rosie? Rosie Laforge?"

"Very funny. How many Rosies do you know?" she asked, immediately regretting it. She didn't want to give the impression that she was still angry at him for cheating on her back then.

"No, you're the only Rose in my life."

Don't call me that, she wanted to scream, but stopped herself.

"Have you made a decision about Lori?" Calvin asked casually, seemingly not noticing her silence.

"Not yet. We need to first clear up a few details."

"Oh, I think we'll be able to come to an agreement. By the way, it's really great to hear your voice. Why don't you come over, and we can talk about everything."

"Okay, sounds good." She quickly grimaced. "I can do that this weekend." She had said those last words so quickly that she first thought Calvin might not have understood her.

"I'll be at the riding school till 5 o'clock on Saturday. My father has gotten a few new students and training horses. Looking forward to seeing you again," he said.

"Then I'll see you Saturday. Bye, Calvin."

"Bye, Rose."

She took a deep breath and slowly exhaled, but her heart continued to race. She slowly slid off the fence onto the ground. Was she really going to go see her ex? It was hard enough to talk to him just on the phone, but now she'd be seeing him again in a few days. But so what? She was doing this for Lori. Now she just had to make sure that Jim didn't catch wind of her plan to visit Calvin. Her brother would forbid her to go there by herself.

The sound of a horse snorting got her attention. She turned around and looked to the forest that lined the edge of the property to the west. Four wild horses were standing near a group of trees. Rosie observed the small group, which often appeared there. The horses grazed for a few minutes before disappearing into the forest. With a hop in her step, she felt light on her feet. She hoped that the wild horses appearing to her just now was a good omen for her upcoming visit with Calvin.

On Saturday afternoon, Rosie glanced at the clock. Darn it, she had wanted to leave at two to make it over to see Calvin at his father's riding stables, but it was already almost three. If she hurried up and finished feeding the animals, she'd be able to leave in a half an hour and everything would still be okay. Why did the farrier have to pick today of all days to trim the hooves of every one of the mares and even spend extra time on the foals? She sighed, but there was no point in being angry. She distributed the specially formulated feed, gave the yearlings slices of apple, and hurried to her truck. But her truck wouldn't start. After trying it numerous times, she got out and opened the hood, but couldn't spot what the trouble was. Shit. Her cell phone rang. That would probably be Calvin asking where she was. But to her surprise, it was Doug.

"Hi, what's up?"

"Have you got any plans for the rest of the day?"

"I do, but ..." she replied, then got an idea. "Do you think you can do me a huge favor?"

"If it means that I get to spend some time with you, then yes."

A little while later, Rosie was sitting next to Doug in his truck, and the two of them were headed to see Calvin. Maybe it was a good idea after all that she wasn't going over there alone. Her ex had made her quite nervous on the telephone, and she wanted to remain professional during their negotiations about Lori's new accommodations.

As Doug's truck rolled up the drive, Rosie saw all the improvements that had been made at the riding school in the last year. Inside several small, individual paddocks stood horses grazing the short grass, some of them covered with blankets to keep the flies off. The expensive race horses lacked for nothing, apart from contact with other horses. Rosie had hoped that the stables would have opted for keeping the horses in groups, but apparently the owners here preferred to keep their horses separate.

Doug parked and cut the motor just as his cell phone rang. "I have to take this. You go on ahead," he said.

She nodded and got out of the truck.

Calvin emerged from the riding hall holding the reins of a saddled horse, spotted Rosie, and grinned broadly.

"Hi, Rose, I'm glad to see you made it after all."

"Yeah, sorry, today was really busy."

He stepped closer and kissed her on the cheek. "No troubles, I'm happy you're here."

"Uh, yeah, I can't wait to see Lori again." She tried to sound casual, but the warmth from his lips still tingled on her cheek. His eyes rested on her for a moment. Could he see the storm that was raging inside of her? Smiling, he raised his hand and pulled a strand of hair out of her face.

She pushed his arm away and took a step back.

"Where are the mares?"

Calvin's eyes darted from her to something behind her, and his smile faded. Doug came up next to her and offered him his hand.

"Doug Fry. Nice riding school you've got here."

"Thanks, it belongs to my father. Did you come with Rosie?"

Before she could answer, Doug slipped his arm around her waist and pulled her closer.

"Yep. We're just friends, but that could change," he said. "And I didn't want to pass up meeting her favorite mare."

Rosie clamped her teeth together against the inside of her cheeks, and Calvin frowned. Then he shrugged his shoulders, continued leading the horse, and motioned at them to follow him.

"Well then, let's go have a look at this wonder horse." Doug grabbed Rosie's hand.

"Could you please not interject yourself into our business discussions too?" she growled at him.

He stopped, still holding onto her hand. "Sorry, but what was I supposed to do? From the way that guy looked at you, it was clear that he would have liked to pull you behind the nearest hay bale."

"You're exaggerating," she snapped, snatching her hand away.

"Besides, I promised your brother that I'd look out for you. Jim wouldn't be too happy if he heard you were here."

"You swore to me on the way here that this visit would stay between us."

He bent over to her and gave her a kiss on the cheek.

"It will. Jim won't hear anything for me. I'm only looking out for your well-being, don't forget that."

"Okay. I do appreciate you coming here with me today."

He gave her a wink, and they followed Calvin into the stables. He had, in the meantime, unsaddled the horse and left it in one of the stalls.

"Lori is here in the open stable," he called over to them, and they headed for the rear of the building.

Rosie saw the Paint standing at the hayrack, and tears immediately filled her eyes. She had just now realized how much she had missed this sweet horse. Rosie had been there when Lori had given birth to twins and had almost died in the process. Rosie entered the open stable and threw her arms around the horse's neck, stroking her predominantly brown coat. "I've missed you so much." The horse snorted a greeting and turned back to the hay. Lori was showing her age and the effects of the many foals she'd given birth to over the years. The brown fur around her eyes was interspersed with gray, and her withers protruded sharply. However, she still exuded an intrinsic peacefulness that only an experienced mare such as her possessed. Rosie ran her hands across Lori's bulging stomach and returned to the fence to where Calvin and Doug were standing.

"She's due at the end of the month, right?"

"Yes, you sure have a good eye for these things," Calvin replied. "Lori would be in the best hands with you."

"You know that I would really love to take her, but you would have to pay for the food until her foal can be sold."

"That's not quite what I had in mind. I was thinking you might take over the feeding costs, and in exchange, you could keep Lori."

"I can't afford that. Plus—" She was interrupted by a loud crack. "What was that?" She turned around and looked down the stable corridor. A shrill whinnying echoed down the passage.

"That's our wild one," Calvin said as he hurried toward the source of the racket.

Rosie followed him. Standing in a box by herself was a brown mare with a black mane and tail. Her neck glistened with sweat.

"What's wrong with her?"

"Sky hates being locked up all by herself. But out on the pasture she behaves like Rambo. We've been trying for weeks to get her used to a saddle and bridle," Calvin explained.

"Where did she come from? Has she had a bad experience in the past?" Rosie wrapped her hand around the pole of the stall door and observed the animal.

"A rodeo buddy gave her to me after he tried to ride her and ended up losing a couple of teeth."

"Crazy animal." Doug attempted to pull Rosie away from the stall.

She shook off his hand. The mare was small, but sturdy. Her

head with its star-shaped blaze was the perfect size for her muscular neck. In Rosie's eyes, she was a beaut. "How old do you think she is?"

"Guess she must be between three and five years old," Calvin said. "A real challenge if you wanted to ride her."

"Before you could even think of riding her, there's a lot of groundwork that would need to be laid first. She needs to learn to trust."

"I really don't have the time for that, nor the desire for this creature to break any of my bones. On the other hand, she's too good for slaughter."

Rosie suddenly came up with a crazy idea. Nothing ventured, nothing gained. "Would you let me take Sky along with Lori if I agree to pay for their feed?"

Calvin raised his eyebrows in surprise. "You want to take Sky too?"

She nodded. "And I'd like for us to put all this in writing."

Doug put a hand on her shoulder. "I don't think that's a good idea. This Sky seems rather unpredictable."

"But she could be my ticket for getting into Gordsteen's to become a certified horse trainer," Rosie said, mostly to herself.

"Are you still dreaming of doing that?"

"Yes, and I think with Sky I'd have a really good chance of it. Have we got a deal?"

"You sure come right to the point," Calvin replied. "Are you in such a hurry to get out of here?"

"No, but—"

"We have plans for the evening," Doug interrupted.

Rosie shot him a sharp look. He raised his hand in a goodwill gesture and took a few steps backwards.

"How long have you been with this guy?" Calvin asked, throwing Doug a disparaging glance. "I always thought you liked cowboys and not some wannabe—"

"Doug is a firefighter and works all around the world as a smokejumper," Rosie cut him off. "I would really like to take Lori and Sky off your hands."

"Okay. I can give you three sacks of feed to start with, but after that you're on your own."

She swallowed hard. Two horses—and one of them needing special pregnancy feed. Her salary wasn't going to cover that. She straightened up; she would just have to dip into her savings for a while. Nick's words suddenly came to mind. "I also want a cut of the amount the foal brings in later as well," she said.

"Wow, what a shrewd businesswoman you've turned into!" Calvin's eyes lingered on her face, and it felt as though she could almost feel the tips of his fingers, which had so often stroked her entire body. Where were these memories suddenly coming from? She shook her head, trying to get rid of them.

"So what do you say?" she asked, momentarily holding her breath. From the research she had done over the past few days, she knew that a foal from Dragon could bring in a minimum of five thousand dollars.

Doug, who had gone off to look at the stalls, now returned. A few of the horses were tied up along the main corridor of the stable building, waiting for brushing or saddling. The riders, all in cowboy hats and boots, some even dressed in their English riding apparel, shot sidelong glances in Doug's direction. In his jeans with the holes at his knees, polo shirt, and sneakers, he truly looked out of place. All the same, he exuded a self-confidence as though he spent every day around horses. Rosie couldn't help giggling. He caught her gaze and grinned.

Calvin cleared his throat. "Let me have a think about your suggestion. I need to quickly check on one of the geldings that I'm trying to break in. I won't be more than fifteen minutes."

"Well, have you come to an agreement?" Doug asked as he watched Calvin walk away.

"I told him that I want a portion of the profits that the foal brings in," she volunteered.

"Very good. Make sure you get what's coming to you."

She looked at him with her head tilted slightly. "I don't know whether he'll agree to it. Perhaps I've gone too far."

"Don't be silly. You just have to be brave enough to ask for it."

"But what if he refuses and sends Lori somewhere else? I would never forgive myself for that. Shit." Suddenly Rosie wished she had kept her mouth shut.

"Don't go there, always think positive. If you take over the costs for the mares, then you ought to get a cut of the proceeds," Doug said.

"You're right. Maintaining two horses with my salary is crazy. Plus, I still need to fix up the stall. Jim would take my head off if he knew about this."

"You can't live your life constantly trying to please your brother. Dream big!"

She gnawed her bottom lip and ran her hand over her ponytail. Doug had no idea that dreams didn't account for anything in her family. Make realistic plans, know your boundaries, and you'll succeed. That was one of her mother's favorite mantras. Rosie took a deep breath as she looked at Lori and tried to imagine what it would be like to have her standing in the pasture next to Eric's cabin and hearing her greet her every morning with a nicker. She hoped that Sky and Lori would get along, and that the brown mare would be a loving aunt to the foal once it was born. Perhaps she would be able to get a second job to cover the repairs on the stall and pay for their feed to avoid using her savings. But if she succeeded in turning Sky into a riding horse, that could be her ticket to being accepted into the training certification program at Gordsteen's; she was sure about that. Her heart raced when she saw Calvin walking her way again. She tried to ignore the lump in her throat.

"And, have you decided?" she asked.

"Fine. You can have twenty percent of the selling price. I can't offer you any more than that."

She nodded and held out her hand to shake. Her ex took hold of it, pulled her in for a hug, and kissed her on the mouth.

"Hey," Doug objected. Calvin let go.

"It's okay, I was just sealing the deal. If you want, I'll bring Lori and Sky over in the next few days."

"Um, well ..." Rosie hesitated, wanting to refuse his offer. But then, how was she supposed to transport the mares to Eric's cabin? Asking either Lee or Jim was not an option.

"Okay, that would be really nice of you. Would you also bring along our contract and the papers for the mares?"

"You'll get the mare's papers after she gives birth," said Calvin. "But I'll include our agreement about your share of the foal's selling price in the contract."

"That sounds perfect," Doug said, grabbing Rosie's hand. "Let's get out here and go celebrate."

Calvin touched the brim of his cowboy hat.

"Well then, I'll let you know when I can come by with the mares."

"See you then, and thanks a lot," Rosie replied.

"Bye, Rose. See you soon." Calvin watched her for a few moments before turning around and walking away as he whistled a melody.

"Dammit, Dad, the milking machine needs to have a professional come by and look at it. I can't just do that along with everything else." Cody stared at his father.

Larry was sitting on a chair in the living room, his broken leg propped up on the foot rest. "That was never a problem for Scott," he grumbled.

Cody balled his fists. "It's not about that. It needs to be done by a certified professional so that we can get the quality seal."

"Our milk is outstanding. We follow all the rules and regulations. What the hell more do the authorities want from us? Your brother managed it all without—"

"Scott is not here anymore," Cody snapped at him through clenched teeth. Nonetheless, his words were loud, too loud.

His mother entered the room just then carrying a tray and stopped dead in her tracks. Cody saw the pain in her wide eyes and cursed himself for losing his temper.

"Sorry, Mom," he mumbled, hurrying past her and through the door. Why did his father have to be so stubborn? He had been at the farm for only two days and could hardly stand it already. His father shot down practically every one of his suggestions without letting him explain himself. And his mother was constantly on the brink of collapsing in grief.

He strode over the farmyard and, as always, avoided looking at his brother's old bungalow whenever he walked past. He came to a stop once he reached the barn, his fists finally relaxing. His parents would be leaving in about fifteen minutes for his dad's doctor's appointment in town. He wanted to use the time to look through the dairy's books. It was clear to him that the farm had never actually been as prosperous as his brother had always claimed.

He walked along the milking stalls and remembered the three times that Scott had tried to call him last April. Cody had been busy at the time and had kept forgetting to call him back. And now his brother was dead, and he missed him more than he ever thought possible. A cow mooing drew his attention to the pasture where the herd was allowed to free range. A group of the black and white animals was gathering around the water trough, mooing loudly as if complaining that things weren't moving fast enough for them. They pushed at each other, making a commotion around their water. He shook his head at their impatience.

He had always been drawn more to horses. Not to mention that his father had long shooed him away whenever he followed Scott into the barn to help take care of the cows. "Go out and play, we don't need you here," his dad had said so often that Cody eventually gave up any interest in his family's dairy farm. He heard an engine starting and turned to look through the open barn door as his parents' van drove away.

A little while later in his dad Larry's office, he could see from all the handwritten notes that Scott had also used this desk. The old computer took an eternity to boot up, which gave Cody time to look around. Why hadn't his brother ever gotten himself a laptop from which he could remotely control the milking machines? Perhaps there was one at the house—he ignored the idea. Finally, the icons appeared on the screen, and he found the files containing the most recent invoices he was looking for. The numbers were shocking.

His mother hadn't exaggerated when she'd said that they couldn't afford to hire an extra hand. He ran his fingers through his hair, wrote down a few numbers on a pad of paper, and shook his head. The family farm was in dire straits. But that wasn't his problem, was it? Just then, his phone rang. Cody looked at the display and smiled. "Emma, hi, it's nice to hear from you."

"Hi, am I keeping you from something?"

"No, never."

"Ah, I thought maybe you'd be sitting in the saddle, teaching Jazz some new tricks."

Cody laughed and said that he wasn't.

"What are you doing instead?"

He hesitated. Emma knew about his brother's suicide, but he didn't really want to tell her about his family farm's financial difficulties as well.

"Oh, just some boring paperwork. Tell me instead how you're getting on with your travel plans."

She cheerfully told him about them, and he soaked up her bubbliness. His anticipation of seeing her in two weeks momentarily overshadowed his worries.

"How are Lee and Naira doing?" she asked once she was finished with her story.

"Everything's great at Willow Ranch. Are you and Sonja still due to arrive on July 6 in Calgary?"

"We are. It's so sweet of you to come pick us up."

"It's no problem at all."

"Super. I've already talked to Naira, and she's letting us borrow her Jeep while we are staying at the guesthouse. Renting a car would be super expensive," she explained enthusiastically. "I'll call you again just before we leave."

"Emma?"

"Yeah?"

"I'm really looking forward to seeing you."

"I'm really looking forward to seeing you too," she replied, causing his heart to almost leap out of his chest. After they said goodbye, he sat in silence and thought about everything that he wanted to show Emma. Then his gaze fell on the computer monitor again, and he let out a sigh. What was the use? He would do everything in his power to rectify the situation here on the farm until his father was back on his feet again, but there was no way that he was going to leave Lee hanging in July. Besides, he wanted to spend as much time as he could with Emma. It was time to get serious. He picked up the phone.

July

Woodwind arrived at the wildlife rescue station before dawn. He was surprised to see someone sitting on the steps as he arrived. Just as he was parking his car, the man got to his feet. Woodwind nodded at him. "Rabbit. What are you doing here so early?"

"It's already been a shitty morning," the young man replied, rubbing his face.

Woodwind walked past him, unlocked the door, and waved him in. "I think the first thing you need is a coffee. And then you can tell me what happened."

While he scooped the coffee into the filter, he wondered what the hell Jeremy Bull's son could possibly want with him. He could only hope that it had nothing to do with his relationship with Una. Bull himself didn't want to have anything to do with Woodwind, and Woodwind couldn't stand that pompous bastard either.

The sound of the coffee machine brewing loudly pulled him out of his thoughts, and he took two cups from the cabinet. He poured the coffee, adding sugar only to his own cup, and looked at Rabbit standing in the doorway. "There's milk in the fridge, in case you need any."

The young man shook his head, then pointed at the dog bed in the corner. "You have a dog?"

"No. We got in a wolf pup a few weeks ago. She slept here for the first few nights and is now outside in one of the enclosures."

Rabbit only nodded in response.

Woodwind could see that his thoughts were elsewhere.

"Take your coffee and have a seat. You're making me nervous just standing around like that."

Woodwind grabbed his mug and sat down at his desk at the other end of the long room. Rabbit pulled up a chair and sat down across from him.

"Well, what's troubling you?" Woodwind took a sip of coffee.

"My little brother Nuka got caught trying to steal a car on the reserve."

"Your dad won't like that."

Rabbit stared at his coffee, then looked up and cleared his throat. "Nuka and these friends of his ... They've got nothing but stupid ideas in their heads. Up to now, they've gotten away with only a warning since they're all underage. But this time, they're going to be shipped off to a juvenile detention center somewhere far away from here."

Woodwind remained silent as he listened. He was well aware of Nuka's criminal record while he'd lived in foster care. He looked at Rabbit, the situation obviously weighed very heavily on him, but the truth was that the majority of the teens at the reserve were just plain bored. And when the wrong crowds got together, they committed petty misdemeanors as a means of entertainment. "Maybe that would be the best option for Nuka so that he doesn't completely run off course?"

Rabbit shook his head so vehemently that his coffee slopped over the side of his mug and down his hand. "Fuck, ow, that's hot!" he cursed, glaring at Woodwind and grimacing.

"Sorry, I'll clean it up in a second."

"Don't bother, it's just a few drops. What would be so bad about Nuka and his friends serving a little time?"

"Because it's a white detention center. Now, I may not have always cared all that much about my tribal roots, but I know now how crucial it is to not lose our connection to our heritage completely. And that's exactly what would happen in a place like that."

Rabbit's eyes bored into him; Woodwind found it difficult to hold his gaze. He knew well enough himself what it meant as an indigenous person to spend time in a white prison. He'd already an adult at the time, but still found it hard to be able to draw on the power of his native roots on his own while being so far removed. Nuka had already spent the last five years growing up with no contact to his native community. He didn't want to think about what this sentence would mean for him.

"I lost Nuka once already," Rabbit whispered.

The desperation in Rabbit's eyes was plain to see. When Woodwind met him about a year ago, he had learned then about Rabbit's difficult relationship with his father. Rabbit, who had barely been of legal age at the time, had struggled to meet his father's expectations. He was a soft-spoken, introverted young man, but Woodwind could well imagine that Nuka, a rather outgoing teen, could easily cause his dad, a man whose reputation was the most important thing to him, to more than just fly off the handle on account of his many escapades.

"I'm really sorry to hear that, Rabbit. But I am still not really sure why you think I can be of much help."

"You're friends with the owner of Willow Ranch, aren't you?" Woodwind nodded and knit his eyebrows.

"And they are planning to offer camps for native teens this summer, right? Cody told me a little about it."

"Yeah, but it's for teenagers who haven't committed any crimes."

"I know, but ..." Rabbit took a deep breath, set his coffee cup on the floor, and got to his feet. He paced as he spoke. "I haven't slept for the past few nights because I've been researching stuff online. There are healing lodges for indigenous criminals, but they only take adults. I found one reserve that has a program targeted at at-risk adolescents. The teens are allowed to stay at the reserve or somewhere in the area and do community service as well. They learn about their culture, what our traditions mean, and all that."

Woodwind was familiar with these healing lodges. They offered indigenous criminals an alternative to the regular prison system.

Unfortunately, this opportunity was currently only being extended to a small percentage of tribal criminals. Woodwind could guess where Rabbit was going with this, but he remained quiet and continued to listen.

"That's when I thought that perhaps Willow Ranch could also set up a program like that in cooperation with our reserve. Nuka and the other teens would have the chance to get closer to their culture, to learn, to not feel so hopeless. Just maybe we can spare them from a future life behind bars." Rabbit stood there, his shoulders hanging dejectedly. He sat back down and looked at Woodwind hopefully.

Woodwind ran his hand over his long braid, tightened one of its leather bands, and thought for a moment. Then he let out a sigh. "I can't promise you anything except that I'll talk to Lee and his partner Naira about it."

Rabbit nodded, and Woodwind could tell by the disappointed expression on his face that he had hoped for more. But Woodwind wasn't able to offer him more than this, mainly because he didn't know himself how much he wanted to get involved in the situation. Just then the two men heard the sound of a motor revving. Rabbit jumped to his feet. "Shit, that's my dad's truck. I bet he's looking for me."

"And so he comes here?" Woodwind had also stood up. "But you don't live with him anymore, do you?"

"No, but I promised I would look after Nuka today. And anyway, my dad knows that I like you a lot. I'd better go." The young man turned to leave.

"Hold up, I'll come outside with you."

Out in the parking lot, Woodwind watched Jeremy Bull greet his son with a stony expression. Without saying a word, Rabbit got into the truck. Bull took a few steps, stopping directly in front of him.

"I should've known my coward of a son would look to you for shelter. You seem intent on avoiding all kinds of confrontation."

Woodwind crossed his arms over his chest.

"What's that supposed to mean?"

"That means that you'd better keep your nose out of mine and my kids' business, got it?"

"I decide for myself in whose business I get involved in or not."

The man was now very close to Woodwind. The two men were almost the same height, with Jeremy being ever so slightly shorter. His beefy face made his eyes look beady under their bushy eyebrows.

"I'm on the council at the reserve and just because you've won over Chinook doesn't mean that I can't make your life a living hell." He raised his chin and poked his right finger into Woodwind's shoulder. "Nothing will stand in my way of becoming chief. No delinquent teenagers and no wannabe social workers like you."

Woodwind raised his arm and swatted Jeremy's hand to the side. "You can threaten me all you want, Bull. But you can't tell me what to do."

"Oh, no? You're mistaken there."

Cody wiped his sweaty palms on his jeans. The flight out of Frankfurt had landed and his skin tickled with the anticipation of seeing Emma. The first passengers made their way through the sliding glass doors and were being corralled by an energetic tour guide. The woman spoke in a mishmash of German and English, which didn't seem to bother the travelers. The group headed for the exit amidst loud chatting and laughter.

"Cody!" Emma's voice caused him to spin around. He spotted the petite brunette waving as she came his direction. Behind her was a tall woman with black curly hair and a big grin. That must be Sonja, Emma's friend. Cody's eyes remained fixed on Emma. His heart skipped a beat when she hugged him; he held her tightly and spun her around. She felt so good in his arms. He breathed in her scent of lemon and coconut that he still remembered from last summer when Emma had come to Willow Ranch as an equestrian tour guest. It was hard for him to let her go, but when he finally did, her cheeks were so rosy that it made her green eyes shine even brighter. She turned and pulled her friend a few steps closer by the arm. “This is Sonja Seher. We’ve known each other since *Gymnasium*, which is what we call our high school.”

He held out his hand. “Nice of you to accompany Emma.”

Sonja looked at him with a smile. “After all my best friend has had to say about you all these months, I wanted to come and have a look for myself.” Emma playfully elbowed her in the side.

“You’re exaggerating. And you only agreed to come because your boyfriend is off hiking through the Andes with his friends.”

“Don’t remind me!” Sonja replied, rolling her eyes. “That idiot thinks I’m not adventurous. Well, poo on him. I’m here now and ready to conquer Canada’s wild wilderness!”

“And hopefully get over your fear of horses and country life.” Emma grinned at her, then turned to Cody. “Sonja is such a city girl. This is going to be a huge test of her courage.” She gave her friend a peck on the cheek.

“Then I’d say, off to new adventures!” Cody exclaimed. “Are you all set?”

The two women nodded, and only a little while later, they were headed for Spruce View.

“Do you have the directions to the guesthouse?” he asked an hour and a half later, as they exited the Queen Elizabeth Highway.

Emma rummaged through her purse and pulled out a piece of paper. “Here, Mary sent this to me,” she said and told him where it was. “Apparently, it’s not too far from Willow Ranch.”

“No, only about twenty minutes away. For Canadians, that’s just around the corner,” he said, grinning. “Should we stop off first at the ranch and pick up Naira’s Jeep?”

Emma shook her head. “That’s not necessary. She said she would leave the Jeep out in front of the house sometime today so that we can go right there. She should have left the key under the mat.”

“Super, then we’ll go straight to the house.” He took his eyes off the road briefly and smiled at Emma. He saw her trying to suppress a yawn. "Why don't you rest? Sonja's already conked out in the back. We ought to be there in forty minutes."

Emma placed her hand on his thigh, nestled herself into the passenger seat, and closed her eyes.

Cody gently touched Emma's arm. She startled awake.

"Are we there?" She rubbed her eyes sleepily.

"We are," he answered, parking his truck next to Naira's yellow Jeep. The guesthouse was painted light beige, and had a broad, covered porch with comfortable-looking rattan furniture. Toward the back of the house, a narrow footpath led to a Jacuzzi. "Wow, you've got your own whirlpool to sit out in and watch the stars!"

Emma followed Cody's gaze, grinning. "If you're a good boy, you can come over for a dip."

"Are we there yet?" A voice came from the back seat. "I must've fallen asleep."

"You did that the moment we left the airport," Emma said, and her friend stuck out her tongue.

Cody chuckled, and they all got out. He helped the two women with their luggage, and they entered the house. It was decorated in a rustic style, and felt very cozy with the small, open-plan kitchen, breakfast bar, round dining table, and wood burner directly in the middle of the room. To the back was a small hallway leading to the bathroom and one bedroom. A set of wooden stairs led up to the loft. "And which one of you is gonna sleep up there?" Cody asked.

The two women looked at each other.

"I prefer staying down here," Sonja said.

"Okay, then I'll take your suitcase up, Emma."

He grabbed her suitcase and placed it in the small sleeping area of the loft. He noticed that there was also a bathroom up there and admired the beautifully carved beechwood bed. Emma followed him up the steps and gave him a kiss on the cheek. "Thanks, you're a dear."

He turned to face her. "I'm sure you guys will like it here. I was surprised to notice that the house even has internet. Especially at that price, it's really a good deal. Or did Mary give you a special price?"

Emma beamed at him. "No, when I found the house online, I had no idea that it belonged to Mary. It's perfect. Sonja can study here for her final exams to become a hypnotherapist, and I—"

"And you?" he asked, pulling her into his arms.

"And I can spend my time with you at Willow Ranch." She leaned forward and kissed him.

Cody savored the feeling of her soft lips on his. Her delicate frame pressed against his, and for a moment, he forgot everything around him. He just wanted to hold this woman in his arms forever.

"Ack! What is that? Come here quick!" Sonja screamed from below.

Cody and Emma let go of each other and hurried down the steps. The back door stood open, and they found Sonja standing next to a small fenced-in grassy area which they hadn't noticed from the car. On the other side of the fence, five goats stood eyeing her curiously. Off to one side was a shed that seemed to serve as their shelter, and next to that was another small wooden structure. Cody surmised it contained the animal's food and straw. "Do the goats come with the price?" he joked.

Sonja stared at him. "That's not funny. I don't like them." She turned to Emma. "What do we do now? Did it say anything about them on the booking website?"

Emma shook her head. "Mary also never said a word about goats. Oh!" She slapped her hand against her forehead.

"She did mention it, didn't she?" Sonja pursed her lips.

"Not exactly. She only said the house came with a stipulation that we needed to like animals."

"Oh my God, Em!" Sonja exclaimed. "And you didn't think you should ask for more details?"

"There's nothing else around for miles at this price," Emma replied, raising her chin in defiance. "And anyway, it's just a few goats, no need for all the drama. It's not like Mary is keeping snakes or breeding spiders or something."

Sonja hopped from one foot to the other, letting out a high-pitched scream. "Stop it, I don't even want to think about it."

"Calm down. It'll be just fine. And you like goat cheese, don't you?"

"Yeah, great." Sonja ran her fingers through her curly hair. "And what are we supposed to do with these things?"

"Wait a minute. There was a letter on the kitchen counter," Emma said, hurrying into the house. She came back a few seconds later with an envelope with her name on it. She took out the three closely written pages and quietly read them, then she looked at her friend and shrugged her shoulders. "Well, it looks as though the goats are the reason for the low rental price."

"That has to be a joke," Sonja sputtered.

Cody took the letter from her hand and skimmed over the pages. "No, it says here that the two of you are responsible for the goats while you're staying here. Mary left you instructions on what to do."

He read the lines one more time. The animals belonged to the previous renter who hadn't been able to take the animals along when she had moved into an assisted living home. And Mary couldn't bring herself to sell the animals, so she listed the house at half the usual rate for the area with the stipulation that the guests had to look after the goats during their stay.

"Instructions?" Sonja tore the pages from his hands. "You can forget that. I won't be setting one foot in this enclosure."

Emma approached the fence, kneeled down, and put her fingers through the mesh. One of the goats approached and rubbed its head against her fingers. "Don't be such a diva, Sonnie. Look, they're totally sweet."

"Then you can take care of them."

"If I've got to do it, you've got to do it," answered Emma, standing up again and taking her friend by the hand.

Cody rather expected Sonja to run away, but she let Emma pull her step-by-step closer to the pasture. Side-by-side, the two women kneeled down, and he watched as a second goat came trotting over. It was the smallest of the group, a little fuzzy gray ball, but before it reached the fence, it was abruptly butted aside by another black and white goat.

"Hey, don't be rude," said Sonja. "She was just coming over to say hello."

Emma threw her arm around her friend's shoulders. "We can manage them, can't we?"

"No idea. But life's about facing new challenges, isn't it?" Sonja's smile wasn't quite convincing.

All the same, Cody liked her attitude and was certain that the two women would get along just fine with the goats. He secretly hoped that Sonja would take over the majority of the work with the animals so that he could spend as much time with Emma as possible. There was something about this woman that had hooked him from the moment he had first seen her.

Rosie leaned against the fence next to her cabin and watched Lori and Sky grazing peacefully. Calvin had brought them over a few days ago and put them in the stall, along with three sacks of horse feed. To her surprise, he had also brought along some prenatal feed. However, he had forgotten to bring their contract. Rosie's annoyance immediately vanished, however, as she watched the two horses look around the pasture and inspect their new home. When they both started rolling around on the ground, Rosie was overjoyed.

Lori had bitten Sky on her rump, making it clear that she wasn't going to take any grief from the young mare. Since then, the two of them had gotten along really well. Sky respected Lori's dominance and enjoyed being out in the small pasture all day, as opposed to being locked up in the stall like she had previously been. Rosie wanted to give the mare enough time to get used to her surroundings before starting to train her. She heard the cabin door open. Doug stepped out with two steaming cups in his hands and gave her one.

"Here, there's nothing better than a cup of coffee after dinner."

She gratefully accepted the cup, took a sip, and made a face.

"Oh, man, is that strong! How am I supposed to fall asleep later?"

He grinned. "Oh, I can think of something we could do to make you fall asleep."

She gave an elusive smile, then raised her cup. "It's nothing more than friendship on my side, you know that."

He shrugged. "Things could always change." He raised his cup and grinned. She turned her attention back to the mares. Was it possible to keep a man at arm's length who obviously wanted more than just friendship? She hoped so, because she really liked Doug. The sound of a motor caught her attention, and she turned around and caught sight of Nick's truck heading up the driveway.

"Who's that coming here so late?" Doug asked, his mood immediately darkening. "It's already after eight."

"That's Nick." She set her cup down in the grass and went to greet him. Hazel, who was snoozing on the porch, barked and came running down the steps.

"Hi, I'm sorry to show up here so late," Nick said after he'd gotten out of his truck. "There's an insane amount of stuff going on at the Tanner Ranch, but I wanted to finally get over and see that mare of yours." He looked to the pasture. "Oh, you've got two horses?"

"It's a long story," she laughed. "But I'm glad you've found the time to stop by."

Hazel sniffed Nick's jeans, and the cowboy scratched her on the head. "Hey, girl, how do you like your new roommates?"

"I think she's enjoying having them around." The three of them walked over to the paddock. Doug, who was still standing at the fence, watched the cowboy suspiciously.

"This is Nick Flint," Rosie introduced him. "We worked together last year at Willow Ranch. Nick, this is Doug, um, a friend."

The two men nodded to one another. Doug held Rosie's cup out to her. "Your coffee." He bent forward and kissed her on the cheek, then turned to Nick with a smile. "May I offer you some as well? Rosie and I always drink a cup of coffee after dinner."

"Yeah, sure," Nick answered.

Once Doug disappeared into the house, Rosie poured her coffee into the grass. "Just a warning, it tastes terrible."

"You've got a new boyfriend? Nice guy."

Rosie rolled her eyes. "We aren't a couple," she replied.

"Hm, I don't know if he sees it that way."

"What's it to you, anyway?"

Nick shrugged, throwing up his hands. "Absolutely none of my business," he answered, opening the gate.

Sky's head shot up and she perked her ears. When he approached her, she took a few steps backwards, never taking her eyes off him. "Why is the brown one so scared?" he asked, moving closer to Lori.

Rosie also walked across the pasture. "Sky's not yet broken in, and she's very suspicious of everyone she doesn't know."

"What are you going to do with her then? Did you get a two-for-one on them?"

"No. I plan to train Sky and secure myself a spot in Gordsteen's certification program."

"Whoa, you've really set the bar high for yourself." Nick stroked Lori's big stomach and pulled a few treats out of his jacket pocket. "Well, at least she is as calm as can be."

"Yeah, she's a wonderful horse. I'm very interested to see how the foal will turn out. When do you think it'll come?"

"Sometime in the next week or two, no longer than that, I expect."

He ran his hand again along Lori's stomach. "I say it will come exactly eight days from now."

Rosie came and stood next to him. "I say in ten," she replied.

"Then let's wager a dinner together," he suggested, giving her a wink. "Of course, only if Doug has nothing to say about it."

She jabbed him in the side. "It's a deal."

They shook on it, and the way his watercolor-blue eyes looked at her took her breath away for a second.

"Your coffee," Doug called, coming down the porch steps.

Rosie's lips stretched into a crooked grin and she shrugged her shoulders.

Nick briefly traced his finger over the back of her hand before pulling away and walking toward Doug.

"Sorry, buddy, I'm afraid I'm meeting someone else this evening and didn't notice the time. I'll have to try your coffee another time." He turned back to Rosie. "Let me know when Lori gives birth, then we'll see who will be taking out whom for dinner. No cheating now." He touched the tip of his cowboy hat with two fingers, got into his truck, and drove away.

Rosie could see from Doug's expression that he didn't like Nick's last words. On the other hand, she didn't owe him anything. Instead she wondered whether Nick really did have another date. "I have to get up early. It would be better if you headed on home," she said, closing the gate and taking the coffee cup out of his hand.

"But I thought I was spending the night? On the couch, of course."

"Sorry, but I am dead tired. Good night." She fleetingly drew her finger over his arm, took her cup as well, and disappeared into the house with Hazel.

Rabbit's desperate request left Woodwind no peace. For days he had dreamt strange things about young people going missing as well as some of his worst experiences in prison; every time he woke up with the harrowing feeling of being alone.

This morning, too, he jolted awake out of a nightmare. The display on his alarm clock said it was exactly five o'clock. He knew he wouldn't be able to fall asleep again, so he got up and made himself some coffee. His view from the kitchen window over the unkempt backyards of the other houses, whose cheap cladding was covered either in holes or in graffiti slogans and symbols, only worsened his mood. He turned away, taking a sip and letting the bitter coffee run down his throat. He then poured the repulsive brown brew into the sink.

The beep of his cell phone indicating an incoming message interrupted the bleak silence. Who would be writing him so early in the morning? He picked it up and read: *I see light on at your house, come over for a cup of tea. Chinook.*

Woodwind walked over to his front window, from where he could see the shaman's house. Light was burning in one of his windows too, and he grinned. The elder was one of the only people he didn't mind keeping tabs on him. He slipped into jeans and a t-shirt, grabbed his zippered sweat jacket, and walked over to Chinook's house.

The front door was open just a crack. He walked in and took off his shoes, and found Chinook in the small kitchen, sitting at the table with two steaming cups of tea in front of him.

"Good morning, old man." Woodwind sat down across from him.

"You call that a polite greeting?" Chinook closely scrutinized him. "By the way, you don't look all that young yourself this early in the morning."

Woodwind ran his hands over his tired face and took a sip of the herbal tea. "I hardly slept."

Chinook nodded his head slowly. "I can see that. Tell me, what's robbing you of your sleep."

Woodwind sighed. "I'm sure you've heard that Jeremy Bull's youngest son and a couple of others were caught trying to steal a car."

"I have. It's not the first time those boys have been in trouble."

"Yeah, and that's why his brother came to me for help." Woodwind told him about Rabbit's idea.

"Very impressive." Chinook leaned back in his chair with a groan. "Let's go into the living room. These chairs are poisonous to my back."

The two men got to their feet and picked up their cups, and while Chinook sat down in his rocking chair, Woodwind settled down on the couch.

"Have you already spoken to Lee and Naira about the idea?"

"No, I wanted to ... Um, well, I thought—"

"You thought you could find a way to stay out of it, didn't you?

By burying yourself in work at the rescue center. Don't you think that you should extend a helping hand to your people?"

Woodwind lowered his eyes and stared at the floor. Yet again, he had the feeling that the shaman could read his thoughts.

"Would such a project even be supported by the Sunchild Council?"

Chinook raised an eyebrow. "Why would you even question that?"

"Jeremy Bull made it clear to me that he didn't want me getting involved in his business. He wants Nuka and the other teens to pay their debts far away from the reserve."

"Bull is an idiot. He runs headlong into things and puts his greed for power above the needs of his sons. And a daughter like Una is also too good for him."

Woodwind choked on his tea and started coughing.

"What makes you bring up Una?"

The old man's eyes hit him like an arrow to the heart. He had no doubt that the shaman knew of his relationship with her.

"I may be old, but I'm not blind."

Woodwind nodded, his eyes dropping to the floor again. Chinook set his tea on the side table and pulled himself out of his chair. His feet shuffled along the floor as he went into the kitchen before returning with the phone in his hand.

"Who are you calling?"

"Lee," Chinook answered.

"But it's not even seven o'clock."

"We'll see if anybody answers. I don't have time to wait. And neither do these kids."

Lee's probably an early riser too, Woodwind thought, as Chinook waited for the ranch owner to answer the phone. With only a few words, the shaman explained the situation to Lee. From what Woodwind could understand, Lee and Naira agreed to come over in a half an hour. Once he was finished, Chinook groaned as he sat back down on his rocking chair. "My old bones are creaking especially painfully today. Could you make us some coffee? And toast some cornbread."

Thirty minutes later, Woodwind, Lee, Naira, and Chinook were all sitting around the older man's kitchen table. The shaman had tucked a pillow behind his back, and he took a bite of cornbread, thickly coated with butter and honey. Woodwind explained to Lee and Naira what Rabbit had asked of him. Lee took a sip of coffee and nodded.

"Yes, I can understand Rabbit's concern for his brother. What do you think, Naira? Would we be putting the grant money for our program at risk by taking on minors with criminal records?"

She took some time with her answer. "I don't think so. In fact, it may offer us the possibility to apply for further financial support. I would have to contact the government office in charge, but I know of two reserves that have done exactly the same thing in order to keep the young people in their own communities on the right path."

"That means Willow Ranch could be another place where minors would be able to fulfill the community service hours they're required to work. At the same time, they'd be learning about their native traditions," Lee added.

Chinook nodded. "The Council will back this program. I give you my word on that."

Naira smiled and laid her hand on her grandfather's arm.

"Thank you, Grandpa, but please let me speak to the Council. Such discussions only rob you of your strength."

"If you wish," he relented, then pointed at Woodwind. "I think it would be good if he were part of the program and its planning. Rabbit didn't go to him for no reason."

Woodwind waved this off. It was all going too fast for him. He hadn't even decided yet if he wanted to be involved. What about his work at the rescue center?

"You're exaggerating, wise one," he said dismissively. "I don't have anything to do with the teenagers around here, and I certainly don't have any training to offer."

"Like so often, you are hiding your light." Chinook threw him a look of reproach.

"We would be happy to have you on our team," Lee said.

Naira backed him up. "The pedagogical leadership will be taken over by one of the reserve's teachers. She and I already have a lot laid out. She will be organizing the lessons, and thanks to my work as a college lecturer, I will lead the lectures on our native traditions."

Woodwind was reminded of the warning that Jeremy Bull had given him, and mentioned to the others what he had said. "You might run into some problems with me working at the ranch, ones you might prefer to avoid."

"Thank you for your honesty. But once we get the okay from the authorities to take on adolescents with criminal records, our first priority will be to help them." Lee glanced at Naira, who was nodding in agreement.

"And that alone will have Bull doing everything he can to stop us," she continued. "Your working with us won't make any difference."

As long as Bull never finds out about my relationship with Una, Woodwind thought, quickly dismissing that thought. Perhaps Chinook was right. He himself had been given a helping hand after he had returned from prison with nothing more than a duffel bag over his shoulder. It was time, not only to say thank you, but to repay his gratitude. "Okay, I'm in," he said.

A broad smile appeared on Naira's face. "Wonderful. We can talk about the details in the next few days as soon as I've spoken to the authorities."

"Mom, calm down. I will pay the helper's salary this month," Cody repeated, almost screaming into the phone. Why did his mother have to call him from the barn where it was so loud that she could barely understand him? During his last visit, Cody had arranged for Kurt to come and help his parents. He had already given him an advance and intended on continuing to pay him if it meant he was able to retain his own freedom.

"Mom, I have to go now. Just make sure that Dad doesn't scare Kurt away. He's there to help you and is only asking to be paid minimum wage. I'll call you later. Bye." He tossed his cell phone on the passenger seat and turned down the gravel road that led to the guesthouse. Over the past few days, he had only talked to Emma on the phone. The two friends had now recovered from their jet lag and were ready for action. Emma was waiting for him outside the house. Her denim shorts and tank top outlined her nice figure. Her hair was tucked up under a colorful scarf, and she was holding a garden rake. She waved at him with a sparkling smile. He grinned as he parked and got out.

"What have you got planned?" he asked.

"I found a gorgeous little wild herb garden not far from the goat pasture."

Her eyes shone brightly, and Cody remembered she had mentioned last year that she was interested in herbology. Before he could ask, she had grabbed his hand and pulled him behind her. She stopped next to a fairly large plant bed with freshly turned soil. "This here is like paradise to me. I told you that my mother is a naturopath, didn't I?"

"Yes, and that your father's a doctor. But you're studying business administration, or so I thought?"

"Business management," she said, waving her hand dismissively. "More for my parents than for me, but whatever. My passion is finding ways to integrate herbs into our everyday lives and our diets, as much possible. Aside from studying, I am working on a plan to open a small herb shop that will be connected to a bistro."

"Wow, that doesn't sound like it has too much to do with the corporate world."

She rolled her eyes. "My parents, well, my dad really, would prefer that I focus on my studies and go into management. But it's so boring."

"I don't think I could envision you being stuck in an office all day either."

"Exactly. But I will at least be able to make some use of the contacts I've made at school to finance my stay here."

Cody looked at her, confused. "What do you mean?"

"I do online research for two professors, and you wouldn't believe how much some students will pay to have their papers edited. I seem to have a knack for it and have made quite a bit of money doing it. I can even do it here in Canada from my laptop." She winked at him. "It's the perfect way to be both independent and creative."

Her effervescence sparkled in her eyes, and even Cody felt the sensation like a mouthful of soda fizzing on his tongue. He threw his arms around her, picked her up, and twirled her through the air. She laughed, threw her head back, and let her hair fly in the wind. He slowly put her back down on the ground, and kissed her on the neck.

"You are amazing," he whispered into her ear.

"Mmh," she murmured, searching his lips.

After a long kiss, they slowly parted. Emma picked up her scarf that had flown to the ground and re-tied it around her head.

He looked around. "Where's Sonja?"

"She found an old bicycle in the garage and went out for a ride."

"On the gravel roads?"

"Yeah, why not?"

"Because no one around here uses a bicycle. Where does she want to go?"

"Oh, nowhere specific. Sonja just loves to ride bikes." Emma shrugged.

"You Europeans sure are an odd bunch." He took a step closer and kissed her on the lips. "But you're also pretty damn sexy."

She laughed and playfully shoved him. "Are you just here to keep me from gardening, or was there a reason why you came over?"

"I wanted to see if you wanted to ride out with me on the horses. And after that, Lee and Naira invited us to dinner. Sonja, too, of course, if she's interested."

Emma clapped her hands and picked up the rake that she had let fall. "Super! I've only spoken to Naira briefly on the phone to thank her for letting us use the Jeep. I would really love to see the two of them again."

Just then, they heard the sound of a bell ringing and turned to look. Sonja waved her hand wildly at them as she rode the rusty bicycle up the gravel road toward them. Cody could only stare at who was running next to her as if it were the most natural thing in the world.

"Hello, Cowboy," Sonja called, coming to a stop.

Cody gaped at the puffy, gray goat standing next to the bike, seemingly waiting for Sonja's instructions. "Did you put a spell on him?"

"Just the opposite! Merlin put a spell on me!" She looked affectionately at the goat.

"He really did," said Emma. "Sonja has even started going out onto the pasture by herself, and is only scared of the two big goats now."

"Maybe Merlin can put in a good word in for you with the other two," Cody suggested, and they all laughed.

Sonja leaned the bike against the side of the house, then she bent over and scratched the goat's back. "I'll just put him back in the paddock and go take a shower."

"Wait a second," Emma said. "We were invited to dinner tonight at Willow Ranch."

"Oh, how nice! What should we bring?"

"Perhaps a bottle of wine if you want."

"We still have a bottle of white wine in the refrigerator," Emma told her friend. "Cody and I are going to go out riding. Would it be okay if you went over to Willow Ranch by yourself in Naira's Jeep when you're done feeding the goats?"

"I think I can manage that. I'll meet you around six at the ranch then. With the wine." Sonja replied.

"That would be perfect." Cody smiled. Then he explained to her the quickest way to Willow Ranch.

"Cool. I'm sure I can find it. See you later, you two." Sonja disappeared around the corner of the house with the goat, whistling a tune.

"She's really great. And she sure got used to the animals quickly."

Emma nodded. "That's what I love about her. She likes to challenge herself with new things and step outside of her comfort zone. Country life used to be a foreign concept to her, and she admitted to me that she was scared of a lot of different animals. But Sonja sees life as a test of courage and is convinced that every day is a chance to grow."

"Will she also be working online while she's here?"

"No, she had a rich aunt who left her plenty to get by on." She took his hand. "Let's go. I can hardly wait to sit in the saddle again."

Woodwind could feel the energy tingling in his fingertips. It was an amazing opportunity for him, despite the fact that the upcoming meeting with the young people scared him to death. He sat at the kitchen table eating breakfast. His mind had been racing the past few days about how he could entice the teenagers to learn about their roots. In any case, he planned to teach them the traditional art of carving. But was he ready to lead them in smaller rituals?

He remembered Chinook's little booklet and his initial resistance to perform the breathing rituals himself. That wasn't a good place to start for a teacher. He stuck the last piece of toast in his mouth, finished his coffee, and put his dishes in the sink. That afternoon, he had planned to speak to Maja at the wildlife center and hand over his duties to her for the time being since he would be busy focusing on his work at Willow Ranch and wouldn't have time to devote to the center. Lyla had given him her blessing to appoint Maja as his replacement. Since the center was a nonprofit and financed primarily through donations, it was up to Lyla as the managing director to make the final decisions about the center's management and employees.

He looked out the small kitchen window at Chinook's house.

The elder was sitting on the front porch with a colorful blanket draped over his legs and the sun shining on his face. It was high time he learned to breathe. He found what he was looking for in one of the kitchen drawers, put it in his pocket, and walked over to see the shaman.

"Good morning, wise man." Woodwind walked up the porch steps.

"It's a wonderful start to the day, don't you think?" Chinook replied with a smile. His thinning gray hair danced in the mild breeze.

"I have both an offering and a request." He knelt down before the old man and held out a small package wrapped in cotton. The strong smell of herbs wafted from the shaman's cup as he took a drink. He swallowed, set the cup aside, and took the package. His arthritic fingers struggled to open the string, but he finally managed and looked at the dried birch rinds. His head slowly bobbed back and forth. "You do know that people usually give tobacco as an offering."

"Yes, but I thought bringing you more birch bark seemed more useful."

The old man grinned and nodded. "A wise decision. Thank you." He laid the package to the side. "So, where do you need my help?"

"You advised me a while ago about practicing the sacred breath ceremony. And I had wanted to read the notes you'd written, but—"

Chinook put up one hand, and Woodwind fell silent. "You do not need to explain if you need help." He raised his arm and pointed to a small patch of grass a few meters from the house. "Let us go touch the earth, and we can begin."

Woodwind helped him out of his chair. "Why can't we just do it here on the porch?"

"We can only feel what is in our hearts when we tap into the power of Mother Earth." With short steps, Chinook descended the porch stairs, shuffled over to the grass, and sat down. "Sit down across from me, my boy."

Woodwind followed Chinook's instructions, and waited.

"Sitting as close as possible to Mother Earth allows us to think more clearly and to feel more deeply." The shaman laid his open palm on the grass, and Woodwind did the same.

"Allow me to recite a prayer of the Lakota people," Chinook said, resting his hands in his lap and closing his eyes. "Wakan Tanka, Great Spirit, teach me to trust my heart. My mind, my intuition. My inner knowing, the senses of my body, the blessings of my spirit. Teach me to trust these things so that I may enter my Sacred Space and love beyond my fear. And thus, may walk in balance with the passing of each glorious sun." He breathed deeply a few times and opened his eyes.

"What did you mean by *Sacred Space?*" Woodwind asked.

"That is the space between inhalation and exhalation. In this sphere, according to our legends, all our selfishness falls away. It is where we trade our isolating, self-serving attitude for mindfulness, for being a part of the world around us."

For the first time in a long time, Woodwind focused on consciously inhaling and exhaling. It was strange how every breath otherwise usually occurred without need of this process to assign value to it. He noticed that Chinook was watching him.

"Breathing represents life. The rhythm of breathing, the cycles of inhaling and exhaling, that is the essence of life. Never underestimate its incredible power." The shaman shifted his posture to sit more upright. In doing so, he grimaced and softly groaned. Woodwind wanted to ask if he was in pain, but the elder continued speaking. "The sacred breath ceremony will connect you with your inner force and make you see that you are a part of the world. Relax, close your eyes, and breathe."

Woodwind found a more comfortable sitting position and followed his instructions.

"While you breathe, allow yourself to feel the process. How the air rushes in through your nostrils, going deep into your lungs. Then breathe a little deeper, feel it in your stomach. Open your mouth and loudly exhale the air."

He turned his full attention to his breathing. Everything around him went silent. It was only him and the air that filled his body.

With every exhale, he also expelled a little bit of his gloom and doubt. He felt lighter and stronger all at once. After a few minutes, he opened his eyes. The shaman was smiling at him.

"Well done, Woodwind. Try to keep up regularly with the ceremony. It will connect you to the earth and to the Creator."

"Thank you, wise one."

The shaman nodded. "And don't forget to also breathe some life into that flute of yours. Find the magic in the melody."

Woodwind came away with a profound sense of peace and confidence that he was on the right path. Where it may lead him wasn't important for the moment. Later that afternoon, he drove to the rescue center and parked his car in the gravel lot next to Maja's, which had a number of animal carriers, blankets, and countless pairs of gloves littered across the back seat. Maja was a born animal rescuer, always ready to help an animal in need. He smiled as he entered the center and found her in the kitchen.

"Hello, Boss." She laid down the paring knife she was using to chop an apple into small pieces.

"Hey, how's it going?"

"Everything's under control. Did you contact the vet for him to come look at Kachina again?"

"No. I think it would be better if you took over doing that."

"No problem. I'll do my best to take your place."

"No doubt about that." Woodwind grinned. "I'll leave a few things for you on the desk, but for the most part you already know what to do."

Maja nodded. He could tell from her bright eyes that she was happy to be carrying out the role of the station's director. She would do a great job, he was sure about that. The feeding schedules for all the animals hung on a bulletin board. He read the notes for the wolf.

"Is she at least eating a little better?" he asked.

Maja shook her head. "I'm afraid not. Will Ayita be coming by occasionally? She and her son seem to have a better connection with her."

"I'll ask her," he replied, checking the food stores for the other animals.

"You two would make a good couple."

He stopped. Did he hear her right? Taken aback, he turned and faced Maja. "Where did that come from?"

"Nowhere, it's just a feeling."

"It would be better if you kept your feelings to yourself." He shook his head. "She's a good ten years older than I am."

"Ah," Maja raised one eyebrow, "and that would ruin your reputation for seducing younger women?"

His expression darkened. "Could we change the topic please?"

Maja threw up her hands. "Sorry. I don't care what the guys on the reserve say about you. To me, you're one of the good ones."

"One of the good ones, eh?" He grinned.

"And I'm sure someday you'll meet the one woman who makes you forget about everyone else. No matter how old she is." She winked at him and turned back to her apples.

Woodwind stepped into his office and sat down at the desk. That woman had once existed, and he was the reason why she was dead. He briefly closed his eyes, concentrating on his breath and the positive energy that had fulfilled him this morning. Gradually he was able to dispel the dark memories. From now on he was going to look to the future. "You have a mission," he repeated softly until his thoughts were clear again. He reached for the telephone; he was ready to call Lee and share his ideas about what he had planned to do with the teens.

Cody let himself get caught up in Emma's exuberant mood. They raced up the hill at a gallop. Jazz, his Palomino gelding, couldn't keep up with the black horse that Lee had let Emma use for their outing. At the top of the hill, they slowed down their horses, coming to a stop next to a large birch tree.

With her cheeks pink from the wind, Emma sat in the saddle and cast her eyes over Willow Ranch's extensive pastures. "I'd almost forgotten how breathtakingly vast it is here," she said softly. "And how much I've missed it all."

"Yep, it's really beautiful here."

"Let's take a break."

They dismounted and tied up the horses, after which Emma sat down in the grass against a birch tree. With a smile, she ran one hand over the top of the high grass and pointed to crows sitting on a branch watching them. "When I was a little girl, I used to be scared of blackbirds of all kinds, even starlings," she said, giggling. "What were you scared of as a kid?"

"Snakes," he answered, sitting down across from Emma. "We had an awful lot of garter snakes at the farm. My brother always used to think it was funny to collect them and scare the hell out of me with them."

"Did you guys have a happy childhood? I can imagine there's always lots to do on a dairy farm."

"My dad made Scott start working pretty young, and I was usually left to entertain myself, but we had a happy childhood. My mother especially made sure of that."

"That's nice," she said, turning her face toward the sun and closing her eyes.

Cody couldn't help but admire her delicate features. When he had met the petite German woman for the first time a year ago, he'd had his doubts that she'd get through their trip into the Rocky Mountains on horseback. But he'd quickly learned that there was a strong-willed, first-rate rider inside her who enjoyed a spontaneous challenge. "My longing for adventure is stronger than my common sense." That's what she'd said about her decision to take a break from her studies and to come again this year. He could remember her exact words on the phone: "I'm coming again next summer to get to know you better and because there's something about that country that won't let me go. It's as though a piece of Canada lives inside me."

He looked at her and realized how happy it made him that she'd come back. All of a sudden, a smile appeared on her face.

"I can feel you looking at me," she whispered.

Her bluntness made him forget everything else.

She opened her eyes, grinned, and nudged him with her boot. "Enough looking. Do you think I could help out over the summer at Willow Ranch a little bit?"

"Are you already getting bored?"

"No, it's just that Sonja will be spending a lot of time on her laptop, and I would really like to make myself useful at the ranch. The goats at the guest house don't need me there around-the-clock, and I prefer to do my online work in the evenings anyway. Plus, we can see each other while you're working." She winked at him and got up.

Cody likewise stood up. "Ask Lee and Naira tonight at dinner," he suggested, pulling her toward him. "I would love to have you near me as much as possible."

She nestled into him and gave him a fleeting kiss, then she pulled away and strode over to her horse. Cody's lips tingled for a few seconds longer.

Back at Willow Ranch, they unsaddled their horses, and Cody carried the heavy Western saddles into the tack room. When he returned, he saw that Lee and Naira's foster child, Samantha, was standing next to Emma. Sam's mother had died last year of cancer, but the girl would be living at the ranch until her aunt returned in a few months from a scientific research expedition abroad.

"Hey, Sam, are you finished with your homework for the day?" Cody asked, trying to keep a straight face.

The girl rolled her eyes. "Ye-ah, I am. Naira didn't give me much to do."

"How is Peanut doing?" Emma asked her. "I can still remember how your pony came with us into the mountains."

Sam beamed. "The best pony in the world is doing great. Are you now Cody's girlfriend?"

"Um, well, we're just getting to know each other better for right now."

"Exactly. Don't be so nosy," Cody followed up.

"Well then, maybe you can take me with you when you go out for a ride next time. You can also get to know each other with three people." Sam gave each of the two horses a slap on the rear. "I'll just take these carrots to Peanut. See you later." She skipped away.

"She seems to be getting along well since her mother's death," Emma commented.

"Lee and Naira take really good care of her, but she also has her bad days, believe me." He untied Jazz's lead. "Let's get these horses out on the meadow so that we can get to the house. I am starting to get hungry."

As they strolled together across the yard to the ranch house, Sonja pulled up the drive in Naira's Jeep. Emma waved at her friend.

"You go on ahead, I'll be right in."

He took off his boots outside the front door and went into the house. Greeted by the smell of braised beef, his stomach started to growl. Jeanne, Lee's aunt, was in the kitchen cooking.

"That smells heavenly. I'm starving." He stood next to the much shorter, gray-haired lady.

"The pot roast isn't for you. Lee is out back grilling steaks. But take a piece of garlic bread, that'll hold you over."

He shook his head. "It's okay, I can wait until everyone gets here. Is Eric coming too?"

"No, I'm going to take this home with me," Jeanne said. "We've hardly seen each other for the past few days, so we plan to enjoy being alone tonight."

He returned her smile. Jeanne and Eric had been married for only a year. He admired them for tying the knot despite being over sixty; they were obviously enjoying their new life together.

"I'm happy to see that your girl is back." Jeanne winked at him. He grinned and turned red. "Me too."

Thirty minutes later, Lee, Naira, Samantha, Emma, Sonja, and Cody gathered around the large dining table.

"Chuck and Sarah also want to stop by," Lee announced, "but they said not to wait for them to start."

"Doesn't Rosie work here anymore?" Emma asked just then.

"Yes, yes. But she's got a very pregnant mare at home in her stable whose foal could come at any moment, so Rosie has been spending all her time there," Lee replied.

"Oh, how exciting!" Sonja exclaimed, taking another bread roll. "We'll have to go see it once the baby's born, Em."

"Did I hear someone mention babies? Looks like we've come at just the right time." Sarah entered the dining room carrying an infant in her arms. Chuck was right behind her with a big grin on his face. They took their places, and Lee introduced them: "Emma, Sonja, this is my best friend, Chuck, his dream woman, Sarah, and their son."

"I remember you," Chuck said to Emma. "You were with us last year on our trip to the mountains."

"That's right. And while my friend Sonja here will be spending the summer cramming for her exams to become a hypnotherapist, I will have time to fall even more in love with this country."

"And in a cowboy," Chuck teased.

"Well, I for one, would really like to have a steak on my plate," Cody announced self-consciously, but briefly laid his hand on Emma's thigh under the table. Whatever was developing between him and Emma, he had no intention of allowing it to become a topic of discussion around the dinner table. Her smile confirmed to him that she felt the same.

Naira placed a steak on Samantha's plate and one on her own before passing the platter on to Lee. One by one, everyone's plates filled up with salad, meat, mashed potatoes, and grilled vegetables, and they began to eat.

Emma leaned over to Sarah, who was cradling her sleeping newborn in her arms. "He is so sweet. How old is he?"

"Two and a half months. John is truly a dream baby," she replied, stroking his face.

"How are the preparations coming along for your youth program?" Chuck asked, looking at Lee. "Has it been signed off on by all the right places?"

"It has. We got the grant money from the government which supports projects for the First Nations tribes. And we'll be offering some workshops in cooperation with the Sunchild Reserve here at the ranch."

"And we'll be spending a few days with the teenagers in the mountains," Naira interjected. "Woodwind is also on board the team, by the way."

"A wise decision," Chuck answered. "And I'll be around to help you with anything you need regarding your trips to the mountains. I can easily combine that with my forester job."

"Unfortunately, not so much with your job as daddy, though," Cody threw in.

Chuck waved his hand dismissively and threw his arm around Sarah. "Of course, little John is my first priority." He gave her a kiss and stroked his son's cheek. "Just as long as you don't start mothering me."

Sarah pushed him away with a smile. "I'll be going back to Mary's diner in another month. We've already found a great babysitter."

"You could quit your job altogether." Chuck put his hand on her arm. "And devote yourself to your own projects."

"I would only do that to Mary if I could find my own replacement." She planted a kiss on his cheek. "Who will be doing the cooking for the teenagers here at the ranch? Or will Jeanne be doing everything?"

"No. She'll be taking care of the guests staying at the bed and breakfast," Lee said. "We would like to introduce the kids to traditional native foods. Chinook gave Naira a lead on who could help us with that."

"We are going to make a great team. And the teens will learn what foods their ancestors used to make."

Naira took the jug of water and filled both her and Samantha's glasses. "Oh, we'll also be focusing on adolescents who have criminal records, by the way."

Cody could see her enthusiasm written all over her face. Presumably, Rabbit had followed his advice and spoken to Woodwind about his brother. Nuka would benefit from the program, and Willow Ranch was the perfect place for it due to its remote location. Cody thought that Lee and Naira made a strong team and threw Emma a sideways glance. She was chatting with Sarah and he caught himself toying with the idea of what a future with her might possibly look like.

"Will you also be incorporating sweating lodges and drumming rituals in the program?" Sonja asked.

Naira nodded. "We will be teaching the youth about all our traditions. They are taught them at the reserve schools, but a lot of that just gets glossed over because they don't specifically focus on native culture. We aren't here to instruct the kids, but rather to give them the opportunity to experience the connection to their roots for themselves. How much do you know about our rituals and ceremonies?"

"To say I know anything would be an overstatement. In my studies to become a hypnotherapist, I have come across the use of hypnosis in shamanism in my readings."

"What do you do exactly as a hypno-lady?" Samantha asked, sticking the last piece of her steak into her mouth.

"Oh, that's a bit difficult to explain." Sonja leaned back in her chair and twirled a lock of her black hair around her finger. "Hypnotherapy is considered one of the oldest methods of healing in the world. As a therapist, I put people into a trance, a state where their spirit and body can communicate with one another. Hypnosis can help with anxiety, as well as chronic pain."

"Unfortunately, in our Western culture, hypnosis has a rather pejorative connotation and there are some discrepancies between scientific research and hypnotherapy," Emma added.

"Yes, that's true. The state of being in a trance is something magical, but many consider it as irrational. And in addition to that, trances occur in an area of consciousness that's difficult to study," Sonja continued.

"I don't think I quite understand it, but it sounds cool. Do they also hypnotize animals?" Sam asked. "Because my pony Peanut is always very anxious when his friend Cashew isn't nearby."

Cody smirked at Samantha's comment. Sonja threw Emma a questioning look.

"Cashew is a horse, and the two animals are joined at the hip," she explained.

"I don't think it works as simple as that." Naira stroked Sam's hair. "But your concern is heartfelt and that's most important." Then she turned to Sonja. "If you're interested, you can come to one of our ceremonies."

"That would be amazing. And even though I can't hypnotize Peanut, I would still really love to meet him." She winked at Samantha.

The girl tried to get up from her chair, but Lee laid his hand on her shoulder, smiling at her. "Sonja and Emma will come again soon and you can show them your pony then," he said. "We still have dessert coming."

"Oh, yummy. What are we having?"

"Grilled pineapples with melted chocolate," Naira said, getting up. "Will you help me with it?"

Sam nodded enthusiastically and followed her out. The others piled up their dirty dishes and cleared the table. Cody carried a stack of dishes into the kitchen, and Emma filled the dishwasher.

"Didn't you want to ask Lee and Naira whether you can help out on the ranch? Or have you changed your mind?" Cody asked.

"No, I certainly haven't done that. I'll ask them during dessert." Emma loaded the rest of the plates into the dishwasher and stood back up.

Her cheeks had a lovely rosy glow. She looks good enough to eat, Cody thought, grinning. "Good. I think it would be fun to work together with you."

Emma leaned forward and kissed him. "I'm not officially allowed to work since I don't have a work permit. But there's nothing that says I can't spend time with my cowboy."

"Your cowboy, eh?" He laid his arm around her waist and pulled her close. "I like that." He pressed his lips against hers.

"Oh, sorry, don't mind me," said a voice from behind Cody.

He pulled away from Emma and turned his head. Lee was standing in the doorway, grinning. "I just wanted to say that we'll be having dessert out on the porch."

"Okay, we'll be right there," he replied over Emma's giggling.

"It would be great if you guys could make some coffee whenever you're finished kissing."

"No problem," Emma answered, and Lee closed the kitchen door again.

When Cody and Emma came out onto the porch carrying the thermal carafe of coffee, Naira was in the middle of distributing pineapple slices among the dessert plates, while Samantha smeared chocolate over the warm fruit with a knife. "Could I have a pineapple without any chocolate, please?" Emma asked.

"Don't you like chocolate?" Samantha's shocked expression made Cody laugh.

"I do, but I've had so much to eat tonight that I think I can only fit the fruit into my stomach."

"I don't get it." Sam shrugged her thin shoulders, but left one of the pineapple slices without any chocolate.

"Who wants coffee?" While Cody went around handing out cups of coffee, he caught sight of Emma speaking with Lee and Naira.

"Sure, we could always use another hand at the ranch," Lee said.

"Great, thanks a lot. I want to learn everything I can about working on a ranch."

Cody smiled. It was going to be a wonderful summer with Emma, he was sure about that. The sound of his phone ringing interrupted his daydreaming and he pulled it out of his jeans pocket. It was a text from his mother saying, *Dad's leg doesn't want to heal. Can't you come at all in August?*

He glanced over at Lee, Naira, and Emma, not wanting to disappoint any of them. He quickly calculated in his mind how much it would cost to pay Kurt for the next month as well. It would be tight, but he refused to put his job at Willow Ranch at risk. *No, I really can't, but I will pay Kurt if he can cover things*, he quickly typed back. She answered, *Okay*. He sighed as he tucked his phone back into his pocket.

"Everything okay?" Emma asked as she approached him. "You have such a brooding look on your face."

"Oh, my mom was just updating me on my dad. I told you how he broke his leg."

"Yes, you did. And, is it healing well?"

"He is impatient, but otherwise everything's fine," he lied. The words burned in his throat.

Rosie watched with concern as Lori paced inside the small enclosure and scratched the ground with her hoof. Yesterday, it had looked as though she still had another two days at least until her labor would start. However, Lori had been acting nervous all morning, which was unusual for the experienced broodmare.

The mares at Willow Ranch who had already had a number of foals throughout the years were typically calm before giving birth. Many of them even happily nibbled on hay until the stronger contractions eventually set in. Lori herself had brought six foals into the world over the past six years. Each one of those births, as far as she was aware, had gone over without any complications. She had even assisted during three of them. She considered whether to call the vet, but then decided it was still too early for alarm.

Opening the gate, she walked over to Lori. She ran her hand over her massive stomach and felt that her flanks were sweaty. Nonetheless, Rosie didn't see any further signs that foaling was imminent, but she also didn't want to risk anything with the old mare. "Well, Sweetie, I think it's about time that we put you in your stall. We'll get through this together." She grabbed hold of the halter and led the horse to the stall which was padded with a thick layer of straw. Lori was able to still see Sky from the stall, which was helpful in keeping the mother-to-be calm.

Sky whinnied nervously and didn't seem too happy to be separated from her friend. Rosie busied herself with the preparations for the foal's delivery. The iodine tincture and umbilical binder stood at the ready. She brought in a bucket to fill with warm water later, scissors, towels, and soap. Lee had given her a spare box of foal milk powder, and she had already procured a bottle. After she had double and triple checked all her supplies, she forced herself to calm down.

"It's not like this is your first foaling," she told herself, but she just couldn't shake her tension. Hazel came in, and Rosie stroked her head. All of a sudden, she felt terribly alone.

At Willow Ranch, there was always someone around to help if a mare had trouble during labor. She felt as though she was a beginner again who had never experienced a foal's birth before. Shit.

Her thoughts were interrupted by a short whinny. She ran to the stall and saw that Lori was again scraping at the ground with her front hooves. She was sweating more now, and kept twisting her head toward her stomach. Rosie softly stroked her neck.

"You can do this. I won't bother you anymore, I'll just be right here," she said calmly. She wrapped a bandage around Lori's tail and left her alone.

Outside the stall, she noticed that Sky was trotting back and forth around the paddock. She repeatedly let out a series of short whinnies, arched her back, and shook her head so violently that her mane bounced from side to side. If she kept on like this, she could hurt herself. Shit. Should she bring Sky into the stall as well? Or would she act even crazier being locked up? Rosie needed help.

She tried to call Lyla, but got her voicemail, which only caused her to start panicking. Who else could she call? As she racked her brains, she dashed into a stall to grab a halter for Sky; she was going to risk it and put Sky in Lori's stall so that she could keep an eye on the two of them. However, when she entered the paddock, it was clear that the agitated mare wasn't going to be so easy to corral. Shit. Rosie was hanging the halter on the fence post when her cell phone rang. She answered without checking the display. "Lyla? I need your help here."

"No, it's Calvin. What's wrong, you sound out of breath."

"Lori's gone into labor, and Sky is going crazy out on the pasture."

"I can be there in an hour."

"But what if something goes wrong by then? How can I help both of them? I have no idea if everything's—"

"Calm down," Calvin interrupted her. "You have so much experience. Just keep a clear head. Go and check on Lori."

His deep voice calmed her down. "I will, but hurry," she said and hung up. Then she turned to Sky, who was standing in the middle of the enclosure with flared nostrils. "I'm going to go and have a look at your friend. Don't get yourself all worked up, or you'll get colicky." She strode over to the stall and saw that the birth was progressing, but there wasn't any sign of the amniotic sac yet. She stroked Lori's neck. The old mare was drenched in sweat and seemed worn out. Calvin never should have bred her again. Rosie hoped that Lori would survive the stress of giving birth this last time around. She grabbed the metal bucket. It was time to get some warm water.

Outside, she saw Sky trotting back and forth along the fence that ran next to the stalls. Her neck glistened with sweat. Rosie ran across the yard. Out of the corner of her eye, she saw a woman coming up the driveway on a mountain bike. She stopped the bike in front of Rosie, took off her helmet, and shook out her curly, black hair. "I'm sorry, I seem to be lost. I'm staying with my friend Emma at a nearby guest rental and—"

"You've come just in time." Rosie pushed the bucket at her. "Go in the house and fill this with warm water, then bring it to me in the stall."

The woman simply stared at her.

"Quickly! My mare is foaling." Without any further explanation, she turned around and ran back to Lori. The mare was already pushing, and the nostrils of a small horse's head along with its two front hooves gradually appeared. Then everything went very fast. After a few more contractions, the foal lay on the ground completely cocooned in its embryonic membrane. Lori bit at the membrane. Rosie drew closer and kneeled down on the straw. She checked closely to see whether the foal's nose and nostrils were sealed, and used her fingers to remove the last bits of the membrane and made sure the foal's lungs were free. The woman appeared in the barn's narrow passage with the bucket.

"Bring the bucket over here." Rosie waved her in.

"I'm scared of horses." She vehemently shook her head.

"It's okay." Rosie got up, strode over to the woman, and took the bucket from her with a little bit too much energy, splashing water all over her jeans. "Dammit. Give me that towel over there, and go wait outside with Sky instead."

The woman gave her the towel and hurried off. Rosie inspected the severed umbilical cord and cleaned the spot with some warm water. Everything looked good. Lori was calm and continued licking her new colt clean. Rosie was deeply touched every time she witnessed this process, which served to strengthen the bond between the mother and baby. She stood up to leave the two in peace and went out to check on Sky. The mare was standing near the barn struggling to peer through the window. The woman sat on the porch steps, and Rosie went over to her. "What's your name?"

"Sonja Seher. You're Rosie, right?"

"That's right, do we know each other?"

"No, but my friend Emma knows you. She was at Willow Ranch a year ago on vacation and is here with me now."

"What a coincidence. Cody told me that Emma was coming with a friend of hers." She held out her hand to Sonja. "I'm sorry that I snapped at you earlier. Thank you for your help."

"No problem. Did everything go okay with the birth?"

"Yes." Rosie led out a sigh of relief and only now noticed her tension draining away. Lori and her foal were doing well. A warm, happy feeling spread through her, and she smiled. "If you want, you can sneak into the stall and have a look. I'll just go and put on a pair of dry pants."

"Thanks."

Rosie stepped into the cabin, put on a pair of fresh jeans, and went back outside. A scream from the barn made her jump. She ran over and saw Sonja waving at her wildly to come closer.

"Something's wrong! What is she eating there?" The woman lifted her hands to her cheeks. "And I don't see the foal anywhere."

Rosie pushed Sonja to the side and entered the box. Lori had turned away from her with her head near the straw. She cautiously approached the mare. Inclined to the panic in Sonja's voice, Rosie's heart beat like a jackhammer inside her chest. It took a moment before she realized what Lori was doing. Then she laughed in relief. She knelt down in front of the placenta. "That is just the afterbirth and the rest of the amniotic membrane," she said.

"Are you sure? But why is she eating it?"

"The afterbirth is full of iron and protein and is often eaten by the mother horses. Lori is just replenishing the nutrients she lost during birth. And apart from that, they do it to get rid of any traces that would indicate to predators in the wild that a baby is in the area."

"I didn't know that. But where's the foal?"

Rosie stood up and gently pushed Lori two steps to the side. The newborn colt lay tucked in the corner in the straw and was sleeping.

"Oh, how wonderful!" Sonja exclaimed, relieved.

"What's going on here?" A man's voice asked, attracting the women's attention away from the foal.

"You're too late," Rosie greeted Calvin, giving him a quick hug, relieved that everything had turned out fine.

"Whoa, don't knock me over." He laughed, straightening his cowboy hat. "This, by the way, is Andrea." A young woman appeared from behind him next to the stall.

"Hello." Stunned, Rosie shook her hand and also introduced Sonja.

"Now let me get a closer look at this little creature," he said, entering the stall.

The three women stood just outside in the walkway.

"Calvin hasn't talked about anything else but the foal for the past few days," said Andrea. "I tend to be more cautious around horses."

"How did you guys meet?" Rosie asked.

"We met online." A broad smile appeared on her face. "It seems the name of the dating site was accurate after all since we've been a match for three months now."

Rosie tried not to let her surprise show. Had she been mistaken, or had Calvin only a few weeks ago tried to flirt with her? Even worse, her heart ached – her ex had a new girlfriend. She examined the full-figured woman while she was busy getting a look at the foal in the stall. She wasn't his type in the least and was miles away from any of those slim cowgirls he could never get enough of at all the rodeos. Calvin, who was kneeling next to the colt, stood up and stroked Lori's neck. "You did a great job, old girl." He raised his head and looked at Rosie. "She looks pretty exhausted. I hope she'll be able to make enough milk for him."

"She is old," Rosie replied, not unaware of how judgmental her voice sounded.

"Yeah, I know, but look at this little guy," Calvin ran his hand along the colt's recumbent figure. "He's going to take over the world." Then he left the stall, laid his arm around Andrea, and pulled her close. While they kissed, Rosie hastily turned away.

"Congratulations on the next generation, Honey."

"Thank you, my Cherry Blossom," he replied.

Rosie rolled her eyes. *Cherry Blossom*, how very original considering he had always simply called her *Rose*. Her ex was behaving like an idiot. "We should leave mama and baby to themselves," she said. "Could you please bring in a hay bale from outside, Calvin?"

With a nod, he went out behind the stable, and brought in a hay bale. Rosie remained next to the paddock fence with Andrea and Sonja while Calvin took a quarter of the hay bale and gave it to Sky. "That ought to be enough for now, eh?"

"Yes, thank you. I just want to keep her occupied now that she will be spending a good deal of her time outside by herself."

Calvin came over, brushing the bits of hay from his jeans. "Sky seems almost as exhausted as Lori."

"She spent the last hour trotting nonstop back and forth in the paddock," Rosie told him.

"I suppose she doesn't like to be alone. It's not as nice as being with someone else." He gave her a wink.

She tried to ignore the tingling she felt starting up in her stomach by turning to Andrea instead. "What do you do for a living?"

"I have a small goat farm and use the milk in various products that I sell."

Calvin stepped up next to her and put his arm around her waist. "Now don't make it sound like less than it is. Her goat milk products are for sale in shops all throughout Alberta."

Andrea waved her hand dismissively, but her cheeks were turning pink. She fiddled with her bun that was starting to come loose. With her reddish-brown hair, her freckles, green eyes, and outfit in earthy tones and accents of forest green felt, she looked a little bit like a woodswoman out of some old fairytale, Rosie thought. She had always assumed that Calvin was exclusively attracted to slim blondes.

"What a coincidence," said Sonja. "If Emma and I ever have problems with our goats, now I know who we can call."

"Sure, of course." Andrea nodded, smiling. "I can bring you some of my goat cheese. You too, of course, Rosie."

She didn't know what to say. Her first reaction was that she didn't want to have anything to do with this Andrea. But the woman's good-natured smile won her over. "That would be great. Thank you very much. I'll pay you for it of course."

"Don't be silly. As my guy's foal's foster mother, you've earned it. He can pay the bill." She nodded her head in Calvin's direction and playfully elbowed him in the side.

"What's this? My girlfriend and my ex are joining forces against me now?" he asked.

"What can I say, I like your ex a lot. I guess that means you get the short straw." She giggled, and Calvin started to tickle her, causing her to burst with laughter.

Sonja went over to Rosie. "It's not easy seeing your ex with someone new, is it?"

"Nah, it's fine. I'm over him." But it was hard for her to take her eyes off the two of them playing around.

"It can still hurt." Sonja briefly placed her hand on her shoulder. "Well, I'd better make my way back. Could you show me where I am on my GPS, please?" She held out a small device. "Emma and I will come visit soon. I'm sure your new little one will attract a lot of admirers."

Calvin cleared his throat, and Rosie noticed that his expression had darkened. But when he didn't say anything, she turned her attention back to the GPS locator. She pointed out the location of her cabin and marked the way to the guesthouse.

"I see, I turned right when I should've turned left." Sonja traced the line on the display with her finger. "Great, then I'll just go back the way I came and turn the other way." She spontaneously gave Rosie a hug. "See you soon."

"Thanks again for your help."

Sonja got on her bike and waved as she rode away.

"Do you mind if I wash my hands before we also head off?" Andrea asked her.

"Certainly, inside the cabin, next to the kitchen on your right."

Once she had disappeared into the house, Calvin came up to Rosie. He swiftly grabbed her arm and pulled her closer. Hazel, who was snoozing in the grass at the foot of the porch, raised her head and growled.

"Hey, what do you think you're doing?" Rosie tried to free her arm.

"Shh," he shushed her. "You listen to me now. This foal is worth a lot of money, and I won't have you letting a bunch of strangers come around to have a look. I heard what that Sonja said. Forget about any admirers. You won't be showing off that colt."

Rosie stared at him aghast. "You're bullshitting me, right?"

He tightened his grip on her arm. "I'm not playing around. Those are my horses. You take good care of them, and when the foal is old enough, I'm going to come for it and you can keep the mares. If anything goes wrong, I'll be taking back Lori and Sky too. At least I can get a good price for them for slaughter."

She gasped. Fear crawled up her throat. She forced herself to look Calvin in the eye.

"Let me go," she said as calmly as possible. "You have lost your mind." Hazel stood next to Rosie and flashed her teeth.

He let go of her arm. The look in his eyes softened. "Sorry." He lifted his cowboy hat and ran his hand over his forehead. "I don't know what just got into me. Having a foal from Dragon is simply a huge deal. And Sonja's comment just caught me off guard. I didn't mean it."

"Didn't mean it?" Rosie asked loudly, then lowered her voice. "What's wrong with you? You're acting crazy. Is somebody out to get you?"

He grinned. "I really am sorry. I'm under a lot of stress with my dad, and my nerves are frayed."

The cabin door opened, and Andrea came out.

Rosie rubbed the spot on her arm where she could still feel his fingers. "Don't take out your anger with your dad out on me," she hissed at him. "I'm perfectly capable of looking after Dragon's progeny."

"You just keep your mouth shut that it's his foal. There are jealous people all over." Calvin turned around and waved to his girlfriend. "Let's go, Cherry Blossom."

Rosie and Andrea exchanged phone numbers, and Rosie watched the truck disappear around the curve. Calvin's words didn't make any sense. Why was he so paranoid about the foal's safety? There were certainly foals out there that were far more valuable than Lori's.

She took a few deep breaths and shook her arms until she could feel the tension evaporate. Then she realized that she'd forgotten to ask Calvin about the written contract regarding the horses. She sighed. However, she didn't feel any need to call him.

Instead, her cell phone buzzed with a text from Nick: *I saw that you tried to call. Did Lori give birth? Were you calling to invite me to dinner?*

Rosie smirked as she typed out her answer: *Sorry, Cowboy. We were both wrong. It was nine days. But I have no objections to dinner.*

With a smile still on her face, she stuck her phone in her pocket. She glanced at Sky and realized just then that the mare was staring into the forest. Rosie climbed over the fence into the paddock and saw a group of wild horses standing in the shadows under the trees, resting. One of the mares also had a foal who was hungrily nursing. Rosie smiled and enjoyed the feeling of relief that the birth of Lori's foal had gone off with no problems.

August

Woodwind soon learned that only two of the eight teenagers were interested in woodcarving. He and Lee had set up a small workshop in one of the barns at Willow Ranch. He had wanted to show the young Cree teens from Sunchild Reserve the traditional art of woodworking, and besides making flutes, they would also make talking sticks. In response to the never-ending questions from the teenagers as to why they had to carve the short sticks he had provided them, he could only answer that they would find out during their trip to the mountains. They grumblingly relented and went out to pick one of the thin branches that Woodwind had set out for them.

"That looks like your limp dick," one of the boys joked, waving his knife in front of another boy's fly.

"At least I have one," said the other.

Woodwind sighed and stepped in between the two adversaries. "Cut it out, you two, otherwise you can take your things and go."

The boys threw him dirty looks. However, they did lay their knives on the workbench.

"Sticks for talking and flutes, great. Who carves a flute these days for his girlfriend?" Nuka groaned, also tossing his knife onto the workbench.

"Yeah, this is bullshit. We thought we were going to learn how to hunt and shoot arrows," one of the others piped up.

"Or drumming," Nuka interjected. "Flutes are so not cool. Did you use it to play a love song for your boyfriend in prison?"

Woodwind tried to calm his boiling anger by taking a few slow breaths before speaking. "You want to know what life was like in prison? Then keep it up, and you'll find out faster than you know."

Nuka only grinned, then started rhythmically drumming his hands against the wooden workbench. Shortly thereafter, the others joined in. Woodwind didn't bother raising his voice above all the noise at first, but simply stepped out of the small workshop. He closed the door behind him and fastened the latch. Let them all kill each other in there or bash each other's heads in.

Shocked at his own thoughts, he stopped. Dammit, he wasn't exactly cut out for working with adolescents. He had no idea what these kids were going through. Maybe Nuka and his friends were better off in a correctional facility. At the very least, they didn't seem to have the slightest interest in learning about the traditions of their ancestors, about what it meant to be a Cree. He heard them shouting from the barn as they tried to pull the door open.

Naira rushed over to him. "My goodness, what's all that racket?"

"Those kids are behaving like wild animals, so I locked them in the barn."

"That doesn't count as a solution." She shook her head. "Luckily their teacher had to leave early today and didn't see you do that."

He hated the reproachful tone in her voice. Naira went to the barn door and unlocked it. She was almost run over by the stream of teenagers pouring out.

"Whoa!" She jumped to the side. "Go inside the house and get yourselves some sandwiches," she called after them, before turning to Woodwind. "What happened?"

He huffed. "Forget it. I'm no good at being a teacher. You'd best start looking for someone else who can work with this age group. Maybe Miss Deerfoot can do it instead of always hiding behind her desk." He turned away, but she grabbed his arm.

"Miss Deerfoot and I have an agreement which was also discussed with the school board. She teaches at the school, and we are responsible for actively bringing these kids closer to their cultural heritage."

"That may be easy for you. You have experience teaching. This is all new for me and, I have absolutely no clue how I'm supposed to teach them anything." Woodwind shrugged.

"No one thinks this is easy. It's not about being their teacher, you're their role model. Show them that they can be proud of being a member of a First Nations tribe. Awaken in them a sense of self-confidence that will allow the teens to feel connected to their people."

He shoved his hands in his jeans pockets and quickly jerked his head from side to side. "I don't know whether—"

Naira laid her hand on his arm. "Have a talk with my grandfather at least before you throw in the towel. Promise me that much."

Woodwind was sitting on his back porch at the reserve, taking the last swig from his can of Coke and watching the sun slowly disappear on the horizon. It was too late now to go over to Chinook's house, he shrugged. What could the old man possibly tell him anyway?

"Do you have another one of those in the refrigerator?" a somewhat scratchy voice asked, bringing him out of his contemplation. He turned his head and saw Chinook standing at the base of the porch.

The shaman ascended the three steps and paused to catch his breath. "Getting old is no walk in the park," he mumbled.

Woodwind grinned, stood up, and pushed his chair toward his elder. "Sit down, and I'll get you one."

A moment later, he returned with two cans. He passed one to Chinook and opened the other for himself, then pulled up another of the flimsy plastic chairs. "Did Naira send you?"

"You're sitting on your back porch all alone watching the sunset. I don't need my granddaughter to tell me that your thoughts are all in a knot."

Woodwind took a long gulp and nodded. "I appreciate your wisdom, but if I needed any advice, I would've come to you."

Chinook took a sip and scrunched up his nose. The wrinkles on his face danced in response. "I always forget how much the carbonation tickles," he said, placing the can on the chair's wide armrest. He then folded his hands in his lap and looked at Woodwind. "You are very close to shutting yourself off to everything, including yourself. What's got you scared?"

"I'm not scared at all," Woodwind replied brusquely. He shrugged his shoulders apologetically and leaned back in his chair, causing the back of the chair to creak threateningly. "No matter what I do, I can't seem to connect with these kids."

"Have you tried putting yourself into their shoes?"

"What good is that supposed to do? I know what will happen to them if they continue to commit more crimes. They'll land in jail. I can certainly tell them everything there is to know about life in prison."

Chinook shook his head, pulling back a strand of his white hair. "They are trying to be young men, but they still have the hearts and minds of children. The concept at Willow Ranch is a good one, don't misunderstand me. But the teenagers equate learning about their traditions with punishment at the moment."

"They also need to be aware of the fact that they won't simply be able to get away with stealing a car and all the other shit they're doing. Life has consequences, and they can count themselves fortunate that they didn't immediately end up in a juvenile detention center." Woodwind stood up, walked over to the wobbly railing, and laid his hands on it. "Maybe Bull was right, and those kids –"

He was interrupted by Chinook's coughing fit.

He turned around. "You okay, wise man?"

The shaman raised one hand and held the other pressed against his chest. "It's okay," he strained to say.

"I'll get you some water."

Chinook willingly accepted the glass and took small sips. Woodwind eyed him apprehensively, but the shaman was already smiling again. "Don't look at me like that. It's not like I'm going to just fall over dead in my chair."

"You used to tell better jokes. Maybe you need to rest?"

"Not before I've told you what you need to hear. Think back to when you were a teenager, Woodwind, to the things that roused the Indian in you. What made you proud to be a Cree back then?"

He knit his brow as he mulled it over, searching his memories for such moments. Before long, images appeared in his mind. Before he could find the words to describe them, Chinook continued speaking. "And now, I want you to think of situations where you cursed the fact that you were Native, that you were different, that you weren't white."

"I never wanted to—" he started to refute, but the shaman's lifted his hand silenced him. And he admitted to himself that he had had these moments. He nodded reflectively.

"We are all connected through energy. It's your job to show this energy to these young people. Use your imagination, integrate them into some little ceremonies. Experience with them the heartbeat of our Mother Earth."

"That's easy for you to say, wise man."

"It's not about me. I stand completely behind you, don't forget that. But here in the reserve, we can't afford having any lone wolves. We can only be strong as a community if we remain as one."

"I appreciate your support. I'm well aware that it's you I have to thank for not having been run out of here by a few people already."

Chinook waved this off. His stony expression made it clear that he didn't want to hear any thanks.

"Everyone here, even the children at the reserve, respect you and turn to you for advice. But I'm just an ex-con on Jeremy Bull's shit-list."

"If that's all that you think you are, then I guess we can just give up right now," Chinook said seriously.

"Oh, well, thanks for that," Woodwind muttered. "But I still think it would be better if I didn't get involved in too many reserve things."

The shaman shook his head. "You're not listening to me." His face was impassive, but Woodwind could see an unspoken anger flaring behind it. "You were given a calling by the Creator, just as I was. I didn't choose you; a higher power did that. So don't you dare screw it up."

"I don't know how I'm going to do it." He gazed helplessly at Chinook.

"Have you started playing your flute again like I told you to?"

Woodwind shook his head, recalling Nuka's sarcastic remarks about it in the barn. Those may have just been the words of a rebellious teenager, yet they still scratched at his soul like shards of glass.

"Find the melody inside you, flute maker. Your brother is not the only one who has magic in him."

"Oh, Chinook, there's nothing magical about me." He shook his head slowly. "I don't even know whether I'm the right person to be working with these kids."

"The decision isn't yours to make." Supporting himself with a hand on each arm rest, Chinook rose slowly. "Those teenagers need you. Cut it out with the self-pity. Only once you decide to contribute to the community here at the reserve will you always be welcome." With these words, the old man shuffled away.

Woodwind stared after him, trying to decide whether he should offer to accompany him the short way home, but then decided against it. He knew that Chinook would only refuse. Had the shaman just given him an ultimatum? If he quit working with the youth at Willow Ranch, would he have to leave the reserve? All of a sudden, the meaning of those words hit him like a punch in the gut.

Cody observed Emma as she chatted with one of the First Nations teens. The two of them were sitting on the pasture fence at Willow Ranch, and the boy was listening attentively. Cody admired the ease with which she talked to people and knew how to ask just the right questions. Getting tight-lipped teens to open up seemed to come so naturally to her. The bell at the main house rang, indicating that lunch was ready. The boy jumped off the fence and two other camp participants came running out of the barn. Cody grinned. The bell's authority seemed to be the only kind that these five boys and three girls accepted without any backtalk. They never showed up late for lunch. Cody walked over to Emma. "Are you hungry?"

"A little. But I think I'll wait until the hungry masses have been fed," she replied, jumping down from the fence. "How about you?"

"Same. Plus, I wanted to have a look at the pack horses' hooves before heading to lunch. Maybe you want to help me?"

"Gladly."

Her radiance was like a drug that he couldn't get enough of. He reached for her hand, and together they walked to the pasture. Cody inspected the shoes on the packhorses while Emma stroked and cuddled them. Next week, Lee and Naira, along with Woodwind and the hired cook, would be taking the teens on a trip into the mountains. It was his job to transport the tents and provisions to the campsite. He glanced at Emma and thought how nice it would be to have her come along with him.

"What's going through your mind?" She came up very close to him and gave him a kiss on the neck.

"Oh, I was just thinking about the trip to the mountains next week and wondering when I ought to give these three horses with loose shoes new ones."

"Oh, right, I forgot all about that trip. You really have the best job in the world."

He smiled. "It's my dream job, I have to say." He took her hand as they walked over to the gate.

"Was it okay with your family when you told them that you didn't want to work at the farm? You had said that the Tippet Dairy has been in the family for over a hundred years." Emma opened the gate.

"Scott was always supposed to be my father's successor, and I've long been more drawn to horses than to cows."

"I can understand that. If I had to choose between being a wrangler or being a dairy farmer, I would also choose horses over cows."

Hand in hand, they strolled along the narrow path leading from the pasture back to the ranch. Cody saw the young people emerge from the house and follow Naira to one of the barns. "I think the coast is clear for us to get some food."

"Sounds good." A conspiratorial grin crossed her face. "Last one has to wash the dishes." With a whoop, she took off running.

He chased after her, laughing. At the top of the porch Emma ran into Lee who was just coming out of the door.

"Whoa, who are you running from?"

Cody, who was right behind her, stopped in his tracks and looked at Lee's face. His boss was amused by Emma's exuberant performance.

"Sorry, Lee. Cody and I were just having a contest to see who could make it to the kitchen first."

"The two of you must be starving then."

Cody nodded as he came and stood next to her. "I just checked the shoes on the packhorses. Only three of them need to re-shoeing."

"Very good," Lee replied. "By the way, Emma, I wanted to ask you if you wanted to come along on the trip to give Cody a hand. Rosie will stay here and keep an eye on all the foals, including hers."

Cody watched as Emma's expression brightened, and she immediately nodded. "Great, thank you! Cody and I were just talking about his job. I'm so glad he became a cowboy and not a farmer."

His eyes met Lee's, and he hoped that his boss wouldn't elaborate further regarding Emma's comment. Lee just raised one eyebrow slightly.

"Well, you'd better go grab some lunch. We can talk about the details in the coming days." Lee touched the tip of his hat, went down the stairs, and walked across the yard.

Emma and Cody entered the house, pulled off their boots, and headed straight for the kitchen. A young indigenous woman stood at the sink, scrubbing a frying pan.

"Hello," said Cody. "I don't think we've met yet."

The woman turned toward him, wiping her hands on a towel. "Hello, I'm Una. Today's my first day here."

"Hi," he replied, then introduced Emma. "Ah, then you will be coming along to the mountains to cook for the group, right?"

"Yep, that's right." Una walked over to the refrigerator and pulled out some butter. "Have a seat. There's plenty of food left still."

They sat down on the bench. Una handed them a basket of cornbread and two bowls of bison vegetable stew. Cody had barely had one spoonful before his cell phone rang. He fished it out of his jeans pocket and saw that the call was from his mother. "Sorry, I have to take this." He stood up and left the kitchen. "Mom, hi, what's up?"

"Bad news. We just got a letter from the milk inspector. They found some impurities in the milk."

"Dammit." He knew it. The milk machines hadn't been professionally cleaned for over a year. "Okay. That's just a warning. We can fix it."

His mother cleared her throat. "We already had a warning a few months ago. Scott said that he would take care of it. But then, you know ..."

"You can't be serious."

"Could you come home and discuss the matter with your father?" His mother's voice had once again taken on a pleading tone.

He gritted his teeth, then sighed. "No, Mom. I really can't get away from the ranch right now. We're leaving the day after tomorrow for a few days in the mountains."

"But we need you here. Your dad needs you."

Cody closed his eyes. His dad had never needed him all these years. And now, he was supposed to just drop everything and take Scott's place? He had a life of his own, dammit. He bit his lip and swallowed his anger.

"Are you still there?"

"Yes, but I have to get back to work. I'll see what I can do from here about making an appointment for getting the milk machine cleaned and ready for inspection."

"But your father is—"

"Make sure that he stays out of the way when the guy is there and lets a professional do it."

"But we can't afford it," his mother exclaimed.

"I'll see if we can pay in installments. Don't worry about it, Mom. I'll give you a call when I'm back." Before his mother could object any further, he hung up and returned to the kitchen.

"Is there trouble?" Emma asked.

"My mom just wanted to wish us a good trip." He put on a crooked smile, sat down, and finished eating.

"Have you got time this evening to come over to the house?" Emma inquired. "Then we can talk more about the trip."

He thought about all the telephone calls he still needed to make and shook his head. "Sorry, but I have to prepare the pack saddles." Another lie. His last bite of soup almost got caught in his throat.

Woodwind gave Ayita a plastic bucket filled with pieces of chopped chicken. Together, they went out to the enclosure where Kachina had been living since July. The little spot in the corner of his office was much too small for the now four-month-old wolf whelp. Wynono was sitting outside the gate while the animal dozed in the sun.

"Your little boy sure seems to have a special bond with Kachina. She isn't as calm with anyone else as she is with him."

"How is she doing? She sure has grown a lot." Ayita kept her distance from the enclosure.

Woodwind also stood back and quietly said: "She is much too lean for her age and still seems rather apathetic. I'm a little worried because she's started chewing on her back paw. But if anybody puts one of those collars around her neck to keep her from doing it, she completely freaks out."

"Poor thing." She went over to her son, kneeled down, and set the bucket of food on the grass next to her. Kachina's ears perked; she raised her head and sniffed. "Hm, are you hungry?"

The little wolf stood up and trotted closer. Woodwind reached for a long pole leaning next to the enclosure and placed a few pieces of chicken into the bowl at the end of it.

"We are no longer feeding her by hand. She needs to develop a respect for humans."

"May I?" Ayita asked, stretching her arm out to take the improvised feeding stick.

He gave it to her, and she guided the apparatus into the cage.

"Don't place it down right in front of her," he said. "I want to see if she's hungry enough to take a few steps towards us."

And indeed, once he and Ayita had moved back a few steps, the wolf slowly approached the food. Wynono curled his fingers around the wire mesh and stood up. The animal stopped, but only threw a glance at the adults. Then she went to the bowl and began to eat. Woodwind gave Ayita a sign for her to follow him.

They sat down on a bench, where they could still see Wynono, and silently observed Kachina pausing after every bite, looking at the boy, and then eating again. The two seemed to be engaged in a silent conversation once more. Woodwind turned to look at Ayita. Her black hair was braided into one thick braid, and she was wearing a gray t-shirt that looked two sizes too big and a pair of loose-fitting jeans. On her feet, she wore moccasins covered in stains and no socks. Her fingers drummed ever so lightly on the wooden bench while her right leg just barely swung.

"How's life with Lyla and my brother?" he asked. "Do you feel a little bit more at home now?"

"The two of them are busy around the clock with preparations for her shop. Lyla helped me get a job in an online call center where I can work four days a week from the house."

He looked at her, unsure of whether she was avoiding his question on purpose. "It's okay if you don't want to talk about it," he said, holding her gaze.

The tiny wrinkles around her eyes did nothing to hide their radiance behind all the sadness. A smile crossed her face, but he could see that it cost her some effort. She averted her eyes, studied her fingers, and folded her hands on her lap. "I don't know what I feel. Maybe I had hoped that it would all be easier, but my past still feels like a wall between me and the residents of the reserve.

What happened back then destroyed so much ..." she stopped, shaking her head. "I want to believe in a future here, I really do." She sighed, knitting her fingers.

Woodwind resisted the urge to ask her about what had happened back then, hoping that she might open up to him some other time. "You see the way Lyla and Lonefeather are building a future together, making their dream come true. Perhaps you might try to find something you're passionate about in addition to your job at the call center."

"That's a lot easier said than done. I have to think about Wynono too."

Giving in to a whim, Woodwind laid his hand on hers. He noticed the way she briefly stiffened, yet she didn't pull away from his touch. "Do you think you could envision the two of you taking care of Kachina?"

Her eyes widened, and her astonishment made him grin. "I'm scheduled to go with the native teens and the Willow Ranch crew on a trek into the mountains. Maja would take care of most things here, but Kachina is the most calm when the two of you are here."

"You don't think Maja would mind?"

"Not at all. In fact, she suggested the idea."

"When do you leave?"

"The day after tomorrow. I'm sorry that I didn't ask you earlier, but I wasn't sure even if working with the teens was the right thing for me." He took his hand from hers and tucked a strand of his hair behind his ear. He told her how he'd had difficulty connecting with the teenagers, and he further admitted that he still didn't know how he was going to persuade the kids to want to go on the trip. "They know that it's part of the program, but I don't want to make them feel like they're being forced to go. Because if they do, they'll be going with the wrong sort of energy."

"Maybe this is a dumb idea, but what do you think about giving the teenagers some sort of task along the way?"

He thought about it, and soon Chinook's words echoed in his mind. *Think about something that makes you feel connected to your roots*, the shaman had said. And all of a sudden, he realized what it was that he could do with the kids.

"That's a great idea," he said. And there it was, that sparkle in her eyes. A warm feeling washed over him. "I think a sacred tobacco ceremony could be just the right thing."

"Oh, yeah, I can imagine so too," Ayita replied.

"I had better explain it to them tomorrow evening at the ranch, so they'll have a chance to come up with some ideas during the hike. Would you like to join me there tomorrow?" He could see from her expression that she wanted to say no, but then she nodded.

"I'd be happy to go with you."

"Great, I'm glad. I just need to start preparing."

They stood up, and Ayita went over to Wynono who was poking a stick into the grass. When she stretched out her hand to her son, he looked at her briefly, but stood up without her help. She left her arm in that position for a moment, then pulled it back and turned around again. "Actually, isn't everyone supposed to bring something for the ceremony on their own?"

"Yes, but it would be simpler if I just brought it all. Should I swing by and pick you guys up at Lyla and Lonefeather's place?"

"That would be great. Then you can also tell me everything we need to do to look after the wolf while you're away."

Once more, Woodwind felt warmth radiating from deep within him, but this time he embraced it. "Sure thing. Then I'll see you tomorrow. I'd better get to work." He gave a short wave, then turned away and left.

The next afternoon, Woodwind parked his car outside of the cabin. It was situated in a semi-remote location, close to where the wilderness began, about a half hour's drive from Willow Ranch. He had let Ayita know that he would be coming a little bit early. He wanted to share with her one of his favorite places before heading to the ranch.

Just as he got out of the car, Lyla opened the front door. "My aunt is almost ready," she called out, waving him to come inside.

He ascended the porch stairs and entered the house. Lonefeather was sitting with Wynono on his lap at the dining table. The little boy was shoving bits of bread thickly coated with butter into his mouth.

"Having kids is a good look for you, little brother," Woodwind said, grinning.

"I think so too." Lonefeather stroked the boy's thick black hair.

The image of himself holding a baby in his arms appeared in Woodwind's mind, of his own child who never got the chance to be born. He gulped and quickly pushed this thought back into the shadows.

"And that embroidered vest with the suede pants is a good look for you, too," said Lyla. "I've never seen you in anything else but jeans and a t-shirt before."

Ayita emerged from the guest room, wearing a traditional tribal dress of light brown leather. Her hair was decorated with feathers and beads. He stared at her, speechless. She ran both hands over her long dress. "Is it too much? I made it myself many years ago."

"No, you look great." He wished she could see herself through his eyes. She would raise her chin proudly and bring the room to light with a radiant smile. Instead, her eyes dropped to the floor, then back to him. "Thanks," she mumbled and went to her son. "I'm ready to go if you are." She wiped butter from Wynono's cheek with a napkin, put her purse on her shoulder, and picked up the boy.

"Do you guys want to come too?" Woodwind asked Lonefeather and Lyla. They shook their heads in unison.

"This evening is for the youth," said Lonefeather. "I wish you a safe journey into the mountains. Let us know when you return."

Lyla gave Woodwind a hug. "Take care of yourself." Then she turned to Ayita and Wynono. "And you two have a nice afternoon and evening."

Woodwind first drove west, then turned onto a smaller gravel road. Ayita looked around. "Lyla took me this way a few days ago."

"What did you guys do?"

"We took a picnic lunch with us and went out to watch the wild horses. Wynono and I got to meet our family horse."

"Shining has grown into a very impressive stallion," Woodwind replied, familiar with the Cree tradition of the shadow horse and the horse as kin here in the valley.

"He is breathtaking. Unfortunately, he didn't let us get too close."

"Not yet." Woodwind smiled at her and parked his car at the edge of the road. "Today I'd like to quickly show you my favorite place."

They got out. Ayita hoisted Wynono onto her hip, and they followed a path through dense pine trees. Woodwind could already hear the babbling of the North Raven River. The trees opened up, and they stood in a small clearing.

"This spring originates from a glacier deep inside the Rocky Mountains," Woodwind explained, kneeling down and letting the ice-cold, crystal-clear water run through his fingers.

"Doesn't that also run past the Three Siblings?"

He looked up, nodding, and was pleased to hear that she remembered this bit of information about how sacred this area was for the Cree people. "Right here, the stream is pretty wide, but it narrows some a little further east, and you can get onto the other side with a fairly good leap. I could listen to it and walk along its banks all day."

"It does have an invigorating effect," Ayita said. She put Wynono down on the mossy grass, and the little boy immediately teetered toward the water. She held him back by the hood of his jacket. "Any idea why it's called the North Raven River?"

"Well, I don't exactly know, but I have noticed that there really are a lot of ravens that come here from up north to have a drink." He raised one hand and pointed at a large, black bird, its feathers shimmering in the sun.

"It could be that there are wolf dens just to the north of here," said Ayita.

"Where did you get that?"

"I've heard that where there are ravens in the wilderness, there are also wolves since the two live in a symbiotic relationship. The birds build their nests near the wolves' dens so that as soon as the pups leave the den, the birds are the first things they see apart from their own family members."

Woodwind listened attentively to her words and was impressed at the enthusiasm with which she shared her knowledge with him.

"Wolf pups and ravens have been known to play together even," she continued. "The pups can make an imprint of the bird's strong scent, and as adults, wolves never hunt ravens; instead, they divide up the work. The ravens are the wolves' eyes in the sky, and they warn the latter of nearby danger to their young, bears or bobcats for example. In exchange, the ravens get to enjoy some of the kill."

"That's what I call a successful partnership," Woodwind declared as they watched two ravens drink from the stream then settle down on the thick branch of a knotty pine tree, chatting to each other.

"What a beautiful picture," Ayita whispered. "This is a good place to restore your soul and be close to Mother Earth."

He nodded, stroked the back of her hand with his finger and tried to clasp it. She pulled away from his touch and picked up Wynono instead.

"Off to Willow Ranch then, eh?"

They were eagerly received at the ranch. Lee led them across the yard to one of the barns. Woodwind saw that a tipi had been set up, and the eight teens were sitting and talking in a semi-circle around a campfire. Lee turned to Woodwind. "We plan to take a tipi with us on the trip. The teenagers will be responsible for setting it up while we're in the mountains."

"Very good. They all seem to be in a great mood." Woodwind looked around at the smiling teens as they clowned around.

"I think they've already made their bets about who is going to make it all the way to the end." Lee grinned, glancing at Ayita. "It's nice to see you and Wynono here tonight."

"I agree," said a voice from behind them.

Woodwind turned around in surprise. Naira had come up

behind them, and Una was standing next to her. He attempted a casual hello, but it almost got caught in his throat.

"Hi," she said with a smile, bending forward and giving him a kiss on the cheek. Then her gaze turned to Ayita and Wynono. "What a cutie! My name is Una."

Woodwind saw from Ayita's pursed lips that she wondered what sort of relationship he and Una had, but this wasn't the time or the place for explanations, so he only smiled.

"Una will be accompanying us into the mountains and doing the cooking," Naira clarified, then addressed Ayita directly. "Maybe Wynono would like to come and see the foals while Woodwind gets ready?"

"Sure," she answered with a smile.

Woodwind nodded at the two women and tightened the leather band holding his hair back. "Have fun looking at the horses. I'll need about fifteen minutes till we can start."

"Okay. I'll go and tell the kids the plans for our departure in the morning," Lee countered.

The four of them left, and Woodwind found himself alone with Una. He took a step closer to her. "I can't imagine that your dad would be very excited about your new job."

"I told him that I would be keeping an eye on Nuka while we're in the mountains," Una replied.

"You know that Bull is against this initiative with the teens. And here you are now taking part in it; you're only going to provoke him."

She shrugged. "I don't let him tell me what I can and can't do. It'll be nice to spend some time together." She winked at him. "But I'd better go. I still have a few things to pack for tomorrow."

Just as she was about to turn around, he grabbed her by the arm. "It's not just about what you want, dammit. I thought we'd agreed that the two of us couldn't be together?"

Una pulled her arm out of his grip. "Calm down, I was just making a joke. I am not here because of you, I'm here for the money so I can pay off some debts faster. Besides, I'm not interested in following my dad's rules." With these words, she turned and marched away.

Woodwind's hands curled into fists. Una's working here was going to cause trouble, he was sure of it. But now wasn't the time to come up with a solution. He couldn't change anything anyway, so he closed his eyes, breathed deeply a few times and released his anger.

Next, he went to his car and retrieved two bags. With a bag of utensils in each hand, he turned around. Next to the tipi, the campfire cast everything in an orange glow. The young people were sitting on horse blankets in a half moon on top of the sandy soil.

Thoughtfully and with deliberate movements, Woodwind walked over to a low table set up next to the tipi and unpacked the supplies. There were small squares of cotton fabric in just about every color, eight rolls of twine, and eight small bags filled with dried tobacco. He knew the teenagers were curiously following his every movement. Nervousness crept in. Would they even be open to listening to him? He hadn't missed Nuka's comment on his traditional native garb.

What had he been thinking in wearing this outlandish-looking vest with an embroidered headband around his braided, feather-adorned hair? All of a sudden it felt much too tight around his head. The necklace he had worn specifically for the occasion seemed to now creep up and choke him. He wouldn't be able to get out a single word. His ice-cold fingers arranged the pieces of fabric as he avoided turning around. The eyes of the teenagers pierced his back like arrows. Without warning, someone laid a hand on his shoulder.

"You'll be great!" Ayita's smile dispelled all his anxieties.

He nodded gratefully. "Where's Wynono?"

"Naira's foster child Samantha is watching him; they're with the horses."

"Good. Then I'll get things underway before those kids start trying to leave." He picked up one of the cotton squares, the roll of twine, and a little bag of tobacco, before turning around and joining the teens. With a short, sharp whistle, he got them to stop talking. Ayita placed two logs on the fire and joined Naira and Lee, who were standing behind the semi-circle of teenagers. Woodwind cleared his throat.

"Tomorrow, we will embark on our expedition into the mountains, and I would like to give each of you a task for the journey."

A groan rolled through the audience.

"Now, just listen to what I have to say before you start complaining. You will each prepare yourselves during the hike for a traditional tobacco ceremony."

"Smoking is always cool," Nuka called out, and the boys snickered.

"It's not for smoking; it will be an offering to Mother Earth, in the form of a small pouch of tobacco." He raised up the three objects. "Some of you already know our tradition of offering tobacco as a sign of gratitude, but have any of you already actually made such an offering of tobacco? Humbling yourselves and being grateful for everything that you receive, whether knowingly or unknowingly, in your everyday lives?"

The majority of the teenagers shook their heads.

Nuka got to his feet. "I don't ever get anything. Why should I give anything to anyone? I don't owe anybody anything, and neither does anyone else here." The boy looked around the group, a few of the others nodded. Woodwind caught Nuka's gaze. He stared penetratingly straight into his eyes until, the boy's hostility disappeared and he sat back down.

"I know that you guys haven't had it easy in life. You're angry. But whenever you're asked about whatever is causing that anger, you clam up."

"That's because nobody really wants to know," one of the boys interjected.

"I care." Woodwind looked at the faces around him. "I want to know why you are so angry."

"Or scared," one of the girls mumbled.

He caught her fearful look and nodded at her. "During our trip, we will be talking about everything that is going on in your hearts. No one will be judged or laughed at or mocked. And I'm sure that you'll be able to find something to be grateful for." He pointed to the supplies on the table.

"You can take as many squares of fabric as you want. Everyone gets a roll of twine and a little bag of tobacco, which I have already prepared for you, to make your offering pouch." He was astounded to see how patiently the kids waited in the line until it was their turn to take the items. Almost reverently, some of they held up the squares of fabric, which glowed brightly in the firelight. One of the girls came over to Woodwind. "So, during the walk, we should think about what we're grateful for?"

"That's right. It can be for something as little as the cookies your grandmother made for you, a beautiful sunset, a half-day of school, or one of your teachers giving you praise, for example."

"And if I don't have much to be thankful for?" Nuka asked.

"Then you just make fewer bundles during the ceremony. It's not about how many pouches you have to offer in the end," Woodwind explained. "But perhaps you might experience something along the way that you can be thankful for."

"Yeah, like blisters and sore muscles," one of the kids joked as the others laughed.

Woodwind had to grin, and he waited until everyone had their things and had sat back down again. "Once we get to our campsite, we will take a day to go from there to one of the sacred places and spend the night there. During that time, you will all find a spot where you will tie up your offering pouches, but I'll talk about that more once we get into the mountains."

"Okay, if everyone has their things for the ceremony, then I'd say it's time to head off to bed for the evening," said Naira. "We've got an early start tomorrow."

Without any complaints, the teenagers disappeared into their sleeping quarters. Woodwind saw Samantha coming toward him with Wynono by the hand. The little boy had flushed cheeks, straw in his hair, and was eating a cookie.

"Did we miss it already?" Sam asked.

"Yes, but it looks like my son's had a really good time anyway." Ayita smiled and thanked her.

Sam helped pick the bits of straw out of Wynono's hair. "He didn't say anything, but he laughed and giggled a lot, so I think he liked it." The girl gave him a kiss on his head, then got down on her knees in front of him. "I understand." Then she stood back up, bade everyone good night, and skipped off toward the ranch house.

Ayita looked at Woodwind and then at Naira, confused. "What did she mean by that?"

Naira shrugged. "Our Samantha understands much of what is hidden inside of us. She will let us know what she means when it's right."

Ayita picked up her son. "I think someone needs to get right to bed."

"We all should," said Lee. "See you in the morning, Woodwind."

"Good night, you two."

On the drive back to the cabin, Woodwind and Ayita quietly discussed taking care of Kachina as Wynono slept in the backseat.

"Maja knows how much to feed her. You can just discuss the feeding times with her," Woodwind said.

"Okay. We can come and spend time with Kachina to make sure she's doing okay."

He parked the car and carried the sleeping boy up the porch stairs. Ayita took her son from there.

"Thank you for being there this evening," he said softly. "It meant a lot to me."

"To me too. Your words have given me a lot to think about. Perhaps it's time for me to make an offering to the land and ask it to accept me into its embrace." She smiled, bent over to him, and gave him a hint of a kiss on his cheek. "Take care of yourself, Woodwind."

Before he could reply, she opened the door and slipped inside with her son.

Rosie had wanted to use her free weekend to finally get started on her intensive training program with Sky. In order to document her progress, she had mounted her cell phone on the paddock fence with an elastic band. She would use the videos as a part of her application to Gordsteen. Since the foal's birth, Sky had become somewhat calmer, and Rosie had to grin at her attempts to get closer to Lori's baby. The old mare still kept an eagle eye on her colt. But Rosie knew that the experienced horse mama would soon allow Sky and the foal to have closer contact with one another.

Standing at the fence, Rosie switched on the camera function and briefly glanced at the clear, blue August sky. The wind rattled the leaves on the poplar trees. And the spicy fragrance of the pine trees wafted over from the forest bordering the western edge of the property. She loved this little patch of earth and smiled.

With a halter in one hand and taking small, careful steps, she approached the brown mare. Sky raised her head and pricked up her ears, as the muscles around her neck and jaw tensed.

"No reason to be alarmed," Rosie murmured in a soothing tone. "Having a halter isn't anything new to you." She took another step toward the mare. As the horse retreated, she remained still. Why was Sky so apprehensive all of a sudden? Rosie set the halter on the ground, reached out her arms, and waited for the mare to come to her, but Sky only stared at her. When Rosie tried once more to get closer, the animal responded with a high-pitched snort.

Rosie could see that she wasn't going to get anywhere like this. "Okay then, we can just spend a little time together at a distance." She detached her phone from the fence, stuck it in her pocket, and got herself a folding chair, which she placed in the small pasture. Lori didn't pay her any attention, but her foal snorted and stared at the unknown object from a safe distance. Rosie sat down and kept an eye on Sky. She went over the basic concepts in her mind of what to be aware of when starting out to train a young or unbroken horse. The animal needed to feel safe, because only then would it be open to establishing a relationship with its trainer. Something was disrupting the communication between her and Sky.

She remembered something that an old horse trainer had once said to her: "A horse instinctively needs a leader. If it feels safe and enters into a relationship with that person, only then does the trainer have the opportunity to slowly take over the lead role."

She was sure that most of the cowboys she knew would mock her for her conservative handling of Sky. Many of them preferred to force a horse into subordination, despite all the dangers and obstacles that this approach entailed.

But that wasn't the way Rosie wanted to proceed, and she also knew that Gordsteen's no longer used such antiquated techniques. Her goal was to awaken in Sky the desire to make contact with her and to learn.

After a half an hour, Rosie stood up and began to scoop the horse poop into the wheelbarrow. Then she rolled her collection over to a manure pile on the other side of the pasture. As she did that, she completely ignored Sky and instead walked over to the foal and gave Lori some affection. After another quarter of an hour, Sky approached her and took a carrot from her hand by stretching her neck to reach it. A tiny success, Rosie smirked.

"Tomorrow you're going to need to do a little bit more to earn a treat," she said.

The next morning, Rosie first fed the horses and then treated herself to a hearty breakfast. She wrote in her small notebook what she had planned to do with Sky today and flipped through the pages to her previous training sessions. She decided she would first engage Sky without using a halter in the hopes of piquing her curiosity. The sun shone through the window, promising another warm August day. She looked forward to the next few hours with her horses. Standing up, she set her dirty dishes in the sink and pulled a vest on over her t-shirt. She stuck a few carrot pieces and oat cookies in her pocket. "Let's go, Hazel. We've got work to do."

She entered the stall and began cleaning it, all the while leaving the gate between the pasture and the barn wide open. After some time, Lori and her colt came trotting in to see what Rosie was doing. She gave the two a few bits of carrot and some extra hay. Out on the pasture, Sky neighed to her companions and made her way to the stable gate.

"Oh, would you also like to earn yourself some carrot bits?" Rosie put away the pitchfork and picked up a brush. She approached Sky with it, who took a few steps back.

"It's okay," she said softly, walking across the grass, intending to close the gate to the stable behind her. Sky threw up her head, apparently unsettled by this idea. Rosie pushed the gate open again, which seemed to pacify the mare. "Okay, you don't want to be separated from your friends. That's fine, we can do it this way too."

Rosie held out the brush with a piece of carrot on it. Sky eyed the object critically, but then took the carrot. After that, she allowed Rosie to brush her. With long strokes, Rosie brushed her entire body, even finding a few ticklish spots, causing Sky to flare her nostrils and extend her neck in satisfaction. Hazel barked, and Rosie saw Lyla's car coming up the drive. Sky stiffened briefly, but relaxed again with a few soothing words.

Lyla parked, opened her door, and jumped out of the car. "Hello, Rosie, I was just on my way into town and thought I should stop by. I hope I'm not disturbing you."

"No, of course not. I'm always happy to see you, especially now that Sky seems to be having a really good day." Rosie smiled and ran the brush down the horse's leg. Sky let her do it without so much as batting an eyelash.

"She seems to be enjoying it. What sorts of problems did you have with her?"

Rosie told her about yesterday's experience, and then realized that Lyla hadn't even had a chance to see the foal yet. Just then, Lori came out of the stall along with her colt, and Lyla's eyes got big. "Oh, what a colt! He's beautiful. His coat is like dark chocolate. Wow."

Rosie smiled and joined Lyla at the fence. "I just love his four white socks. He's a dapper little man."

Sky greeted her friends with a grumbly whinny and tried to

get as close as possible to the foal. Lori laid her ears straight back as a warning sign, and Sky retreated.

"Looks like somebody is eager to play auntie." Lyla laughed.

"Yeah, Sky is crazy about him."

"Maybe you should breed her too. Have you got her papers?"

"To be honest I don't know if she even has papers." She thought about the letter that Calvin had finally sent after she had asked him multiple times. He had handwritten a few lines as a contract, but had avoided providing much detail; Rosie was pretty dissatisfied with his informal agreement, but he had signed it. She had no desire to continue nagging him about it, so she had left things as they were.

All of a sudden, Sky threw her head up and stared into the small forest near the pasture. She trotted to the fence with a loud neigh and her ears pointed upward. Rosie watched as several wild horses emerged from the trees and looked around briefly, before vanishing again into the shadows. Sky trotted back and forth along the fence, loudly whinnying. It took her a long time to calm down again. Rosie looked at Lyla, who was thoughtfully watching the mare. "What are you thinking about?"

"Oh, I was just thinking about Shining and his herd."

Rosie knew the story of the stallion who had been born at Willow Ranch. His roots lay with the wild horses of the area, and Lyla had set the stallion free four years ago. "Do you sometimes wish that you had kept Shining?"

Lyla shook her head. "His place is in the wild."

"Yes, but he was born in captivity, and there are many cases of wild horses that were captured with permission and who turned out to be excellent riding horses."

"That's true, but I also know of cases in which the owners failed miserably in trying to establish a connection to their horses. The thing about wild horses is that their desire for freedom is far greater than their willingness to work with humans and be part of a team."

Rosie looked at Sky. Was it possible that the mare was also a wild horse? She asked Lyla for her opinion.

"I can't say with any certainty. You and Sky, you have a long way ahead of you that requires an awful lot of patience. Keep your eye on the goal, but don't lose sight of what's best for Sky."

"Yes, I'll do that. As long as we're making progress, I'll assume we are on the right path, don't you think?"

"You have more experience in training horses than I do, but I think you can't let Sky feel like she's being coerced. Take your time with her." Lyla turned around and called out for Mud. The black Lab came running with Hazel in tow. "Sorry, but we've got to keep moving. Congrats on the foal."

Rosie hugged her friend. "Thanks for your visit."

Lyla opened the door for Mud to jump into the car, then got in herself and drove away with a wave.

The horizon lazily shifted into a deep orange. Cody looked at the clock. Two hours from now, he and Naira would be heading off in the van to the starting point of their hiking tour with the indigenous teens, along with Woodwind and Una. From there, it was a twelve-mile trek to their campsite. They estimated the group would take about six hours, including a couple of long breaks. During the last couple of weeks, the teens at the ranch had undertaken a few shorter excursions in order to prepare themselves for today's longer journey.

Cody suspected, however, that this trek into the mountains might be a test of endurance for some of them. He and Emma would be going a different route with the packhorses. He had calculated it would take them four hours to get there despite taking a longer route than the hikers. But the teens would need to take a few breaks.

With a cup of coffee in hand, he walked over to the barn to get a look at the pile of stuff they needed to take with them. The kids wanted to bring that much into the wilderness? He shook his head. Never in a million years would he be able to get all that onto only six pack horses. Emma joined him, also with a mug of steaming coffee in tow.

"Wow, all of that is coming along with us?" She looked more closely at the luggage, picked up one of the bags, and groaned. "I think somebody packed a few rocks in here."

"Lee promised me that he'd tell the teens what to bring and what the weight limit was." Cody took another sip of coffee, then tossed the rest of it into the grass. "These kids seem to have completely ignored him. There's no escaping it; they're going to need to repack their bags before breakfast."

Emma nodded. "Let me take care of that. In the meantime, you can get the horses ready."

He smiled at her gratefully as he had no desire to torture himself with a bunch of grumpy teenagers so early in the morning. He gave her a kiss on the cheek. "Thanks, you're the best."

"And don't you forget it," she replied, grinning.

Barely had he brought in the pack horses and two riding horses from the pasture and prepared them when Emma returned, bringing with her Woodwind and Lee and the kids. With a smirk, he watched out of the corner of his eye as the teens pulled iPads and handheld game consoles out of the bags. One of the girls produced a giant makeup bag, and one of the boys had packed a hairdryer.

"Guys, guys," Lee said, shaking his head. "Where do you think we're going? To the Banff Springs Hotel?"

The teenagers giggled.

"We are headed out into the wilderness, where there is neither electricity nor cell phone reception."

A groan made the rounds, and some of the girls started whispering among themselves.

"Don't worry," said Emma, "you guys won't be bored. And you also won't die without the social media for a few days."

"But all my friends will think I'm dead," Nuka balked.

"I thought you said yesterday at the campfire that you didn't have any friends," said one of the girls, grinning.

Nuka snorted and put his cell phone and his iPad in the designated box. The others followed his example, and after a while, the pile of belongings dwindled into a more acceptable amount. Cody gave Lee a thumbs up.

"Okay, thanks for your help. And now, off to breakfast." Lee shooed the teenagers out of the barn, and Woodwind followed them.

"I'll help you load the things onto the truck. And then we can get the horses into the trailer and meet you at the parking lot at Peppers Lake, sound good?" Lee asked.

"Yep. The cookware is already inside the trailer." Cody saw that Emma was saddling the riding horses. They would be taking Jazz and Asra, the same gray mare Emma had ridden a year ago, with them to the mountains. Emma's excitement was written all over her face.

At Peppers Lake two hours later, Cody handed Emma the lead to one of the packhorses. "Shall we head off?"

She beamed at him, bent down, and gave him a kiss. "Let's go, Cowboy."

He swung himself onto Jazz's back, guided the gelding over to where the packhorses were, and untied their leads from the horse carrier. The four horses were bound together by their leads, and they followed the lead animals. Setting off, they took one of the narrow pads leading from the parking lot into the forest. He took a deep breath. The fragrant aroma of resin and pine needles filled his nose. He glanced back and saw the happy smile on Emma's face and shared in her excitement at being part of the tour. They rode single-file in order to help the pack horses remain calm. From what he knew about Emma, like him, she enjoyed riding through the wilderness in silence. He thought about his mother, with whom he had spoken yesterday on the phone. She had said that his father refused to take it easy and was out helping Kurt in the barn, even on crutches. Everything seemed to be okay at the farm for the moment, but Cody knew that he couldn't afford to pay Kurt in the long term. He would need to find an alternative solution. For a moment, he closed his eyes, bringing his thoughts back to the here and now. Before him lay three days out in the wild with Emma, and he wanted to enjoy that.

They made faster progress than expected and arrived at the clearing where they would set up the campsite after only four hours. They dismounted, tied up their horses, and unloaded the equipment, before coming up with a plan on how to best set up the tents.

"The kids will be setting up the large tipi tomorrow on their own. That is one of the milestones in learning about their native traditions," Cody explained.

"How do these teens know so little about their own culture?" Emma held a tent pole in place.

"Naira once told me that these kids have barely had any chance to learn about their roots. Many of them were raised in non-native families, primarily in white foster families. And for that reason, they had little to no contact with their native traditions." With experienced hands, Cody pitched the first tent.

Two hours later, each of the two-person tents stood in place. For the kitchen, they spanned a tarp over a campfire ring to keep it dry from the rain. The pack boxes along with tree stumps would serve as places to sit.

"What will the teenagers be doing while they're here?" Emma asked, opening a bottle of water.

"I don't know what the exact program is, but I know they will be spending at least one night sleeping under the stars."

"That's sure to be a memorable experience for them."

He nodded, then heard voices approaching. The travelers emerged one by one out of the forest. A few of the teens were dragging their feet with their heads hanging, and two girls were chatting with Woodwind. Once they spotted the camp, many of them cheered and jogged the last few yards. Cody walked over to Lee and Naira. "Well? Did everything go smoothly?"

"The last half hour or so they were starting to complain, but now we're all here," Naira replied, turning to Una. "Let's get started on dinner before these hungry kids start ripping out the grass instead." The women grinned at each other.

"I'll fetch the firewood," said Woodwind.

"Take a couple of the boys with you," Lee suggested, and he nodded.

"Is there anything else planned for the day?" Cody asked, strolling alongside Lee to one of the tents.

Lee set down his backpack in front of it. "No, nothing else is scheduled for today. It doesn't look like the hike took much out of them, but most of them have never been camping before or cut off from the outside world and their electrical devices. I think coming to grips with that is enough for today."

Cody nodded. "Okay, then I'll get the horses settled for the night."

Emma joined him a little while later and helped him hobble the horses and place their bells on them. They would be allowed to graze in groups of three, one after the other.

"Don't they need you in the kitchen? We men are practically starving, you know that, right?"

Emma rolled her eyes, grinned, and playfully elbowed him in the side. "You can drop the macho act. Two of the boys volunteered to bake the bread rolls, so I don't expect they need me. Naira and Una have everything under control."

He grabbed the hem of her shirt and pulled her close. "Oh, that's great. Then I can get in a little snack before dinner." He got in a kiss before she managed to free herself, smiling.

"There are kids present." She wagged a finger at him. "We don't need them getting any dumb ideas."

"Okay, you're right," he winked at her. "But maybe we can share sleeping bags tonight."

After dinner, everyone sat on blankets in a circle around the campfire underneath the clear night sky. Cody had his arm around Emma, and noticing that Woodwind repeatedly threw glances at Una, he momentarily wondered whether there was something between the two. The teenagers held marshmallows on long sticks in the fire. Their tired faces reflected the strenuousness of today's long journey, but he also saw a collective pride of having made it this far.

"What are we doing tomorrow?" one of the boys asked.

"Sleeping in," Nuka spat out.

The others backed him up.

"I'm afraid not. Tomorrow we'll set up the tipi," Woodwind told them. "And go fishing in the afternoon."

"I don't like fish." One of the girls contorted her face.

"Well, then you ought to be happy to see them dead, right?" Nuka grinned.

The girl picked up a pinecone from the ground and threw it in his direction. Soon, pinecones were flying back and forth across the campfire.

"Hey, that's enough," Naira put her foot down, and the teens stopped. "Listen instead to the wilderness."

Cody also followed her instructions and could hear a distant howling.

"Are those coyotes or wolves?" Emma asked softly.

"Hard to say from so far away." He listened to the slowly approaching howling. Deeper voices answered from another direction, sonorous and dark.

"Wolves," he whispered back to her. The chorus got louder, echoed, and increased again in volume until it started to fade and die away.

"Wow, I am covered in goosebumps." One girl said, rubbing her arms.

"Me too," one of the boys admitted, and others nodded.

"Will we get to see the wolves?" Nuka asked.

"That would be amazing luck," Naira answered. "The packs around here are not used to people and are very shy."

"Hm, maybe we'll see some lone wolf cross our path." Nuka stuck a toasted golden-brown marshmallow in his mouth.

"Hopefully not." Naira poked her stick into the embers.

"Why not? Lone wolves are cool," Nuka mumbled with his mouth full.

"Because lone wolves are often extremely lonely. Wolves need a family; having a pack ensures them a more fulfilled life. A single wolf out in the wilderness is doomed and not likely to survive." Naira looked around the group. "But now, it's about time to crawl into our sleeping bags for the night."

The teens only half-heartedly protested. Many of them had been yawning for some time already and were more than ready to retreat to their tents.

Once the teens had all gone to bed, Lee addressed the others. "Everything went really well today. Thanks, you two, for setting up camp. You make a great team."

"I love being here." Emma laid her hand on Cody's thigh. "It doesn't feel at all like work. The hours spent in the saddle looking at a landscape like this ... it's an absolute dream job."

"I'm glad to hear that." Lee yawned. "Oh man, a day in the saddle isn't nearly as tiresome as a hike like today's. I'm off to bed." He stood up.

"Same here." Naira reached out her hand to him, and he pulled her to her feet. "See you in the morning, good night."

Una and Woodwind also got to their feet.

"I'll wake everyone up in the morning," he said. "Breakfast is at eight?"

"Yes," Una replied simply, then mumbled a good night and disappeared into her tent.

Woodwind also left the warm light of the fire and went in the other direction to his tent. Emma cuddled up closer to Cody. "It's so nice to be out here with you."

He gave her a squeeze and a kiss on the side of her head. "I'm very happy we could take this trip together."

She sat up straight and turned to face him. "I realize that this is just a dream of mine, but I want to ask you anyway."

"Sure, what is it?"

"Do you think that I could cut it as a wrangler? I would so love to learn how to work with horses, but there's so much else to learn as well to be able to offer equestrian tours into the mountains."

"Would you give up your life in Germany to do that?"

Emma hesitated with her answer. "Being so far away from my

family and friends ... to be honest, I don't know at the moment. On the other hand, being here is such a wonderfully liberating feeling."

Cody lifted his hand and stroked her cheek. "The work is rewarding, but it also has its downsides. For example, there's no way to know at the end of the summer whether you'll have a job again next year. And also during the winter months, there's no way to survive without having another job."

"Hmm, I hadn't thought about it from that perspective. You're right. But I can't think of anything better than being here with you. You want to continue doing this work in the future, right?"

Now it was Cody who hesitated before answering. What about his family? What would happen to the family farm if he continued his life as a horse wrangler? And if he did decide to remain a cowboy, was he likely to always remain an employee, never becoming the boss of his own operation? Cody was realistic. Running a guest ranch was certainly a step too far for him, but the idea of giving up a life in the saddle to run the family farm was also not his ideal lifestyle. If that decision was even his to make. Hadn't his father decided years ago that his youngest son wasn't cut out to be a farmer? He took Emma's hand.

"I love being out here in the wilderness and working with horses." He saw from her expression that she wasn't satisfied with his vague answer, but it was the most honest thing he could say to her.

He was relieved when a smile appeared on her face. She turned her back to him and leaned into him. He put his arms around her and breathed in her scent, hints of coconut and lemon. He softly placed his lips on her neck. She turned her head, and they kissed. He melted into her warmth, and his hands starting to explore. She returned his now more passionate kisses. His hand slowly pulled down the zipper of her jacket, and his fingers found her nipple. It was hard and tight underneath the thin material of her shirt. She moaned softly. "Let's go to our tent."

A barely audible beeping awakened Woodwind. He grumbled, blinked a few times, and turned off the alarm on his watch. He slowly sat up and groaned. Every muscle ached. In addition to yesterday's hike, his uncomfortably hard earthen bed had finished him off. His entire body hurt like hell. With more moaning and groaning, he crawled out of his sleeping bag and fumbled through his shaving kit for the painkillers he'd fortunately packed. He swallowed two tablets with a gulp from his water bottle, pulled on his jeans, and slipped a buttoned shirt on over his t-shirt.

He unzipped his tent and gazed out into the early morning. The other tents with the teenagers stood to his left and his right, and he didn't see any movement. Over in the makeshift kitchen, he noticed movement and watched Una take the coffee pot off the fire and pour herself a cup. That was exactly what he needed to get himself going before the kids woke up. Lumbering stiffly, he went to her.

"Good morning."

Una smiled at him, took a cup, and filled it. "You've looked better," she said.

"Thanks a lot." He took a sip of the strong coffee. "Aren't you sore at all?"

"A little. I rubbed some peppermint oil into my legs last night before bed."

For a moment, he thought about their time together as a couple, and how she had once pressed her soft body against his while they both forgot about the world around them. However, this time, he knew these were just memories and not something he could allow himself to long for.

"Can I help you?" he asked, but Una only shook her head. He poured himself some more coffee and walked over to the nearby stream. It was the North Raven Creek, snaking its way eastward between the large stones. He saw a few trout swim past, and Woodwind hoped they'd have a good catch when he took the teenagers out fishing later that afternoon. He thought about how he could best communicate to the teens this aspect of their Cree tradition.

His parents, both of them victims of the residential school system that had cut off the First Nations children from their roots, had never been very proud of their native heritage. In the boarding schools, indigenous children were harshly punished if they nurtured their traditions, and they were forced to cut off all contact with their families. He had his grandparents to thank for the little bit of life as a Cree that he was familiar with. They had done their best to impart to him and his brother the traditions of their people. But as soon as Woodwind had hit his rebellious teen years, his grandparents had no longer been able to get through to him. To top it off, he had started experiencing racism and prejudice due to his ethnic background.

He sat down on a boulder half-covered with moss, his thoughts wandering further into his past. He thought about his Nimosom, the Cree word for *grandfather*, with whom he had gone fishing as a kid and whose stories he had loved to listen to. He had also been the one who had discovered Woodwind's talent for woodworking and had encouraged him to play the flute. On the one hand, Woodwind was happy that his grandfather wasn't around anymore to witness his time in prison. But on the other hand, he wished he could still ask his Nimosom for advice.

Woodwind meditatively stared at the water as it tumbled over the rocks and listened to the sound. "That's a beautiful melody you're playing," he mumbled to the water, set down his coffee cup, and pulled out his flute, which he usually carried with him. It was longer than a ceremonial flute and was devoid of any decoration. He slowly raised the instrument to his lips and began to play. The notes felt awkward and refused to harmonize with the rushing water. He stopped in resignation. There was no melody inside him.

The sound of voices and laughter drifted over to him from the camp. The teenagers were awake. He stuck his flute back into the inside pocket of his vest, got up, and went back to the others. The young people had formed a line, each one with a paper plate and silverware in their hands. On the grill stood a pan of cooked sausages and a tray of corn cakes.

"There are only two corn cakes each to start with," Una told them. "If you're still hungry after that, then you can come and get more. The sausages are bison meat, and the syrup on the table is made from wild berries."

"Two corn cakes aren't going to fill me up," Nuka complained.

"I don't like corn cakes. Don't we have any regular pancakes and maple syrup?" one girl asked.

Woodwind joined the group of youth. "Give them a try at least. I'm sure they taste good."

A couple of them grumbled, but everyone filled up their plates and sat down to eat. Lee and Naira appeared, walking over hand in hand.

"Good morning." Naira took a plate and silverware. "That smells great. I'm starving."

"Help yourself," Una replied. "Coffee's next to the fire."

"Has anybody seen Cody and Emma?" Woodwind asked, biting into one of the bison sausages.

"They're off taking care of the horses," Lee answered. "We'd better leave some food for them."

A little bit later, Lee called the teenagers together. "Today we will be setting up the tipi. Naira will tell us about the history of the tipi as we work on it."

She stood next to Lee. "I would also invite you to share your own knowledge of our traditional native housing."

"Could there be anything more boring?" Nuka protested. "I thought we could go hunting or look for wolves."

"Why should we go hunting?" Woodwind inquired. "We have enough provisions for three days. It is only justified to hunt and kill an animal if there is no other food available."

"And what about fishing?" The boy challenged him.

"We catch the fish and let them go again," Woodwind replied.

Nuka glared at him, but gave no further argument. The boy turned to his friend and Woodwind heard him mumble the words "pansy" and "know-it-all." He took a deep breath to suppress the urge to defend himself. "Go get your gloves from your tents, and whoever is wearing flip-flops had better put their boots on. We'll meet back here in ten minutes," Lee instructed, and the teenagers dispersed.

Woodwind went to Lee and Naira. "Unfortunately, Nuka keeps spouting off all the time."

"You're not responsible for his behavior," Naira said. "We made the decision together that we wanted to help kids like Nuka. And if I recall, we never told ourselves that it would always be easy."

He smiled at her gratefully. She was right. But still, he couldn't help but take Nuka's resentful behavior personally.

"We hewed the birches last week and piled them nearby," said Lee. "It would have taken simply much too long to also prepare the tipi frame with the teenagers."

"Will send them in groups of two to go out and collect the fifteen poles and bring them here." Naira pointed to a spot with enough space to build the tipi.

"Okay, then Lee and I will stand back and observe, and only help them when they need it," Woodwind suggested.

An hour later, all the wooden poles had been collected and Woodwind was pleased with how well everyone had worked together.

"How many of you have constructed a tipi before?" he asked the group. One girl half-raised her hand. He waved her over. She obeyed with her eyes lowered as though she now regretted having raised her hand.

"Don't be shy, Mina." He smiled at her encouragingly. "We will instruct the others together on what to do step-by-step. Are you with me?"

Mina nodded.

"Good, where do we start?"

"First we have to make a tripod," she mumbled, her eyes still glued to her feet.

"Very good, that's exactly right," he praised her.

Mina straightened her shoulders.

"We need to lay two of the poles here, next to one another on the ground." Her voice was sounding stronger.

Woodwind pointed to two boys who immediately got to work.

"Then the third one comes on top." Mina was starting to sound more confident.

Naira wrapped a rope around the poles to hold them in place. She looked at Mina and nodded.

"Now we need to stand the tripod up. Then the rest of the poles, except for one, are placed counterclockwise between the ribs and connected with the long end of the rope."

Everyone pitched in, and soon the frame was finished. It stood a good fifteen feet tall against the blue sky. Naira laid her hand on one of the poles.

"Tipi is a compound word; *Ti* means dwelling and *Pi* means to use. The end of the poles all point in different directions. We are like these poles and require the help and strength of our family members and others in our communities in order to stand strong. At the same time, we recognize that our paths in life each run in different directions." Naira walked in a circle from pole to pole. "The construction shows us that it doesn't matter which version of the Great Spirit we believe in, we all look to the same Creator and come from various beliefs." She pointed to the sky. "And there, where the poles come together, they form a sort of nest. Don't the ends of the poles look like a bird who is just settling down with its wings still extended? We are all connected to one another through our relationships, and we depend on one another. The rope is a sacred tie that unifies our traditional values."

Cody and Emma brought forward the canvas, and three of the teens hurried over to help them carry it.

"Unfold the tent and lay it flat on the ground," said Naira. "Originally, these were made of bison skins. The first canvas tipis as we know and use them today appeared in North America around 1800. Since canvas is much lighter than animal skin, people started sewing together larger coverings. They subsequently expanded to a circumference of twenty, twenty-five, and then even up to thirty feet. Our ancestors transported the tents with the help of dogs and simple carriers, like a sled. Later, they employed horses, which made the task much easier and allowed them to cover greater distances."

Nuka walked around the cream-colored canvas as it lay in the sunshine. "And how do we get this thing up onto the poles?"

Mina pointed to the pole that they hadn't attached to the tripod. "We wrap the cloth around this pole, lift it up, and lean it up against the others."

Woodwind nodded. "Do you guys know which direction the door needs to be?"

"Facing east, toward the rising sun," said one of the boys.

"Exactly," Naira confirmed. "Tipis were almost always erected with the door facing east to greet the rising sun. The sun is the giver of all life and, for that reason, is sacred to our people."

Two boys took hold of the other remaining pole and, following Woodwind's directions to lay it in the middle of the cloth, hold it in place, and loosely roll the canvas around it. Then together, they raised it up and leaned it against the back side of the tipi frame. Before Woodwind had the chance to give further instruction, the teenagers had already each grabbed hold of a corner of the canvas and ran around to meet again on the other side of the frame so that the cloth completely enveloped the poles. Naira handed them short wooden pins which they used to hold the ends of the canvas together above the door opening. The tipi was finished! One of the boys cheered and the others joined in. Excitedly, the teenagers jumped around the tipi, clapping and laughing. Woodwind looked at Lee and Naira, who were watching the kids with smirks on their faces. He, too, grinned and celebrated the group's success.

From over at the campfire came the sound of a bell, and he turned his head. Una was waving a horse bell and waved them over for lunch.

"Guys, lunch is ready," he called out to the teenagers. "We'll go fishing afterwards."

Soon, everyone was sitting either on the ground or on top of the pack boxes, balancing a bowl of soup and a bannock.

"Do we all have to go fishing?" one girl asked.

"What else would you be doing? Brushing your hair?" Nuka emptied his water bottle and threw it over his shoulder.

"Plastic bottles belong in that bag over there." Una pointed to the left. "The rest of the garbage goes into the orange bag next to it."

Nuka grumbled, but he stood up and minded Una's instructions.

Woodwind stood in front of the group. "We will need about an hour to reach the spot that's best for fishing. Bring along some water to drink, and we can get going."

"Aren't there any alternatives to fishing?" Nuka probed.

Woodwind looked at Lee and Naira, unsure of what else he could offer the group. If in the end, everyone wanted to do something different, the sense of unity they had established while they were constructing the tipi was sure to fall apart.

"We are here as a group to experience the wilderness," he replied, "and for that reason, we will all stay together. When we get to the river, you can decide then if you'd like to fish or would rather watch."

As the young people got themselves ready, Naira walked over to Woodwind. "That was exactly the right thing to say to keep them together," she said. "I'm sure they'll all have a lot of fun at the river."

He hoped she was right, and he and the teens started on their way. They walked uphill for a while along a narrow path, until the forest thinned out and they had a clear view of the mountainous landscape. The view of the forests seemed to go on forever, and above, the snow-capped peaks stood out against the sky.

He looked around. Some of the teenagers, like him, were enthusiastic about the landscape, turning their heads left and right with big eyes. Others simply stared at the sandy, stony path before them with closed faces, breathing hard and heavily setting one foot in front of the other. They came around a curve, and a turquoise lake came into view. Knotty pine trees stood near the shore and almost looked like old people who had fallen asleep in various positions and had turned into trees.

Woodwind thought he saw something moving toward them from the direction of the lake. Indeed, there was a figure. Perhaps

Cody and Emma had gone for a hike? The person came closer, and Woodwind stopped in his tracks.

"What's the matter? Are we there? I don't see any river." Nuka suddenly said next to him.

Woodwind pointed to the person approaching them.

"That's Rabbit," said Nuka. "I bet he just wants to make sure that I'm behaving myself. What an asshole!"

"Now, now, don't get upset." Woodwind raised his hand and waved at Rabbit.

"Hello," he said, shoving his other arm through his backpack strap. "I thought your campsite was further down in the valley."

"Are you here to spy on me?" Nuka asked, folding his arms over his chest. "Isn't it enough that our sister is here to watch me like a hawk?"

"I'm not here because of you, brother." Rabbit turned his attention back to Woodwind. "Did you guys see the wolf tracks yesterday on your way to the campsite or this morning?"

"We heard howling last night, but didn't see any tracks. Why? Is that why you're here?"

Rabbit nodded. "I've been staying in Chuck's forester's cabin for the past two nights. There's a rumor going around that someone is out hunting wolves."

Woodwind frowned. Hunting wolves was prohibited in this area. "Do you know anything else about it?"

"No. Shots were heard, and someone from the reserve thinks they saw a black wolf covered in blood along the forest road to the south."

Woodwind thought about the wolf pup at the rescue center. Perhaps her mother had been frightened off by hunters and then shot? Was that the reason that the pack hadn't dared to come back for Kachina? But that was many months ago now.

"We'll keep an eye out," he assured Rabbit.

"To be honest with you, it would help me a lot if you guys returned to camp," Rabbit replied.

"Are you crazy?" Nuka exclaimed. "Don't go showing off. We're going fishing, and you can't stop us from doing that."

Woodwind placed his hand on the boy's shoulder, but he shook it off and continued staring at his brother.

"It would be better if you guys didn't leave any more footprints up around here." Rabbit looked at Woodwind, and then at his brother. "I'm not looking to ruin your trip, but with all of you traipsing around the area, I don't have a chance of tracking down any potential poachers."

Nuka huffed. "Why do you have to be like this? All this 'save the wolves' and stuff." He kicked the trunk of a tree with his boot.

"This land once belonged to our ancestors, and the least we can do is to protect its nature and wildlife." Rabbit tucked a strand of his long hair behind his ear. "Don't you understand that?"

"No," Nuka retorted. "First you force me to take part in this program, and then you show up and ruin it."

"That's not how it is. I'm only asking you to—"

"Fuck you. Stay out of my life." Nuka turned around and pushed his way through the group back to the path.

Woodwind saw Rabbit's face contort into a grimace. "Nuka has to find his own way in life. He's angry now, but things will get better."

"I can understand him. It's true that I'm the one to blame for messing up his life."

"No, he did that himself when he decided to engage in theft." Woodwind glanced over to the path and saw that Nuka was still walking away. "We'd better go after him. Keep me updated about the wolves."

"Will do."

The two men said goodbye, and Woodwind and the rest of the kids followed Nuka back to camp.

Cody, dressed in only his underwear, shirt, and cowboy boots, chased behind Emma, shrieking with laughter. She dashed up the path to the tents from the river with his jeans in her hand. While Lee and Naira had set off together on horseback, the two of them had indulged in a dip in the cool water. Emma exuberantly waved his jeans in the air, then abruptly came to a stop between two pine trees at the edge of the camp. Cody saw his chance and sprinted at her. He tore his jeans from her with a whoop.

"Next time I'm going to hide all your clothes." With his pants tucked under his arm, he marched away.

"Wait," she called and waved at him to urgently come back.

Una must have returned from her walk in the woods and seen them, he immediately assumed. Emma grabbed him by his t-shirt and pulled him underneath one of the low pine trees. A branch hit him in the face.

"What in the world?" he said. "I'm sure Una has seen a man in his boxers before." He rubbed his stinging forehead.

"The group is back, but I think only two of the girls may have seen you." She pointed at the giggling girls.

Cody's entire head flushed red with the heat of embarrassment. He hastily pulled off his boots, slipped on his jeans, and then tugged his boots back on. Emma stood next to him, watching, and when he looked at her with a severe expression, she laughed even louder. His anger disappeared; he simply couldn't hold a grudge against this woman. He ran one hand through his wet hair. "I'm glad that I could be of some entertainment to you and the kids." With a grin, he gave her a playfully shove.

"Nobody can carry off the cowboy boots slash underwear look as well as you do," she said.

"Very funny. Let's go and see why the group has come back so soon."

Together, they strolled over to Woodwind, who had started a fire inside the stone circle.

"Did something happen?" Cody asked.

"Where are Lee and Naira?" The other man grumbled, glancing around. "And where is that damn coffee pot? I need some coffee."

"I'll take care of it," said Emma. "Looks like Naira and Lee are just returning over there."

"Thanks." Woodwind marched over to the two on their horses, and Cody followed him.

Lee and Naira dismounted and tied the horses to two trees.

"What are you doing back so soon?" Naira asked.

"We ran into Rabbit. Apparently, somebody is out hunting wolves," Woodwind replied. "He's on their trail, and he asked us to not get in his way."

Naira sighed. "Hopefully, that's just a rumor. How are the teens taking it?"

"They're disappointed, and Nuka is pissed off at his brother for ruining everything for him."

"You take care of the kids," said Cody. "I'll unsaddle the horses and let them graze."

"Thanks." Lee nodded at him, and the three of them walked away.

Cody unbuckled Asra's cinch, lifted off the saddle, and laid it in the grass. He noticed Una sitting next to Emma, chatting by the campfire. Una showed her something inside one of the pack boxes, let her smell it, and then handed her a pot. Emma's interest in native cooking and preparation seemed insatiable.

While he took care of the horses, all he could think about was the wolf hunt. As far as he knew, illegal hunting was punishable by a high fine and even time in jail. Who would want to risk that, and why? He brushed the horses where the saddles had been, hobbled and belled them, and left them to graze. Asra and Jazz inched away to a patch of green grass and began nibbling.

He put away the gear and saw that the teens had divided into two groups. A few of them had begun painting the tipi with finger paints. One girl drew a horse, while one of the boys sketched the silhouette of a wolf in black paint onto the canvas. Woodwind sat with three other teenagers, each with a blade in their hand, whittling a piece of wood on the ground.

Cody wondered whether it was a good idea to hand them knives, especially Nuka. He immediately regretted the thought. Rabbit had once told him that his brother was just a misguided youth who didn't know where his path was taking him. Even though his situation wasn't comparable, Cody wondered where his own path would eventually lead him too.

He looked at Emma. She loved being out in the wilderness; he could see that from the peaceful look on her face. She was a natural at camping and seemed to soak up the wilderness. He slowly strolled over to the campfire. Una and Emma were each sitting on a pack box, holding bowls in their laps and mixing ingredients, which they then formed into small balls.

"What are you two making there?"

"Pemmican with dried fruit." Emma beamed at him while holding up one of the balls.

He took it and inspected the creamy-white mass. "And what is that?"

"Pemmican is a traditional food that our ancestors took with them on their journeys. It's a mixture of dried meat, such as buffalo or venison, dried berries, and suet. You can use any other animal fat for this as well," Una explained, popping one of the bite-sized balls into her mouth.

"That sounds like a strange combination." Cody sniffed at the ball and bit off a tiny piece. The taste of the animal fat would take some getting used to. He was glad he hadn't put the whole thing in his mouth.

Una grinned and held up a bottle of water for him to take. "It's not everyone's taste. If you aren't used to it, you should take it slow at first."

"It'll be interesting to see if the young people eat it." Emma stood up. "Shall I go offer them some?"

"Go ahead," Una replied. "There's enough for everyone."

Cody followed her over to the teenagers. Only three of them took the nutritious snack while the others asked for cookies or chocolate. Naira gratefully took a pemmican ball, stuck it in her mouth, and chewed happily. "Mmh," she murmured with her eyes closed.

"I really love that horse you made," Emma said to the girl who had been working on the tipi..

"Thank you. I love painting."

"Do painted tipis have some special meaning?" Cody studied the various motifs.

Naira stood up and ran her hand over the bottom half of the canvas. "The images painted onto tipis illustrate which family group and tribe the owners belong to. Beyond that, they also have a cosmological meaning. When we get back to the ranch, I'll show you guys some traditional painted tipis where you can see how the bottom halves show the earth, and the upper halves evoke the sky and the spirit world."

Cody noticed that the kids who had been busy whittling now walked over to the tipi to listen. Naira slowly walked around the tent and ran her hand along the material at waist-height. "Between heaven and earth lies the region depicting a vision that its owner or a family member has experienced. If at some time the buffalo skin, or later the canvas, ever needed to be replaced, the images from the old tipi were then transferred onto the new cloth or hide."

Cody stood next to Emma. She admired the depictions the teenagers had hand-painted onto the tipi.

"They are so talented," she said. "I can barely even draw a stick figure."

"You have other talents instead." He took hold of her hand and squeezed it.

"You Romeo." She playfully jabbed him in the side, but he could tell from her smile that she secretly appreciated his complement.

"We will be using your talking sticks this evening inside the tipi. Are you finished with them?" Naira asked.

Most of the teens nodded.

"Good, then you are free to do what you want until dinner."

The teenagers put away their carving knives and paints and decided to go for a swim in the river. They bellowed and cheered on their way down to the water a little while later.

“I’ll go and see if I can help Una with the dinner preparations,” Emma announced, disappearing in the direction of the campfire.

Cody decided to bring in Jazz and Asra, and let two other horses graze in their place instead.

After their dinner of bison spareribs, roasted squash, and bannock, Woodwind stepped inside the tipi. He made a circle of stones in the middle of it and lit a campfire. Thanks to the opening at the top, the smoke quickly found its way outside. The door flap opened, and Una came inside. She handed him a small wooden bowl, and the aroma of cinnamon and molasses filled his nose.

“Is that corn pudding?” he asked, taking the bowl and spoon.

“It is, I’m impressed.”

Woodwind tasted the pudding. It was exactly like how he remembered his grandmother’s had been. “It’s delicious.”

“Thanks, but Emma’s the one who made it, after I told her the recipe.” Una smirked. “She’s really remarkable.”

Woodwind ate the rest of the pudding in the bowl. “Do you think she’ll stay in Canada permanently?”

“That would be a huge change for her,” Una replied.

“Sometimes a new beginning like that is exactly what a person needs.”

“I think that’s easier for some people than for others.” Una took the empty bowl from his hands, her finger brushing over his wrist.

“You want to be there for Nuka, and I understand that, but don’t lose sight of your own plans. You deserve more than playing your father’s secretary,” he said, piling up firewood, then sitting down on the ground.

She kneeled next to him, placing her hand on his thigh and resting her head on his shoulder. “Thank you, flute maker, that’s sweet of you to say. And just for the record, I am giving thought to my future. Maybe—”

A gush of air against his back made him look around. Nuka stood in the oval door opening, staring at them.

Una quickly got to her feet and went to him. "We're just good friends."

"I can see that." Nuka shrugged. "Anyway, I don't care. Just as long as you keep living with Dad. Being alone with him would be even more unbearable."

"You don't have to worry about that," she told him. "Did you try some of the pudding?"

When Nuka shook his head, she shoved him back outside, and threw Woodwind a brief, penetrating glance before the cover flap fell closed behind her. Una had a big heart, and he knew that she gave Nuka some stability. At the same time, he hoped that Bull wouldn't succeed in suffocating her endeavors for independence. Just as he was starting to mull over the issue, some of the young people came into the tipi and sat down, followed shortly afterward by the adults. Naira instructed everyone to sit in a circle around the fire.

"Before we begin, I'd like to discuss the events of this afternoon."

"Like how my amazing brother totally ruined it," Nuka griped.

"No, about the fact that there are wolves in this area and that they are legally protected by the government and by the Cree nation." Woodwind admired the way Naira kept her cool despite Nuka's words.

"The area in which we are currently located officially belongs to our friend Chuck Morton. However, he recognizes that the Cree people are the original protectors of the land. The area is environmentally protected, which means that all hunting of any of the animals is absolutely prohibited."

"If the wolves are protected that means that their hides can't be sold legally. What do the hunters want with them then?" asked one of the boys.

"Unfortunately, it's still possible to sell wolf hides on the black market. And there are others who just want to put on a show that they've hunted a wolf."

"Assholes," Nuka mumbled, and Woodwind could only silently agree with him. He, too, couldn't comprehend why anyone would do that.

"If there are hunters out there who are actively hunting wolves, then someone must have shown them the routes that the packs take. That includes things like showing them where the animals have made their dens—such information is only known to very few people. The area is constantly under observation by both ground and aerial surveillance. No one would be able to hunt the animals for very long without attracting attention. If any of you have heard or know of anyone hunting wolves, I beg you to let one of us know."

Everyone nodded.

"Have you all brought your talking sticks with you?" Woodwind asked the group, removing his own stick from the inside pocket of his vest. "Do any of you know the significance of these sticks?"

"Only the person holding the talking stick is allowed to speak," Mina said.

"Yeah, but we all have a stick," Nuka interjected, holding his stick in the air.

"I have asked you to bring your own sticks with you so that we can have a look at them." Naira looked around the group. "Please lay your sticks in front of you on the ground."

The young people had used various types of wood, and some had decorated their sticks with feathers or colorful ribbons.

"They look great," said Woodwind. "These talking sticks belong to our traditional talking circle. It's a ceremony, but one that doesn't require any opening rituals. These circles can be invoked anywhere, in order to restore closeness in a community or to discuss some specific topic. The talking circle imparts a sense of belonging among its members."

The teenagers looked around. Those who were out of line scooted a bit forward or backward in order to form a perfect circle around the fire in the center of the tipi. One of the boys glanced around and wanted to get up to move, but Naira gestured at him. "Please stay seated. This isn't about sitting next to your friend, everyone in the circle is given the respect they deserve."

"And that's what the talking stick is for." Woodwind raised his in the air. "The person who has called the meeting, passes their stick around. Only the person holding it is allowed to speak. He or she is not to be interrupted, criticized, or ridiculed." He threw a look at Nuka, who first rolled his eyes, but then nodded.

Naira took a bundle of sage, lit it, and waited until it started to smoke. She laid it in a bowl, and with elegant movements, she waved the smoke over her face and hair before passing it to the next person. "Cleanse yourself and your body, your spirit, and your thoughts."

Woodwind noticed that many of the teens were hesitant, unsure of what they were supposed to do with the smoldering sage bundle. How sad that for many of them, this seemed to be their first encounter with the tradition of smudging. Once he had fanned the smoke over himself, Naira said a short prayer and declared the talking circle open. "Who would like to begin? Maybe tell us about what else you'd like to learn. Or let us know what your expectations are being here at this camp. Whatever comes to mind."

"May I begin?" said a voice so quietly that it was almost inaudible over the sound of the fire crackling.

"Of course. Here, take the talking stick." Naira passed it over, nodding encouragingly.

Mina held the stick with both hands against her chest and stared at her shoes. "I would really like to learn my language. Our language, I mean Cree."

"Why would you want to do that?" Nuka laughed. "Nobody understands it anyway."

"Be quiet." Woodwind threw the boy a piercing look. "You can talk later when it's your turn. Stick to the rules and show respect."

The boy grumbled, but said no more.

Naira turned to Mina. "Would you like to tell us why you'd like to learn Cree?"

"My grandfather taught me a few words and told me that the

language is very pictorial and descriptive of our environment. I imagine it must be amazing to hear the legends of our people in the Cree language."

Naira nodded. "I can understand your wish. We can certainly consider offering a language course as part of the program."

The girl smiled and passed the talking stick to the boy sitting next to her.

However, he only shook his head. "I don't have anything to say," he mumbled.

"That's perfectly fine," Woodwind said. "No one here is forced to speak. Just pass the stick on to the next person."

To his disappointment, none of the other teenagers were interested in contributing anything else to the talking circle. He looked at Naira, who only smiled and barely noticeably tilted her head and shrugged her shoulders. Her gestures reminded him a lot of her grandfather's. Chinook also never had any problem with accepting things the way they were, nor did he attempt to read more into a situation than what the person was willing to reveal. For this reason, Woodwind didn't indulge his urge to ask the teens more questions in order to get them to talk. They would find their words when the time was right.

The next morning, Woodwind was awoken by loud voices. He hastily unzipped his sleeping bag, slipped on his suede pants and boots, and crawled out of his tent. Lee, Naira, and Chuck were standing next to the campfire, while a few steps away from them, Nuka and his brother Rabbit were loudly arguing.

"Haven't you meddled in my life enough?" Nuka's arms were crossed over his chest, and his back was straight. He was nearly as tall as his brother.

"Chuck and I found footprints belonging to poachers. It would be best if you all didn't spend the night outside tonight." Rabbit's voice was calm, but firm.

"Why? Are they hunting teenagers too?" Nuka spat at him.

Woodwind stood next to Lee and Chuck. "What's going on?"

"Rabbit came to get me at the cabin, and we stumbled upon a campsite belonging to four men. We eavesdropped on their conversation. They are here hunting wolves, but haven't yet managed to catch one from the pack."

"Did you confront them?" inquired Woodwind.

"No, that would've been too dangerous. They were all intoxicated and armed, and they sounded rather aggressive. Especially when one of them turned the conversation onto the topic of native individuals."

Lee rolled his eyes. "Typical hillbilly from what it sounds like. But they're out for blood, and I have to agree with Chuck. It would be safer if none of the indigenous teens crossed paths with them."

"It sounds like Nuka doesn't share your concern." Woodwind turned to the quarreling brothers. The other teenagers and adults now came and gathered around the fire, most of them still half-asleep and confused about so much noise so early in the morning.

Una also joined them. "I'll make us some coffee and hot chocolate," she said.

"We'd best get started making breakfast. It looks as though today's hike just might end up back at Willow Ranch," Naira replied, and the women got started with the provisions from the pack boxes.

Lee pointed to Cody and Emma who had started feeding the horses. "Then I'll give the instructions to start packing up camp."

"Okay. And I'll see if I can mediate between these two sibling rivals." Woodwind stepped next to Nuka, who was spitting out one cuss word after the other. "Calm down, now. For the safety of the group. Your brother is not here to ruin anything for you."

"Of course, it's obvious that you would be on Rabbit's side," Nuka retorted. "Why can't we stay here and make a trap for these men? We far outnumber them and—"

"And they have guns and are completely unpredictable," Rabbit cut him off. "Chuck and I will inform the authorities. If one of these poachers manages to shoot a wolf, they certainly won't be getting off so easily."

Nuka snorted. "Real great. We might as well smoke the tobacco that we were going to use in our ritual since we won't have a chance to offer it to Mother Earth now." He turned around and marched away.

"Tell the others they should start packing up their things," Woodwind called after him.

Without turning around, the boy raised his hand and gave him the middle finger.

"Are you really planning to get the authorities involved?" Woodwind asked, and as he had expected, Rabbit shook his head.

"That wouldn't do any good anyway. They only care once you come to them with a dead wolf in your hands. Besides, I have the feeling that I've seen at least two of these guys before."

"Well, if they're going to engage in a hunt like that, they have been around the area for a few days. Do you think you might have to run into them somewhere in town?"

Rabbit turned down the corners of his mouth as he thought. "No, it was a while ago. And last night one of them said something about one hand washing the other."

"Do you think there are others involved who would benefit from hunting a wolf?"

"That's exactly what I intend to find out."

An hour later, the youth were packed and ready to go. Woodwind saw the disappointment in their faces due to their premature departure. To top it all off, rain had set in and the gray sky above reflected the mood of the group below. The positive energy they had experienced yesterday was like a distant dream, and Nuka's words echoed in his mind. He hadn't expected any mention of the teens looking forward to the tobacco ceremony, least of all from him. But apparently, the young man had eagerly been awaiting their night spent under the stars along with the offering ceremony. The location they had chosen for their overnight stay commanded a view of the sacred Three Siblings mountain grouping, but alas, it would remain out of their reach. A spiritual place such as that was, however, the required basis for the ceremony. At least that's how Woodwind remembered it to be.

Wrapped in silence, the group made their way back. They waved goodbye to Cody and Emma who were busy breaking down the tents, until the forest blocked their view of the couple. Woodwind followed at the back of the group. His heart ached to see the teenagers with their heads hanging, unaware of the little ways that Mother Earth was trying to get their attention. For the past few minutes, they were being followed by two squirrels who chased behind them, jumping from branch to branch, welcoming the group into their forest with their chatter. The fragrant smells of resin and rain-drenched moss filled his nose with an unforgettable, refreshing scent.

A feeling of deep gratitude flowed through him for being allowed to traverse this section of the earth. The sound of something rustling caused him to pause. He looked through the trees and saw in the not-too-far distance a white-tailed deer. The animal raised its head, its ears standing straight up. Perhaps it was a good thing the group was covering this path in silence. Nevertheless, the unfortunate conclusion of their trip to the mountains weighed heavily upon him. At least it had stopped raining, and the teens had lowered the hoods of their rain jackets. He looked ahead at Mina as she followed the curve into the valley before them. What was she holding in her hand? He jogged a few strides and saw that it was one of the fabric squares meant to be used to commence the tobacco ceremony. Stunned, he stopped in his tracks. Hadn't he himself been filled with gratitude for being in this exact place only a minute ago? "Stop!" He called out to the group.

Everyone came to a standstill, confused and wondering why. Lee turned around. "Did something happen?"

Woodwind trotted past the line of teenagers to Lee and Naira. He quickly told them his idea and was happy they agreed. They waved the kids into a circle around them.

"I know that you are all very disappointed that we had to forego tonight's ceremony and leave earlier than planned," Woodwind said. "So instead, I want to make a suggestion."

"Whatever could that be?" Nuka retorted.

"It is a promise that I would like to keep, if you guys are okay with us arriving back at the ranch later than planned this evening."

"An adult who keeps his promises. Now that's something new!" Nuka had found a twig and was sticking it into an ant hill.

Woodwind went over to him. "Don't you think these little forest helpers deserve your respect?"

The boy looked at him, seemingly surprised that Woodwind didn't just take this stick out of his hand. "You're right, sorry," he mumbled.

"Okay. Maybe you'd like to make a campfire instead? We ought to find enough dry kindling in the forest."

"And then?"

"And then we'll make our tobacco ties and offer them to Mother Earth." Woodwind saw something shift in Nuka's eyes. His harsh, stubborn look made way for a softer and almost childlike expression. A thin smile appeared on his lips. He waved two of his buddies over. "Come on, let's go find some firewood."

Less than twenty minutes later, a campfire was roaring. Naira and Una distributed lunch packages, and the group sat down on their rain jackets in the still-wet grass. Woodwind chose a seat on an old log.

"When you're done eating, find yourself a spot in the area that speaks to you. Make yourself comfortable there, and begin by putting a pinch of tobacco onto the cotton square and make a tobacco tie for each thing you are grateful for. Take your time. This is a sacred ceremony that deserves your full attention." He pulled a long piece of twine out of his backpack. "Then come over here and take a piece of this twine, tie it around your little pouches, and hang them here on a tree or a branch."

After a while, the group of young people dispersed and began the ceremony. Nuka sat down on a tree stump and looked out over the valley with his hands in his lap. He kept glancing back at the others in the group, who were busy tying up their pouches and working without any hesitation. On a whim, Woodwind pulled his flute out of his vest pocket and began to play. He didn't miss that Nuka turned to watch him for a moment. It was a simple melody he sent out into the valley. Though his fingers felt a little stiff, his playing was more fluid now than it had been yesterday at the river. Nuka observed Woodwind out of the corner of his eye a few times, and the man saw the boy's stony expression slowly fade. Nuka tied up one pouch and that was it. Woodwind finished playing, and the teenagers went around looking for a branch or a vine to tie their offerings to.

Once everyone was happy with the placement of their tobacco ties, Woodwind called the group together. "You guys did a great job. And for anyone who only made one tobacco tie today, that's okay." He looked at Nuka, nodded at him, and was relieved to see a slight smile cross his face. Woodwind pulled out a piece of paper with a few lines on it that he had copied down from Chinook's little book. "When you give your offering to Mother Earth, you have recognized where your gratitude should be focused. Celebrate this ceremony whenever you feel alone, are full of doubt, or feel afraid. Focus your thoughts on gratefulness, on being one with Mother Earth and all her creatures." He looked around the circle, then tucked the paper back into his pocket.

Mina raised her hand, and he nodded at her. "I don't feel any different than before. Isn't this ceremony supposed to trigger something inside of me?" Her eyes seemed to look directly into Woodwind's soul.

He tried to find a response, but his mind was blank. He knew exactly what Mina meant, for he had asked himself the very same question before.

"This was only your first experience with a tobacco ceremony," said Naira. "Be patient and stay curious. If you'd like, you could speak with one of the elders about this and other rituals."

"Okay." Mina's somber expression was replaced by a shy smile. "I really enjoyed your flute playing."

"Yeah, that was really nice," another girl concurred. "It felt like eating chocolate."

"Thank you," Woodwind replied, moved by the girls' words.

"It's time we kept going," Lee called out, and they left the valley.

The next morning, Woodwind stood under the hot shower at his house and hoped his muscle aches would lessen. The hike back to the ranch had robbed him of his last reserves of strength. He turned off the water and reached for his towel. He was sure the teens would also be having a hard time getting out of bed today. For this reason, he thought he would take advantage of the extra time and stop by the rescue center on his way to the ranch. He had asked Ayita to meet him there to hear her account of the past few days with the wolf pup. He dried himself off and got dressed, then made a travel mug of coffee and headed off.

Ayita and Wynono were just getting out of Lyla's car when he pulled into the parking lot. He parked and joined them.

"Can you bring them back to the cabin later?" Lyla asked through the open passenger window.

He raised his hand and nodded. "Sure, no problem. Say hello to Lonefeather for me."

Ayita waited for him at the door, while Wynono tugged at her jacket.

"I guess the little guy can't wait to see his wolf friend." Woodwind smiled.

"Yes, we've spent a good many hours here over the past two days." She returned his smile, but quickly turned serious again. "I'm afraid Kachina isn't doing much better."

"Let's go in, and we can talk about it." He pushed open the heavy door, allowing Ayita and Wynono to pass through first. Maja was in the kitchen along with two volunteers, preparing breakfast for the animals.

"Morning, everyone," he called out, before addressing Maja specifically. "How are our little charges doing this morning?"

"Everyone's doing great, except for the little wolf, but I'm sure Ayita mentioned that already. Only when the two of them are here does she eat a bit more than just one bite of food."

"Okay, we'll go check on her first." He pointed to a plastic bucket filled with pieces of meat. "Is that for the wolf?"

Maja nodded, handing him the container. "Good luck."

He thanked her as Ayita and Wynono went on ahead to the wolf's cage. One look at the animal and he could see that she had gotten even thinner; her coat was bristly and dull. Wynono took his usual seat next to the fence. Kachina stood in the middle of her enclosure, observing the child. Woodwind stood next to Ayita. "Thank you for taking care of her."

"It breaks my heart that she's not doing any better. She really seems lost. It's like her loneliness is eating her up." She said that as though she knew the feeling. Her eyes were fixed on the animal, but he decided not to dig any deeper, hoping instead that the time would come when she opened up to him. "I'll contact the vet again. He should be able to give her something that will stimulate her appetite," Woodwind thought out loud.

"Ask Naira instead. She knows all about herbal remedies and could probably help us."

Us. It echoed in his ears, and he was pleased that Ayita seemed to count herself as a member of the wolf's team of caretakers. "Good idea, thanks." His cell phone rang. It was Lee.

"Lee, hi, what's up?"

"We've got a problem here. Can you come over right away?"

"Are you having trouble with one of the teenagers?"

"No, just get here as fast as you can, okay?" He sounded worried, and Woodwind immediately felt sick to his stomach.

"I'm at the rescue center. I'll come right away."

He stuck his phone back into his pocket and turned to Ayita. "I'm sorry, but I have to go. Do you want to stay here for a while, and I'll pick you up later?"

She looked at her son, then at the wolf, who was half-heartedly gnawing on a piece of meat. "Can we come with you to the ranch? Maybe Samantha would be around to look after Wynono for a bit. I think it would do him some good."

"Yes, why not?" Woodwind was relieved to not have to face whatever was awaiting him at the ranch alone. "I am sure, Samantha would be delighted."

When he turned into the parking lot at Willow Ranch, he immediately recognized where the problem lay. Jeremy Bull was standing next to Lee and Naira, along with a woman in a business suit holding a briefcase. Woodwind sighed as he cut the engine.

"Who's the man standing next to Lee?" Ayita asked.

"Trouble," he simply said. "Sam is over there near the meadow. I'll come and find you when all this is finished." Without waiting for an answer, he got out and walked over to the four. "Hello, what's the problem?"

The woman looked him in the eye and asked: "Are you Woodwind Jones?"

"That depends on who's asking."

"Mr. Bull has informed us that you are engaged here as a youth leader despite the fact that you have a criminal record."

Woodwind looked at Bull, who returned his gaze with a dark grin, making it instantly clear how he had found out about his working there. He must have somehow heard it from his daughter. Dammit. Why did Una have to work at Willow Ranch too? As he looked at the woman's serious expression; it made no difference anymore. She cleared her throat. "Forgive me, I haven't even introduced myself yet." She held out her petite hand to him. "Miss Rultie. I work for the Alberta Child and Youth Services."

Woodwind shook her hand. "I didn't know that I needed a special permit to work with teens. We, I mean Lee and Naira, naturally have a court-appointed advisor for the program, since we also have delinquent minors enrolled. He gave me his blessing to go on this trip to the mountains. My duties here are very specifically limited to teaching about our native traditions and ceremonies."

"That may be, but it seems your role wasn't quite as clearly specified to him." She threw Woodwind a critical look as though she were wondering whether he had purposely not told the court-appointed advisor the truth. She cleared her throat again. "The way Mr. Bull explained the situation to me, you have direct contact with the teenagers. However, as a convicted criminal, you are restricted in your social interaction with minors to very specific circumstances." Miss Rultie pushed her glasses further up her nose with one finger.

"And that clearly was not the case here," Bull interjected. "It's irresponsible to let a convicted felon work around children. The entire program is just one big joke and a danger to the well-being of the teenagers."

"Our project was fully approved by the authorities," said Lee.

"We have followed every one of the legal guidelines to a T and have acquired all the necessary permits," Naira added. "I can gladly show you all the documents."

Miss Rultie waved her hand dismissively. "Just to set things straight, I approve of the program, but it should have been clear to you that hiring Mr. Jones would raise a number of problems."

"I will not allow my son to be left in the care of a dangerous felon," Bull was starting to get agitated.

"At least here, there's someone looking out for him." Woodwind crossed his arms over his chest.

Lee raised one hand. "Now, let's just all keep calm and find a solution for the situation. Miss Rultie, is there any chance that Mr. Jones would be allowed to work here officially?"

The woman nodded and pulled a sheet of paper out of her briefcase. She held it out to Woodwind. "Here you will find a website with the legal requirements along with an online course including an exam at the end, which you will need to complete. Assuming you successfully pass the course, you will receive an assessment and the authorization to be around minors under supervision. Since your program already has a court-appointed advisor, he will keep an eye on you during your duties. Again, once you've passed."

Woodwind took the paper. He hated tests. Even just the thought of having to take a test made him nauseous.

"Wait a minute, that can't be right." Bull huffed.

"Yes, those are the rules. There is, however, a time limit. You will need to have successfully passed the exam by the end of January.

I will speak with the court-appointed advisor and take care of all the formalities." Miss Rultie produced a small notebook from her jacket pocket and opened it. "I've marked down that part one of the program is due at end of next month. Is that correct?"

Lee nodded. "By that point, the teenagers will be staying at the reserve or with their foster families, and will have regularly scheduled seminars they are obligated to attend. In February, we will be starting with various daylong workshops that will be led by First Nations elders. We had planned for Woodwind to join us again in June, when the teenagers would be staying here for a three-month stint."

Miss Rultie jotted something in her little book and nodded. "Good. Well, until you have successfully completed the course and passed the exam, you are not allowed to work as a mentor and caregiver for these children. I am going to leave it at a warning for the work you've done the last few weeks. Even though you won't be working here again until June, you will still need to show proof of your certificate by the end of January. After that, the next exam takes place in the winter."

"What would be the consequences if I—" before Woodwind could finish his sentence, Miss Rultie raised her hand to stop him.

"Do not let it come to that," she replied, tight-lipped. "Your illegal work here could have consequences for the entire program if you do not meet the deadlines and obtain the proper permission."

"You can do it." Naira smiled at him supportively.

He twisted his lips, but couldn't manage to return even a crooked smile.

"Well, if that's everything, then I'll say goodbye. Should you have any questions, here's my card." Miss Rultie handed Woodwind her business card. "Oh, and Mr. Bull, just in case you were considering taking your son out of the program prematurely, his court-ordered community restitution would be considered terminated and he would then face jail time. Just keep that in mind." With that, she turned around and walked to her car.

Bull stepped closer to Woodwind, grabbed hold of his jacket

collar, and yanked him closer. "Don't think for a second that this matter is closed. I'll be watching you."

Lee stepped in between the two men and pushed them apart. "That's enough. I will not tolerate any sort of violence on my ranch."

Bull turned to the side, pulled back his arm, and punched Woodwind in the shoulder. "You seem to think your lone wolf act makes you invincible, but I'll find out what makes your heart bleed."

"That's enough," Lee repeated, this time louder, and Bull backed away.

"It's all good, but I want to speak with Nuka at least for a minute before I go."

"The kids are in the barn working on their projects." Lee pointed to the building to the left of the stalls.

"Yeah, whatever," Bull relented, turning around.

"We'd better head over there too," Lee said to Woodwind. "You can also use this opportunity to say goodbye to the kids."

They followed behind Bull for a moment, but Lee hurried ahead. Woodwind caught sight Ayita coming out of the stall and noticed that Bull had seen her too.

"Hello, do we know each other?" He heard him ask just before he caught up to them.

Ayita hesitated, scrutinizing him. "No, I don't think so."

"Ah, then I must be mistaken. I'm Jeremy Bull, councilmember and soon-to-be-chief of the Sunchild Reserve." He held out his hand to her, and she shook it.

"Ayita, my son and I have been here visiting my niece for the past few weeks."

Woodwind watched as she tried to pull her hand back, but Bull held it firmly. There was something in his eyes he didn't like, so he came up and stood next to Ayita. "Nuka's over in the barn. Lee's already there."

Bull let go of Ayita's hand and smiled. "I'm sure we'll see each other again. Goodbye, Ayita." Bull turned to Woodwind. "I don't think I should interrupt the kids if they're working on something."

What was that supposed to mean? "I'm sure that Nuka will be

able to take a few minutes for you. You just have to go through that door there." He pointed to the small door next to the larger barn doors. "I'll be right there."

Bull nodded, then disappeared.

"What's your connection with that man?" Ayita inquired.

"More than I'd like," Woodwind replied. "His son Nuka is in my group, and Bull has something against that ... Oh, it's too complicated to explain right now."

"Well, it's in every father's interest to want the best for his son."

He was taken aback. Why was she defending Bull without knowing anything about the situation? Wasn't he good enough to look after Nuka and the other teenagers? Her words went straight under his skin, but before he could come up with anything to say, he heard loud voices coming from the barn. "I'm just going to say goodbye to them," he said. "I don't know how much longer this is going to take."

"Okay, then I'll go with Wynono to see the foals," she said.

"That's fine, I'll come for you when I'm done." He waved at her and hurried to the barn.

Rosie pulled the pan of blueberry muffins out of the oven. Also covering the counter were a tray of chocolate chip cookies, an apple pie, and vanilla cupcakes.

"Maybe I've overdone it a little bit with the baking," she said to Hazel, who lay on the floor, panting. But today was a special day and she had invited over some friends to celebrate. Lori's foal would finally be getting a name.

Naira had suggested making a party of it, and Rosie immediately went into action. She had thought about asking Calvin if he was okay with her naming the foal, but then she'd have to tell him about the party and he would certainly not be happy about having so many people around, even if all the women who would be there were her friends. She decided to just hope that Calvin would accept the name and register it with his papers.

She heard a car pull up outside and went to the door, with Hazel right behind her. Naira got out of her Jeep with a large grin. Samantha followed, and to Rosie's surprise, Sarah too.

"Hello, are we the first to arrive?" Naira helped Sam lift something out of the Jeep.

"I made a flower chain for the foal." Sam held up a long garland, proudly grinning.

"Oh, it's beautiful," Rosie exclaimed.

"I hope my little man is also welcome." Sarah rocked her baby in one arm with a blanket covering him.

Rosie descended the porch stairs and went over to them. "Oh, you brought your little angel with you! Chuck must be beaming with pride."

"Yes, he sure is. He even wanted to cancel his next two weeks in the mountains, but I talked him out of that," said Sarah. "He was here for the birth, which was wonderful. Over the past three months since our son was born, Chuck has turned into a true mother hen. The baby usually wakes up only once during the night, and is otherwise a very happy baby. I'm looking forward to having some time alone with him."

Just then, Lyla's station wagon bounded over the driveway and came to a stop next to the Jeep. Lyla had Ayita, Wynono, and, of course, Mud in the car with her. Together, the group entered the cabin. For the first quarter of an hour, Sarah's baby was the main topic of conversation. After he had gotten enough admiration from the guests, Naira turned her attention to the many treats. "My goodness, who all have you invited?"

"Emma and Sonja are the only two left," said Rosie. "I was simply in the mood to bake."

"Can Wynono and I take a cookie and go see the horses?" Samantha asked.

"Sure, we'll be right behind you."

Sam grabbed two cookies and disappeared outside, hand-in-hand with Ayita's son.

"The two of them seem to get along well," Lyla commented.

"Yeah," Ayita concurred. "Since the moment they met."

Naira reached for a cupcake, then paused. "Are these for later?"

Rosie waved it off. "Not at all, go ahead and take one. But the coffee isn't ready yet."

Grinning, Naira took a bite from the cupcake, and Lyla claimed a muffin for herself. There was a knock at the door, and Emma and Sonja came in.

"Hey, you two," Rosie greeted them.

"Thank you for the invitation." Emma went over and gave her a hug. "My goodness, you made enough food to feed an army!"

"Yum." Sonja selected a cupcake and licked off the vanilla buttercream frosting before taking a bite of the cake.

Rosie grabbed the colorful foal halter that she had bought for the occasion and held it in the air. "I couldn't decide on one color, so I took one with all of them instead."

"Good idea," said Ayita. "Have you already picked out a name?"

"I have a few ideas and was hoping that you guys could help me decide."

Ayita looked at Sarah, who was sitting with her baby on the couch. "What's your son's name?"

"John Levi. We named him after Chuck's father and my grandfather."

"It's always nice to honor your ancestors that way," said Naira. "Are you aware of the meaning of names in our tradition?"

Except for Ayita, everyone shook their heads.

"Before I eat myself into a ball, let's go outside," Naira suggested. "Then I'll tell you about it."

"Gladly." Rosie carried out the halter, and the group of women went outside to the horses. Mud and Hazel were playing together out on the meadow, while Wynono and Sam were petting the foal. The women stood next to the fence, where Sam had hung her flower rope.

"For a long time, we weren't allowed to give our children traditional native first names," Naira explained.

"It was a terrible time with those residential schools," Ayita mumbled. "Both my parents were given English names and they refused to be called by their indigenous names. They wanted to name me Amanda, but my grandmother put her foot down and I was called Ayita, which means She Who Dances."

"You never told me that," Lyla said.

"My years growing up were a very painful time, almost cruel in fact." Ayita pursed her lips, closing her eyes for a moment and breathing deeply. "It was important to me to give my son a traditional name."

"What does Wynono mean?" Lyla asked.

"Firstborn." Ayita smiled. "But enough about me. Forgive me for interrupting you, Naira."

"No problem. I find it important to talk openly about everything. After the years of the suppression enforced on our culture, many parents have begun to hold ceremonies again where the elders give their children so-called Spirit Names. The celebration is something very similar to a baptism, but the ceremony usually happens when the child is a bit older. Even teenagers can still be given a spirit name. They're usually provided by the shamans and elders and come to them in a dream or through meditation."

"How interesting," Rosie said. "I'm sure those names must be very powerful and have a very special meaning for the child."

Naira nodded. "The names are passed on to the elders from the spirit world, where the wisdom and love of our ancestors lives on along with the wisdom of all animals."

The foal led out a high-pitched neigh, causing the women to laugh.

"He knows," Naira said. "Today is all about him."

Rosie opened the gate and approached Lori's colt. The foal eyed the colorful thing curiously, and let her slip it over his head without any fuss. Sky kept to the background, her ears perked.

Rosie then led the foal to the pasture fence where he whinnied again, and Lori came and stood next to him. The foal stuck his nose in Rosie's pocket, looking for treats. She laughed, gently but firmly pushing his muzzle away. Lori nudged him in the side, as though she were telling him to behave. The foal answered with a short nicker.

"He has a very strong and beautiful voice," Lyla commented. "You ought to be very proud of him."

"Thanks." Rosie bit her lip.

"And what names have you chosen?" Naira asked.

"I would call him Raweno." Ayita interjected. "The name means 'great leader', but also 'great voice.' I think it suits him."

"Raweno," Rosie mumbled as she stroked the foal's neck. "Yes, I think I like that better than the other names I had in mind."

"I think Raweno is a great name," Samantha said. "What was his father's name?"

"Dra—" before Rosie could finish, a green truck rolled up the driveway much too fast, then churned up a cloud of dust by coming to an abrupt stop. Out of the corner of her eye, Rosie saw Mud and Hazel come running. Raweno stepped backward.

"It's okay, little guy." Rosie soothingly stroked his neck.

Sky snorted nervously. Doug got out of his truck and slammed the door behind him. Only then did he seem to notice Rosie, and he came over to her with a broad grin.

"Do you have to make such a fuss?" Rosie admonished as she climbed over the fence and approached him. "You're scaring the horses."

Doug raised his hands apologetically. "Sorry, I wasn't trying to. Could I still get a kiss hello?" He playfully grabbed her t-shirt and pulled her close to him. "I've missed you," he muttered.

Rosie turned away before he could kiss her.

"We're only friends—have you forgotten?"

He sighed loudly, then looked at the women standing along the fence and raised his hand to greet them. "Sorry, I didn't know you had company. I wanted to come by and see you again right away, now that I'm back."

His sheepish expression reminded her of a naughty puppy. "It's fine. Have you got a new truck?"

"Yeah, do you like it?" He proudly ran his hand over the shiny hood.

"It's even greener than your old truck," she joked. "Come on, and I'll introduce you to my friends." They walked over to the other women, and Rosie explained to him why they were all there.

"Oh, that's a really nice way to welcome the little guy," Doug said. "I know how much the foal means to Rosie. Is there anything I can do to help?"

"You could get the coffee ready," Naira suggested.

"Sure. Anything for the kids?"

Rosie was pleased that he offered to help while trying not to think about how strong the coffee had been the last time he made it, and nodded. "That would be great. Thanks a lot. But don't make it too strong."

He smiled at her. "You girls continue what you're doing here, and I'll take care of the refreshments." He had hardly disappeared into the house when the women started asking questions.

"Why didn't you tell us you have a boyfriend?" Lyla asked. "He's a looker. How long have you been together?"

"We're just friends."

"I don't like him," Samantha announced. "He scares the horses, and the dogs don't like him either."

Rosie only just then noticed that Hazel and Mud had gone to lie down a good distance away.

"That's not very nice of you, Sam." Naira gave her a gentle yank on her ponytail. "You don't even know Doug."

The girl pouted and turned back to the foal.

"Doug isn't exactly a horse guy," Rosie halfheartedly admitted.

"Well, let's just hope that he's better at making coffee than he is with horses." Naira playfully elbowed her friend in the side, and all the women laughed.

"So, back to the name giving," Lyla implored. "Do we want to stick with Raweno?"

"Yes, I like it," Rosie agreed, and the others nodded.

Sam took the flower garland and laid it around the colt's neck. He immediately started nibbling on it.

"We'd better hurry up before he eats it all," said Sam.

Rosie opened a bottle of champagne and walked over to the foal. She poured some of it over his withers. "Raweno, may you bear this name with pride and joy."

Her cell phone abruptly started ringing, but she ignored it, giving both the foal and the mare a carrot. It soon started up again.

"Don't you want to answer it?" Lyla asked.

"I'm sure it's not important. Let's go and see if the coffee's ready."

"I'd rather stay with the horses," Sam said.

"If you'd like, but if you want some of the sweets, you'll need to come inside," Naira replied. The women filed into the house.

To Rosie's astonishment, Doug had set everything on the small dining table, including plates, napkins, and the pot of coffee. She gave him a kiss on the cheek. "Thank you, that was nice of you."

"My pleasure." He picked up one of the chairs. "I thought that since the weather's so nice, we could sit outside, what do you think? I'll put a few chairs out on the porch."

"Good idea." Lyla placed a muffin on her plate and poured herself some coffee. "We can sit out in the sun."

Rosie had barely stepped onto the porch with her cup of coffee when her cell phone rang yet again. She set down her cup, pulled her phone out of her pocket, and looked at the display. It was Calvin. With a sigh, she took the call. "Hello? What's up?"

The other women were talking and laughing so loudly that Rosie couldn't quite understand him. "Wait a minute, it's too loud here." She went down the porch stairs.

"Where are you?" he asked.

"At home. What do you want?"

"Are you throwing a party, or what is all that noise in the background? Is everything okay with the foal?"

She rolled her eyes. "Yes, he is healthy and happy. By the way, I've named him Raweno. What are you calling about?"

"I don't want you showing off that colt to everybody."

Lyla called out her name and raised her coffee cup to Rosie, who smiled and mouthed back: "In a minute."

"Rosie, I'm serious. That is my foal."

"I know that. You don't need to keep telling me that. But you can't tell me I can't invite some friends over. What's your problem?"

Calvin went silent, and she almost thought that he had hung up. Then she heard him sigh. "Okay, okay. I'm sorry. I was just calling because I plan to come by in a few days with a buyer for the colt."

Rosie nearly dropped her phone. She gulped a few times. "You can't separate Raweno and Lori until February at the earliest. And didn't you just say yourself that you don't want too many people getting a look at Dragon's foal?"

"This is different."

"Raweno is barely two months old. I will not allow you to sell him before he's at least six months old."

"Calm down. That's also not what I have planned. But like I said before, Dragon's offspring are in high demand and I would just like to plan ahead. I'll see you later."

"Calvin?" She stared at the display. That idiot had hung up on her. She leaned against the wooden porch railing and tried to blink away the tears that had gathered in her eyes. Her anger at Calvin was equal to her helplessness against him. It was something she despised.

"Is everything okay?"

All of a sudden, Lyla appeared next to her and put her arm around her shoulder. "I couldn't help overhear, but that guy on the phone was really loud. Was that your ex-boyfriend?"

Rosie nodded, feeling increasingly confused about what he had said.

"Does Raweno really belong to him?"

"Yes. He had wanted to find a quiet place for Lori to give birth." She explained about their agreement and how she came to also have Sky. "Lori will stay with me the rest of her life once Raweno, once he's ..." She could barely comprehend him being taken from her. She needed to pull herself together.

"But you could buy Raweno, couldn't you?" Lyla suggested.

Rosie shook her head, her shoulders slack. "I could never scrape together that much money. Plus, I want to start the courses to become a horse trainer as soon as I possibly can."

"How's it going with Sky, anyway?" Lyla looked at the brown mare, who was still lingering in the furthest section of the pasture.

"We're making small progress."

"That's good, and you still have some time until Raweno is sold off in February. It's not like you to give up so easily," said Lyla with a defiant gaze.

"I don't know. It's a big responsibility."

"Then you'll have to see if you can get Doug excited about horses." Lyla winked at her.

"He's really just a friend to me."

Lyla shrugged. "That's fine. You have to decide for yourself. And if your dream doesn't instill at least a little bit of fear in you, then you're not dreaming big enough."

"That's easy for you to say. You and Lonefeather are soulmates and are fulfilling your dream together."

Doug walked over to them with two cups of coffee in his hands. "What's this I hear about dreams?"

Rosie threw Lyla a desperate look. She nodded ever so slightly and raised her cup. "Here's a toast to the foal. To a wonderful home, and a bright future."

September

"I'll be back in a few days." Cody spoke to Emma using the hands-free device in his truck.

"Is everything okay with your parents?"

"Well, they had a couple of problems with the last inspection. There are a few things that need to be done to improve the milk machine, and of course if I do some of the work myself, we can cut down on the cost." He hoped she wouldn't ask any more.

"I see. Sonja and I will look for things to do until you get back. Have fun with the cows."

"I'd much rather be having fun with you, I swear."

Her laughter filled the cab of his truck. "I miss you already, Cowboy," she said.

"I miss you too, Cowgirl. See you soon."

He hung up, thinking about her rosy cheeks and the way her eyes shone during their ride to the mountains. The two of them had made a great team leading the pack horses, which only caused Cody to dream about what a future with her might look like. Still smiling, he pulled into the driveway of his family farm. When he saw his mother standing at the door with her arms crossed, his smile disappeared. He parked, grabbed his bag, and got out. "Hi, Mom." He gave her a kiss on the cheek. She seemed to have aged more than a decade over the last few weeks.

"You're finally here." Her rough hands clasped his. "Your father's been sitting in the office all morning. He needs to eat something and hasn't done any of his leg exercises."

"Let's go have a look." He placed his hand on her back. She had grown so thin. He followed her inside and dropped his bag on the floor in the hallway before pulling off his boots. He stood in front of the office door, straightened his shoulders, and knocked.

"I'm not hungry, Jackie," his father called.

He pushed open the door and walked in. "It's me, Dad."

"Ah, the prodigal son." He waved him in. Cody took off his cowboy hat and held it in front of him with both hands.

"How long are you here for this time? One night, maybe two?"

"I plan to stay until we clear up the problem with the milk inspection."

Larry snorted and pushed his heavy leather chair away from the desk with both hands. His leg lay on an upholstered footrest, still in a brace.

"How's the leg doing?" Cody asked, trying to avoid an instant argument about the farm.

"It's getting there. I have no idea why your mother thinks you need to come around again. You never wanted anything to do with the dairy business. Scott had—"

"Dad," Cody interrupted him. "The milk inspector is coming again tomorrow. Before that, I would like to read his report and have a look at what needs to be fixed."

"It's out in the barn. I read it already. There's nothing wrong."

Cody clenched his teeth forcefully. How could one man be so stubborn? And how had Scott managed to put up with it? Perhaps his father had behaved nicer with his favorite son.

"Can you even go out into the barn with your leg?" he asked sharply.

"What are you trying to imply? That I can't run my business anymore? You'd like it if I had to sell and you were able to stick some of that money into your own pocket, wouldn't you?" His father's voice got louder. "Well, you're wrong. They'll have pry this farm out of my cold dead hands before I sell it to anyone else."

The door opened. "What in Heaven's name is going on here?" Jackie asked, her concerned look darted between the two men.

"Everything's fine." Cody put his cowboy hat back on. "I was just going out to the barn. Are you coming with me, Dad?" Without waiting for an answer, he hurried outside for some fresh air. He reached the milk parlor where Kurt was piling hay into the feeders.

"Hi, Kurt," he said to the gaunt man in his mid-fifties. He had known him since he was a little boy and liked the man a great deal. He had lost his own family farm to the bank many years ago and since then had been around to offer a helping hand on the Tippet family farm. The soft-spoken man nodded at him and continued working.

Cody entered the room with the automatic milking machine. On the small shelf, he found the report of the last inspection and skimmed over it. His father had claimed that there was nothing wrong. But here it mentioned a batch of milk was detected to have remnants of antibiotics in it. If that was true, they would have to destroy the entire load off the milk truck and the farm would be slapped with a hefty fine. How could that happen? He flipped through the five-page report. He read the comment on the last page describing two incidents where the cooling chamber had failed to keep the milk at a constant temperature of between one to four degrees Celsius as required. He got on his knees in front of the stainless-steel canister and looked at the display. At the moment, everything seemed to be fine. He got back up, and his gaze fell on the numerous photos, some of them askew, inside a large frame on the wall.

Snapshots of his father and Scott at around ten years old, smiling, surrounded by a herd of black and white cows; his brother welling with pride, holding up his college diploma in agriculture; Scott standing next to a milk truck with a big grin on his face. Two other photos of his brother looking serious into the camera. The picture with the milk truck looked like something had been cut out of it. He took it off the wall and opened the frame. Scott had his arm stretched out and it looked as though he was holding someone else's hands. Cody recognized the ring on one of the thin fingers. He flipped the photo over. *Scott and Kathlyn's Engagement* was written on the back and dated three years ago.

Cody remembered her. Kathlyn was a pediatrician, and she and Scott had dated for many years. He had met her a few times, and to Cody, she had seemed like an amazing woman: intelligent, friendly, not to mention attractive. He remembered wondering what had happened when Scott had sent him a text message that they had broken up. When he had asked, his brother had only answered that they had grown apart. Strange. Who would have cut her out of the picture? What had really happened between the two of them?

A loud bang brought him back to the present. His father stood in the doorway, proposed up on one crutch and panting. He was obviously having trouble keeping his balance without putting his full weight on his bad leg. Cody hung the photos back on the wall.

"I thought you were here to see what was wrong?" Larry said between gasps. "Not to look at old pictures."

"Whatever happened to Kathlyn?" Cody asked. "That's her in the picture, right?"

His father waved dismissively. "She couldn't help him either."

"What do you mean by that?"

"She always knew better; she totally turned his head. But he figured out in due time that she wasn't the right one for him ... whatever, it doesn't matter anymore."

Cody would have liked to know what had led them to call off their engagement, but he could see that his father wasn't going to talk about it any further. "Well, from what I can see, we need to take a closer look at this refrigeration tank. And how could traces of antibiotics get into the milk?"

Larry hobbled over to the shelf and tapped his finger on the report. "Why us? I've got everything under control. Why don't you just go back to your horses?"

Cody huffed. "Oh, really? You have nothing under control, Dad. Let me help you before the farm completely goes under."

"What do you care? You don't even want to be here, so just go away." Larry raised his crutch and banged it against one of the stainless-steel containers.

The loud bang echoed sharply in Cody's ears. "I'm here now and ready to help. Dammit, Dad," he said as the sound died away.

"It's too late now. Scott is dead. It's too late." His father stared at him, the anger in his face giving way to an ashen desperation. He opened his mouth, closed it again, and swallowed hard. Before Cody could say anything, his father turned around and stiffly hobbled away.

Cody watched him go. What did he mean by "it's too late"? They still had time to keep the farm out of bankruptcy, though it wasn't going to be easy. Cody's heart ached as he realized what else his father could have meant. Did he blame himself for Scott's suicide? His eyes returned to the photos. The pain hit him like a punch to the gut. He dropped to his knees and threw his hands over his face. His cowboy hat fell onto the cement floor. He fought against the sobs that still managed to escape.

"Sorry, is there anything I can do for you?" a voice asked.

He hastily wiped his eyes, stood up, and turned around. Kurt was holding out his cowboy hat to him. He nodded as he took it, combed his hair back with his fingers, and put his hat back on. "Thanks, I'm okay."

"Running a family business isn't easy. On the other hand, there's nothing quite as worthwhile."

Cody looked at him. The pain of losing the farm that he himself had inherited was written all over his face. While he tried to find the right words to answer, Kurt cleared his throat. "To your father, the farm is his life. I don't think that he can comprehend that it could also mean as much to you too. You have your own life, you're happy. I think he doesn't want you to have to give that up." He tapped the bill of his baseball cap with two fingers before turning around and going back to work.

Cody folded the inspector's report and tucked it in his pocket. He planned to have another look at it later, but for now he needed some fresh air.

Cody strode into the pasture next to the open barn and strolled among the grazing cows. Kurt's words had left an impression on him. He scratched the back of one of the cows and dismissed his previous thoughts. Reflectively, he watched the cows, who didn't seem bothered by his presence. He thought about Betty Lou, the cow that he and Scott used to ride when they were kids. Whenever they were supposed to bring the herd in from the pasture, they had taken a halter with them, put it on to Betty Lou, and one of them had ridden her back to the barn. Even their father used to think it was funny and allowed Betty Lou to live out the rest of her life at their farm. Then his father had bought him a pony. Oh, Dad, at that point, we weren't yet worlds apart.

Cody walked through the feeding hall and inspected the corridor down which the cows passed twice a day to be milked. He noticed a few things that needed to be repaired or improved. It would take weeks. Time that he didn't have due to his job at Willow Ranch, especially now that Emma was visiting. He wanted to spend as much time with her as he possibly could. He pulled out his cell phone and sent her a message: *Arrived safely. Thinking of you. Have fun with Sonja.*

Her response came only a moment later. *Hello, Cowboy. Don't let those cows keep you away too long. I plan to ride off with you into the mountains a million more times.*

He sent her back a kissy face emoji and stuck his phone back into his pocket. Without a doubt, Emma loved the Canadian wilderness just as much as he did. Was his job as a wrangler the reason why she would consider moving to Canada to be with him? Dammit, it made no sense trying to figure out what Emma wanted when he didn't even know what he wanted himself. Cody shoved his hands into his pockets and looked out over the pasture. To the west stood tall grain silos. How many times had he hidden behind them or ignored strict orders not to climb up the ladder so that he could watch his father and Scott taking care of the cows. His memories, along with the feeling of not being wanted here today, erupted inside him like a flood and his hands balled into fists. What the hell was he doing here anyway?

Rosie heaved another sack of feed onto the pallet. She took inventory once more of what Lee had ordered and compared it to the delivery receipt. Everything was there. She signed the paper and handed the clipboard back to the driver.

"See you again in three weeks, Rosie."

"See you then, and thanks again for the dog food samples. I'm sure Hazel will be happy."

"No problem. Have a nice day."

The old delivery truck rumbled away from Willow Ranch. She wiped the sweat from her forehead. It was due to be another warm September day. She could only hope that fall would stay like this a little longer. She called Hazel with a whistle. The dog promptly appeared just as another truck was approaching. Rosie smiled. Nick parked and got out, as the bloodhound walked over to him with her tail wagging.

"Hey, Sniffer, how you doing?" He gave her a good scratching.

"Hi, what are you doing here?"

He stood upright. "It's nice to see you too. I wanted to talk to Lee and also see about the debt I owe you."

Rosie needed a minute to realize he was talking about the bet they had made regarding what day Lori would deliver her foal. Then she nodded, smiling. "Oh, well, since we were both wrong, we could cook together at my house. How about tonight?"

"That's what I call spontaneous."

"You haven't even gotten to see him yet."

"Yeah, sorry about that. I've had so much to do with the stallions."

His crooked grin set off a swarm of butterflies in her stomach. "You can do that tonight. Bring a couple of steaks, will you? I'll take care of the rest."

"Very good, ma'am. Would 7 o'clock be okay?"

"Perfect. I'm looking forward to it."

He touched the brim of his hat with two fingers, then headed for the ranch house. Her anticipation of an evening with Nick sent excited shivers down her spine. She strolled back to the barn, whistling a tune.

The day seemed to drag on. She kept glancing at the clock, thinking about what she needed to pick up at the store, and decided to cut out a little early for the day. By three o'clock, she had finished all her work, loaded Hazel into her truck, and turned the radio up loud. She sang at the top of her lungs as she left Willow Ranch and headed for the little supermarket in town. As she got out, her cell phone rang. A glance at the display told her that it was Doug. If she ignored his call, he would probably simply show up at her place this evening. She needed to make sure that didn't happen. "Doug, hi."

"Hey, are you done working? Want to get together later?"

"Sorry, I've got plans," she said.

"Too bad. I've got some free time right now; you could easily—"

"Some other time. I need to go, take care," she interrupted him before hanging up. So many times she had tried to make it clear to him that, for her, they were just friends. But he still seemed to hope for something more. Whatever. She didn't have time to think about him now.

An hour later, she had assembled a Caesar salad, the baked potatoes wrapped in aluminum foil were piping hot in the oven, and a baking tray of garlic bread was waiting to go in once Nick arrived. When she heard Hazel barking outside, she tore off her apron, ran her fingers through her hair, and walked out onto the porch. When she saw the truck approaching, she raised one eyebrow. What was Calvin doing here? And who did he have with him? Her ex-boyfriend got out of his truck, as did the stranger. Rosie's stomach constricted as she remembered that he had wanted to come by with the buyer for Raweno. Rage instantly shot through her veins. Yes, the horses belong to him, but he couldn't just show up unannounced whenever it pleased him.

Calvin raised a hand to greet her and guided the man directly to the paddock. Hazel let out a deep growl as Rosie descended the stairs to follow them. "Hey, this isn't your property, Calvin." She held her dog by the collar and planted herself in front of him.

"Calm down. I told you that I wanted to come by in the next few days." He smiled apologetically at the man, then pointed at the foal. "The colt will be very valuable for studding."

"I'm well aware of that," said the man. "I figured your father would manage to get his hands on the last droplets of Dragon's semen."

Calvin's responding laugh sounded artificial. He rubbed the back of his neck with his hands. "Oh, you know, he's focused now on expanding the riding school, so he let me take over."

The man nodded.

For her part, Rosie couldn't imagine Mr. Dunn letting such a lucrative opportunity slip through his fingers so easily. At least, in the four years that she had known Calvin and worked at his father's riding stables, such a thing had never happened. Before she could say anything, another truck pulled up in front of the cabin. *Nick!* flashed in her head and she hurried over to greet him. The cowboy got out of his truck and nodded in Calvin's direction. "Um, I only brought two steaks with me."

"That's fine. The two of them will be leaving soon."

"And who is that?"

"The guy with the cowboy hat is Calvin. The horses belong to him. Well, actually, just the foal, but ... Oh, I'll explain later. And the man is a potential buyer."

Lines appeared on Nick's forehead. "But the colt isn't even three months old."

"Calvin likes to plan in advance."

Just at that moment, the two men turned around, and Nick cursed. "Shit, that's Floyd."

Rosie looked at him, confused. "You know him?"

Nick laid his hand on her forearm and leaned in close to her. "I visited his studding ranch once to have a look at one of the stallions. I would never sell a horse to him," he said quietly, then he raised his head and a thin smile appeared on his face.

"Mr. Floyd, hello. Nice to see you again."

"It's a small world. Are you also here to see the colt?" The man's eyes darted from Calvin to Nick and back.

"No worries, I'm just here for a steak dinner," Nick said unabashed.

Rosie now noticed that Calvin was staring hard at Nick. "This is Nick Flint, a friend and former colleague."

"Ah, a friend?" Her ex said, amused. "I hope your boyfriend Doug won't be jealous."

Rosie wished that she could have strangled him right then and there, but forced a smile instead. "It was nice to meet you, Mr. Floyd. Take care."

"Thank you, Miss. And make sure you take good care of that precious animal."

"I'll be right back, Mr. Floyd." Calvin came up next to Rosie. "Don't forget our agreement," he growled. "And keep that colt under wraps, you understand?"

Hazel growled at him from next to Rosie's leg. Before she managed to say anything, Nick had placed his hand on Calvin's chest and pushed him away from her. "I think it would be better if you left now."

"Hands off!" He knocked Nick's hand away, then he turned around and marched over to his truck.

Rosie's breath didn't even out until the vehicle was out of sight. She thanked Hazel with a good ear scratching and looked at Nick. "I could also scratch your ears to say thank you, or we can get started making dinner."

He grinned. "First, I want to see the foal, and then we can start the grill. You can tell me what this is all about over dinner."

As they sat together at the dining table, Nick was still raving about Raweno. "You can already see that the foal has inherited all of Dragon's best traits. He looks just like his father. That dark chocolate-colored coat of his is highly sought after."

Rosie smiled blissfully. This must be what parents feel like whenever anyone says something nice about their children.

They talked further about the mare's lineage and Raweno's bloodline. Rosie couldn't get enough of Nick's enthusiasm. His passion for horse breeding was accentuated by his bright eyes. And it made her proud whenever she was able to surprise him with her own knowledge about this or that. After they had cleaned their plates, he leaned back in his chair and took a sip of his beer.

"I've never met a woman who could carry on such a good conversation about horse breeding before," he said.

"I can only return the compliment." She stood up and began to clear the table.

Nick also got up. "It's only fair: we cook together, we cleanup together."

She piled up next to the sink all the dirty dishes as he rolled up his sleeves. "You can dry." He threw her a towel, then turned on the tap. "So, Doug is your boyfriend now, eh?"

The question took Rosie by such surprise that she almost dropped the plate she was drying. "No, he's still just a pushy friend."

"Sorry, it's none of my business," Nick replied. "Actually, what interests me more is hearing about this agreement you have with your ex."

Rosie would have preferred to set the record straight about Doug, but Nick didn't seem to care. She grabbed some silverware out of the draining rack and dried it. She explained how she had gotten Lori and Sky. "I love the old girl and wanted to give her a good home for the rest of her life. And Sky." Rosie sighed. "She is a tough nut to crack. I have been filming our training sessions together in order to apply for a scholarship at Gordsteen's, but it seems like any day we make the smallest bit of progress, the next day she reverts back four times as much."

"I only saw her briefly out on the pasture, but she had a wild look in her eye. Perhaps she's a little out of your wheelhouse ...?"

Rosie groaned. "You can come right out and say it if you don't think I'm up to it. But if I don't get a scholarship, there's no way I can pay for the program myself."

"I think with your knowledge about breeding, you'd do better by buying Raweno."

Rosie, who was presently putting away the clean dishes into the cupboard, paused for a moment. "That sounds so easy, but

I can't afford to do that. My plan is to become a horse trainer." She opened the refrigerator. "You want another beer? I'm afraid I didn't make any dessert."

"Don't you like sweet things?"

"I do, but I didn't have any time to bake anything. Have you got a favorite dessert?"

"Pumpkin pie."

Rosie grimaced. "For real? It needs to be something chocolatey for me."

"To each their own. But I'll have another beer." He took bottle she held out to him. "Is your plan to become a horse trainer also your dream? Or are you just trying to prove something?"

"I don't need to prove anything. My dream would be to be able to keep Raweno, Lori, and Sky, and to be accepted to Gordsteen's. But in reality, I lack the contacts and the money to be able to establish myself as a breeder."

They went and sat down on the porch. Rosie took a long swig of her beer. "I definitely want to work towards becoming a horse trainer. Focusing on my dreams will only distract me."

"You shouldn't give up your dreams so easily. Sometimes it's enough to rethink your goals and readjust. That isn't the same as defeat." Nick leaned back on the bench and stretched his legs out in front of him.

Rosie's gaze fell on the paddock where the three horses were enjoying the warm September evening. Was Nick right? Should she try to buy Raweno? Especially now that she knew where the colt could possibly end up? Her thoughts raced. What if she were able to not only achieve her goal, but to even fulfill her dreams?

"It's nice here," Nick said into the silence and interrupted her brooding. "I mean, the Tanner Ranch has its charms, but it doesn't really feel like home. Perhaps it's just too big for me by myself."

She wasn't sure how to answer that and wondered whether he had a girlfriend. She noticed he was looking at her and she returned his gaze. His clear blue eyes twinkled, and his smile was both warm and hungry. Shit. Rosie felt the lump in her throat. Her mind had gone blank, and yet it was full of questions.

Nick raised his bottle and finished his drink in one go. "I better get going, gotta get up early tomorrow."

"Oh, okay." She hoped her weak knees would carry her.

She stood up and, along with Hazel who had been snoozing on the porch next to them, walked him to his truck.

"It was a really nice evening," he said.

"I thought so too."

He opened the driver door, turned around again, and kissed her on the cheek. "Take care of yourself. If you get into any trouble, just give me a call, okay?"

"Thanks, I will."

"See you next time."

Long after the taillights of his truck had disappeared, Rosie could still feel the warmth of his lips on her skin. Shit.

October

Cody set the box with the apple pie from Mary's diner on the seat of his truck and read through the shopping list one more time that Emma had given him in preparation for the large Thanksgiving dinner she and Sonja were hosting. The only thing left to get was red wine. He would have preferred to simply spend the time alone with Emma, but he knew how much she had been looking forward to this day. He looked at the bags of groceries covering the back seat of his truck. No one would be going hungry after all that. He grinned.

After stopping at the liquor store to buy the wine, he arrived shortly after noon at the guesthouse and was surprised to see all the colorful decorations. Emma and Sonja were in the middle of decking out the porch stairs with a variety of miniature pumpkins and gourds. A garland of fall colors spanned the front of the house, tall candles burned inside of large lanterns on either side of the front door, and handmade wreaths of dried grass and various-colored berries hung from the windows. He parked his truck and got out. "You guys are lucky that winter is late this year," he said.

Emma came over and threw her arms around his neck. "Did you get everything?"

"Yeah, I think so. Mary added some extra cinnamon and walnuts to her apple pie. She sends her love and told me to tell you that you and Sonja ought to come by sometime for brunch."

"Oh, that would wonderful. Mary is so nice, as are you too, of course." She gave him a long kiss and nestled up against him.

"If the two of you keep that up, nobody's going to get fed." Sonja suddenly appeared on the porch with her arms crossed, grinning.

The three of them carried in the boxes and bags of groceries. Inside the house, the two women hadn't been stingy with their decorations either. It smelled wonderfully of roasted turkey and ham.

"My mouth is watering already," Cody said.

Emma put away some of the groceries, opened a bottle of wine, and poured two glasses. She handed one to Sonja, then turned to Cody. "Would you like some wine or a beer?"

He looked at the clock. It was early afternoon. He shrugged. "I guess I'll have a beer."

Along with a bottle of beer, Emma handed him the vegetable peeler. "It's good that you've come so early."

He sighed dramatically. "Well, then tell me who all is coming?"

"Lee, Naira, and Samantha. Woodwind, Lyla, Lonefeather, Ayita, and her little boy. Rosie might bring Doug with her, and Nick said he might stop by later for a piece of pumpkin pie."

He looked around the small house. "Where do you plan to put all these people?"

"It's going to be cozy," Sonja replied casually. "Everybody can just find a place to sit wherever, that's all. The weather's supposed to be nice, so we can also sit outside."

"It'll be great." Emma beamed at him with rosy cheeks. "I love the relaxed attitude of the people here."

About an hour later, the food was ready. The peas and carrots were finished, and the plates and silverware stood ready. Cody heard the sound of cars pulling up. One by one the guests arrived, and thirty minutes, later the house was full of people and activity. Hazel and Mud trotted around the herb garden while Samantha and Wynono went to look at the goats. Cody, who actually intended to continue helping out in the kitchen, was given a second bottle of beer and sent outside. He found Lee chatting with Rosie on the porch and went over to them.

"We've got some snacks inside so that no one goes hungry before the bird is out of the oven," he said.

"I'd better not," Lee answered. "I've been looking forward to this turkey for days and don't want to ruin my appetite with other things."

"I'll go see if I can do anything to help and leave you two to talk." Rosie grinned and disappeared into the house.

"Wasn't she supposed to bring her new boyfriend with her? Doug?" Cody asked, looking around.

"Oh, I had no idea she had a boyfriend."

"I guess he's not worth mentioning. At least I've never seen him before."

The men stood together for a while in silence, and Cody saw Lee watching Samantha collect colorful leaves with Wynono.

"How long is Sam supposed to still stay with you and Naira?" Cody asked.

"Not sure. Apparently, there were some problems at the research station where Sam's aunt is working, and she needed to stay there a while longer. Naira and I are in no hurry to get rid of her either."

"And when are the two of you planning to have kids?" Cody accidentally blurted out, immediately regretting that he went too far. But Lee smiled. "No one knows that for sure either. For right now, we are focusing on building a future together."

"Well, you've got the best foundation for that with Willow Ranch."

"Yeah, I am really grateful that my father left it to me, even though he didn't really think I would make it as a rancher."

Just like my dad, Cody thought. Except that he didn't really want to take over the family farm. His memories of the farm felt like sandpaper against his soul.

"It's an honor to continue a family ranch or farm, but it's also a mighty big undertaking. That said, I would do it again if I could." Lee placed one hand on Cody's shoulder. "I'm not interested in telling you what to do. You're a good cowboy and outfitter, and we'd missed you an awful lot. But having a farm is the ideal basis for starting a family and a future."

He felt the slight pressure of Lee's hand on his shoulder, then Lee turned to Naira, who had just stepped out of the house. Lee joined her, and the two of them went over to Sam and Wynono. Cody finished the rest of his beer and decided to switch to a soft drink instead. As he walked past the open kitchen window, he heard Emma's voice."

"Oh, Sonnie, I see it in my daydreams, it would be amazing to live at the side of a cowboy. In the summers, we'd take the horses into the mountains, lead a tourist group, or take packhorses. And spend the winters in our cozy little cottage."

"That sounds like one of those trashy romance novels," Sonja replied. "Cody might inherit his father's farm though. Would you also feel that way about becoming a dairy farmer?"

"Don't be silly. He doesn't want to take over the family farm. He's a cowboy through and through! He's not going to give that up for a barn full of cows."

"I understand that you love working with horses, and that you also love your independence. We should sit down and have a talk about the chance ..." Sonja's voice faded away.

He gulped. That was a strong statement from Emma, and it sat in his stomach like a rock. He had no idea now how he was going to be able to discuss his concerns about the future with her.

He heard laughter, and someone from the house called out: "Dinner is ready!" He wished he could just jump into his truck and drive away, but he couldn't bear to. He joined the others headed for the house, filled his plate with food, and found an old rattan chair out on the porch to sit on. Emma joined him with her plate. "May I sit with you?"

"Of course." Before he had the chance to stand up and offer her his chair, she threw a pillow on the floor and sat down on it. "I hope you like it."

He barely had any appetite and considered whether he should mention what he had overheard her say when someone suddenly screamed. They both put down their plates, got to their feet, and ran around the side of the house to where the noise came from.

They saw Sonja inside the goat enclosure, kneeling in front of a goat. Lyla was standing next to her.

"What happened?" Cody asked.

"I don't know what's wrong with her. Samantha called me over because she saw that the goat's stomach was badly swollen on the left side."

"It's probably just colic," Cody surmised.

"I assume so, but I can't get a hold of the vet," said Lyla, holding her cell phone to her ear. "Does anyone here know anything about a goat with colic?"

Out of the corner of his eye, Cody saw Rosie come running. "My ex's new girlfriend is a goat expert."

"Right. Andrea told me she had her own goat farm. Could you call her, please," Sonja pleaded. "Hurry."

Ayita came over to the enclosure, holding a baby goat in her arms.

Sonja looked up and let out another scream. "Merlin, oh no." She jumped to her feet and ran to Ayita. When she touched the goat, he raised his head and let out a loud bleat.

"I think the little guy was just sleeping," Woodwind's commented from his spot between Lonefeather and Cody.

Sonja let out a sigh of relief and took Merlin in her arms. He heard Rosie speaking to someone on the telephone.

"Okay, wait a minute." She turned to Lyla. "Andrea says we should give the goat some sunflower oil or peanut oil to drink, about a fourth of a cup."

"I'll get it," Emma called out, running into the house and coming back a moment later with a bottle of oil in her hand.

Sonja set Merlin on the ground, took the oil, and approached the goat with the distended stomach. Samantha had fetched a halter and held the animal firmly while Sonja poured the oil down its throat. "And now?" She said to Rosie.

"Massage its stomach, especially on the left side."

"How will we know if the colic improves?" Cody asked.

Rosie gestured at him to wait, listened for a moment, then briefly smiled and ended the conversation. "When the goat starts farting and burping, then we'll know it's okay."

Everyone's eyes were on Sonja as she massaged the goat with slow, circular movements. Emma wiped away a tear from her eye, and Cody came up next to her. He took her hand and squeezed it. "It'll be fine," he said softly.

"Sonja would never forgive herself if that goat died."

After a few tense minutes of complete silence, the goat stretched out her neck and burped, then the animal visibly relaxed. A loud fart came next, and Samantha giggled.

"I think the goat's better now," said Woodwind.

"Sounds like you when you've had too much to eat," Lonefeather teased and nudged his brother in the side.

"Speaking of eating, I think it's about time for dessert," Rosie said, and the others nodded in agreement.

Soon afterward, the pumpkin pie was distributed, and since Emma was talking to Sonja, Cody sat down next to Rosie. "Did you make this?" He asked, sticking a large piece of pie with whipped cream on it into his mouth.

"I did. Is it any good?"

"Fantastic. Did you eat yours already?"

She shook her head. "I don't like pumpkin pie."

"Then why did you make it?"

Rosie's cheeks turned red.

"Is it Doug's favorite pie?"

"Doug's? Nah." She waved dismissively, but glanced toward the driveway.

Cody tried to remember who else was on Emma's guest list, and then grinned. "Maybe you ought to take a piece over to the Tanner Ranch?"

Now her cheeks were bright red. "Idiot." She stood up. "I prefer to stay single. It's less complicated." Cody watched her walk away, grinning. I don't believe that for a second, Rosie LaForge, he said under his breath. Although she might be right when he considered his relationship with Emma, which felt very complicated at the moment. But at the same time, he didn't want to rule out a life together with her right off the bat either. The sound of a drum interrupted his thoughts. He turned his head to look, and the other guests also heard the drumming and wondered where it was coming from. Cody spotted Naira, standing on the west side of the guest house, waving at everyone to come. He got up and joined Emma and Sonja. "Any idea what's going on?" he asked.

Both women shook their heads. Cody noticed that neither Woodwind nor his brother Lonefeather were among the rest of the guests gathered around Naira. The First Nations woman raised her hand and the murmuring stopped. "A while back, I promised Sonja that she could take part in a drumming circle. And today, I'm fulfilling that promise."

"What? Really?" Sonja sputtered. "Here?"

Naira nodded. "As a thank you to you and Emma for inviting us all to this wonderful feast today. Come on, it's not far."

Cody followed along with the others, and a few minutes later, they were standing in a field, where six men were sitting in a circle around a campfire, drumming a slow rhythm on the instruments in front of them. Cody saw Lonefeather, who seemed to be leading the group. Woodwind was also part of the ensemble, and he was surprised to see how young the other four musicians were. One of them was Nuka, whose eyes were concentrated on Lonefeather as he followed his direction. The listeners stood in a semicircle around the drummers. Cody stood next to Sonja and Emma, with Ayita and Naira on the other side of them.

"I've already got goosebumps," said Sonja, rubbing her arms.

"I do too," Emma admitted. "What an amazing surprise!"

"Just wait until they really get started," Naira said. "They're just warming up."

"How did the teens get here?" Emma asked.

"With me," a voice behind them said.

Una approached, smiling. "It took a little bit of convincing Nuka to come, but once he heard that Lonefeather was leading the circle, he quickly agreed."

"Yeah, Lonefeather's drumming is known all throughout the reserve," Naira said.

Una turned to Ayita. "Where is your cute little boy?"

"He's over there sitting with Lee and Naira's foster child and the two dogs." She pointed to the spot where the four had made themselves comfortable on the grass.

"I'm supposed to tell you hello from my father, by the way," said Una. "After I told him where Nuka and I were going this evening, he was sure that you would also be here with your niece. He says he would like it if you gave him a call sometime." Una handed her a card. "Here's his number."

Cody observed Ayita look at the card for a moment and then stick it in her jacket pocket.

"Would you mind giving us a short explanation of the tradition of this circle before the men really get started?" Sonja asked.

Naira nodded. "Sure. The beat of the drums symbolizes the heartbeat of Mother Earth. It's hard to say how old this tradition is, but of course the drum has deep roots in our culture. Drumming gives us the opportunity to connect with our Creator and the spirits, and offers spiritual enlightenment."

"Not only the rhythm of the beat, but also listening to it can set a person into a trance-like state, right?" Sonja asked.

"That's right. It's similar to hypnosis, a sort of state of ecstasy. While in this state, a lot can happen in a person's unconscious, blockages get opened up and cleared, and some people have visions of how they can solve their problems. There are many different things that happen in this state. Many of us believe that drumming has the power unleash thunder and lightning. The beats of the drum are also said to draw the attention of the gods and can communicate with the spirits."

The group had stopped playing their instruments, and Cody observed Lonefeather speaking to the young men.

"Thank you for bringing the teenagers here," Naira said to Una.

She waved her hand. "It was a good opportunity to bypass the argument that was starting between Nuka and our father."

"What was it about this time?" Cody asked. "Rabbit told me that the two of them don't get along well."

"My dad has his sights set on Woodwind and the youth workshops again. He thinks that it's all too soft and that the teenagers aren't going to learn anything about real life by going to these 'love and peace camps.'"

"And what did Nuka say?"

"He said that his time at Willow Ranch was the best time of his life and that Woodwind is a great mentor."

Cody raised one eyebrow. Wasn't that the same boy who had constantly complained about the program and about Woodwind?

Una smirked and shrugged her shoulders. "I can see the surprise in your face, Cody. I was also baffled, but Nuka said that he had changed his mind and that along with drumming and woodworking, he wanted to learn how to play the flute. Teenagers!" She laughed.

The drumming started up again and grew louder. Cody saw Ayita walk over to Una and ask her a question about her father. The rest of their conversation was drowned out by the sound of the drums. Lonefeather seemed to be driving the other drummers with his own drumming. Cody threw a glance at Emma and Sonja; their eyes were fixed on the drummers. He too heard the echo of the rhythm deep inside.

Woodwind finished off the rest of his coffee and thought about Ayita. He had asked her yesterday during Thanksgiving dinner at Sonja and Emma's whether she could imagine taking on a permanent position at the rescue center and continuing caring for Kachina. Of course, only as much as she was able to with Wynono. She had been so excited that she had given him a kiss, and it had felt so good to hold her in his arms. However, she hadn't seemed to want a second kiss. And early this morning, she had called him to say that he didn't need to pick her up because she didn't have time to come to the rescue center today.

His disappointment felt like a fog around him and he couldn't shake the feeling that Ayita was avoiding him. Had he been too forceful? But she was the one who kissed him first. Dammit, he should've just left it at that. After the drumming circle, she had only said a quick goodbye. While he was busy brooding, his cell phone beeped with a new text message: *Here is the website for the online course. Don't put it off. Best regards, Naira.*

Woodwind sighed. His thoughts about Ayita were now replaced with concern about the course and especially about taking the exam. He didn't own a computer or a laptop, which meant that he would have to use the public computer in the small library at the community center. That alone filled him with dread. The fact that he didn't know how much material he needed to cover, along with his awareness that he was a slow learner, only exacerbated the urgency for him to start as soon as possible. He cursed Bull. On the other hand, what if he were right, and Woodwind wasn't cut out to work with youth? He was aware that many of the teenagers saw his time in jail as some sort of badge of honor. And that was exactly what he wanted to avoid. Nonetheless, his past did provide him with an opportunity to show them up close what the consequences were for screwing up their lives.

After their time in the mountains, Woodwind still wasn't convinced he had managed to get through to the young people, but he had made a promise to be there for the group. Their care would continue in the form of courses following a stint at home in February, and the intensive program would begin again in the summer. Woodwind definitely wanted to be part of that. If he didn't take these courses and pass the test, he'd feel guilty that he was leaving the teens in a lurch. That thought alone was too much for him. There were enough things in his life that he couldn't forgive himself for; being there for these kids was the one thing that he was determined to do.

He arrived at the community center twenty minutes later. In contrast to the cheaply constructed houses, the community center building was made of bricks. Next to it was the so-called Band

Office, a new-ish complex where the offices of the chief, the deputy chief, the council members, and administrators were located. His gaze floated over to the football field, school and gymnasium on the other side of the community center. Not far from that was the police station. He entered the community center and, ignoring the curious looks, walked up to the information counter. He desperately tried to remember the name of the woman who was sitting behind the desk and smiling at him.

"What can I do for you?"

"I need to use a computer."

"Do you have a library card?"

He shook his head while a little girl promptly walked up next to him with three books in her hand and placed them on the desk. "I'm bringing these back," she said. "And Mama said that I can take out some others instead."

"I've already told you that you need to wait until it's your turn," a voice behind Woodwind said. He took a step to the side and turned around.

"I'm sorry, my daughter is an absolute bookworm." The young mother tried to pull the girl back by the hood of her red sweatshirt.

"Oh, that's no problem. I'm not in a hurry," he said.

The Cree woman looked at him for a moment. "You're Woodwind, aren't you?"

He nodded. "Do we know each other?"

"May I go and find some new books now?" The girl asked, tugging on her mother's jacket.

"Yes, you go ahead. I'll be right there," the young woman replied and watched her daughter disappear between the shelves of books. "Sorry, she really loves books and is always so impatient."

"No worries. But how do we know each other?"

She nodded, then took a few steps away from the information desk.

"My niece Mina has been raving about you ever since she heard you play your flute on your trip to the mountains."

Woodwind felt his cheeks getting hot.

"Oh, uh ..." He stuttered, his gaze dropping to the colorful carpeting.

"You really made an impression on her and that is not an easy task with Mina. She tends to be rather hostile towards adults and finds us all incredibly irritating."

He looked up. "Thank you for telling me that. I wasn't sure whether the teens had taken me seriously at all."

The young woman smiled. "They do, Woodwind. The kids around here need someone exactly like you in their lives."

"Mommm, come here! I want to show you something," the girl called out as she hopped from one foot to the other, waving at her mother.

The woman briefly placed her hand on Woodwind's arm. "I'd better go have a look. See you later. And don't let Bull get you down."

He nodded at her as she walked away.

In the meantime, the woman at the information desk had filled out a library card and handed it to him. "You can use the computers at any time. The password, opening times, and all the rest is written on the pamphlet." She handed him a piece of paper. "If you have any questions, I'm here just about every day."

"Thank you, that's very nice of you."

"My pleasure, it's what I'm here for. By the way I think it's great that you are taking on the youth. No matter what Jeremy Bull says, there are many people here at the reserve who appreciate what you're doing, Woodwind."

"Oh, um, thank you." He hurried over to one of the desks with a computer. Did everyone here know about his trouble with Bull? He shook his head and had a look at the online courses.

Only a short time later, Woodwind was overwhelmed by the amount of coarse material, primarily consisting of numerous pages of notes and hours of videos. How was he supposed to read, watch, and remember it all? His eyes, unused to staring at a screen for any period of time, burned like the devil, and he logged off the computer.

Once outside the library, he decided to pay Chinook a visit. Perhaps Ayita had finally decided to have a talk with the elder and for that reason hadn't had time to devote to the rescue center. He covered the short distance to Chinook's house and knocked on the door. When no one answered, he turned the knob. Not unexpectedly, it wasn't locked. He opened the door and walked in.

"Hello? Chinook? It's me, Woodwind," he called out.

"Don't make so much noise, and come into the living room." He pulled off his boots and found the shaman sitting in his rocking chair, with a book on his lap. "Good thing you're here. Would you take this please?"

Woodwind saw that the book was some sort of chronicle and that Chinook had scrawled something in it with shaky handwriting. "What are you doing with this?" he asked, placing the book on the side table.

"I'm writing down what I know. Don't want everything to be lost once I kick the bucket, or more accurately, turn to dust." The old man chuckled.

"Well, take all the time you can with that. We still need you here for a while."

Chinook coughed. "I may be able to influence a lot of things, my boy, but the end comes when it wants. Tell me instead how it was with the young people."

Woodwind sat down on a chair across from Chinook and told him about the trip to the mountains and also about Jeremy Bull's attempt to get him kicked off the program.

"And so, I was just now at the community center looking at the course material on the Internet."

Chinook knitted his eyebrows, drawing attention to all the lines on his forehead, and massaged his knotty fingers in his lap. "For Jeremy, the program at Willow Ranch really goes against the grain. He's struggling at home with Nuka and thinks that having a delinquent son will have a negative effect on his aspiration to become chief of the reserve."

Woodwind gave a throaty laugh, but immediately became serious again. "Bull must be stopped. I mean, do you really think that as chief he'll put away his own interests for the good of the reserve?"

Chinook's head bobbed. "Jeremy is a bitter man."

"Ah. And that's supposed to excuse him for attacking me and treating Una like some peon? If no one has the courage to stand up to Bull, then I will." He stood up, hoping to avoid hearing any further defense for this pigheaded bastard.

"Sit back down." The shaman's words were barely audible, but were not to be disobeyed. "Everyone has his part to play. And yours is to pass this test and be there for the teenagers."

"And what if I don't pass the course?" What if I'm just wasting my time and Ayita doesn't want anything to do with me anymore?"

Chinook stared at him, and Woodwind wished that he hadn't mentioned Ayita's name. It hung in the air between them like an unfinished thought. The shaman coughed again, visibly straining. He raised his hand, indicating to Woodwind to wait until he could catch his breath again. "Why would Ayita not want anything to do with you? Did something happen between you?"

"I thought we had finally managed to open a line of communication with one another." He recounted the story of the wolf pup coming to the rescue center. "But now, I have the feeling Ayita is doing her best to avoid me. I thought she must have finally come to talk to you."

Chinook shook his head.

"Her son still hasn't said one proper word all this time, but he seems to have a special bond with the little wolf."

"A wolf without a pack is lost," Chinook said pensively.

Woodwind nodded, and the two men sat together in silent contemplation for a few moments.

"I don't understand why Ayita doesn't want to contact her relatives at the reserve. Despite being surrounded by so many people, she and Wynono seem to be falling more and more into isolation."

"The sort of isolation that comes from feeling lost cannot be cured by others."

The shaman's words penetrated deeply into Woodwind's mind.

They resonated with him as well; something he didn't want to admit. It was time to go. He stood up. "Can I bring you anything?" he asked, but Chinook shook his head.

"I'll make sure that Una starts making her way on her own. You take heart and keep your eyes on passing the test, you understand?"

Woodwind wanted to ask how the shaman planned to help Una, but the wise man's look prevented him from asking. Woodwind nodded and left the living room. He stopped in the doorway, turning around to look at the shaman. The old man had started nodding off, so he took a blanket from the other chair and laid it over his thin legs. Chinook's wrinkly face had a grayish tinge, and his cheeks appeared even more sunken than he had remembered. His breathing was shallow and accompanied by a rattling in his lungs that Woodwind didn't like. He gently drew the blanket up over the elder's hands in his lap. "Have a good rest, wise man. I'll come by again as soon as I can," he whispered before leaving the house.

Rosie sat at her small, wobbly dining table and went over the figures again for the hundredth time. Nick's advice to reconsider her goals echoed in her ears. They were more like an incentive to her. Why shouldn't she dream big? However, her salary from Willow Ranch went to pay the rent for Eric's cabin, food for herself, and food for the animals.

She leaned back in her chair with a sigh. If she dipped into her savings and kept to a rigorous minimalistic monthly budget, she might have the money together to buy Raweno by February.

But what would that mean with regard to her plans to become a certified horse trainer? The courses at Gordsteen's would begin again next summer. No later starting dates were listed on the website.

There were two ways to secure a spot there. Either you could afford it and put down a deposit, or you had to convince the school that you were talented enough and win a scholarship. The requirement for this was to make a video diary documenting yourself training an unbroken horse and eventually being able to ride it. Would she be able to train Sky over the next few months to become a riding horse? Was it too risky? If she allowed Raweno to be sold, she would receive her share of the selling price, which would cover the first few installments of the program and also eliminate the pressure of trying to transform Sky into an obedient riding horse with a saddle.

Rosie ran her fingers through her hair. She needed to make a decision. Did she want to buy Raweno and try to win the scholarship, or take the easy way by letting the foal be sold while also solving a few other problems as well? There was no question that having three horses meant more expense for her, as well as pressure to increase the size of the pasture. She told herself to calm down, to breathe, and to take one step at a time.

Calvin had called her yesterday and offered to trim the horses' hooves. There were a number of other things she could imagine doing instead of spending the afternoon with her ex, but at least this time he had given her notice that he was coming. Plus, the mares desperately needed hoof attention. She stood up. Hazel, who was sleeping on the couch, raised her head. "Let's go out, you lazy dog. I need to clean out the stable." She grabbed her phone.

She looked around the stall. She would need to make a number of changes for when Raweno no longer needed to be with his mother and would require space of his own. As an adult stallion, she would also need to keep him in a separate paddock. She took the old radio off the windowsill and turned it on. Country music filled the structure. While she raked the muck, she wondered if Jim would be willing to help her rebuild the boxes. If she were lucky, he would also be able to procure some wooden slats for free.

Rosie considered asking her friends for some advice, but then decided not to. They were sure to try and talk her out of her plan. She could already hear their well-meaning words: "be reasonable," "you can't do that," or "that would be too much for you." She didn't want to hear it. She loved a good challenge. What else was there to live for?

The light bulb over the aisle between the stalls flickered, reminding her that she urgently needed to have an electrician come and check the wiring. Jim had warned her more than once that she was risking a fire with those worn wires.

She heard what sounded like a vehicle approaching and peered out the window. It was Calvin's truck. She propped the pitchfork against the wall, grabbed three halters, and went out into the pasture. Raweno trotted up to her and she pulled a treat out of her pocket for him.

"Don't go spoiling him too much, now, or he'll be walking all over you in no time." Calvin stood at the fence. To Rosie's surprise, he had brought his new girlfriend with him. Andrea waved at her and smiled. She was wearing a pair of corduroy pants and a plaid shirt underneath a forest green jacket.

"Hello," said Rosie. "I'm glad you came along."

Andrea held up a package wrapped in wax paper. "Here's the goat cheese I promised you. One is made with lavender, and the other with herbs."

"Wow, thank you. I'm afraid my hands are dirty at the moment."

"No worries, I just didn't want to forget the cheese in the car." Andrea slipped the cheese back into the bag, then reached over the fence and pet the foal. "He sure has grown."

"And he also has a name now. May I present Raweno."

Calvin had gone back to his truck and returned with his box of hoof trimming equipment. "I'll just get right to work. I'm interested to see how the foal takes to his first pedicure."

"You two go ahead," Andrea replied. "I'll just take the cheese into the house and put it in the refrigerator."

While Calvin was busy with Lori's hooves, Rosie thought about bringing up the option of her buying Raweno.

"What do you think, are Andrea and I a good match?" He asked suddenly, standing upright.

"Uh, why are you asking me that?"

He took a step closer to her. "I don't know. I have never had such strong feelings for one woman before. Somehow it scares me."

"That's a good thing, then you'll be less likely to cheat on her with other women." She knew that her words sounded bitter, and she chewed her lower lip as she stared at him.

He lowered his gaze briefly. "Oh, Rosie, that was a long time ago. I've grown up since then, and I know now that I've made mistakes."

She raised her hand. "Let's just leave it at that."

He came up very close to her and slowly leaned over. Rosie held her breath. Her desire to kiss him overwhelmed her, but he stopped, pulled a piece of straw from her hair, and took a step back. "I would just like to ask for your forgiveness."

Her thoughts flashed like lightning through her head. What did he just say?

"Please forgive me for cheating on you. It would mean a lot to me. I love Andrea and just want to clear the air. Ask forgiveness for old sins, that sort of thing."

Out of the corner of her eye, she saw Andrea on the porch. When had she come out of the house? Rosie swallowed her angry words. Clear the air. What an asshole. He'd hurt her so much with his affairs and his insults. At least, that was how it had felt to her. And now he was asking for her blessing on his relationship with a new woman? What in the world was he thinking?

Andrea came over to the pasture. "How's it going?" Her eyes flitted between her and Calvin.

"Good. I was just about to inform your sweetie here that I plan to purchase Raweno myself in February." Rosie forced herself to smile and savored Calvin's stunned face.

"Oh, that would be great," Andrea exclaimed. "Wouldn't it, Cal?"

"Sure, if you can afford it, I don't mind. The asking price is five thousand dollars."

Andrea elbowed him in the side. "I'm sure you two can agree on a better price than that. After all, you used to—"

"I don't want any special favors," Rosie interrupted her. "I will have the money ready in four months."

"I'll need to have a down payment though. Shall we say, two thousand?"

Was this just another ruse of his? Whatever. She would just have to free up part of her savings sooner than she expected. "Okay, I can do that. I can give you a check right now for the deposit."

"Whatever you want," Calvin replied, finishing his work on Lori. "Let me get started on Raweno. Hold the rope real slack. I don't want him to associate hoof trimming with forcefulness."

"I got it. He's not the first foal I've had to hold during a trimming," she snapped at him.

Calvin started by calmly stroking his hand over the colt's long, thin legs and murmuring something to him in a deep voice. Raweno calmed down and lifted his hoof without any problem. She almost felt the need to apologize for her sharp words from a moment ago.

"How's it working out with Sky? Do I need to worry that she might crack my head open if I look at her hooves, or are you making progress with your training?" Calvin asked.

Rosie cautiously approached Sky, put a halter on her, and led the mare to the fence. Instead of tying her up, she let the rope fall to the ground. "We can get started."

Calvin eyeballed her and the horse skeptically, but when Sky raised her front hoof without a fuss, he began filing. Rosie could tell from Sky's body language that the mare was taking the treatment in stride and was relaxed.

After he was finished, he gave Sky abundant praise. Rosie offered her a handful of treats and took off her halter. "Have you guys got time for some coffee?" Rosie asked.

"Sure," said Andrea.

"Do you have got any cookies to go along with it?" Calvin asked. His cell phone rang, and he pulled it out of his jeans pocket. "I have to take this. I'll be right back."

Inside the cabin, Rosie brewed coffee and set a package of cookies on the counter. "Thanks, by the way, for your help with the colicky goat," she said. "The tip you gave about massaging the goat and the oil really worked wonders."

"Well, I don't know that I would exactly call a farting and burping goat a wonder, but I'm glad I could be of help."

Rosie poured the coffee into two cups, retrieved the milk from the refrigerator, and set it next to the sugar bowl on the counter.

"Thank you." Andrea spooned three heaps into her coffee, then paused. "Oh no, I told myself I was going to start cutting back on so much sugar in my coffee." She stirred it with a crooked smile. "It's such a bad habit. I won't be getting any skinnier continuing on like this."

"Oh, you're trying to lose weight?"

"Well, I just have the feeling that Calvin might like me better if I were thinner. Look at you, you're perfect. And I'm just a chubby little thing."

Rosie poured milk into her mug and shook her head.

"Stop thinking like that. That's nonsense. Either he loves you the way you are, or he's not the right one."

Andrea sighed. "I bet you have a lot of men telling you how pretty you are."

"I mean, if you've got guys who are constantly telling you that you're pretty or that you're sexy, at some point you can't stand to hear it anymore. It's all just empty words."

Andrea took one of the chocolate cookies. "You've got a point there," she said. "Still, sometimes I wonder what Calvin sees in me. He could have any cowgirl he wants. He doesn't need to be stuck with a boring goat farmer like me."

"You ought to be asking yourself instead whether he fits into your life and gives you what you want from a man."

Andrea smiled. "He's my dream man."

He had been Rosie's as well, at one time. They both turned their heads and looked out the window. Calvin was coming up the path to the cabin. She handed him the chocolate cookies when he entered the kitchen, and he grabbed two of them at once, shoving them into his mouth, chewing and swallowing. "Delicious, that's exactly what I needed. We gotta go. Dad needs us in the riding stable."

Rosie pulled her checkbook out of her purse and wrote him a check. "Here, that's the down payment for Raweno. Can you give me a receipt for that please."

Calvin nodded. "I've got a receipt book in the truck." He inspected the check. "Are you sure you can afford it?"

"Of course." Rosie forced a crooked grin.

They went out to the truck together, and Calvin wrote her a receipt.

"Thanks. For the trimming too."

"No problem. See you later." Calvin stowed his box of tools.

She stuck the rest of the cookie package inside the truck. "You can have these, enjoy."

He grinned, gave her a kiss on the cheek, and went back to his truck. Andrea threw her a look, which Rosie couldn't quite make out. She hoped that Calvin's girlfriend wouldn't get the wrong idea about him kissing her cheek.

Once the truck had disappeared from the driveway, she went back into the cabin and turned on her laptop. She had come to a decision. She would need to find a second job in order to pay Calvin the balance for the foal as soon as possible. She looked at the local job website and saw that the Coyote Bar in Spruce View was looking for a waitress to take over the evening shift. Perfect! she could work there after she was done at the ranch. With what she'd make along with tips, she was sure to earn enough. She planned to stop by the bar first thing tomorrow.

Hazel came over, sat down next to her, and laid her head on Rosie's thigh. She stroked the dog's ears. "I know, sweet girl, it's going to be a tough time, but we'll get through it." Her thoughts wandered to Nick. Would he try to talk her out of it? It didn't matter. He had no idea what she was capable of. Why should she have to choose between keeping Raweno and participating in the horse training program if she could do both? She closed her laptop. Giving up was not an option.

November

Cody couldn't bear to think about what Emma had said at Thanksgiving dinner. Had she fallen in love with him simply because he was a cowboy? With his thoughts elsewhere, he took the next bridle and rubbed it with leather oil as he stared out the window at the gray snow clouds covering the western sky. Winter had arrived in Alberta, bringing with it gloomy cold and snow. The days of long rides on horseback were over.

Emma and Sonja had decided to stay on at the guest house throughout the winter. They had both successfully managed to extend their visas. When he asked Emma what her plans were regarding her studies, she simply shrugged. "I've set some other priorities," she had said. "And I still have enough savings to last a few more months. Germany will always be there."

He was glad to hear it, but for as much as he had wanted to share his feelings with her, he felt something holding him back. Was it the uncertainty of whether Emma could envision herself living permanently in Canada, or his own misgivings about him being able to offer her the life she dreamed of?

He wiped his hands on an old rag and looked at the bridle. Happy with his work, he returned the leather oil to the cabinet and hung the two bridles on separate hooks in the shed for repair. He opened the door and a cold southwestern wind blew at him; he flipped up the collar of his jacket. Burying his hands into his jeans pockets, he walked over to the main house. Maybe he could find some coffee there. He pulled off his boots, hung up his jacket, and entered the kitchen. To his surprise, Lee and Naira were sitting there. They had piles of documents and accounting books scattered in front of them.

"I'm not interrupting anything, am I?" Cody asked.

Lee waved him in. "No, in fact, you've come just at the right time. Get yourself a cup of coffee and come have a seat."

Cody did just that, and picked one of the cookies from the plate on the table. "Are there problems with the program?"

"No, just the opposite. We've already received the grant money to continue for another year. We're just considering whether we should offer smaller camps throughout the year so that the young people at the reserve won't be bored and give in to any dumb ideas."

"Oh, that sounds great! Would you also continue running the bed-and-breakfast?" Cody took a swallow of his coffee.

"We haven't yet decided about that, but can we continue to count on you?" Lee asked him.

"Um, of course, why do you ask?"

His boss leaned against the back of the bench. "I know what it means to run a ranch, or in your case, a family farm. And I also know how it feels when your own father doesn't think you're good enough to continue on with the business."

Cody swallowed hard. He knew Lee's story, how he had arrived from Germany five years ago to be with his father in Canada, who was dying of cancer. And who, instead of being happy to see him, only greeted him with suspicion and bitterness. But Lee had refused to be put off, had hung up his career as a photojournalist, and with his father's blessing, had eventually taken over as heir of Willow Ranch. "But you knew all along that you were a rancher. I have no idea whether I'm a farmer and can run a dairy business the way my father and Scott managed it."

"You don't have to run it the way they did. If taking it on is something near and dear to your heart, you'll find a way to make it work." Lee grabbed a cookie.

"That's right," Naira said. "Lee transformed an old horse breeding operation into this guest ranch, and now we are using it for indigenous youth. You have to find your own way."

"You make it sound so easy," Cody answered, draining his cup. "I can't imagine doing anything else but working here with the horses."

Lee closed his accounting book and ran his fingers through his hair. "It's not an easy decision. How about you let us know by Christmas what you've decided, okay?"

He nodded and stood up. "That's fine. And thanks a lot for your patience."

"Will you be coming to dinner tonight?" Naira asked before he left the kitchen.

"No, Emma and Sonja invited me to come over."

Once outside, he hurried through the cold wind back to the barn. He wanted to start working on two new wooden pack boxes, which would be useful for the next year. He had only just picked up the saw when his cell phone rang. It could only be his mother, so he answered the call without pausing to look at the display. "Hi, Mom, what's up?"

Silence.

"Mom?"

"Um, I was calling to talk to Cody Flint." A man's voice said.

"Oh, sorry. Yes, that's me."

"This is Mr. Monty. I'm interested in buying your father's farm."

The saw slipped from Cody's hand. His dad was looking to sell? "Why are you calling me and not my father directly?"

"I've tried talking to him, but he refuses to let me explain myself. I know that your brother commit—, um—, that he's no longer with us. And it came to my ears that you yourself aren't interested in running the farm, so I figured y'all would probably be looking to sell the farm sooner or later."

Cody's thoughts raced like a pack of scared chickens. What did Mr. Monty want from him? And how did he even get his number?

"I'm sure you're wondering how I got your number," the man said as though reading Cody's thoughts. "Your mother was nice enough to give it to me."

"I don't know how I can help you."

"Well, you can help me by turning down your inheritance, which you apparently don't want to accept anyway, then perhaps your father will consider accepting my offer."

Cody felt something in his side, a quick, sharp pain. "Who told you I wasn't taking over the farm?" he heard himself say.

"Oh, then forgive me, I must've misunderstood something. Well, your parents have my offer. If at some point I could come and see the condition of the farm, that would be very generous."

"Would you plan to continue running it as a dairy operation?"

Cody heard a brief laugh, then the man cleared his throat. "Good Lord, no. I am merely interested in the land and its potential."

"I understand."

"Take your time and think about it, and let me know," the man said before saying goodbye.

Cody placed his phone on the workbench and needed to swallow a few times to fight back the burning acid taste in his throat. The Tippet Ranch was destined to disappear off the face of the earth. The thought of this was suddenly unbearable to him. His childhood with Scott and the memories of all the adventures he and his brother had had in the barns, in the orchards, the wheat fields, and around the cows would all fade away and die, just like Scott. Dammit. He knew what he had to do, but he had no idea how to achieve it. Above all, he didn't know if he was ready to confront his father before it was all too late. And whatever would become of him and Emma after that, Heaven only knew.

Woodwind kept his eyes on Kachina. The vet had come by yesterday and had a look at the wolf's paw, which she kept chewing to the point of bleeding, though it finally seemed to be healing. Dr. Langley was almost beside himself with concern about Kachina's condition, and Woodwind could only agree with him. He had asked Naira for some herbs to help increase her appetite, but they were proving to be of little help. The wolf was now eight months old and gaunt; both her fur and her eyes were dull. "Why don't you want to live?" he asked. "As soon as you are strong enough, I'll let you out into the wild where you can be happy and find a pack."

"How can you be so sure that will happen?" A voice from behind asked, and he spun around.

"Ayita. I hadn't expected you to come at all today." He stepped closer and gave her a short hug. She smelled of beer.

"Lyla had to go into town, and I asked her if she'd drop me off. I had a feeling it might be a good idea to come today with Wynono." Her gaze drifted over to the wolf who barely moved. Only once Ayita's son appeared from behind her long skirt and ran to the fence did the animal raise her head.

"I'm glad you've come," said Woodwind.

How can you be so sure that Kachina will find a new pack?" Ayita repeated her question.

"If she shows that she is submissive, no pack should refuse her."

"But her family has already left her behind once. Perhaps she doesn't feel she can trust other wolves anymore."

He stared at her, unsure of whether she was speaking about the animal or herself. "She won't survive in the wilderness on her own," he said. "And I can't release her into the wild as long as there's hunters after the pack. If the wolves are being chased and Kachina hesitates even for a second due to her familiarity with people, that would be her death."

Ayita nodded thoughtfully and glanced at her son standing next to the gate in a thick snowsuit, then she turned to Woodwind. "Would you like to hear why I left the Sunchild Reserve years ago and the events that lead to that?"

He was stunned that she wished to open up to him. "Let's go into the office. The wind is so cold, and I'll make us some tea. Does Wynono want some juice and a snack?"

A few minutes later, they were sitting together in the office. The little boy wasn't happy to have to leave the wolf, but he cheerfully accepted a few cookies and paged through the picture book Ayita had brought with them. She was sitting on the couch and now looked as though she were no longer sure whether she wanted to tell him about her past.

"It would be nice to learn more about you," he said cautiously. "To get to know you better."

"I was twenty at the time and taking care of my younger siblings while working at a store outside the reserve. That was where I met Marc, and we fell in love. Naïve and in love, I was convinced I had met my soulmate, but after a few months of dating, he gave me my first slap across the face." Her hand rubbed her cheek as though she could still feel the pain of his blow. Her lips curled into a bitter sneer.

"Why did you stay with him? Were the two of you living together?"

"My affair with a white man wasn't regarded very highly within the reserve, so I moved in with him. He had a small apartment in Innisfail, a shack really, but in my mind, anything was better than being near my alcoholic parents."

"And what happened then?"

"Marc lost his job, and although I was paying a share of the rent, we simply couldn't afford to live there anymore." She took a sip of her tea, glanced at Wynono, and then stared at the vinyl flooring. "My younger siblings missed me, and I felt guilty for having left the two of them behind on their own. So, I asked Marc to move in with me at the reserve. The house I had been living in was still there and was empty, so they gave us permission."

"Was he no longer violent towards you?"

"Only when he'd been drinking," Ayita quietly answered, but he suspected this had often been the case.

"However, he could also be a very warm and loving man," she added. "Unfortunately, he had gotten into a scrape or two with some of the other men in the neighborhood who refused to accept a white man living on the reserve."

Woodwind could understand the predicament Ayita must have felt herself stuck in at the time, just as much as Marc's difficult standing among the residents. He propped his elbows on his upper legs and waited for Ayita to continue.

"And then, it happened that a number of women were being assaulted in the area. One young woman was almost raped but managed to escape."

Woodwind raised his hand. What had she just said? "Wait a minute, are you telling me that Marc was out trying to rape women?"

She shook her head first, then hesitated. "Just hear me out, please," she pleaded. "I didn't know if Mark was the one who was after those women. To be honest, I was so scared of him at that point in time that I didn't even have the courage to think of that. And ..."

"And?" Woodwind asked, slightly gruffer than intended. He didn't want to believe that Ayita could have been protecting a rapist.

"And I was pregnant." A tear rolled down her cheek. She quickly wiped it away. "But it was when a close friend of mine was sexually assaulted by him that I had to face the truth. I directly confronted Mark about it."

"How did he react?"

"He denied everything and said that I had better not ever dare accuse him of something like that again, and then he beat me so that I wouldn't forget it."

"Did you report him?"

After a moment, she shook her head.

Woodwind had a feeling that she wasn't telling him the entire truth.

"Everyone at the reserve started giving me the cold shoulder. It was my own fault for having let things get this far, most of them said. It was even up for discussion among the Council about kicking me and Marc out."

"Didn't Chinook put in a word for you?" He couldn't imagine that the wise man would abandon Ayita in such a situation.

"At the time, he had only been the shaman for a short while and didn't have any influence over Council decisions."

"And what happened to Marc?"

"He packed his things and was gone the next day."

"Did the rapes and assaults stop after that?" Woodwind asked, but didn't get an answer.

Wynono, who had gotten to the end of his picture book, stood up and tried to put his snowsuit back on. Ayita walked over and knelt in front of her son. "Lyla will be coming any minute to pick us up." She looked at the clock.

Woodwind also stood up. "That's when you left to go up north? But what about the baby?"

"I wasn't pregnant anymore when I left," she whispered.

"You should have talked to the Council, or with your parents."

"My parents were broken people; they could barely even take care of themselves. And because of their experience in the residential schools, they despised me for having a relationship with a white man."

He understood and remained silent. His parents had also suffered their entire lives due to the abuses they had experienced at these boarding schools. His heart ached for Ayita and for the events that had driven her away. On the other hand, this now all lay in the past. It had to be possible for her to find peace again and to feel at home here. "Chinook was hoping that you would contact him."

Ayita helped Wynono into his snowsuit. "Some things aren't as easy as they might seem at first," she said, pulling on her down coat.

"Not easy, but also not impossible. I have the feeling you haven't told me the entire story."

"I had hoped that my story would just fall into oblivion, but I'm here primarily for Wynono. I have to try to break his silence, and in order to do that, I have to start breaking my own."

Woodwind thought about the bond between the boy and the wolf. "Maybe his healing is not in your power."

Ayita's eyes darkened. "Are you trying to say that I can't take care of my son?"

"No, that isn't what I meant."

Just then the door to the rescue center opened, and Mud came running down the hallway. Wynono tripped over his half-donned snowsuit to get to the dog, and Lyla appeared behind Mud. Woodwind glanced back at Ayita and saw that she was hastily hiding something in her jacket pocket. Was that vodka? He looked at her inquisitively. However, she avoided his gaze and walked past him toward her niece. Lyla kneeled down on the floor between Wynono and Mud, whose tail was wagging wildly, and zipped up Wynono's snowsuit. Then she stood up and briefly waved at Woodwind, who was standing in the doorway to the office. "Hi, have you got a minute? There's something I'd like to talk about with you. Business stuff."

He raised one eyebrow in surprise, but then nodded.

"The two of you can get started, I'll be right there," Lyla said to her aunt, handing her the car keys. "Take Mud with you."

Without saying goodbye to Woodwind, Ayita, her son and Mud left the center. Lyla came into the office and sat down on the chair in front of the desk.

"What did you mean with business stuff?"

She sighed. "It was just an excuse. I need your help."

He sat down across from her. "Okay, shoot."

"I think Ayita has started drinking again. The truth is, I'm not sure if she ever stopped."

"I'm afraid I think so too."

"I told her that she can't be a good mother for Wynono if she's drinking."

All of a sudden, he understood Ayita's overblown reaction to what he had said earlier. "She takes good care of him."

"Yes, for the moment still. But I know how neglectful she gets the more she drinks. I experienced it firsthand when I visited her in the Yukon."

"How can I help?"

"Can you just keep an eye on her? She enjoys coming here to the rescue station." Lyla ran her hands through her long brown hair.

"I offered her a job here. She seemed excited at first, but since then she doesn't seem to want to." He saw the surprise on my Lyla's face and knew that it was the first time she was hearing about it.

"Perhaps you'll think of a few things you guys can do together," Lyla suggested. "Just be a good friend to her."

Woodwind rubbed the back of his neck with one hand. "I can't promise you anything, but I'll try to show her that she doesn't need the alcohol. She is a strong woman and a good mother."

Lyla's smile reflected more her hope than her agreement. "Thank you."

Woodwind couldn't get Ayita's story out of his head the entire afternoon. Everything inside of him felt drawn to her. He wanted to take her into his arms, to drive away her pain, and to hold her until the pieces of her that were broken could heal. She carried around her guilt as though she were wearing someone else's clothing, and he wished for nothing more than to help her shed her alienation and to see her shine in the native dress of her people again. Freed of all the burdens she should never have carried around with her all these years. I love her, he thought, the recognition coming to him suddenly. At the same time, he asked himself what he could offer her apart from his deep affection, which only confused him. She needed a friend, not a lover.

He closed himself off to his longing for her. He would be her confidante and nothing more. Chinook's words came to mind: "Everyone has their role. Yours is to pass the test and to be there for the young people." The shaman was right, he had made a promise to those teenagers. A promise to be there for them. "And I will be," Woodwind murmured, pulling on his jacket and going out to the enclosures. He stopped in front of the wolf. "I know that you're lonely, but there's no cure for that for right now. Hold on until the spring."

December

Rosie stood outside on the pasture near her cabin with her hands cupped next to her mouth, exhaling hot air into them to warm them up. Where the hell were her good gloves? She was only risking losing a finger or two to frostbite in these thin knit ones. It was December and a good thirty below.

The water in the horse troughs was frozen solid, and she was now at the point of having to haul out a vat of water every morning and putting the heating coil in it to keep it from freezing. Her brother Jim wanted to come by this afternoon to help her better isolate the troughs. With stiff fingers, she quickly distributed hay for the horses before rushing back to the cabin.

Hazel, who was even less of a fan of the winter cold, still lay snoozing on the couch. The wood stove glowed brightly with a fresh log, and Rosie held out her hands toward its warmth. She wished she could just stay home for the day, with a good book and a cup of tea. The late shift at the Coyote Moon Bar the past few weeks had taken a lot out of her, and she'd been getting little more than four hours of sleep every night since. *You are doing it for Raweno*, she reminded herself. She poured coffee into an insulated cup and stuck a granola bar in her jacket pocket. She pitched another log into the stove to last until she got back home and turned to Hazel. "Oh, you haven't had any breakfast yet. Pardon me!" She quickly filled Hazel's bowl and used the time while the dog ate to make herself a sandwich. Her phone rang with Calvin's name on the display. "Good morning."

"Hey Rosie. How is the keeper of my little treasure doing this cold morning?"

"Drop the cutesiness. I need to get to work. What do you want?"

"Whoa there. Somebody got up on the wrong side of the bed."

Idiot. She'd do a happy dance the day she didn't have to deal with him anymore. "I need to go," she prompted him.

"Listen. I'm really sorry, but I need the rest of the money for the foal as soon as possible. Mr. Floyd already assured me he'd take him, but if you want the colt, I'll need the rest of the money before Christmas."

"What?! You're joking, right? I already gave you two thousand dollars for the deposit, and now I am suddenly supposed to pay it all in full?"

"Sorry. Do you want to back out of the deal?"

Rosie swallowed. How was she supposed to swing that in three weeks? She had to somehow. "I'll have the money for you, okay?"

"Okay, good. Talk to you then."

Rosie spent the entire morning at Willow Ranch trying to come up with other ways of scraping the rest of the money together. Even if she used what was left of her savings, she was still short fifteen hundred dollars. Should she try asking Lee for an advance on her salary? No, she didn't want to do that. She already felt bad enough for not giving the mares and foals at the ranch the attention they were used to. She had even forgotten to make sure the barn door was locked once. If she hadn't left her cell phone in the stall and had had to go back to get it, she wouldn't have realized her mistake, and the horses could have roamed freely over the ranch all night long and could have hurt themselves. Rosie thought about the huge Christmas party that Coyote Moon put on every year. She had already asked about it and figured that she would theoretically have to work a full three days straight if she planned to combine that shift with her work at the ranch. Before Calvin's call this morning, she was still undecided as to whether she wanted to work the event, but now that she had even less time to come up with the money, she saw no other option. She cursed Mr. Floyd and kicked a hay bale.

"Are you angry?" someone asked. Rosie turned around. Samantha was standing there, looking at her questioningly.

"No, not really."

"Really?" Sam grinned, then shook the snow off her thick down coat. There was a spot on her coat that had been taped back together with duct tape. When she pulled off her giant wool hat, her curly blonde hair stood out in every direction.

"Now you look like a Christmas Angel," Rosie exclaimed.

The smile abruptly disappeared from Sam's face.

"Did I say something wrong?"

Sam shook her head. "No, it's just that ... This will be my second Christmas without my mom."

Rosie stroked the girl's cheeks. "I feel so sorry for you. But I'm sure that you and Lee and Naira will all have a wonderful Christmas together in spite of it."

Sam looked at her, her eyes glittering with tears. Rosie had to bite her tongue to keep herself from blurting out the surprise that Lee and Naira had planned. They would be spending Christmas in one of the cabins in the mountains. Rosie had forfeited the days off she otherwise would have had in order to look after the horses at the ranch during that time. It was going to be a working holiday for her this year. Nonetheless, Sam more than deserved a memorable Christmas.

"I wish I could be an angel for a day and fly up to my mom in Heaven."

Rosie hugged the girl tightly. "Your mom is looking down on you every day and sees everything you do. I'm sure she's very proud of you."

Sam stepped out of the hug and tried to smooth her hair. "I know, and I'm also too old now to wish I could be an angel."

Rosie looked at the brave ten-year-old girl, who was always there to help out and who cheered everyone else up with her bubbliness. "You're never too old to wish for the wildest and craziest things. Even if they can never come true, it sometimes helps just to dream."

Sam's bright smile returned, and she gave Rosie a hug. "I often dream at night that I'm with my mom," the girl murmured. "Your greatest wish is to be able to keep Raweno, isn't it?"

"Yes, he and Lori and Sky and Hazel are my family."

"What about Doug?" Sam frowned, causing her forehead to crease, making her look many years older than she really was.

"No, he's just a friend."

"That's good, because I don't like him. Nick would be much better for you." The girl grinned.

"Is that what you think? I don't expect he would like to be part of my family."

"But would you like that?"

Rosie quickly pressed her lips together before a yes had a chance to slip out. With a crooked grin, she ran her hand over Sam's blonde hair. "You're much too curious for your own good. Now, would you like to help me feed the mares?"

Thanks to Samantha's help, Rosie was able to leave the ranch half an hour early. Her cell phone rang as she was getting into her truck. There was no number listed on the display. "Hello?"

All that she could hear was someone breathing. She waited another moment, then hung up. Someone must've accidentally dialed the wrong number. She and Hazel drove home to find Jim already working on the trough. He had brought an electric heating cable with him which they attached to the water supply pipe on the horses' trough.

"But we'll need to come up with something better this summer," her brother said. "It would be best if we laid an insulated pipe a few feet away from the water supply, then it shouldn't freeze again. And the electricity in the barn urgently needs to be updated."

"I know. That's obviously the best solution." Rosie tossed the pliers back into the toolbox and stood up. Her legs were stiff from kneeling for so long.

"You're not very talkative today. You got something on your mind?"

Rosie recalled something her grandmother used to say and smiled. "Let's go inside. I'll make us some soup and grilled cheese sandwiches."

Inside the cabin, Jim fired up the wood stove, while Rosie prepared the food. She observed her brother and caught herself wondering what it would be like if Nick were here instead. *Don't be silly*, she told herself. A man was the last thing she needed in her life. She set the table, and Jim sliced a cucumber for the salad.

"Everything's delicious," her brother said a little while later. "Now, would you finally tell me where my usually so happy-go-lucky sister has gone. You look tired and worn out."

"I plan on keeping Lori's foal," Rosie blurted out. "But I have only three weeks to give Calvin the money." She told him the asking price. "And that's why I've taken on a second job working at Coyote Moon and haven't been sleeping very much lately."

Jim shook his head. "Sorry, Rosie, but that's completely crazy. I mean, the foal might well be worth the money, but ..."

"The man who Calvin had planned to sell him to isn't a good horseman, and I wish for nothing more than to watch the foal grow up."

Jim shook his head again. "You're willing to risk your entire savings for this? I thought your plan was to become a horse trainer?"

She leaned back in her chair and crossed her arms. "And it still is. Sky is making progress." Rosie pushed aside the memory of her last recent disaster with Sky. A few days ago, she had wanted to have the mare walk over a tarpaulin, but Sky had instead ripped the lead out of her hand with so much force that Rosie was thrown to the ground. It was by sheer luck that she had managed to get out of the way of the mare's thunderous hooves and to safety in time.

"Oh Sis, you're such a dreamer."

"This isn't dreaming, I have a plan."

"Didn't you tell me yourself how hard it is to make it as a horse trainer and to be able to support yourself that way? You're not laying the groundwork here for an independent future, you're shoveling yourself further into—"

She waved him off and stood up. "Why doesn't anybody think that I can manage this?" she asked, starting clearing the table.

Jim held her by the arm. "Sit back down. I only mean well. You always seem to want to prove how tough you are. You have the courage and the grit. But you don't have to prove anything to me. You're only putting more obstacles in your way."

Reluctantly, she sat back down. She wasn't used to hearing words like that from her brother. Everyone always meant well. She was, after all, the pretty blonde who was supposedly blessed with good luck.

"I don't think that Calvin is a person you ought to be doing business with. Let me make a suggestion," Jim said, pulling out his checkbook. "Even if you decide to just keep the two mares, the entire barn still needs to be updated and repaired. As does this cottage in the not-so-distant future."

Rosie tried to answer, but Jim wouldn't let her. "I am giving you some money so that you can quit your job at the bar, and tend to your house and the mares, the condition being that you let go of the foal in February."

"Then that revolting Floyd guy will buy him," she threw back.

"You can't tell me that he is the only one who's interested."

"He's already given Calvin a deposit. If I back out, Raweno is his."

"I'm really worried about you. Won't you accept my offer?"

She bit her lip. She knew that Jim wasn't going to make her the offer twice. And it would be a huge relief to have the money for the many repairs that needed to be done, as well as to be rid of her stressful job at the Coyote Moon Bar. On the other hand, wouldn't she be giving up her independence by letting herself be rescued instead of taking her life into her own hands? Would she ever be able to trust her own resilience again if she gave in as easily as that? She slowly shook her head. "Sorry, Jim. But I've made my decision. I want to buy Raweno."

Jim wiped his mouth with his napkin and put away his checkbook. "You're making a mistake, sister dear."

"But then I'll at least have given it a go. You want some coffee?"

He stood up. "No, it's already late. I'd better be headed home. I'll see you again at mom and dad's for Christmas."

"Oh, I can't come. I have to be at Willow Ranch."

Jim knitted his eyebrows. "I don't even need to bother trying to convince you to change your mind; I know how stubborn you are." He gave her a hug. "Take care of yourself."

"I will, and thank you. Even though I can't accept it, I still appreciate your offer."

After her brother had left, Rosie called the Coyote Moon Bar and put herself down for a shift at the Christmas party.

Cody watched as Emma shoveled a small path to the pasture at Willow Ranch in her snowsuit. Actually, Lee had a snowblower to do that, but she had decided she needed the exercise. To his surprise, the persistent cold temperatures—it had been in the minus-twenties for days—didn't faze her in the least. Her cheerfulness was as indestructible as it was infectious. She had told him how her parents were sad they wouldn't be seeing her for Christmas. "But Sonja and I can think of nothing better than to be snowed-in in Alberta." Her eyes shone as she spoke.

Since then, he had been trying to come up with ideas for how they could spend the days together. Before he'd had a chance to ask Emma, his mother had left him a message yesterday on his cell phone. "Are you coming for Christmas? Your dad would like you too." Cody hadn't responded yet. Did he really want to spend the holidays on the farm?

A snowball hit him in the back. He saw Sam standing at the barn door, grinning, forming another ball between her mittens. He glanced at Emma, who was still shoveling the path. He waved Sam over, holding his finger to his lips, and the girl silently approached. He scooped up a handful of snow and shaped a ball, then he pointed at Emma. Sam nodded, grinning, and the two of them threw their snowballs in Emma's direction. Sam had the better aim, and her snowball hit Emma right in the back of the neck.

The young woman squawked and turned around. "Two against

one, you'll pay for that!" She took the shovel and flung snow in Cody and Sam's direction. Cody wasn't fast enough and was immediately covered in white. He heard Sam giggling next to him. Emma also laughed and came running over to him. She brushed the snow off his shoulders and from his face. "Looks like I got you good."

"You can say that again," he replied flatly, grabbed her around the waist and fell down in the snow with her.

"Eww, you guys can kiss all by yourselves. I'm going in for some hot chocolate." Sam dashed off toward the ranch house.

"I also wouldn't mind having something to warm up with." Emma wiped the snow off her hat.

"How about a nice hot kiss?" He pressed his lips on hers.

"Mmh," she moaned.

It took a while before they separated, their cheeks glowing pink. "Say, cowboy, do you think you can take your lunch break now so we can cuddle a little?"

"Cuddle, eh? Sorry, but I promised Lee that I would run into town to pick up the special animal feed for him."

She pursed her lips into a pout. "You're going to leave me here to freeze in the snow?" she lamented dramatically.

He got up and pulled her up with one hand. "No, snow princess. I'm taking you to town with me. Considering how nicely you shovel snow, you can help me load the sacks of feed onto the truck."

She laughed and playfully punched his arm. "How romantic. I'll just grab my purse out of the Jeep."

In town, they decided to have lunch at Mary's diner. As usual, the restaurant was jam-packed. They managed to grab a small table next to the window and ordered the soup du jour and a sandwich.

"What are you doing for Christmas? Are you going to go visit your parents?" she asked, stroking the back of his hand with her finger. "Sonja and I would be glad to have you over. We've already started decorating the house and want to make it nice and cozy with a Christmas tree, eggnog and all that stuff."

He smiled. The prospect of spending Christmas with Emma

was tempting. Since moving out of his parents' house, he hadn't really celebrated Christmas all that much. But then he thought about his parents and how they would be alone without Scott. Perhaps this was a good chance to finally discuss the future of the farm with his father.

"Of course, I understand if you prefer to go to the farm."

Mary brought their food and chatted with Emma. This gave him a few minutes to think. Should he take her to meet his parents? No, that wouldn't be a good idea. His father could just as easily be ready for another argument. Besides, their old farmhouse was in no way the romantic image Emma had in her mind about spending Christmas in Canada.

"Well, enjoy," said Mary. "We can talk more about things after the holidays, Emma."

Cody watched the owner of the diner as she walked away. "What have you got to talk about with her?"

"Oh, it's just a little something we are planning."

"Well, if the weather stays good, we can go out with the horses and have a picnic in the snow, with a campfire and roast some sausages." As he said this, she took a bite of her sandwich.

Cody lifted a spoonful of soup to his mouth. He wondered what the big secret was between her and Mary. But since he himself was keeping a few things from her, he wasn't in much of a position to feel insulted.

She smiled. "I don't actually care what we do, I just think it would be nice if we could spend Christmas together."

He sat back in his chair and stared at his soup bowl, then cleared his throat. "I'm really sorry, but the annual accounts for the farm are due in December. My brother used to take care of it, but—" Cody broke off. Why was he lying to her? Because at the moment he saw no other alternative, he told himself. "But we can definitely spend New Year's Eve together."

Her disappointment was so clearly written all over her face that he nearly changed his mind. He loved her, but something inside of him refused to believe that her feelings for him were adequate enough for him to consider building a life with her. He couldn't live up to her romantic ideal of life in Canada if he didn't remain a cowboy, could he? "I'm really sorry." He extended his arm across the table toward her and was relieved when she locked her fingers with his.

"I understand, and I know how important the annual reports are for a company. Then it'll just be New Year's Eve. But I'm taking you at your word. Sonja was actually invited to a hypnotherapy symposium in Toronto at kind of the last minute, and she will be flying to Ontario right after Christmas. I absolutely don't want to spend New Year's by myself."

For the first time, he noticed a hesitation in her smile, and he squeezed her hand. "I promise," he said, but his stomach did a somersault.

That evening, when he was alone in his place at Willow Ranch, he couldn't stop thinking about Emma's disappointed face. He didn't want to lose her, but explaining himself to her right now simply felt impossible. He needed some more time to figure out his plans for the future. He recalled his talk with Lee and Naira. They were right; he didn't need to carry on the farm in the same way his father had. Maybe it was possible to incorporate the old fruit trees again, and find a more ecological way to produce the milk, maybe somehow integrate horses into the farm business. Cody surprised himself at the whirlwind of ideas that unfolded in his mind. They gave him a new feeling of excitement that he had never had before in connection with the family farm. He had to smile.

He decided he would leave Emma a Christmas present out on the porch at the guest house's front door before he left for the farm. He had no doubt that she and Sonja would have a nice cozy Christmas together, and he looked forward to seeing her again on New Year's Eve. He yawned as he stood up from the old couch and shuffled off to bed.

Woodwind left the library at the community center. He had seen a notice tacked up on the pin board advertising the Winter Fest the elementary school children at the reserve were putting on that day. There would be a campfire, hot chocolate stands, and even an ice rink to go skating on. Woodwind thought it would be nice to invite Ayita to go. Granted, it was quite last-minute, but still he hoped that she and Wynono would be up for it. Maja had let him know that Ayita and her son had been regularly coming to look after Kachina. He was happy to hear that, even if it disappointed him that she never informed him herself as to their visits.

At home, he put away the folder containing the printouts from his course. He was indeed making progress with it, and for the first time, he was hopeful that he would pass the test. After taking a shower, he got into his car and drove over to Lyla and Lonefeather's cabin. He wanted to surprise Ayita with his invitation, and for that reason, he hadn't announced he was coming.

It was early afternoon, but dusk was not far behind on the horizon. The winter days were so damn short. He imagined Ayita's smile when he told her that Kachina had learned to catch mice. Ever since they had put the wolf into a larger enclosure, she was moving around more and seemed less apathetic. This had given Woodwind hope that he would be able to set the wolf free in the coming spring, assuming the hunters, who were still roaming free, were finally caught.

As the cabin appeared before him with lights in the windows, his stomach started to do flips. He ascended the porch stairs and knocked on the door.

"Oh, hello, brother. What are you doing here?" Lonefeather stood barefoot in the doorway. "Come in."

It was pleasantly warm in the house thanks to the wood stove. Woodwind saw Lyla sitting on the shag rug, playing with Wynono. Mud, lying next to her, greeted the visitor with a half-hearted wag.

"Boy, what a great watchdog you are!"

"To his credit, he and Wynono spent the entire afternoon outside in the snow." Lyla tousled the little boy's hair with one hand and then scratched the Labrador's head with the other.

"Isn't Ayita here?"

"No, did the two of you have something planned?" Lyla handed Wynono a puzzle piece and stood up.

"Um, no, I just wanted to surprise her with a visit to the Winter Fest at the reserve." He tried not to sound too disappointed.

Lonefeather came over with his arm outstretched. "Give me your jacket. Now that you're here, you can at least have a cup of coffee with us."

Woodwind kicked off his boots. "Where is Ayita?"

"Jeremy Bull picked her up about an hour ago. I have no idea what they had planned."

Woodwind stared at Lyla, unsure if he had heard right. What the hell did Bull want with Ayita?

"And you just let her go?" he blurted out, quickly remembering that neither his brother nor Lyla knew of his problems with Bull.

"Why not? She seemed happy to see him," Lonefeather replied.

"Isn't Jeremy on the reserve council?" Lyla asked as she pulled three mugs out of the cupboard.

"That's right, but he's not someone Ayita should be running around with." Woodwind sat down at the small dining table.

Lyla set the mugs on the table and gave Wynono a banana, before taking a seat at the table herself. "I know that you're concerned about her. We all are. But I have no control over who she sees."

"Sorry, I wasn't trying to make you guys feel responsible. Is she still secretly drinking?"

Lonefeather poured coffee into the mugs, placed the sugar and milk on the table, and took a seat. "Yes, though I have no idea when she buys the alcohol."

"She has lots of chances to do that when she drives into town with me. I don't keep track of her the entire time we're there." Lyla took a sip of coffee. "And that's exactly the problem. We can't give her the help she needs."

"What do you mean by that?" Woodwind asked, watching Wynono give Mud a piece of banana. The Lab carefully took it, and then sat down closer to the boy.

"She can't get over her alcohol addiction on her own. I looked into it, and she could have a spot starting in January at a women's recovery clinic. The director herself is indigenous."

"That sounds good," said Woodwind. "But by the look on your face, I can see there's a catch."

"The clinic is in Saskatchewan, and Ayita wouldn't be able to take Wynono with her," Lonefeather replied.

Woodwind shook his head. He couldn't find the words to say it, but the idea sounded terrible.

"Wynono hasn't spoken for months, and Ayita can't stay off the alcohol. Perhaps some time away from one another would bring the two of them closer together," Lyla said. "Wynono seems to really like Samantha, and he recently babbled something to Mud."

Woodwind rubbed both hands over his face. Perhaps she was right. "Have you talked to Ayita about it?"

"Not yet. We were hoping that you might speak to her first. You have a good connection to her. Whenever I say something to her, she immediately feels like I'm telling her what to do or criticizing her," Lyla said.

"I don't know if a recovery clinic is the right solution." Woodwind glanced again at Wynono, stood up, and sat down next to him on the rug. The boy raised his head and looked at him. His expression seemed to contain either a question or a request. But what did he know about children? He wished he could have witnessed his own child grow up. This thought and its accompanying pain hit him so suddenly that he flinched. He took one of the large, colorful puzzle pieces and held it out to Wynono. The boy grabbed it and turned his attention back to his puzzle. Woodwind got up. "I can talk to Ayita, but I don't like the idea of her being separated from her son for weeks on end. I'll have a talk with Chinook. If we can all show that we're here for her, we can find another way." *And I have to keep her away from Bull*, Woodwind thought, though he kept this to himself.

Woodwind took his time in returning to the reserve. There were just too many thoughts running through his mind. He recalled the various ceremonies that perhaps could help Ayita. If she would just open herself up to the community that the reserve offered, she was sure to find other women who would welcome her in, like a sort of healing circle. But then he remembered the vast number of Cree people who themselves had problems with alcohol or were dealing with an alcoholic in their family.

He hoped that Chinook would give him some advice and decided to speak with him right away. As he rounded the corner to the shaman's house, he noticed a brightly lit building. Wasn't that where Bull lived? A truck pulled up in front of the garage and parked.

Woodwind slowed his car to just barely walking speed, and watched a man and a woman get out of the vehicle. The woman on the passenger side hung onto the door as she got out. In the light from the garage, he recognized the man as Bull and watched as he went around to help the woman, holding a paper bag with the name and logo of a liquor store in one arm. Bull hooked his arm in hers and together, they walked over to the house. Woodwind only just managed to get a look at her face. It was Ayita. Was she already too drunk to know what she was doing? His first impulse was to jump out of his car and prevent Bull from taking her inside the house. But then he saw him put his arm around her and they kissed. She smiled, seemed relaxed, and made it up the stairs just fine. She must not have been as drunk as he had thought.

His hands gripped the steering wheel as he forced himself to keep driving. He could now scratch that conversation about her with Chinook. Lyla was right. Ayita needed to go to a recovery clinic, to be as far away as possible from Jeremy Bull's influence.

Cody was on his way to the Tippet Farm. Before heading off, he had left a present for Emma at the front door of the guest house. Inside was a thick scarf and a necklace with a horse pendant. He hoped she would like them both. His guilty conscience for having lied to her about why he was driving to the farm for Christmas tugged at his heart like a fish hook. But he hadn't been able to push his concerns to the side enough to admit to her that he increasingly planned to take over the family business.

When he arrived at the farm, a wreath hung from the sign over the driveway. Presumably his mother had put it up. He parked in front of the house, grabbed his bag, and went to the door. A chorus of animated mooing reached him from the barn. What was going on over there? He let the shoulder strap of his bag slip down his arm and left it in front of the door. Halfway across the yard, Kurt came running toward him.

"Hi, you've come at just the right time," he called, looking him up and down, then pointing to Cody's cowboy boots. "You'd better put on rubber boots instead. The hose on the slurry tank has detached itself. There's literally shit all over the place."

"Oh, great," he mumbled, hurrying to his truck to change his boots and swap out his cowboy hat for a baseball cap. He then followed Kurt into the barn. It was a huge mess, the biggest Cody had ever seen. His father stood in the door of the milking parlor cursing loudly. *Standing around shouting always helps, Dad*, he thought. Then he grabbed a pair of overalls that were hanging on the wall and put them on. Next, he drove the cows that had been waiting to be milked out of the barn. "Sorry, ladies, you'll just have to wait a little."

Each armed with a hose, Cody and Kurt sprayed water over the walkways and the paths around the milking machines. Thirty minutes later, the place looked a good bit better. "We'll need to disinfect the milking units before we can use them again," Cody said to Kurt.

"Hey, what you talking about?" His father shouted. "You've already rinsed them clean enough. We can't risk missing the evening milking."

Cody looked at the clock. An hour from now the truck would be coming to pick up today's milk. But there was no way that they could risk filling it with milk that could be contaminated, not after their last warning.

"Then we'll just have to let them take only the milk from this morning," he said to his father. "We'll have to milk the cows by hand this evening after we clean them, in order to take the pressure off their udders."

Larry moaned, but then realized that there was no other alternative. "What are you waiting for? Get to work. I'm going in the house. Did you even say hello to your mother?"

"No, I didn't get a chance to," Cody replied.

It was late in the evening by the time every cow that needed milking was milked. Cody's back and legs ached as he took off his overalls and hung them back on the hook. Just then, he realized those overalls must have been Scott's. How had his brother managed to survive days like this? He dragged himself into the house. His mother had left his bag with his clothes on the stairs leading upstairs. All he only wanted to do was take a shower and go to bed. Though his stomach growled, he was too sweaty and smelly to go into the kitchen to greet his mother. He slowly pulled himself up the stairs and into the guest bathroom for a hot shower. Then he went back down to join his parents in the kitchen. His mother jumped to her feet when he came in.

"Son, you must be starving! I'll warm up some of the roast." She hugged him, and he gave her a quick squeeze.

"Thanks, Mom." He sat down and looked at his father, who was sitting with a cup of coffee in front of him. "The barn is clean again," Cody said.

Larry grumbled something unintelligible, took a drink of coffee, and rubbed his chin with one hand.

Cody realized just then that he was unshaven, which wasn't like him. "How's your leg?" he asked, then thanked his mother, who had set a plate with roast beef, mashed potatoes, peas, and gravy in front of him.

"Can't put all my weight on it anymore," Larry said. "Damn this getting old. Makes your bones not want to heal properly."

"What happened to the hose today?"

His father waved his hand in the air. "The work is getting to be too much for Kurt, so I went out to give him a hand and got my leg caught on the hose."

Cody nodded and began to eat hastily.

"Slow down, you're going to choke," his mother said. "There's plenty left."

"Will you be staying for Christmas?" His father asked.

Cody paused and threw his mother a look. She smiled at him apologetically, stood up, and got him a glass of water. She hadn't said anything to his dad about his visit. Cody could barely swallow the last bite of food in his mouth. His dad wouldn't care whether he was here for Christmas or not.

"Just don't go thinking that we've got anything to celebrate around here," his father quickly added. "Scott always wanted to put up a Christmas tree every year, but—" the older man broke off, staring into his cup.

"I didn't come here to celebrate. We've got a few things to talk about, Dad."

Larry raised his head, his brow covered in deep wrinkles. Then he placed both hands on the table top and pushed himself up. "Not today. I'm tired." He cleared his throat. "Thanks for cleaning out the stall with Kurt ... And for coming to stay for a few days." Taking his cane in his right hand, he hobbled out of the kitchen.

Cody watched after him, stunned by his father's gratitude. But what did it change? He still refused to talk about the future of the farm with him. His mother laid her hand on his arm.

"He's happy that you're here. You know him, he doesn't say a lot. Tomorrow is a new day," she said. "I'm sure you're exhausted from the drive over and from cleaning the barn."

He nodded. "Do you think that Dad will ever come around to discussing the farm with me? Why does he refuse to believe that it just might mean something to me as well?"

His mother sighed. "It's just that you moved out once you were old enough and have made your life around horses. Your dad was counting on Scott, and now he has to face the farm without him. He is still deep in mourning."

"A Mr. Monty called me. Did he really make you guys an offer for the farm?"

"Yes. But your father refuses to do business with a city dweller."

Cody stood up, went to the door, and turned around again. "Does dad feel guilty for Scott's death?"

His mother gasped sharply. "Where'd you get that idea?"

He had hoped she would answer with a clear no and stared at his mother for a moment. Then he shrugged his shoulders. "Was just a feeling. Good night, Mom."

"Wait." His mother got to her feet, pulled something out of the cupboard, and gave it to Cody. "I was in Scott's cottage the other day cleaning, and I noticed the calendar hanging on the wall. He had marked all the important dates for the farm on it. Maybe it will help you get an overview of everything."

He took the calendar and quickly flipped through it. His mother laid her hand on his arm. "I'm sorry that I didn't give you that on your first visit, but I couldn't bring myself until now to even go into Scott's house."

"Thanks, Mom," he said, tucking the calendar under his arm without looking her in the eye. His mother was less of a coward than he was.

"In case you also want to, the key to the bungalow is under the mat."

"Okay," he mumbled. "Good night."

When he opened his eyes the next morning, Cody needed a moment to get his bearings. His gaze fell on Scott's calendar. He had been too tired yesterday to read any of the entries. Yawning, he rubbed his face, sat up, and picked it up from the nightstand. Along with the important appointments concerning the farm, he had also written down a few personal dates. Cody saw that Kathlyn's name appeared a few times, and in the weeks leading up to his death, Scott had also marked down the few brief times he and Cody had spoken on the phone, even including the times he hadn't been able to reach him. He counted the number of attempts and was shocked. Eight calls in total. Why had Scott tried to reach him so many times? And why, dammit, hadn't he bothered to call him back? Once again, the thought crept into his mind that he had left his brother in a lurch. But Scott had said he was doing just fine. Dammit. Maybe he ought to try giving Kathlyn a call. After all, according to the calendar at least, she had still been a very important part of Scott's life.

"Breakfast is ready!" he heard his mother calling.

Memories from his childhood flooded Cody's thoughts as he left the room. The scent of coffee and fried bacon filled the air. He stopped on the steps and inhaled the breakfast aromas. Had his mother also baked croissants? But Christmas wasn't for two more days. He opened the kitchen door with a smile on his face and saw a table loaded with good food. His mother stood at the stove, wearing her colorful apron as always and with her hair pulled up into a bun. She beamed at him. "Sit down. I don't know what you usually eat for breakfast, so I made a little bit of everything."

He walked over to her, and gave her a grateful kiss on the cheek. "You didn't need to do that. But thank you." He sat down and took a helping of scrambled eggs, bacon, and a croissant. "Where's Dad?"

"He went into town. He's got a doctor's appointment."

His mother poured him some coffee and sat down next to him. "Be honest with me, son. Can you imagine yourself taking over the farm?"

He chewed, swallowed, and didn't know quite how to formulate his answer. After a swig of coffee, he realized that he would never be able to confidently convince his father of his idea if he weren't able to even tell his mother. He leaned back in his chair. "I can't imagine Tippet Farm no longer existing one day. Even if Dad doesn't think so, the farm's long history matters to me, and I hate the idea of it having to be sold."

His mother placed her small hand on his. He saw the tears in her eyes. "Oh, you don't know how happy your words have made me."

"Nonetheless, if Dad will leave me the farm, I don't plan to run it the same way that he has up to now."

"But it will still remain a dairy farm, won't it? All the equipment is here, and that's the Tippet legacy."

Cody gently pulled his hand from hers. "The farm's balance sheets prove beyond a shadow of a doubt that something needs to change, it can't go on like this. I have other plans and ideas that will preserve the milk business as a secondary source of income."

His mother shook her head. "Talk like that was the reason for the whole controversy between Scott and your father," she said, covering her mouth. Cody was sure that she regretted those last words.

"What controversy?"

"Oh, you know the two of them. A couple of stubborn mules always battling it out." His mother was avoiding a direct answer.

"I don't believe you. There's more to it than that. Scott had tried to call me a number of times this past year, more than he had ever done in the past. What the hell happened?" Cody realized that he had raised his voice, but he finally wanted to know the truth.

Just at this moment, the kitchen door opened, and Kurt appeared. "Cody, I need your help. One of the cows has gotten herself wedged in the milking parlor."

He jumped to his feet. "Thanks for breakfast, Mom. We'll continue this later."

In his rubber boots and Scott's overalls, Cody hurried after Kurt. The farmhand stopped next to a barrier and started trying to push the cow's left hind leg through the bars. The animal mooed loudly.

"How did that happen?" Cody took hold of the cow's tail and pulled it to the right.

"The grate in the middle closed too early," Kurt panted, continuing to manipulate the cow's leg. "It's happened a few times before." With one more good push, the animal was freed.

Before letting go of the cow's tail, a pile of poo landed on Cody's rubber boots, spraying onto his overalls. The cow then teetered away along the path. He saw that her back foot was now wounded from the incident. "We'll need to keep an eye on that to make sure that it doesn't get infected," he said to Kurt.

"Yeah, of course. I tried to repair the mechanism, but the thing is so old that nothing helps."

"That's fine, I'll have a look at it later. For now, I just want to get out of these soiled overalls."

"Cody," a voice called out from the barn entrance, and he turned around. He caught sight of his father standing there, and next to him was Emma. She was wearing a light-colored winter coat and the scarf that he had given her. Cody looked down at himself. He was covered in manure. He quickly started stripping off the overalls just as his father and Emma reached him.

"This young lady says she knows you." Larry sounded disgruntled. "She was blocking the driveway with her yellow Jeep. Got herself stuck in a snowdrift. These people who don't know how to drive in the winter really ought to just stay home."

"This is Emma, a friend of mine," Cody interrupted his father from saying anymore.

"You're not from here, are you?" Larry asked, and she shook her head.

"I'm from Germany. We don't have as much snow there. I'm really sorry."

"It's okay. I'll pull the Jeep out with my truck." Cody smiled at her.

"Good, you take care of it," his father said. "I'm going in the house to warm up."

Once his father disappeared, Cody turned to Emma. She was studying him from top to bottom. Blushing, he hung up his overalls. "What are you doing here?"

"Well, I just wanted to drop off your Christmas present." She ran her hand over her scarf. "Thank you for mine. I couldn't wait until Christmas to open your gift. That was really nice of you. I also love the necklace, it's beautiful." She leaned forward and gave him a quick kiss. "You look a lot different without your cowboy hat and stuff."

He felt his cheeks getting hot. It was a little bit embarrassing to him to be standing with her breathing in the barn air. She smelled like a Christmas cookie herself. And also a little bit like coffee, which she had probably drunk on the way here. And here he stunk of manure and hadn't had the chance to brush his teeth this morning. "You're welcome. The scarf looks really good on you."

"Your present is still in the Jeep. I don't plan to stay long." Emma stuck her hands into her coat pockets. "Don't your parents know that we're a couple?"

"Well, yes, my mom knows. My dad is, well, you've just met him. Let's go and have a look at the Jeep," he said, and they left the humid stall. Outside, Cody saw that his mother was just leaving the house.

"Hello, Emma, my husband just told me about your accident. Don't you worry, it happens to everyone." With a warmhearted smile, she reached out her hand. "I'm Jackie."

"Emma Michaelis. It's nice to meet you. I don't plan to stay too long."

Jackie waved her hand. "Nonsense. After such a long drive, you should come inside. Cody can take care of the Jeep by himself. He hasn't told me anything about you. You can do that over a cup of tea." She hooked arms with the young woman and turned back toward the house.

"Sure, I can do that," he concurred, nodding to Emma, who threw him a desperate look.

Half an hour later, Cody entered the kitchen to see Emma and his mother sitting at the table. The two of them raised their heads.

"Would you like some tea?" Jackie asked, attempting to stand up.

"Just stay there, Mom. I can do it myself." He sat down at the table across from them with a cup of tea. A plate of Christmas cookies sat in the middle. *When did she bake these?* he wondered, taking a ginger cookie.

"I just invited your girlfriend to stay for dinner. And she'll also be staying the night. Snow is in the forecast for later, and no one ought to be out on the roads," his mother said in a firm tone.

"That's really very nice of you," Emma replied, obviously not for the first time. "But I really don't want to be a bother. Plus, I don't have anything with me to spend the night."

"Oh, sweetheart, that's not a problem. I'll make us a hearty beef stew and whip up some fresh rolls for dinner. You eat meat, right?"

She nodded, gazing at Cody. He only shrugged. When his mother set her mind on something, there was no getting around it.

"I have a nightgown you can use and some extra toiletries. It'll be okay for one night, don't you think?"

Emma seemed uncertain. Had she noticed that he felt anything but relaxed that she was here? On the other hand, he would never forgive himself if something were to happen to her on the way home.

"It would be better if you stayed till tomorrow," he said, hoping he sounded convincing. Not that he wasn't happy to see her, just not here. Not at the farm where he was no longer the cowboy she knew.

"Were you able to get the Jeep out of the snow?" she asked.

"I was, and without so much as a scratch."

"Thank you. I'd better send Sonja a message that I'm staying here for the night." Emma pulled out her cell phone.

"Yes, do that." Jackie got up. "We wouldn't want your friend to be worried about you. I'll just go and make up the bed in the sewing room for you and get you a few towels."

"Mom, that won't be necessary," Cody said. "Emma can—"

"Sleep in the sewing room. I don't need to know anymore," his mother cut him off. "In the meantime, why don't you show her the farm." She smiled and disappeared from the kitchen.

"Sorry, my mom is very old-fashioned."

"Oh, that's okay. I'll just sneak over to your room during the night." She grinned. "And now I'd really like to see the farm."

"Um, okay, I'll give you a little tour. I'll need to see to the milking in about an hour."

In the hallway, they pulled on their jackets and boots. Emma looked at her beige boots and her light-colored down coat and frowned. "Too bad I didn't bring any other clothes with me."

"Well, you couldn't have known that you'd be stranded here.

I'm sure we have a coat for you, but my boots are probably much too big for you."

"Oh, it doesn't matter," Emma replied, pushing him out the door.

They strolled hand-in-hand around the farmyard.

"Whose house is this?" Emma asked, pointing at Scott's bungalow.

"My brother used to live there." Cody said without looking at it as he tightened his grip on her hand and gently pulled her further. But she stopped and turned to face him.

"His death is still quite raw for all of you, isn't it?"

"Yes. My parents miss him every day."

Her eyes rested on him, and he tried to find the words to express all the things he couldn't say out loud. His throat constricted. He found warmth and understanding in her eyes—more than he could bear and much more than he deserved. He pressed his lips together and rubbed the back of her hand with his thumb. "It's cold out here, let's go look at the barn."

"Okay," she mumbled. "If you'd like to talk about it, I'm here for you."

He could only nod and breathe normally again once they reached the door to the barn and went inside.

Emma looked around. "It's quite small in here."

"There's a lot that needs to be renovated. It's getting harder and harder to earn enough money to maintain the business by only selling milk."

She walked along the narrow aisle, looking at the milking equipment and then pointed to the door that led to the pasture. "At least the cows can go outside. In Germany, there are more and more large dairy farms where the animals spend their entire lives locked up inside."

"There's a lot of those here as well." Cody placed his hand on one of the metal barriers. "We're just a small family-run business. There aren't too many of us around anymore." He realized too late that he had said *we*. His hope that Emma might not have noticed disappeared when he saw the questioning look on her face. "Anyway, I prefer horses," he hastily added.

"There's so much else you could do here. Is your father open to changing things at all?" Emma glanced in the small room where the cooling vats for the milk were located. "Organic products, for example? There is a growing market for those here in Alberta, isn't there? And were those fruit trees I saw on the way to the barn? Do they also belong to the farm?"

He stood in the doorway and was speechless at her train of thought. Was it possible that they were thinking the same things? "Yes, we have apple and pear trees. And two barley fields. The rest is pasture."

"Ever thought about brewing beer?" Emma asked, grinning. "Microbreweries are all the rage in Europe."

Cody tilted his head slightly and stared at her. Was she making fun of him or was she being serious? He heard footsteps behind him and turned around. Kurt was walking in their direction with a pitchfork in his hand. Cody waved him over and introduced Emma.

"Nice to meet you, Miss. I'm sorry to interrupt you, but a handful of the Holsteins are still not giving much milk."

"Thanks, Kurt. I'll keep an eye on them."

"Okay. Then I'll get back to work." Kurt nodded at Emma and strode away.

"Since when have you had that problem with the cows?" she asked.

"Not too long. Unfortunately, two of them have mastitis in their udders, so the vet will have to come. I will talk to my father about it the next chance I get."

"Oh, you never said anything about that. Looks like you've got several little fires springing up all at once here at the farm." Emma reached out to touch his arm..

Cody resisted pulling away from her touch. "Ah, well, in the end, they aren't really my problems. I'm just helping out," he said. The words felt gritty on his tongue.

Later on during dinner, Cody's mother relentlessly interrogated Emma on German Christmas traditions. The younger woman patiently answered every question, and Cody only loved her more for it. He succeeded for a moment to hold on to the feeling.

"We've never made a big deal about celebrating Christmas," said Jackie. "And this year, there's even less reason to."

"I can understand that. Cody told me about Scott. Losing him must have broken everyone's heart," Emma said.

"You can say that again, dear. He was the backbone of the farm and the future of a century-old family enterprise. Now, we are suddenly faced with a multitude of difficult decisions."

His father slammed his palm on the table. "That's enough. We will not be discussing our family problems here in front of a stranger," he said with a strained voice.

Cody swallowed, recognizing that this was his own fault. He hadn't ever mentioned Emma, so it was no wonder that his dad saw her as a stranger.

"Forgive me, I didn't mean to offend you." Emma laid down her silverware.

Larry grumbled something incoherent, then turned to Cody. "Did everything go smoothly with the last milking?"

"Yes, but a few of the cows are giving a lot less milk at the moment."

"The old girls will have to be culled out. Any of them that don't produce only cost us money."

Emma cleared her throat. "Perhaps you might try looking first at where the problem lies. Their age can certainly play a role, but Cody mentioned that a few cows have come down with udder infections recently."

Cody's eyes flew to his father, who critically narrowed his gaze at Emma. Why couldn't she have just kept her mouth shut? He had told her that he was going to talk with his father about it the next chance he got.

"Now, listen here, Miss. This isn't Germany, and I don't need anyone like you telling me how to run my farm."

Emma raised both hands in defeat. "I didn't mean it like that. I only thought that—"

"Think what you want, but don't go putting your nose where it doesn't belong."

"Larry! She wasn't being disrespectful," Jackie exclaimed.

Emma's eyes bored into Cody. He could only smile apologetically, to which she rolled her eyes in disdain.

Cody lay in his bed early the next morning, listening to the sounds in the house. He felt absolutely terrible. As he said good night to Emma, he had apologized for what his father had said. She had taken it in stride, giving him a kiss, and he clung to his hope that she would come to his room during the night. As midnight rolled around and he was still wide awake, he crept down to her room only to discover that she had locked the door. He planned to ask her about it today before she left for the guest house.

On the ground floor, he heard his mother puttering around in the kitchen, which was located directly under his room. He was sure the coffee was ready. Cody got out of bed and crossed the hall to the bathroom. When he opened the door, the scent of coconut and lemon hit him, and the mirror was partially fogged up. Emma had just been in the shower. Too bad. He would've liked to share the hot water with her. After a quick shower of his own, he returned to his room and slipped into his jeans and cowboy shirt. He could put on his farm clothes after Emma had left.

Emma and his mother were sitting together in the kitchen over a cup of coffee.

"Good morning," his mother greeted him. "Have a seat. The croissants still need a few minutes."

"Good morning, you two." He sat down next to Emma on the bench and kissed her cheek. "Did you sleep well?"

"Just fine, thank you."

He poured himself a cup of coffee from the pot. Jackie got up, took eggs and bacon out of the refrigerator, and got busy at the stove. Cody leaned over to Emma. "I wanted to cuddle with you last night, but your door was locked," he whispered, rubbing her back.

"Sorry, it's a habit of mine whenever I stay in strange places. Besides, I was exhausted from the trip."

He placed his hand on her thigh. "It's okay." He gave her a quick kiss on her neck. "Hmm, you smell good."

His mother turned around, and Cody automatically scooted away from Emma. "How many eggs should I make for you two?"

"None for me, thank you," Emma replied. "I'll just finish my coffee and be on my way."

"But you can't leave without having breakfast, honey."

"I don't like to leave Sonja alone any longer than I have to. We also have the goats to look after."

"Then I'll pack you a couple of croissants to take with you and a jar of homemade jam. Do the two of you like spiced walnut bread?" Jackie lifted a dark brown loaf out of a tin to show her. "None of my men have ever been very excited about it, but for me, it just wouldn't be Christmas without one. And I always bake much too much of it."

"Thank you, that's really nice. I'd love to take some back with me."

Jackie smiled brightly and turned back to the stove.

"Do you have to go back right away?" Cody asked. "I had hoped we could go for a walk and talk a little."

"We'll see each other again on New Year's Eve."

Cody nodded. The kitchen door opened, and Larry came in. "Morning. Are the cows milking themselves today?"

"Kurt said he would take over this morning," Cody replied.

"Uh, yesterday I gave him today off. It's Christmas after all."

Cody gulped. He didn't even have the right to be angry at his father. It was Christmas, and Kurt had a family of his own to be with. He threw a glance at Emma, to which she replied with a crooked smile.

"I'll be on my way then," she said. "Thank you very much for your hospitality."

Jackie placed a bag on the table with the bread in it. "Here, you can take that with you and share it with your friend."

"Is there any breakfast or not?" Larry asked irritably.

"Here, you grump," Jackie replied unfazed, setting a plate in front of him with two eggs, bacon, and a croissant.

Emma got to her feet and picked up the bag. Cody also stood up and noticed that his father was watching him.

"You can't go out to the barn in cowboy clothes."

"I'll put on overalls," he answered.

"Do what you want. Just get the work done now that you're here."

Cody saw Emma give his father a disapproving look.

"Merry Christmas," she said, holding out her hand to Jackie. His mother smiled and gave Emma a heartfelt hug. "Merry Christmas, my dear. And be safe driving home."

Larry grumbled. "Watch that you don't get stuck in a ditch again somewhere with that Jeep. Cody doesn't have time to keep rescuing you. We farmers don't get days off."

Cody took hold of Emma's hand and squeezed it. "Ignore my father, he's a grinch, in the truest sense of the word," he told her quietly, pulling her toward the kitchen door.

"It's fine. It's not like you wanted to be here," she said, then turned back to address Larry. "I realize that this is a difficult time for you and that it's hard to get into the Christmas spirit, but if you insist that Cody be here over Christmas to go over the annual account reports, you should at least help him feel like he's welcome here," Emma said.

Larry snorted and wiped his mouth with his napkin. "What are you talking about? Cody isn't involved with the business side of the farm. Why in the world would I have him draw up the year-end reports?"

"Umm ...," Emma replied, biting her lip and looking at Cody for help.

"I'll walk you out to the Jeep," he said meekly, wishing the ground would open up and swallow him whole.

"You don't need to." She let go of his hand, jerked open the kitchen door, and disappeared.

"Wait!" Cody ran after her.

In the hallway, she silently slipped on her boots and coat.

"I'm sorry, Emma. This was all a big misunderstanding."

She ignored him, trudged through the deep snow to the Jeep, and left the farm without once turning back to look at him.

Rosie glanced at the clock and closed the gate behind the mares on the pasture at Willow Ranch. It was late, and she needed to hurry. She not only wanted to drop Hazel off at home, but also needed to get a bite to eat before starting the night shift at the Coyote Moon Bar's Christmas party. Yawning, she made a note on a piece of paper that one of the mares wasn't chewing her hay well. She pinned the note onto the corkboard next to the door. "Damn, am I tired," she mumbled, trying to shake off her exhaustion. But she reminded herself why she was putting herself through all this torture. The hourly pay for the night shift was three times what she would make otherwise, and the tips that she had gotten yesterday made it worth the effort. She turned around again. "Good night, my lovelies," she called out to the horses before trudging through the cold to her old truck.

She let Hazel into the back seat, got in herself, and started the engine. It felt like an eternity until the cabin started to warm up. She hoped she'd be able to afford to have the truck's very unreliable heat fixed before next year's winter came, but for now, she was putting aside every cent she could to buy Raweno. She had gone over the numbers over and over again. If she worked the entire event as she had planned and made a decent amount in tips as well, she would have enough money together once Christmas was over.

Lori's colt would grow up at her homestead, and she would be able to begin the program to become a certified horse trainer. She'd manage to get Sky under control yet. If Raweno became a breeding stallion, he wouldn't be able to stay at her place; that much was clear. But if he belonged to her, she had the upper hand in choosing a new home for him in one or two years. Maybe she and Nick could work together, and Raweno could move over to the Tanner Ranch. She smiled at the idea. She would show everyone that she had it in her to be a shrewd businesswoman and not just some mousy housewife. Her brothers had never treated her as such, per se, but she wanted her parents to finally be proud of her and not just see her as an unmarried stable hand. She would show them what she was made of.

Rosie turned into her driveway, surprised to see Doug's truck parked in front of her house. She hadn't had any contact with the fireman for weeks and assumed he was away on another one of his missions. Actually, she had hoped that he had lost interest in her.

He got out of his truck with a big grin. "Hey, Babe, I just got here too. Right on time, from the looks of it."

Rosie knit her eyebrows. "Right on time for what?"

"Well, you're coming home from the ranch, tired, and I was planning on making you dinner and pampering you with a massage. That's what good friends do for one another. It's Christmas, after all." He walked toward her to give her a hug, but Hazel stepped between them, growling.

"I see your bloodhound still doesn't like me. I can change that." He pulled a bone out of his jacket pocket and gave it to Hazel. She sniffed it, turned her head, and nudged against Rosie, who couldn't help but grin. Loyal Hazel could not be bought. She scratched the dog's head as Doug stuck the bone back in his pocket. "Well, if she doesn't know what's good for her. But I can promise you that my chicken in cream sauce will knock your socks off."

Rosie couldn't deny the fact that her stomach growled loudly at the prospect of dinner.

He grinned. "Sounds like I'd better hurry into the kitchen. You can take a shower in the meantime. I also brought some wine."

She looked at her watch. "I'm afraid that won't happen. I only have thirty minutes until I have to leave again for my shift at the bar."

"You got yourself a second job? Are you short on money?"

"I want to buy the foal," she said. "And I need to go check on the horses now too. Sorry."

Doug sighed. "Yeah, yeah, the animals are always your top priority."

"Sorry, but when you just show up unannounced ..."

"I just like surprises. I guess I'll have to cook for you some other time. Or, even better: let's spend New Year's Eve together."

Rosie wasn't in the mood, nor did she have time to discuss her plans with Doug. "Um, I was actually thinking of having a girls' night for New Year's."

He snorted. "What do you want with the girls? We can have a nice time all by ourselves."

"I really need to get moving," she insisted, taking a few steps in the direction of the barn.

"Okay, okay, I get it." He shoved his hands into his coat pockets and put on a grim expression.

"Sorry. Goodbye and Merry Christmas." She waved before disappearing with Hazel into the barn. From the small window, she saw Doug kick the tire of his truck and glance back in her direction. The intensity in his eyes scared her, then he got in his truck and drove away. Rosie shook off her trepidation as she gave the horses fresh hay and some of their special feed. "Very soon I'll have more time for you," she said, stroking the backs of all three of them.

Inside the cabin, she gave Hazel some kibble, warmed up a frozen macaroni and cheese dinner for herself, and quickly ate it.

After a fast shower, she dried her long, blonde hair, and felt the exhaustion creep into every muscle of her body. *Pull yourself together*, she reprimanded herself, as she got dressed in a pair of tight jeans and a white t-shirt with the bar's logo on it.

"Good night, Hazel. I'll be back early in the morning. It would be nice if you could have coffee ready." She rubbed the dog's velvety ears. Hazel yawned and laid her paw on Rosie's arm. "For as much as I would love to cuddle with you, we need the money to expand our little family."

Hazel let out a sigh, climbed onto the sofa, and made herself comfortable. It was a dog's life. Rosie put her jacket back on and opened the door. It had started to snow heavily in the meantime. Shit, she was going to be late.

She squinted as she drove very slowly through the snowfall. The heat in her truck was now blowing at full blast. She yawned, turned on the radio, and opened the window, but the whoosh of snowflakes that blew in made her close it again. She smacked her hand against her thigh to keep awake. It's only twenty miles, she told herself, and began to sing along to the song she loved that was playing on the radio. Her eyes felt heavy. It was after ten and there were no other cars on the road. She had only one more night shift to work as well as helping with the clean-up and disassembly tomorrow evening, which the bar's owner had promised to compensate her generously for, Rosie reminded herself and took heart. Then she envisioned the moment when she would hand Calvin the money and take Raweno's papers in return. Her dream would be coming true. With a smile on her face, her eyes fell closed.

A rumbling, followed by an ear-piercing screech of metal jolted her out of her doze. Her hands gripped the steering wheel as she slammed on the gas pedal instead of the brake in her panic. The truck shot off into a ditch. She tried turning the wheel to one side, but it was no use. She slammed against a tree at full force, was thrust forward, and hit the steering wheel with her chest. In the next second, she was flung back against her seat, and her head flew against the headrest.

Completely disoriented, she sat there and blinked a few times, then looked around. A sharp pain stabbed at her neck and the hammering in her head took her breath away. Shit. Streams of hot tears rolled down her cheeks as she cautiously reached to unbuckle her seatbelt as it constricted her breathing. Even after it was unbuckled, she noticed that it still hurt like hell to breathe. Did she have a broken rib? A fresh flood of tears poured from her eyes. But crying wasn't going to help.

She needed to call for help and felt for her cell phone in her coat pocket. Who should she call? A wave of nausea rolled over her and she quickly swallowed back the bile that had crept up her throat. Her eyes felt like they were swimming in her head as she tried to focus on the phone's display. All of a sudden, the phone vibrated in her hand. Someone was calling her. She couldn't read the name but pushed the green blur. "Hello?" she gasped.

"Rosie, is that you? Are you okay? You sound—"

"Nick?"

"Yes, I just wanted to call and wish you a Merry Christmas."

She let out a sob, paying dearly for it in pain. Keeping her breathing shallow, she whispered: "Nick, I've just had an accident near Spruce View. I need help."

"I'll be right there."

Rosie lowered her arm in relief and gently leaned her head against the headrest.

An hour later, she was at home, lying in her bed. It took her a great deal of effort to convince Nick not to take her to the hospital. In the end, it was the increasingly heavy snowfall that made him agree to take her home. It would have taken them an eternity anyway to cover the seventy miles to the hospital in this weather. Along the way, Nick had called a doctor friend of his, who had told him what to look out for regarding Rosie and instruct him to call immediately if she started vomiting or lost consciousness.

At home, Nick gave her some of the painkillers he found in her medicine cabinet, and called the Coyote Bar to let them know she wouldn't be coming in. He also checked in on the horses, which she asked him to do. With the help of a few pillows, she managed to find a halfway comfortable position on the bed and looked up when Nick returned to the bedroom. "The animals are just fine. How are you?"

"A little bit better." She smiled painfully.

"You don't need to put on a brave face in front of me. I'll stay here tonight. Is there an extra blanket for the couch in case Hazel agrees to make room for me?"

"You don't have to do that."

"I won't hear any objections. Or I'll take you to the hospital." Nick stepped next to the bed and affectionately stroked her forehead. "You sure gave me a good scare, Rosie."

"Thank you for rescuing me," she whispered, grateful that he wasn't going to leave her alone. "That was very ..." Before she could finish her sentence, she nodded off.

The next morning, Rosie woke up at almost eleven o'clock. To her surprise, Lyla was sitting on the chair next to her bed.

"Hello." Rosie's throat felt scratchy, and she coughed.

"Good morning, sleepyhead. How are you feeling?" Her friend stood up and handed her a glass of water.

Rosie managed a slight smile, very slowly sat up, and took a few sips. Hazel's head appeared next to her, and the dog's brown eyes searched hers.

"Nick said that she hasn't moved from your side all night," Lyla said. "She didn't even go over to greet Mud. He's in the kitchen pouting, though he's probably asleep by now."

Rosie ran her hand over Hazel's head, which was resting on top of the bedspread. "I feel a bit better," she told her and looked Lyla in the eye. "Where's Nick?"

"He needed to get back to his stallions. You know how he is. They're his top priority, but he didn't want to leave you alone, so he called me to come over."

"Thank you for coming."

Lyla waved it off. "We didn't really celebrate Christmas anyway. Actually, I'll be glad when the holidays are over."

Rosie noticed her friend's expression darken. "Is everything okay with you guys?"

"I am worried about Ayita. She's drinking again and stays out all night a lot. We'd like to convince her to go to a recovery clinic."

Rosie drank the rest of her water and leaned back against the pillows. "I'm sorry to hear that. Looks like I, on the other hand, literally spent Christmas in a ditch."

Lyla raised one eyebrow questioningly, and Rosie briefly explained about her second job and that she could now forget about it without a truck to get there with. Then she suddenly realized that she wouldn't be able to drive to her job at the ranch either. "Somebody will have to make sure everything's okay at the ranch. Your brother and Naira aren't due back until tomorrow." She swallowed hard against the lump in her throat.

"Everything is under control. You just focus on getting better."

Rosie sighed. "Is my truck actually still in the ditch?"

"No, Nick called Dennis, and he pulled it out early this morning and towed it to his shop."

"I have no idea if I can even afford to fix it." Rosie pinched the bridge of her nose, hoping to dispel her dull headache.

"You just need to recuperate. Don't worry about any of that. You are on sick leave for the next three days."

"Says who?"

"Says me. I'm going out right now to go look after the horses and then I'll make us a late breakfast." Lyla stood up. "Try to get some sleep. I'll take Hazel and Mud outside with me." She stopped in the doorway and turned around again. "Your phone rang a few times, but there was no number listed so I didn't answer it."

Rosie nodded. "Wrong number," she mumbled, closing her eyes. Her head felt like it was filled with a giant cotton ball obstructing all her thoughts.

Woodwind had spent the holidays alone. Christmas didn't have any significance for the Cree people, even though many people at the reserve still celebrated it. But he wasn't in the mood for celebrating either way. He couldn't get the image of Ayita and Bull kissing out of his head. His anger and disappointment felt like a leech feeding on his conscience. He would have liked to confront Bull and give that asshole a good beating and a warning to keep his hands off

Ayita. The angry grizzly in him was raring to get out. Woodwind could only just barely contain himself. He locked himself up inside his house and meditated, breathing out his anger and breathing in the hope that things would take a turn for the better.

He decided to drive to the mountains to soak up some positive energy from Mother Earth. He took a bottle of water out of the refrigerator as his stomach growled, but that was because he had intentionally been fasting since yesterday in order to purify himself for the ceremony. He picked up his cell phone and saw that Lyla had left him a voice message. She had already asked him over the course of many messages to please have a conversation with Ayita.

But Woodwind knew he wouldn't be able to find the right words in his current emotionally-charged state. The objective was obvious: Ayita needed professional help to overcome her alcohol addiction. But if she wasn't willing to go into recovery on her own, there was no way that she would be open to any healing. Along with that came the fact that he didn't agree that separating Ayita from her son was the best solution. Even if it didn't necessarily look like the mother and son had a close relationship, Ayita was still Wynono's primary caretaker.

He put on his jacket and fur boots. After returning from his day in the mountains, Woodwind planned to visit Chinook. He had been so caught up in his own thoughts that he hadn't spoken to the elder for a while, although he valued the wise man's advice and the fact that he had known Ayita since she was just a girl at the Sunchild Reserve. Chinook would be the one to know how to help her cope with the pain.

Woodwind made a path through the snow to his car and unplugged the cable from his engine battery. Without this little bit of help, his car would never start in the current negative twenty-degree temperatures. As he pulled out of his driveway and headed down the street, he saw three trucks parked in front of Chinook's house. What was going on there? He stopped next to the sidewalk, left the motor running, and went up the stairs to the front door. Since no one reacted to his knocking, he opened the door. There was a young girl sitting on the floor in the hallway, holding her face in her hands. He knelt down before her. "What happened?" he asked quietly.

She sobbed and looked up. "Chinook is dead."

He thought at first that he must have misheard her, but the fat tears that ran down her cheeks could only mean that it was true. The shaman was on his way to another world. Woodwind's heart constricted so tightly that his entire chest hurt. He heard voices in the living room, stood up, and stumbled outside. He didn't belong here on this day of mourning. He saw Lee pull up and park behind his car. He and Naira got out and approached him. Naira's face was marked by the loss of her beloved grandfather.

Woodwind's eyes met hers. He walked over to her and gave her a hug. "I'm so sorry," he mumbled and let go.

"Thank you," she whispered, then ascended the stairs to the house.

He reached out his hand to Lee, the rancher took it and pulled him in for a brief embrace.

"My condolences," Woodwind's said. "I had no idea that he had been so sick."

"Chinook never made a big deal about his health. He hadn't been doing well for many weeks now."

Woodwind gulped and had to admit that he had tried to ignore how weak the shaman had looked during his last visit. "I'll leave the family alone now. It is a great loss for all of us."

Lee placed his hand briefly on his shoulder. "Yes, it sure is."

Woodwind got back into his car. Even after ten minutes, he couldn't yet bring himself to drive away. He sat there with his hands on the steering wheel and stared off through the windshield. He had lost his chance to talk to Chinook; he'd thought he still had time. Idiot. He banged his right hand against the console so hard that the glovebox popped open. Among the pair of gloves, a flashlight, his vehicle registration, and some old bags of salted peanuts, a stuffed animal popped out and landed on the passenger seat. Woodwind picked up the little wolf; he had completely forgotten about it. He had bought it for Wynono a few months ago. Why hadn't he ever given it to him? Because you're a coward, he said to himself, shoving the toy animal back into the glovebox. And what had this putting things off brought him? Chinook was dead, and he was helpless to stop Ayita from self-destruction. This all needed to end.

He drove over to the cottage. It was now time to put his money where his mouth was. When Lyla opened the door, he could tell that she was already aware of Chinook's death. Her eyes were red, and her nose stuffed. Without saying a word, he took her into his arms and held her closely. "I'm sorry. I know how much he meant to you."

She wiped the tears from her cheeks. "Chinook had been in so much pain recently. Now he has been released." She smiled briefly. "Come in."

Woodwind was greeted by Mud sniffing him; he pet the dog then hung his jacket on the coat rack. He saw Lonefeather in the kitchen taking a teabag out of his cup. "Hey, little brother."

"Nice to see you. Want some herbal tea?"

Woodwind nodded and looked around. "Aren't Ayita and Wynono here?"

Just at that moment, the door to the guest room at the rear of the house opened and Wynono came running out, followed by Ayita.

"Oh, hello," she said.

Woodwind could see that she, too, had been crying and wondered whether she regretted not having spoken to Chinook. "Hey, you two," he said. "I know this isn't perhaps the best day to talk about stuff, but it's important." He threw Lyla a glance. Despite having made the decision for himself, he wasn't going to continue without her permission. But she nodded. He then looked at Ayita, who was staring at him skeptically.

"How about we all sit down," said Lonefeather. They all took a seat at the table. Wynono and Mud sat down on the floor in front of the wood stove. The boy picked out one of his books and sat down, captivated by the pictures. Lonefeather passed around cups of steaming hot tea.

"What have you got to talk about?" Ayita asked. "I'm meeting someone in a little while."

Who might that be? Woodwind wanted to ask, but held back. "We're concerned about you," he said instead, looking straight at her.

"You don't need to be."

"You're drinking again, or perhaps still. It can't go on like this," he responded.

"And that's why we think you need to go into recovery. You need professional help," Lyla said.

"I have it under control." Ayita's expression turned stony in the blink of an eye.

"No, you don't. And you're mistaken if you think that Bull is a good person to be hanging out with. Trust me."

"You're just jealous," Ayita threw back at him. "Jeremy doesn't nag me; he lets me be how I am. And he and I can laugh together."

"And drink," he mumbled under his breath.

"Wynono needs you," Lyla said. "You've hardly done anything with him for the past two weeks. And he seems to be retreating more and more into his own world. All the interaction he has is with the animals and the little bit with Samantha."

"He just doesn't feel at home here yet," Ayita objected.

"That's just an excuse and you know it." Lonefeather's voice was calm. "You can close your eyes to it all you want, but the truth is still there."

Ayita crossed her arms over her chest. "I won't go to any rehab place."

"Oh, yes you will," said Woodwind. "Everything's been settled. Wynono will stay here with Lyla and Lonefeather and you will begin the healing process."

Ayita stared at him in disbelief, then vehemently shook her head. "No and never. I'm not going anywhere without my son."

"How can you be a good mother to him if you aren't willing to work on yourself? You need help." Lyla placed her hand on Ayita's arm, but she pulled away.

"You guys sure came up with a great plan. Sticking me into a clinic so you can take my child away from me. Never!" Ayita pushed her chair back abruptly and stood up.

"Wait! Let's talk about this," Woodwind implored.

But she turned around and disappeared into the guest room, slamming the door behind her.

"And now what?" Lyla asked the others.

"We can't give up." Woodwind felt the same fear of losing Ayita that he'd felt after Chinook passed away and his throat constricted.

"It won't be easy," Lonefeather said. "She's a grown woman and if she won't go, then—"

"Then we'll threaten to report her to the authorities. They don't look too kindly on alcoholics taking care of children," Woodwind finished his brother's sentence and was himself a little bit shocked at what came out of his own mouth. Would he really go that far? The bear in him was tearing to get out with its razor-sharp claws, and he knew that if it meant saving Ayita, then he'd do it.

"What do you think about it, Lyla?" Lonefeather asked.

"If there's no other way, then I guess we'll have to."

"Then it's decided." Woodwind stood up. "Will you call the clinic?"

Lyla nodded. "As soon as I know more, I'll let you know what day she can start. Can you drive her there? I'll stay here with Wynono."

"Yes, we'll do it that way," he agreed. "We ought to spend the rest of the day accompanying Chinook on his last journey. Do you know when he's supposed to be buried?"

"Naira told me a while ago that he didn't want a big ceremony. Don't celebrate the dead, celebrate the living instead, he said." Lyla gave him a somber smile.

"That sounds like him." Woodwind came up next to her, put his arm around her shoulder, and pressed his cheek against hers. "We'll get through this together."

"Together," she repeated.

January

Rosie struggled to drag the hay bales to the mares. Her accident had happened two weeks ago, but her ribs still smarted when she picked up anything heavy. She had slept through New Year's Eve. The way her friends had all gathered together and pitched in to help her was deeply touching, but she couldn't shake the nagging feeling that she had failed. She had tried resuming her training sessions with Sky yesterday, but the mare had refused to cooperate. Rosie took out her pocket knife and cut the twine around the hay.

Calvin had called a few days ago asking for the money for Raweno. After she told him about her accident, he seemed sympathetic and told her to focus her energy on getting better for now. But Rosie didn't trust any olive branch from him. Not only that, she had no idea how she was going to scrape together the money in the near future. Jim had paid for her truck to be repaired. He told her it was meant to be an atypical Christmas present, but Rosie insisted that she'd pay him back the money as soon as possible. The owner of the Coyote Bar told her there wouldn't be any need for her until May, and there weren't any extra hours to be had at Willow Ranch either. She spread out the hay inside the paddock, and the horses happily began munching on it.

With every fiber of her being, she refused to let go of her dream. The idea that Raweno could possibly go to Floyd gave her nightmares. He belonged to her family. Rosie swallowed hard.

Don't start crying, think instead, she lectured herself. Her phone rang; it was stuck in her vest pocket which was underneath the coat and snowsuit she was wearing. She pulled off her glove and unzipped both zippers, but by the time she finally had it in her hand, it had stopped ringing. She saw on the display that Calvin had left her a voice message. Shit. Was he calling to tell her that he couldn't wait for the money any longer? Her fingers were stiff from the cold, so she went into the stall where it was a little warmer and pressed the Play arrow.

"Dammit, where are you? I'm coming to pick up Lori and the colt in a few days, but I don't know when yet. The deal is off. I'll be giving you back your deposit."

She stared at her phone in disbelief. He couldn't do that, could he? And would he also be taking Sky back as well? She dialed his number, but he didn't pick up. She left him a message to call her back as soon as possible. Her stomach churned as she grasped that he had every right to simply come and take Lori and Raweno.

Calvin still possessed the mare's papers, as well as those of her foal. She only had the scrap of paper with the handwritten terms of agreement on it, except that he hadn't signed it using his full name, and she had no idea whether it was even legally binding. Why had she taken him at his word? Hazel trotted over and sat down next to her. Afraid that her legs might soon fail her, Rosie took a step back and leaned against the wall.

The sound of an engine got her attention, and a cream-colored car pulled up in front of her house. What was Calvin's girlfriend doing here? She left the stall and went to greet her. Andrea opened the driver's side door, but failed to get out, yanking at the seatbelt that held her back. Finally, it unbuckled, and she got out. Her purse hung on her arm by only one handle, and its contents poured out onto the snow. Andrea cursed as she began to collect her things.

"Hold on, I'll help you." Rosie bent down. "What's the matter? You seem upset."

Once everything was back in her purse, Andrea stood up. "What a crappy day I've had," she replied. "The streets are full of ice, I haven't eaten anything since breakfast, and I really have to pee."

"Let's go inside, and I'll make you a cup of tea and you can tell me why you're here."

A short time later, the two women were sitting at the table inside the warm cabin. Hazel had made herself comfortable on the couch. Andrea put three hazelnut cookies on her plate and sipped her tea.

"Should I make you a sandwich?" Rosie asked.

Andrea waved her hand. "No, these cookies are delicious. It's okay."

"I'm very happy you're here, but it seems like a strange coincidence since Calvin tried to call me just before you came."

"He tried calling you? What did he want? Did he say where he is?" Andrea's face was pale, and her eyes were wide.

Rosie told her what he had said. "I tried to call him right back, but his phone was turned off. What the hell happened? Did you guys have a fight?"

Andrea stuffed another cookie into her mouth and washed it down with a gulp of tea. "Ah, if only that was all it was," she mumbled and stared into her cup. Then she raised her head. "I've suspected for a long time that Calvin might be cheating on me with another woman."

Rosie sighed. "I'm sorry to hear that. I know exactly how you feel and—" the way Andrea looked at her caused her to stop. "Wait, you don't think that I'm the other woman, do you?" Rosie recalled all the phone calls she'd received with no number listed on the display and the person not saying anything. "Are you the one who's been calling me?"

Andrea diverted her eyes, but then nodded. "I'm sorry. I thought that the two of you might secretly be back together again. He's been away so often recently. And when you told him about your accident, I saw how concerned he was about you."

"I'm afraid you came all this way for nothing. I am not who Calvin is cheating on you with." She knew that her voice sounded annoyed, but she wasn't interested in discussing her ex's relationship.

"I already know I was wrong, but that's not why I'm here. It's because you should know that, strictly speaking, Calvin is not Raweno's owner."

"What? Has he sold him already?"

"No, the foal belongs to his father. As the story goes, the infamous stallion was supposed to have mated with one of Mr. Dunn's mares. But Calvin saw his chance to earn some good money and told his father that the pregnancy didn't take and instead used Dragon's semen on Lori."

Rosie raised her hand. She needed a moment to wrap her head around this revelation. Calvin had fraudulently used the semen for the foal. That's why Lori had needed to be relocated out of his father's barn as soon as possible—so that her pregnancy wouldn't be noticed. What a dirty trick! "How do you know that?" Rosie asked.

"I was in the riding stable and overheard Mr. Dunn lamenting again how there wouldn't be any more offspring from Dragon. I was angry at Calvin, and at you, so I informed his father that his son had indeed produced a foal from the stallion."

Rosie could well imagine how the man would subsequently put two and two together. "And how did he react?"

"He said that his son had better watch out and that he wasn't going to let him get away with it." Andrea rubbed her hands together. "He seemed calm about it, but his eyes ... I don't know, something in his eyes made me scared of him."

Rosie nodded. She had spent many years living under the same roof with this man. Mr. Dunn was not an unreasonable man, but anyone who ever got in his way paid for it dearly. He showed no mercy, not even to his son, whom he would turn out on the street with only the shirt on his back without batting an eyelash. "Did you tell Calvin about this?"

"I did. I was worried about him. He went insane and said I was the first woman that he had ever been loyal to and now I had gone and destroyed it all. Destroyed his life and any future we had together. He packed his suitcase, and I haven't heard from him since."

"When was that?"

"A few days ago. I started to wonder whether he had done something drastic, but then I thought you might've heard from him."

"Why didn't you just call?"

"Because I was embarrassed about all the anonymous phone calls and wanted to apologize to you in person. Besides, I didn't know whether you'd even believe me if I told you the story over the phone."

Rosie had to concede that she probably would have had her doubts about the story. Despite the fact that she herself didn't trust Calvin as far as she could throw him, the notion that he would defraud his own father like that was, nevertheless, hard to believe. "I'm sorry, Andrea. I don't know where he is. I'm sure he'll come by to pick up Lori and the colt before his father finds out where they are."

Andrea nodded. "Maybe you could also talk to Mr. Dunn. Perhaps he'd let you buy the colt sometime in the future."

Rosie shook her head. "Never. He knows exactly how much that foal is worth, and he'll want to auction him off as soon as possible to the highest bidder. I wouldn't stand a chance."

"I'm sorry. I didn't want this to happen."

"You couldn't have known it before the fact. I just wonder why Calvin would do that."

Andrea shrugged. "He and his father have had almost daily arguments over the past year. And because he doesn't own any stake in the riding school and is only an employee of it, he's always had to suck it up and suffer through stuff."

Oh, Calvin. She almost felt a little bad for her ex. All these years, and he'd never managed to get out from under his father's thumb. What happened to his dreams of starting something of his own? Rosie shivered with goosebumps. Was the money that he would have gotten for the foal supposed to help him fulfill that?

She put aside her thoughts. It was more important to come up with a plan of what she should do now. Wait until Calvin stopped by to pick up the horses? Was there any other option?

Yes. She could call Mr. Dunn and cut Calvin off at the pass. Either decision would ultimately lead to the same conclusion: she would lose the colt and probably Lori as well. Her stomach twisted into a knot. What if Sky didn't belong to Calvin either? Her little family was falling apart right before her eyes.

"Do you think he really meant what he said?" Andrea asked, abruptly putting an end to her daydreaming.

"What?"

"When he said he's been loyal to me," Andrea said softly.

Rosie stared at her, dumbfounded. *I have much bigger problems at the moment than that*, she wanted to say, but bit her lip instead. "I do," she replied, not knowing why, but she was certain that Calvin hadn't lied about this point at least. "But you need to figure out for yourself whether you can trust him and if you love him or not."

Andrea sighed and nodded. "You're right." She looked at the clock. "I'd better get going. If Calvin shows up or calls you, would you please tell him to call me?"

"Will do. Say, by the way, do you know if Sky belongs to Calvin?" Rosie asked.

"As far as I know she does. He won her in a bet at a rodeo."

Rosie let out a sigh, packed up a few cookies, and gave them to Andrea. "Here, take these and look out for yourself."

"All right, I'll be around early to pick up Ayita tomorrow," Woodwind told Lyla over the phone. "We're going to need about ten hours to get there. It's a long way to Oak Lake, Saskatchewan. And they've got everything ready for her there?"

"Yes. I called the director again today to confirm. They're expecting her."

"Good. Are you sure she doesn't suspect a thing? I don't want her running off on me."

"Don't think so. She seems to believe that we are okay with her just going to Alcoholics Anonymous and won't pressure her into going to a rehab clinic anymore."

"Okay. I told her that I was meeting with an expert on wolves and preferred to have her with me when I met him. I'll see you in the morning." After he hung up, he rubbed his hands over his face. It simply had to work. Woodwind knew that Ayita would never agree to it once he told her where he was actually taking her. But if she didn't agree, he would then threaten her with the fact that she could have Wynono taken away from her. That thought alone left a sour taste in his mouth.

As so often in recent days, Woodwind wished he could ask Chinook for advice. The shaman was greatly missed. Whenever he thought of the wise man, his conscience always seemed to get the better of him as he was supposed to be focusing his priorities on his work with the youth and passing the exam. At the moment, he couldn't remember when the last time was that he had looked at the course material.

He looked at the clock with a sigh. It was too late now to go to the library at the community center. He took a glass and filled it with water at the sink. Quickly swallowing it, he saw his reflection in the window. "Tomorrow, you will help your friend Ayita, and after that, you will sit your ass down and cram through the material until the test," he told his reflection. *She's not just a friend, she's the woman you love*, the man in the window stared at him sternly.

Woodwind turned away, trying hard to suppress both his desire for her and his fear of doing the wrong thing. Yes, they were separating Ayita from her son, but Lonefeather, Lyla and he would take good care of the boy.

The next morning, he left his house, got into his car, and drove to the cabin. His cell phone rang along the way. It was Lyla. She was presumably calling to see if he was already on the way, so he let it ring. He'd be there in a few minutes anyway.

He ascended the porch stairs with a nervous feeling in his stomach and knocked on the door.

"Come in," he heard Lonefeather call out.

He stepped into the kitchen to see Lyla leaning against the cabinet, talking on the phone. Her face had a stony expression. His brother sat down at the table and indicated for him to also sit down.

"What's wrong?" he asked, glancing at Lyla.

"Ayita took Wynono during the night and disappeared."

His eyes widened. "What? Shit, where did she go? Did someone pick her up?"

"That's what Lyla is trying to find out. She's talking right now to Una," Lonefeather replied.

Lyla looked at the two of them and shook her head. A few minutes later she hung up. "Una hasn't seen Ayita and Wynono."

"Was Una at Bull's house just now when you talked to her?" asked Woodwind. He thought that if she was, it was very possible that Una might not be telling the truth out of fear.

"No, she is out looking at a house to rent for herself and Nuka in the area. Chinook left her a bit of money in order to do that."

You've kept your promise to look after Una, wise man, Woodwind silently said, and his own failed promise immediately felt like a knife in his back. He expressed his desperation by slamming his fist on the table. "Dammit, we need to find Ayita and Wynono as fast as possible."

"Calm down," said Lonefeather. "We shouldn't do anything rash."

Woodwind stood up so suddenly that his chair fell backwards and loudly banged against the wooden floor. "It serves us right. Fucking hell. This idea of taking her to the clinic was completely misguided. Why did I let myself be talked into it?" He began pacing the floor.

Lyla picked up his chair, walked over to him, and grabbed his arm. "That's not going to do us any good now."

He resisted the urge to pull away, and breathed deeply in place a few times. Then he turned and looked at her. "Sorry, the time for talking is long past. I am going to find Ayita. Let me go."

Her hand fell to her side again. Woodwind noticed his brother's calm, but concerned look and ignored him. "I'll call if I find her."

His first stop was to the rescue center. Perhaps Maja had picked up Ayita and her son and brought them there. But when he got there and saw that the center was empty, he realized that he had a hard time admitting to himself that his real suspicion of where Ayita was hiding out was correct. He sent Maja a short text that he had stopped by so that she didn't wonder whose tire tracks those were in the new-fallen snow and continued on to the reserve.

He parked in front of Bull's house and got out of his car. It was barely eight o'clock in the morning and only one window was lit. He stared at the steps to the front door and thought back to the last time he had witnessed Ayita and Bull here together.

He quickly shook his head to dispel the memory, went up the steps, and rang the doorbell. He continued to press the bell until he heard a voice approaching the door. And he was still pressing the button when the door was torn open and Bull's massive head appeared. The man glared at him through narrow slits. Even dressed in just a pair of jogging pants and a faded T-shirt he exuded a daunting authority.

"Hey, asshole, what's this all about?" He took a step forward.

"Is Ayita here?"

"What's it to you?"

He tried looking past Bull and into the hallway. Was that Ayita's coat hanging on the hook?

Before he could look any further, the man put one hand on his chest and shoved him backward. "Go away."

"Let me talk to him," a voice came from the darkness of the hallway, and Ayita appeared. She was wearing a bathrobe that was much too big for her, and Woodwind's heart descended into a black hole.

"I'm taking care of it." Bull tried to hold her back. "You go make coffee instead."

"It's my business." She refused to be dismissed, went around him, and placed herself between the two men. She was so close that Woodwind could smell the alcohol on her breath. He balled his fists, then let go.

"Fine," Bull relented. "Just as long as this jerk disappears again, fast." He turned around and stomped down the hallway.

"Come with me," Woodwind implored.

"No. I know what you and Lyla have planned, and I'm not going to let you." Her words were slightly slurred, but the fury in her eyes was clear to see and dead set on him.

"Please, Ayita, we can talk about this. You and Wynono can't stay with Bull, he—"

"He took me in! He would never try to separate a mother from her son. Now leave me alone." She crossed her arms and raised her chin.

"We just want to help you," he said one last time, though he could see that he had lost.

"I don't want or need your help. Get out of my life." Ayita took a step back, put her hand on the door, and closed it.

He stood there staring at the door. It could have just as easily been a wall. He slowly returned to his car and typed a short text to Lyla. He told her only that Ayita and Wynono were at Jeremy Bull's house and that her aunt refused to allow them to interfere in her life. Then he drove back to the rescue center in order to avoid the emptiness that waited for him at home.

Cody had tried a million times to reach Emma ever since she left the farm. She finally sent him a text message yesterday telling him only that she was going to accompany Sonja to her hypnosis symposium in Toronto and that she planned to stay in Ontario for a while. Una, who was looking for a house to stay in, would be living at the guest house and looking after the goats during that time. Great. He thought about how to answer her, but every time he found something he wanted to say to her, his thoughts scattered like a flock of frightened birds. All he knew was that he loved her. But maybe that wasn't enough. So, he answered with only: *Okay, let me know when you're back.*

He ran his hand over Jazz's back, took the brush, and massaged the gelding's stomach and the various other spots he enjoyed having brushed. A warm front had caused the January temperatures to rise, and Cody had spent the entire afternoon on horseback. Lee wanted to discuss the planning for the coming months with him over dinner, and Cody hoped he'd be able to shake his uncertainty by then. He searched his pocket for the last treats he had and gave it to Jazz. "Here you go, boy. Thanks for a nice afternoon." He released the gelding into the paddock and walked across the yard to his trailer.

Once there, he put the kettle on and sat down with a cup of tea at the kitchen table. In front of him lay a letter announcing that the milk inspector would be coming to the farm in a week from today. Hopefully Kurt had followed his instructions and was keeping up with cleaning the equipment. He considered calling the farm for a moment, but decided not to. His father refused to let him take over the operating procedures of the dairy. The few times Cody had been at the farm, he had felt like he was nothing more than some grunt who was just barely tolerated. Let his father find out what being stubborn would get him. Cody emptied his cup, stood up, and went into the bathroom. He hoped a quick shower before dinner at the main house would cheer him up.

Less than an hour later, Cody, Lee, Naira, and Sam were sitting together at the kitchen table of the main house. It was much cozier here in the kitchen than at the large table in the dining room.

"Everything looks delicious. Did you help Naira cook?" Cody asked, placing a fried drumstick on his plate.

"Yes, I made the potatoes and the salad." Sam filled up half of her plate with potato wedges and reached for the ketchup.

"You're a really good cook. Thanks for inviting me for dinner," Cody said.

"Nah, I'm no cook, I'm a cowgirl," Sam replied, squirting a large pool of ketchup on her plate.

Naira laughed and poured glasses of water. "Even cowgirls need to know how to cook."

"That's right," Lee chimed in. "So, Cody, how are your plans looking for this year? With the new grant money we received, we can expand our program for indigenous youth. Can we count on your help?"

Cody swallowed a bite of chicken and tried to pinpoint what made him hesitate. Yes, he would like to take over his family farm, but his father stood in his way. And sitting around waiting for him to finally die so Cody could inherit the farm made him uncomfortable. On the other hand, Cody also didn't know at the moment whether the dairy would be financially ruined by then, or if his father intended to sell instead of letting his wayward son take it over. He felt Lee's eyes on him and looked at his boss. "I know that you guys have been very patient with me until now, but would you mind giving me just a little bit more time?"

"Time is very short," said Lee.

"We made up a new contract for you to read," Naira said. "We'll need your consent, that is your signature, by mid-March."

Cody nodded. "I would really love to be part of the Willow Ranch team again. It's just that at the moment, it's a little difficult to say."

"We would like to give you more time," said Lee, "but if in the end you pick the farm, we risk being shorthanded here. It won't be easy to find someone like you again."

Cody felt himself blushing and took a drink of water. "Thank you. I'll make my decision as soon as I can."

"That's fine. We need an experienced cowboy, and the time it would take to find someone else, in case you decide not to continue with us, is very short."

Cody nodded. He knew that Lee and Naira were doing him a huge favor by giving him another two months to make his decision.

"I'll be discussing the details of the equestrian tours with you in the next few weeks to see whether we need to buy more horses and whatever else needs to be done. There's going to be a lot of work to do," Lee said. "Even if you do decide not to accept this new contract, I'll at least need to use your knowledge for planning the upcoming season."

Cody grinned. "No problem, you can count on me."

Sam stood up and began clearing the table. Then she went to the refrigerator and pulled out a cake. The aroma of caramel and chocolate filled the room. "Marble cake with caramel frosting," the girl proudly announced.

"Are you guys trying to use all this delicious food to get me to stay?" Cody asked.

Naira, who had gotten up to retrieve the dessert plates and forks, smiled. "It's worth a try."

Sam dumped a giant piece of cake on his plate. "I also want you to stay."

He grinned and put a large bite of the cake in his mouth.

"By the way, there's been new developments regarding the wolf hunters," Lee stated. "Two of the men were caught after they illegally shot an elk cow, and the foresters also found traps and other things that clearly indicated they were hunting wolves."

"Finally, some good news," Cody answered. "And what about the others?"

"The officers have their names, and there are rumors as to who put them up to it."

"Aha, so there is someone behind all this." Cody scraped the last crumbs of chocolate cake together on his plate and licked his fork. "It would be interesting to see if my buddy Rabbit suspected the same person."

Lee raised one eyebrow, but Cody shook his head. "It's only an inkling. Does Woodwind know about it too?"

"Yes, I told him the same thing I told you," Lee replied.

That evening, Cody read through his new contract. To his surprise, it was open-ended. His salary had been increased, and his vacation days were moved to the winter months since there was too much going on at the ranch during the summer. Everything sounded great. How could he risk a job like this that other people could only dream of? There weren't very many ranch owners who gave their cowboys and wranglers such good working conditions, not to mention a full-year contract. Most of his buddies in this line of work went from ranch to ranch each summer, looking for work.

He fiddled with the pen in his hands. Would Emma be happy about it and maybe forgive him? Didn't she also dream of a life such as this? He could well imagine being able to convince Lee and Naira to hire her as well, if she applied for a work visa the next time she returned. He held the pen poised to sign, but then hesitated. Would his signature here mean the end of the Tippet Ranch? Just then, his cell phone rang. His parents' number appeared on the display.

"Mom, what's up?"

"Uh, it's your dad here."

It took him a second to realize that it was his father on the phone. He couldn't remember his father ever having called him before.

"Hi. How's it going on the farm?"

"You need to come. Some of the cows are coughing. The winter hay seems to have too much mold."

"And what am I supposed to do about it?"

"When can you be here?"

He sighed and swallowed back the anger that rose up his throat like heartburn. "Dad, I can't just leave here like that. My job at Willow Ranch is important to me, and I won't be risking it for a couple of coughing cows."

Silence.

"Dad, are you still there?"

Cody heard a grumble and some noise in the background, and finally, his mother's voice.

"Honey, your dad isn't doing well. He ... Well, it's just hard for him. I can't explain it over the phone. Can you come home?"

"I can't just up and leave and come to the farm."

"Ask your boss, please, dear."

"Is it dad's leg? Is it causing trouble again?"

"No, that's not it."

Cody was annoyed that his mother wasn't upfront with him. But he obviously wasn't going to get any more information out of her over the phone. "Okay, Mom. I'll see what I can do."

"Thank you."

"And as for the cows, call the vet if it doesn't get better, yeah? And look through all the bales of the winter hay."

"We will. See you soon," said his mother, hanging up before he could say anything else.

Cody didn't plan on asking Lee for more days off. What could be wrong with his father? The entire time he'd been there at Christmas, he hadn't had more than three nice things to say to him. Every new idea that he'd had tried to implement on the farm had been shot down. He could figure it all out for himself. Nevertheless, Cody laid down the pen and stood up with a yawn. He would take his time in signing the contract. But for now, he needed to go to bed.

Woodwind unzipped his sleeping bag and sat up. His back hurt. He had spent the past week sleeping on the couch at the rescue center, not wanting to risk running into Ayita or Bull at the reserve. He didn't doubt that it was childish of him to hide out at the station, but he didn't care. He didn't care about anything anymore. Putting on his jogging pants and a t-shirt, he went to the kitchen, stretching and groaning, turned on the electric kettle and scooped three spoonfuls of instant coffee into a cup. His stomach growled. Did he even have anything to eat last night? He pulled the milk out of the refrigerator. There wasn't much else in there. He'd need to go into town and do some shopping. His thoughts trailed off as he poured the hot water into his cup.

"Good morning," a cheerful voice said.

Woodwind startled, spun around, the spoon nearly flying out of his hand. Maja stood in the doorway grinning at him.

"Do you have to scare me like that?" he grumbled.

"I can see you left your good mood at home," Maja said.

"No, I sent it out into the wilderness yesterday. Along with my sense of humor." He ran his fingers through his long hair and took a drink of his coffee. He screwed up his face in disgust.

"What's wrong? Did you mix up the tins?"

"No, it has no sugar in it."

Maja walked over to the cabinet, pulled out the sugar bowl, and gave it a shake. "It's empty," she declared.

"Aw, great." Woodwind poured his coffee out into the sink and threw some water on his face.

"How long do you plan to live here like a hermit?" Maja asked as she started preparing breakfast for the animals.

"Until I can build myself a cabin in the wilderness and live there." He rolled up his sleeping bag and dug through his backpack for clean clothes. All he found was a flannel shirt; that was it. *Looks like I'll need to buy groceries and do laundry,* he thought, grabbing his old jeans draped over the arm of the sofa. He disappeared into the cramped bathroom and got dressed. He looked at the grim face in the mirror with the dirty hair and the lifeless eyes.

"Who cares," he said to his reflection. "Nobody's looking anyway."

By the time he reappeared, Maja was already loading bowls of food onto a wagon. She looked up. "I can take care of everything here in case you have things to do."

"I need to go into town," Woodwind answered. "But I'll look at Kachina before I go."

"Okay. Have you given any thought as to when we can set her free?"

"In the spring, and only after these wolf hunters have been caught. What do you think, will she make it in the wild?"

Maja stopped for a moment, seemingly surprised that he would ask her opinion. "No idea. But she can't stay here forever. Or do you prefer handing her over to a zoo? I couldn't stand that. If we let her go, at least she'd have a chance of surviving in the wild and rejoining her pack."

Maja was right. Nevertheless, his heart ached for Kachina.

"We've done what we could, don't you think?" she continued. "That little wolf is a fighter. She fought her way back from the brink of starvation, and we owe it to her to set her free." With these words, Maja grabbed the handle of the wagon and went out to the enclosures, pulling it behind her.

Woodwind reflected on their conversation, but didn't come to any final decision. He took the bucket of chicken pieces and went to the wolf's cage. Kachina raised her head and stood up. She was still lean, but new muscles were starting to show. Her coat was now shiny and her yellow eyes alert. He lifted the hook on the door which resulted in a deep growl from the wolf. Even though this was a warning, it didn't sound very threatening. However, Woodwind was pleased to see this behavior from her and held back. It was a positive sign that Kachina was alert in his presence. When he poured the contents of the bucket into her bowl and pushed it into the enclosure with a pole, her growling sounded more like hunger.

"That's what I want to see," he said, studying the wolf as she approached her food. It looked like she wasn't putting any weight on her back paw. Had she somehow hurt herself again? That wasn't going to help when they released her into the wild. He carefully went back to the door of her cage and opened the latch. Perhaps he could get a better look at her paw if he could get a little closer to her. He had barely put one foot inside her enclosure when she froze. The hair on her back stood straight up and she showed her teeth, but made no sound. Afraid she was about to pounce on him, he quickly retreated. Would she be healthy enough to be released in the spring? He hated this uncertainty and feared making the wrong decision.

An hour later, Woodwind was at home stuffing his dirty clothes into the washing machine. He would need to stay there for at least as long as his laundry was washed and dried. Thankfully, he had a real coffee machine here. But no more coffee, as he discovered when he opened the tin. Shit.

He pulled himself together and drove over to the gas station on the reserve, which also sold a few groceries, warm snacks and alcohol. With his hair hanging in strands and his dirty jeans, he wouldn't attract any attention. Nonetheless, he quickly grabbed a bottle of Coke, a bag of bread, coffee, and margarine. At the self-serve counter, he put two slices of pizza and a few chicken wings into the box. All of a sudden, he heard a familiar voice speaking with the cashier. He lifted his head and saw Bull standing at the register. He had a bottle of whiskey and a six-pack of beer in front of him. Woodwind's anger started to rise, but he forced himself to wait until Bull had left the store. As soon as the door closed behind him, Woodwind placed his things next to the register.

"I'll be right back," he said to the cashier and hurried outside. "Hey, asshole!" he shouted at the man, who was just getting back into his truck.

Bull turned around. "You don't want to mess with me," he replied.

Too late now, Woodwind thought, running up to him to punch him in the stomach before he could get into his truck. The man saw the attack coming, grabbed him by the collar, and as fast as lightning, spun him around, pressing Woodwind against his truck with his arm across his throat. "I could have you arrested for bodily harm. You looking to go back to jail? Maybe you've got some sweetheart there who misses your ass?"

"Let me go," Woodwind croaked.

Bull lessened his grip. "Stay away from me. And everything that belongs to me, including Ayita." He lowered his arms.

Woodwind rubbed his neck. "She's not your property. What do you intend to do with her? You don't give a shit about her or her son."

"That's my business. Stop acting like a lovesick fool and find yourself another woman. You've never had any trouble finding a warm bed to crawl into before." Bull snarled his lips into a crooked grin.

"Don't you have enough to do with Nuka and your efforts to

become chief? Rumor has it that your nomination cost you a pretty penny. When it comes out that you bribed people for their votes, that'll be the end of it," Woodwind retorted in an icy tone.

Bull's eyes darkened. His jaw muscles tensed, and Woodwind thought he could hear his teeth grind. The man raised one hand, but then let it fall again and straightened his shirt. "You'd do better to not believe anything Rabbit says. You two losers have no proof of anything."

Woodwind furrowed his brow. What was Bull talking about? Was Rabbit right in his suspicion that his father was behind the wolf hunting? Before he could act on this thought, Bull pressed his finger against his breastbone.

"I told you already I'd find something that will rip your heart right out of your chest, and I keep my promises. Ayita said that your willingness to take her son away from her cut her like a knife. She needs the alcohol to drown the pain. What kind of a friend would I be if I refused her this deliverance?" A hateful laugh rattled from deep inside Bull's throat. He turned around and got back into his truck, and Woodwind just managed to jump out of the way to avoid being hit. His words stuck like arrows in his heart.

Stunned, he stumbled to his car. The clerk came running out to him and asked if he needed help. He looked at her in confusion. Her words reached him as through a filter.

"Are you okay? Your things are waiting inside, do you still want them?"

At first, he shook his head, but then followed the woman into the shop, paid, and took the bag. The smell of the pizza and the chicken wings only made him nauseous, but he carried everything into his kitchen and set the bag in the sink. Then he dragged himself into the bathroom and took a long hot shower. Bull's words pounded in his head. He found a package of painkillers in the medicine cabinet and swallowed four tablets in one gulp. He went to the bedroom and fell naked onto the bed, waiting for the medicine to finally start making him drowsy, before drifting off into a deep sleep.

Woodwind woke up shivering. Shit, was it cold. He turned his head. It was eight p.m. He grabbed hold of the blanket he was laying on and wrapped himself up in it. But he just couldn't get warm. His tongue felt furry, and he was thirsty. He groaned as he got up, but the only things in the bathroom were his dirty clothes. The clean ones were still wet in the washing machine. Cursing, he stuffed them into the dryer, turned it on, and threw on an old bathrobe. In the kitchen, he greedily drank a glass of water and made himself some coffee. His head felt like it was full of cotton. He ran one hand over his face. The tablets had knocked him out for five hours.

Once the coffee was finished, he sat down at the kitchen table with a cup and stared anxiously at his cell phone. Should he call Lyla and tell her about his run-in with Bull, maybe ask her if she'd heard anything from Ayita? At exactly this moment, the phone went off. Naira was calling.

"Hey, what's up?" He answered with a scratchy voice.

"Hi, are you sick? You sound terrible."

"Hardly slept," he said, realizing too late how idiotic that sounded; it was early evening.

"Ah, okay. I just wanted to ask how the exam went. It was yesterday, right? I had hoped you'd call and let us know how it went."

Woodwind needed a moment to figure out what she was talking about—the certification exam to continue working with the youth! He had registered for that time slot because the online exam was only available on certain days in January and wouldn't be offered again until next winter.

"Woodwind, are you still there?"

"Yeah, but I have to go. I'll call you later," he said and hung up. Goddammit. He missed it. Chinook's words echoed in his ears like a hammer against a metal gong. "Your work is with the youth," the shaman had said. Woodwind rubbed both hands over his face and pulled at his hair. He had let down his own people. What kind of a terrible person was he for not keeping his promise to his own people's youth? What would happen to the youth program now when the authorities found out that he hadn't taken the exam? He yanked on his hair so hard that the pain brought tears to his eyes. His phone then beeped with a text message from Maja: *Kachina is gone. Did you forget to close the gate?*

With a swipe of his hand, the phone flew from the table, hitting the wall and clattering onto the hardwood floor. He let out a guttural scream.

February

It was early February, Cody and Lee were standing in the large tack room at Willow Ranch, examining the array of bridles and saddles.

"What about providing riding horses for the teens to use? Is something like that being planned?" Cody asked.

"Not really, but Naira is working on putting together a course where the kids can learn how to communicate with the horses non-verbally. It will especially be useful for those who have behavioral problems or who are shy."

Cody thought about which horses would be best suited for that. "My draft horses are the calmest, but I think their size could scare a few of the kids."

Lee nodded. "Yeah, Naira also mentioned that. I think we ought to choose two or three other horses to keep in mind for the program."

Cody made a note on the board hanging on the wall. "The camps start in June, right?"

"Yes. Just before that, the teens will have daylong seminars with the various elders and will be visiting other reserves. We plan to continue running the bed-and-breakfast at the ranch until the program gets started." Lee's phone rang, and he pulled it out of his pocket. "Oh, okay, I'll let him know."

"What is it?"

"Your mother is on the phone up at the house. She has been trying to reach you for over an hour on your cell phone."

Cody patted his jacket pockets and realized just then that he had left it back in his trailer. "Is it something important? We were just about to go through the packing equipment."

"Naira said she sounded hysterical. I think you'd better see what's going on with her. We can continue this later."

As he hurried across the farmyard to the ranch house, he wondered whether his mother was just being dramatic again in order to get him to come home. Or maybe she was trying to appeal to his guilt? He found Naira in the kitchen. She was speaking very calmly, and Cody suspected that something really had happened. She handed him the receiver with a stony look. He took it and nodded at her before she left the kitchen.

"Mom, what happened?"

"Cody, thank God," his mother sobbed.

"Calm down. What's wrong?"

"Your dad's in a coma."

"What? What happened?"

"Please come right away. The doctors don't know whether he will recover. It's all—" a sob choked her words.

"Did he have an accident? Did he fall?"

"I don't know." She sobbed more.

"I'll be on my way in half an hour." His head was spinning. He went back to the hallway with weak knees and slipped on his boots. Lee came inside.

"Shit, Cody. Naira just told me about your dad. Is it very serious?"

"I have no idea," he replied.

"Well, drive carefully and keep us up-to-date, will you?" Lee put his hand on his shoulder. "Look after yourself. Family is the most important thing."

Cody nodded absentmindedly, said goodbye, and went to his trailer. As if in a trance, he stuffed a few things into his bag and grabbed a Coke from the fridge. His phone was sitting on the kitchen counter, and he saw that there were three text messages waiting for him. He didn't have time for that now. He needed to get to the farm and to his dad before it was too late.

It was around eleven o'clock at night when he finally arrived at his parents' house. His mother opened the door for him in her nightgown and old housecoat, and gave him a long hug. Her eyes were red from crying and her skin slightly flushed. "Your father's condition is stable so far. We'll drive over early in the morning to see him," she said. "Should I fix you something to eat?" She sounded so exhausted that Cody worried she might collapse on the floor in front of him.

"Mom, tell me what happened."

She looked at him, and her red eyes once again filled up with tears. He put his hand on hers.

"It's okay, we'll talk about it in the morning. Go to bed and try to sleep. I'm here now. Everything will be fine."

His mother gradually shook her head, then raised her eyes. She laid her hand on his cheek, her smile seemingly forced. "Thank you for coming. I'll see you at breakfast."

Early the next morning, his mother seemed to still be sleeping when he went out to the barn. There, he found Kurt filling up the hayracks. A foul, dusty smell reached his nose. "Wait a minute," he said, taking a handful of hay. He smelled it and grimaced. Then he looked more closely and discovered it had white speckles. Mold. "Is that from the barn where the winter hay is stored?"

"Yes. I know that it's not really good anymore, but your dad said we can't afford anything else and that that little bit of mold isn't going to kill the cows."

"That may be, but it can harm the milk. I'll go straight over to the other barn and see how bad it is. Hopefully, it's just a small number of bales that are bad."

When he inspected the winter hay, it looked as if all of it was contaminated with mold. It must have been too wet when it went into storage. Dammit. He hurried back into the cow barn and asked Kurt how much of the hay had already been used as feed.

"We've been using that for a good long time now."

"Then we have to test the milk today! It might've already contaminated the milk." Then he remembered that the milk inspector had come a few days ago. He asked Kurt about it, and the older man confirmed that he'd been around for that. "And haven't we gotten the report back yet? Has anyone from the authorities been in touch?"

Kurt shrugged. "There's a pile of unopened mail on the table in the milking parlor. Maybe there's something in there."

"Why doesn't anyone here open the mail?" Cody asked, but then waved this off. "I'll take care of it," he said instead and went into the milking parlor, finding a letter from the Milk Board. It was dated four days ago and looked as though his father had indeed opened it. He skimmed over the information:

Dear Mr. Tippet,

We regret to inform you that the milk processed at your dairy has repeatedly failed to meet the quality standards set by the Ministry of Agriculture. Your license to sell milk is herewith suspended until such time as a new inspection can take place. If you are found to be in noncompliance with this suspension, you may be subject to a heavy fine and could face imprisonment.

Cody cursed and kicked a tin milking bucket across the cement floor.

"Bad news?" Kurt asked.

Cody told him what was in the letter.

"Holy shit. I'm sure that sent your father over the edge." His hand then immediately flew to his mouth once he realized what he had said. "Sorry, I didn't mean it like that. I'm sure your father will recover. How is he?"

"It's okay. Mom and I are going to the hospital in a bit." Cody glanced at his watch. "I'd better go inside and change."

"Okay. I'll hold down the fort for as long as you need me."

Cody waved at him and hurried into the house, which smelled of coffee and toast.

His mother stood fully dressed in the kitchen, where she was sipping her coffee. "There you are. I'd like to go in fifteen minutes," she said.

"No problem." He spread butter and jam on a piece of toast and quickly gulped down a cup of coffee.

On the way to the hospital, his mother still couldn't explain to him what had happened exactly. Her concern for her husband seemed to rob her of her ability to speak clearly. "Your father fell and was found unconscious," was all that she could say.

He tried to comfort her, but wasn't sure whether she could even process what he was saying. Silently, they walked side-by-side down the third-floor hallway at the hospital. The smell of disinfectant burned his nose, and he had to swallow back the wave of nausea that hit him. A young doctor was standing in front of one of the doors to the room and looked familiar to Cody. She greeted Jackie with a warm smile and gently rubbed her back. "You may go in to him. Unfortunately, his condition hasn't changed. I'd like to speak with Cody."

Jackie entered the room. Once the doctor turned to face him, he recognized her. It was Scott's ex-girlfriend.

"Kathlyn?"

"Hello, Cody."

"Have you been working at this hospital for long? You had your own practice. Did you give it up?" he asked.

"No, I only help out a few days over here in the children's ward."

"How is my father? Did he have an accident?"

"You don't know what happened? Didn't your mother tell you anything?"

He shook his head and stared impatiently at the door to his father's room, resisting the urge to simply barge in.

"I'm very sorry. But from the looks of it, it seems your dad tried to take his own life."

Cody stared at her in disbelief, refusing to take in what he had just heard. Then he recalled that strange phone call from his father recently. It had been a call for help, which he had ignored.

Just as he had done when Scott had tried to reach him, and he had disregarded him too. This realization gripped him like a wild animal and its claws dug deep into him.

Rosie lowered the halter she was holding and gazed at Sky. The mare was staring into the nearby forest with her ears standing straight up. The wild horses were there again. Rosie had heard a faint neighing from afar. It made no sense trying to get Sky's attention now. She thought back to Lyla's words: *The thing about wild horses is that their desire for freedom is far greater than their willingness to work with humans.*

"Whatever shall I do with you?" she mumbled as she walked over to Lori and Raweno. The uncertainty of how much time she and the horses had left together overshadowed her joy, leaving her almost sick to her stomach. She felt as though she'd been abandoned. Calvin had used her for his own purposes, and she seemed to have overestimated her abilities by taking on Sky. It was hard for her to admit that she had made one wrong decision after the other. And on top of that, she had fallen for Calvin's empty promises. Her ex had given her reason to hope that she would soon be able to call these three horses her family.

And Nick? In her naïveté, she had mistakenly taken his kindness as interest in her, but he hadn't been around since her accident. Shit. She couldn't think clearly. Her plans seem to be collapsing like a house of cards.

Rosie went over to her truck and whistled for Hazel. "Let's go out for a little drive. Perhaps that'll help me clear my head." She locked a chain around the gates and let the dog jump in the back seat. In case Calvin came now to pick up the horses, he would have to wait until she came back. She made sure that the gate between the pasture and the stable remained open so that the mares could go back and forth.

She took the gravel road to the highway and turned. A familiar green truck came her way. She quickly turned her head, but the vehicle was already too far away to say for sure.

After an hour of driving, she didn't know which way she should go anymore and decided to go back home. Nor had she come up with any solution for her problems. As she made her last turn, she caught sight of the smoke. She parked her truck at the side of the driveway, stumbled out of the door, and dashed over to the house with Hazel right behind her. A fire had broken out in the barn. She called the emergency services in a panic and gave them her address. Where in the world were the horses?

"Lori, Raweno, Sky!" Her voice faltered. Thick smoke lay over the pasture. Were those their silhouettes she vaguely saw in the distance? Her eyes burned. She grabbed the hose from off the wall, attached it to the spigot, and frantically turned the valve. The water came out at first as a trickle, and she feared the groundwater was still frozen. But soon the water started to flow freely, and she ran with it to the barn. She called out the names of the horses over and over again. Why weren't they in the pasture? She needed to check the stable. Perhaps the gate had fallen closed on them, and they were trapped inside. She propped the hose on the fence so the water could still reach the exterior wall, and ran to the door. Suddenly a pair of arms caught her and held her back. She screamed and freed herself.

"Doug, what are you doing here?"

"I was coming by to pay you a visit when I saw smoke."

She only listened to him with half an ear as she rushed toward the door and tore it open. A searing heat of smoke and embers rushed out at her. Doug pulled her away from the structure. "You can't go in there. Dammit, Rosie."

"Let go of me. I have to save the horses."

"Are you crazy, they aren't even your animals. They aren't worth risking your life for!"

She watched in horror as the flames ate away at the wooden

walls and surged into the sky. Then a loud cracking sound, like wood breaking apart, reached her ears. Sky galloped onto the pasture. The mare snorted and was covered in soot. But where were Lori and Raweno? Rosie tried again to free herself from Doug's grip. "I have to find the other two," she screamed at him.

"They must be dead by now. Forget them. That's how it goes."

"You're the fireman!" She tore at his jacket. "Do something!"

"It's too late. Come away from here. There's nothing we can do."

Rosie blinked. Smoke was burning her eyes. Doug's fingers felt like handcuffs around her wrist. She had nothing more to lose. She ripped her arm from him with a jerk and shoved him away when he tried to hold her back again.

She ran along the narrow barn aisle, blindly through the thick clouds of smoke, feeling her way toward the broken gate. Presumably Sky had kicked it open in terror. She turned left then right, trying to make out Lori and her foal through the plumes of smoke.

A thin break in the smoke allowed her to see all the way into the corner. The mare lay on the floor, with Raweno right next to her. She dashed over to them, kneeled down next to them, and discovered Lori wasn't breathing. The foal nudged her repeatedly with his nose.

"You have to get out of here," she choked out, loosening the belt of her jeans and buckling it around his neck.

With all her strength, she succeeded in pulling Raweno outside to the pasture. A moment later, the barn roof caved in, burying the dead mare underneath it. Rosie fell to her knees and buried her face in her blackened hands. Sirens screamed through the air, and a fire truck raced up the drive. She stood next to the horses, with Hazel at her side, and watched the firemen swiftly get the flames under control.

One of the men came over to her and draped a blanket over her shoulders. "Are you hurt? Can I help you?"

She looked up and shook her head. "No, I'm—," and broke out into a coughing fit. The man reached out his arm and pulled her to her feet. She gratefully took the bottle of water he gave her and drank from it.

"Better?"

She nodded. "Did you see where Doug went?"

The man looked at her confused. "Who? There's no one else here."

Rosie saw that his green truck was gone, but she was too exhausted to think about that. She looked back at the fireman. "Can you tell what might have caused the fire?"

"Perhaps old wiring. The construction looks pretty old."

She gulped. Was her negligence the reason for the fire?

"When everything has cooled off, the experts will go through the wreckage and determine the exact cause," said the firefighter. "Did all the animals make it out?"

Her eyes filled with tears, and she shook her head.

The man laid his arm briefly around her shoulder. "I'm really sorry. Is there anyone you could call? You shouldn't be alone tonight, especially after inhaling some of the smoke."

"I'll call a friend to come over," Rosie mumbled.

"Okay. Then we'll be packing up to go."

Raweno let out a hearty neigh, and her attention flew to the horses. She mumbled out a thank you to the firefighters and went to the pasture, barely registering as the fire truck drove away. She examined Sky closely and found a gash on one of her hind legs, probably from the gate. Raweno stood off to the side and seemed so lost that it broke Rosie's heart. He was now old enough to not need to be with his mother, but his experience amid the flames would certainly leave its mark.

It was her fault that the fire had cost Lori her life. She should have invested her money in renovating the barn, rather than in her narcissistic endeavor to purchase the three horses. Now Lori was dead. Rosie dressed the wound on Sky's leg and gave the animals hay and fresh water, before dragging herself over to the cabin and collapsing on the porch floor. She suddenly had no strength left. Hazel lay down next to her, and Rosie cuddled against the dog's warm body. *I have to call Uncle Eric*, the thought popped into her mind, but her grief over Lori and her concern about Raweno's future took precedence.

She felt broken and wished that someone would come around who could put everything back together again for her. For the first time ever, Rosie admitted that she couldn't do it all by herself. How often had she been told by other people that a pretty girl like her ought to find herself a man. How she had loathed these words. But right now, she wished that she had done just that. From the pasture, Raweno neighed repeatedly as he paced the fence next to the charred remnants of the barn. Lori's body still lay under the rubble. Hot tears poured down Rosie's cheeks, and a paralyzing helplessness took over her body.

She kept her eyes on the horses, specifically on Raweno, who abruptly stopped in place, turned his head, and looked at her. She felt as if she'd been struck by lightning. *Don't you dare sit around and wait for some friends to save you*, a voice inside her said. She got to her feet and went to the hose to wash her hands and face. The water was ice cold, and it roused her fighting spirit. She turned the water off. Now, the idea of not being able to make it alone no longer felt like a defeat. *Asking for help doesn't mean that I'm weak*, she thought for the first time.

Rosie had worked so hard to achieve what she had on her own, never realizing that she was actually working against herself instead of getting closer to achieving her goals. Her friends had tried to tell her that she was overdoing it. Instead of listening to them, she had always felt like they were attacking her or not taking her seriously. Now she saw they were right and that she needed help. Standing in front of the charred barn ruins, along with the mare who longed for freedom and a young colt stallion, she knew now that her strength lay in this realization.

March

Cody inspected the next cow's udder. The mastitis seemed to be pretty much under control among most of the cows. The vet had agreed to let Cody pay the bill in installments, but that also wasn't going to save the farm. He took off his baseball cap and ran his fingers through his hair. They still couldn't bring the milk to market for a few weeks or even months. This meant that there was income flow to buy new hay. In the end, their only option would be to sell some of the cows, perhaps even the entire farm.

Nevertheless, he didn't want to make that decision as long as his father was in a coma. Had he really tried to kill himself? Cody couldn't imagine it, nor did he want to. His stoic, religious father would never go against God's plan and take his own life, would he? Then again, he had never expected that from Scott either. His phone vibrated in his pocket.

"Lee, hello."

"Hi, how's your dad?"

"No change. The doctors aren't willing to make a prognosis yet." Cody went into the cooling chamber and sat down on a stool.

"Sorry to hear that. I wouldn't otherwise be calling, but the time is running out for Naira and me."

Cody sighed, rubbing his stubbly chin with his other hand. "I'm afraid I can't get away right now. Sorry. It looks as though you're going to need to find another ranch hand." The words felt like a punch to his stomach.

"Dammit," said Lee. "Forgive me, I was really hoping to be

able to have you on the team, but I fully understand that you're needed at the farm."

"Believe me, I wish it were the other way around. I'll come back as soon as I can to clear my stuff out of the trailer. Can Jazz stay at the ranch for a while?"

"Sure, no rush. Just take care of your parents and the farm. Jazz is doing fine here."

Cody thanked him, and they hung up. His thoughts wandered next to Emma. She and Sonja were still traveling together, and she occasionally sent him pictures from her travels along with short text messages. He longed for her and had thought about calling her a couple of times. But what would he say to her? So he usually just sent smiley face emojis instead and told them to have fun. In his last message, he had written that he definitely wanted to see her again before she returned to Germany. She had answered with an "Absolutely," but that was all she'd said. *Forget about her*, a voice inside him said, and he put his phone away.

Everything around him felt like one broken dream after another. He left the barn and shuffled across the farmyard with heavy steps. Two crows were perched on top of Scott's cottage, staring at him as if to summon him closer. Cody stopped in his tracks, transfixed by a flicker of light in one of the windows. What could that be? His legs felt as if they were rooted to the spot. He took a few deep breaths. It was time. He slowly walked over to the door. Like his mother had said, the key was under the mat. He picked it up, unlocked the door, and opened it. On the hook in the small hallway still hung a jacket, a bandana, and Scott's cowboy hat, which he only wore on special occasions. He stepped through the door and glanced around. It looked as though his brother was just on vacation and would return at any moment.

Cody unhooked the bandana and caught the faint scent of aftershave on it. With his breath faltering, he pressed it to his nose, swallowed hard, and tied it around his neck. Then he slowly moved to the kitchen and saw what had caused the reflection through the window. A ray of sun had bounced off the glass mobile hanging next to the window. It was of a galloping horse with its mane and golden tail blowing in the wind behind it. Hadn't he made this mobile himself in high school? He stepped nearer to have a closer look. Indeed, he recognized his initials written in permanent marker on the hoof: C.T. He remembered that at the time his greatest dream had been to someday own a Palomino just like this one. At this point, he had owned Jazz for many years. Why had Scott hung up this old mobile in this house?

Cody's gaze swept over the clean countertop and the colorful tablecloth on the kitchen table, and then landed on the living room. There stood a small desk with a pile of letters on it. He walked over, and seeing that they were old bills, sat down on the uncomfortable chair. He started looking through the envelopes until he stopped at a sheet of paper that was handwritten. He pulled it out, causing a photo to fall to the floor. He picked it up and realized it was of Kathlyn; behind her was Scott's arm and the milk tanker—it was the other half of the photo that hung in the barn. Scott had never gotten over Kathlyn, Cody realized as he began to read.

Kathlyn wants to have a family and children, and it breaks my heart that I can't be the man she deserves. She's right, I need to get help. Dad says it's just a dark phase and that we Tippets are strong enough to get over it. Maybe he's right. On the good days like today, I find myself making plans for a new, more animal-friendly barn and a farm that's profitable. I think it would be nice if we had horses. Who knows, maybe Cody would start coming here more often if we did. I miss my little brother, but am so proud of him. He's forging his own path. I even envy him a little that he has the freedom to live his dreams. Sometimes I wonder if he really never wanted to become a farmer and always wanted to become a cowboy. I've seen how easily and lovingly he handles the cows. All my attempts to include Cody in the dairy business failed because of Dad's impatience and stubbornness. I know that Dad's behavior doesn't mean that he doesn't love Cody; he wants us both to be happy. But on the awful, dark days, nothing can make me happy. Everything feels like black tar and every step pure torture. Kathlyn says it's depression, but we farmers don't have any time for that. We work hard on the good days, and on the bad days, we just pull through by doing more work. I can feel it when the dark days are coming, and every time, they seem to eat away more and more at my will to live.

Cody closed his eyes for a moment. It was as though he could feel his brother's desperation within his own body. He forced himself to keep reading. The handwriting in the next section looked different, as though the letters were scrawled down with much effort.

I sent Kathlyn away–I don't want to drag her into my black hole. No one can help me. I've tried calling Cody a number of times, but only to make sure that he's doing well. Hopefully, he won't think he's abandoned me ... You haven't, little brother. Every time I look at the mobile in the kitchen I have to smile. Often these are my only bright moments ... This gloom ... It's like a wild animal ... it eats away at me. If I can't handle it anymore, I'll go ... And hope nobody will think it's their fault. It's–

This is where the letter stopped. Or was it more of a diary entry? Had Scott wanted them to find this? Cody leaned back in his chair. His sorrow over his brother swallowed him up so abruptly that he could barely breathe. But there was also the slight inkling of release in his words. Scott had suffered from depression and was convinced that no one could help him. It was both tragic and unbearable.

"Hello?" someone suddenly called from the front door.

He jumped to his feet. "I'm in here."

His mother appeared in the living room. "The door was open. What are you doing here?"

"Did you know that Scott was suffering from depression?" Cody was fed up with her secrets and silence.

His mother nodded. "Kathlyn and I had tried to get him to see a psychologist, but he only chalked it up to being a bad phase."

"Had Dad convinced him of that?"

"No, maybe, oh ... I don't know. Your dad felt so helpless. His own grandfather had committed suicide, and he could never bring himself to acknowledge this stain on the family's history. When he saw that Scott was having problems, he didn't know how to handle it. And your brother refused to seek any kind of therapy." His mother threw up her hands to cover her face.

Cody put his arms around her until her sobs died away. "Why didn't anyone tell me about any of this? I might've been able to help."

His mother took a step back. "Scott didn't want that. He told us that we shouldn't call you under any circumstances. You had your own life to live and the right to be happy. He loved you very much."

Cody gulped. "And I loved him too."

His mother reached for his hand and squeezed it. "I have good news," she said quietly.

"Dad?"

"Yes, he woke up from his coma."

"Did he really try to kill himself?"

A smile appeared on Jackie's face. "No, it was just a sequence of unfortunate events. But he can tell you that himself. Let's get over to the hospital."

About an hour later, and after the doctors had given Larry a complete checkup, Cody and his mother looked at him from either side of his father's bed. Larry's skin tone was almost the same light gray color as the cement floor of the barn, but his eyes were alert.

"Tell me what happened." Cody pulled his chair up closer to the bed. To his surprise, his father reached out his hand to him.

He cautiously took hold of it, carefully avoiding touching the IV needle and tube.

Larry cleared his throat. "Kurt was out in the pasture, and I wanted to get the tractor out of the shed to move the hay in the barn." Larry started coughing and Jackie handed him a plastic cup of water and a straw. After a few sips, he continued. "I opened the large garage door with the opener, got on the tractor, and started it. Then suddenly, the door fell closed. I pushed the button again, but nothing happened. So, I got off the tractor and my damn leg gave out from under me. I slipped down the metal steps next to the tractor and must've banged my head." Larry raised his arm, and it trembled as he felt the back of his head. "And then everything went black."

Cody gently squeezed his father's hand. "Kurt says he found you unconscious inside of the closed garage with the tractor running."

"And he thought that I'd wanted to—? Oh God, no, I would never do that." His father buried his face in his hands.

"Dad," Cody said, "I have something I'd like you to read. Scott wrote it." He laid the paper in front of his father on the blanket. "Take your time. I'll be back later."

"Where are you going?" His mother looked at him in disbelief.

"I need to call Emma." He left the room and took a seat in the sterile-looking hospital cafeteria. He couldn't exactly say where his sudden urge to call her came from, but he wanted to tell her the truth and that he loved her. His longing to hear her voice was suddenly overwhelming. He took a deep breath and dialed her number. She answered on the second ring.

"Cody, hello. What a nice surprise!" The sound of her voice made his throat constrict.

"How are you? Are you guys still in Ontario? I'm sorry that I didn't call you earlier."

"Well, I could've also called, but Sonja and I have been on the go quite a lot. Listen to this, my parents even came to visit us in Toronto."

"Oh, how nice. I'm glad you're having a good time. I—"

"Is everything okay on your side? How is the ranch and how are your parents?"

Cody swallowed. "I'm really sorry how Christmas ended," he said instead.

"I'm not angry with you anymore if that's what you think. I was just hurt that you lied to me."

"That was stupid of me. It's just that so much has happened since Scott's death. I had really been looking forward to your visit and spending time with you, but then ... Aw, dang it, Emma, I miss you."

Silence. Cody listened closely. Had she hung up?

"I miss you too. I have so much to tell you, but not over the phone. Sonja and I will ... we ..."

"Emma, you're cutting out. I can't understand anything."

"We can talk when Sonja and I are back at the guest house. You ... it's ... I'll be ..."

"When are you coming back?" Cody waited a few seconds, but the connection gave out, and he hung up. She had said that she missed him. That was a good sign, wasn't it? He sighed and stuck his phone back in his pocket. He bought himself and his mother a couple of coffees at the counter and made his way back to his father's room. He knocked on the door and entered. His father was now sitting up and holding Scott's letter in his hand. His eyes looked teary. Cody quickly averted his gaze and handed his mother her cup. She smiled tiredly. "I told your father that Kurt didn't really believe that ... Well, never mind, it doesn't matter. It was an accident and that's all that matters."

"Leave it alone, Jackie," Larry said, rubbing his finger across the piece of paper. "Scott's words here have made me realize how self-righteous I've been. The eldest son always inherits the farm, that's how it's always been. And in my stubbornness, I made you feel as though you weren't cut out for farm life."

Cody looked at him, astonished. His father reached out his hand, and Cody stepped up next to the bed. Hesitantly, Cody took his father's hand. Larry's thin lips curled into a fleeting smile, and his fingers closed around Cody's. "I long denied the fact that Scott was depressed. I was afraid that talking about it would make it worse." He shook his head. "I've acted like an idiot. Your mother and Kathlyn tried to get him help, while I kept trying to convince him he just needed to stay strong."

"It doesn't do any good to beat yourself up about it, Dad," Cody said, fully aware of his own guilt for not having been there for his older brother. There was a knock at the door, and Kathlyn popped her head in the room. She was wearing a white sweatshirt jacket instead of her doctor's coat and smiled at them. "I just wanted to say goodbye before I go home."

Larry waved her in. "I also need to apologize to you."

Kathryn looked at Cody, bewildered, then back at his father. "Why? I wasn't part of the team of doctors who looked after you."

"No, that's not what I meant. You were an amazing partner for my son, but I never gave you a chance, and I'm sorry for that. Scott loved you very much."

"And I had always hoped that my love for him could save him. He broke my heart when he ended our relationship." Kathlyn's voice sounded strained.

"I was so dumb to believe that you wanted to come between Scott and the farm. With all your ideas of how to change everything, I thought that as a doctor, a dairy farm wouldn't be good enough for you." Larry shrugged his shoulders apologetically.

Kathlyn approached the bed and rested her hand briefly on Larry's arm. "There was nothing I had wanted more than to start a family with Scott at the farm. But now we have to look forward. Take care of yourself, and I wish you a good recovery." She said goodbye and left the room.

Cody saw his father try to suppress a yawn. "You should rest now, Dad. I'll take care of everything at the farm."

"Thank you for all you've done. I'll be back on my feet again soon. I want you to know that your happiness means a thousand times more to me than the farm does."

"Thank you, Dad. That means a lot to me."

"Speaking of happiness, you're in love with that German girl, aren't you?"

Cody nodded.

“Then make sure she knows how you feel. I made the mistake of getting involved in Scott’s relationship. I won’t do that to you.”

“Emma will be returning from Ontario in a few weeks. I will take care of everything here until you recover. Kurt was able to find us new hay that we can afford. Not exactly top-quality, but better than what we have now. And I have an appointment with the milk inspector in a few days. We’ll get that up and running as well.”

“Your optimism gives me hope,” his father said.

Cody stood in the doorway of his father’s hospital room and turned back around. “Dad, in case Mr. Monty calls again, tell him the Tippet farm will remain in family hands.”

Woodwind hadn’t left his house for over a week. Before that he had met with a dealer who talked him into buying a little weed. He felt rotten for supporting the drug dealers at the reserve with his money. What a shitty, irresponsible mentor he was for the teenagers. He chuckled at the thought. His throat, raw from the smoke, emitted only a husky sound. How pitiful. He got up from the couch, coughing, shuffled into the kitchen and took a drink of water directly from the tap. But then nausea hit, and he gagged it all up. He heaved a few more times, turned around, and slipped down onto the floor. With his head against the wall, he sat for a few minutes with his eyes closed. *I am such a miserable, stinking piece of shit*, he thought.

“Then get up, take a shower, and purge your soul,” Chinook said so clearly in his mind that Woodwind’s eyes widened. He looked around to see if the shaman wasn’t actually standing near him. Of course, no one was there. “Even you have abandoned me,” he mumbled. “You can’t tell me what to do anymore, old man.”

“You know what you need to do, dummy.”

Was it the effects of the last joint that was making him hear these voices? He rubbed his face and got to his feet. Wherever they came from, having a shower certainly wouldn't hurt.

He stood under the water for a long time, scrubbing himself with the bar of soap until the hot water turned cold. Then he dried off and went into the bedroom to put on some fresh clothes. None of the three pairs of jeans that he owned were clean. Great. It suddenly disgusted him to put on any of the pairs of jeans, since they all reeked of marijuana. His jogging pants were also covered with coffee stains from having spilled his cup a day ago or so.

As he searched for something clean to wear, his hand brushed again soft suede. He pulled out the suede pants he'd worn in the mountains. How long ago was that now? At the time, he thought he could finally become a real Cree and live sensibly and confidently as such. *The whole time, you were only kidding yourself, playing dress-up*, said a voice in his head.

Regardless, he slipped on the pants and was surprised to notice that the soft leather against his skin gave him a sense of peace. Instead of a t-shirt, he chose a plain cotton button-down shirt. Something was still missing. He bent over and pulled out his moccasins from the bottom of his closet. As he stepped into them, he noticed that there was something in one of the shoes. He reached inside and pulled out a small box. It had a rubber band around it, which was holding a folded piece of paper around the box. It took him a moment to remember. It was the box that Naira had given him from Chinook after his death. He hadn't felt ready to open it before now. Seeing what was inside of it felt as though it would be like a final goodbye.

I will always be with you, the voice inside his head told him again. Woodwind sat down on the bed with the small box in his hand. At least read what was written on the paper, he told himself, and he pulled it out from under the rubber band. He recognized Chinook's shaky handwriting.

If you're reading this, then I have moved on. But you still have your journey before you, which I can only accompany you on in spirit. Do you remember our conversation when I told you you should lead a ceremony? You said you weren't qualified enough. But I said, you are breathing, that means you are qualified. It's time that you find the truth of my words and embark on a vision quest. My instructions will guide you, and we'll see each other with Mother Earth.

Chinook must have dictated the following lines to someone else who had written them in clear penmanship. There was a list of what he needed to prepare for a day-long vision quest. Was he ready for it? Chinook had once told him that the human fear of separation and loneliness was a learned fear. It sneaks up on us as soon as our lives begin and the umbilical cord is cut. We desire the feeling of being cared for, of validation. This fear is a shackle we need to courageously break.

Woodwind stood up from the bed, went into the kitchen, and placed the box on the table. He read through the steps one by one. At the very end, Chinook had added one more line.

The purpose of the ceremony is to allow you to be courageous.

Woodwind's gaze drifted from his last, half-smoked joint waiting in the ashtray to the dirty dishes piled up next to the sink, and then to his overflowing garbage can. Disgusted, he got up, opened the window, and gazed outside. It was a sunny March day, and the snow was almost all melted. He'd practically forgotten how it felt to have the warmth of the sun on his skin. With a few shrugs of his shoulders, he returned to the box and Chinook's letter. So, a vision quest, eh, wise man? Why not, what did he have to lose?

As part of the preparation, he would need to choose a spot in nature where he could spend an entire day and night. He already knew where he would go, but he decided he would still visit the place today and bring Mother Earth a tobacco offering to express his gratitude for this place. All he needed to do now was buy some groceries and prepare a meal that he could eat after he was finished fasting. It felt good to be doing something, to have a purpose. He spent the rest of the day concentrating on his upcoming ceremony, and his thoughts finally stopped spinning in his head in an endless loop.

On the morning of the vision quest, he got up before sunrise to collect himself by doing a few breathing exercises. Then he ate a hearty breakfast, his last meal for the next twenty-four hours. He packed a notebook and pen, a blanket, a sweater, and socks into his backpack. On a whim, he also packed his long flute, the same one he had played for the teens in the mountains, and then he set off. He left the box at home, as Chinook had instructed him to do in his letter, and drove west into the Rocky Mountains. After a while, he parked his car alongside a gravel road and wandered toward the North Raven Creek, the one he had shown to Ayita and Wynono.

He spread the blanket on the ground over the scant snow and sat down with his legs crossed. He listened for a while to the sounds of the birds and the rushing of the stream from underneath its ever-lessening ice cover. Once he had soaked in enough of his surroundings, he reached for his notebook and wrote down everything he saw and heard. With his eyes closed, he breathed deeply, inhaling the many smells around him. The moss, the wet tree bark, the earth.

He set aside his book, stood up, and purposely walked in a small radius around his chosen spot. He picked up stones, twigs, and pinecones, placing them on the blanket before sitting back down. With long, slow movements, he touched each one of the objects again, smelled them, and began to feel closer and closer to the earth. Again, he wrote down his impressions in accord with Chinook's instructions. It was becoming increasingly easier to express his thoughts and feelings about the here and now.

The hours passed, and he started to feel hungry. He felt an increasing restlessness and deliberately took a drink from his water bottle. The day slowly drew to an end, and darkness settled over the small clearing around him. Woodwind wasn't afraid of the dark night; at least that's what he had always thought. But this time, it was a dramatically different experience to sit in the darkness without any light source, as opposed to walking around with the possibility of being able to turn on a flashlight. *Breathe calmly*, he said to himself. The darkness seemed to surround him more closely, as if it were slowly smothering him.

All of a sudden, he was back in his prison cell with his cellmate pulling the scratchy blanket tighter and tighter around his throat. He gasped for air, stretching out his arms and digging his fingers into the earth. He felt the winter's frosty, solid grip on the ground.

"I'm not in prison, I am here with Mother Earth," he mumbled, but could only barely force himself not to run back to his car.

A rattling in the trees behind him caused him to turn around. What was that creeping through the forest? It was something large and clumsy. The sound of a snort penetrated through to his ears, or was he just imagining things? He tried to see what it was through the darkness; his throat constricted with fear, but he couldn't see anything. He thought he'd felt something lie down next to him, but there was nothing there. A deep growl resounded from inside him. He hesitantly stuck out his hand and buried his fingers into a thick, bristly fur. "Grizzly, my spirit animal, thank you for coming," he mumbled, and his heart became light.

"Woodwind?" He heard Chinook's voice so close to his ear that he jumped. "Why do you feel so unsettled?"

He knew that the shaman was also just a vision and that it would be wise to converse with him. But he sat there for a while in silence and considered his longing to be part of something bigger than himself. He started to become aware of how much he wanted to belong to something. At the same time, he recalled the desperation which had defined his life and how unsatisfied and unworthy he felt.

"I don't know anything," he said into the stillness of the night. "I have the lives of two people on my conscience. I was torn away from my culture, spent nine years in prison, and haven't been able to connect to my roots ever since."

"Close your eyes and look at me," Chinook said.

He obeyed and was indeed rewarded by the shaman's likeness. The elder smiled at him blissfully and made a circular movement with his hand to encourage him to continue speaking. Woodwind spoke about the humiliation he'd felt from the whites in prison, even from the other indigenous inmates as well until he had literally fought his way into their gang. "There are no half-Indians here in prison," they'd said to him. And that was why he had intended to stay away from all aspects of his culture. But then Woodwind described what it had felt like to be homeless after his release. "I tried to hold fast to our native traditions; I wanted to feel connected. But this feeling was nothing more than hot air and my frustration only increased."

He mentioned the numerous times that he hadn't taken part in the ceremonies because he had felt ashamed of his past. "I grew up with our native traditions and our spiritual path, but I have the feeling that I'm no longer entitled to it or know how I can become part of the Cree community again."

When Woodwind fell silent, Chinook nodded and tilted his head slightly. "You don't know a great deal," he said.

"What do you mean? I just told you everything I don't know."

The shaman smiled. "You told me what you think you don't know, but if that's true, then you know what you don't know. And if you look at it that way, you just told me what you do know. Everything is part of the cycle. Knowledge and ignorance have the same energy. If you know what you don't know, then you possess knowledge."

Woodwind wanted to challenge this, but the shaman raised one hand, motioning him to comply. Thus, he remained silent and let the wise man's words echo in his soul, until he finally understood their meaning. He let out an exclamation of surprise. It was clear to him that he had always carried around the traditions, the ceremonies, and the way of life of his people inside him; he had only been denying them all this time. No one but he had a say over his own roots. He and Mother Earth were one; he was in community with his people.

"We are all one energy, one soul, and one melody. Find the magic in your song," Chinook said just as his apparition started to fade and disappear. Woodwind opened his eyes, accepted the darkness, and felt protected. His grizzly briefly pressed his massive body against his before plodding back to the spirit world behind Chinook.

"Thank you, bear, and you're right, wise man. I need to find my courage. Because I am never alone, but a part of something bigger: we are one big family."

His thoughts flitted to Ayita. He needed to prove just that to her ... that she wasn't alone and would always have a family. He had excluded her out of anger and jealousy, but he wouldn't ever do that again. He felt around for his flute, put it to his lips, and sent out his song into the shadows of the night. The melody expressed his longing, mingling with a new sense of energy and strength. Then he felt it: the magic that Chinook had seen in him. At first, just a tiny speck that grew brighter and brighter the longer he played his flute. Becoming rooted with everything that made him who he was as a person and as a Cree felt like a warm hug. And at the same time, it allowed the seed that connected him with Mother Earth and with his community, and which granted him this talent of evoking joy and happiness in his listeners with his music, to grow.

As he played, he fell into a sort of meditation, losing himself and letting his melody be guided through the darkness by the nocturnal sounds and scents of nature until the first light of dawn appeared on the horizon. It was accompanied by a long, sustained howling, causing the hair on the back of his neck to stand on end. He put away his flute. The wolf's call didn't go unanswered for long, and a few moments later, he listened to the ensuing concert of low notes and high notes, which turned into an almost screeching howl.

Once it all came to an end, he heard a rattling sound in the bushes a few feet away from him. He turned his head to see gray-brown fur and a pair of yellow eyes staring at him.

"Kachina," he whispered. The she-wolf sniffed at him, then

cocked her head. How he wished he could run his fingers through her smooth fur, but he knew that she was a child of the wilderness. He made a quick shooing motion with his arm, and the wolf immediately disappeared into the bushes.

Before he packed up his things, he thanked Chinook and his power animal, before scattering tobacco in a circle around himself to thank Mother Earth. He slowly got up. Feeling dizzy for a moment, he held still.

As he started on his way back, he was empowered by his feelings of being sanctified and revitalized. At home, he took the food he had prepared out of the refrigerator and made himself some coffee. After pensively finishing his meal of cornbread with honey and butter and a small portion of meat with vegetables, he took a shower, got dressed, and cleaned up the house. His gaze kept falling upon the box on the table. *Give this to your brother Lonefeather once you are at peace with yourself*, Chinook had told him in his letter, and he planned to comply with this request.

He placed the box on the shelf. "Soon," he mumbled. Then he looked at the ceremonial flute he had carved lying next to the box, and thoughtfully picked up the small instrument. As opposed to his longer flute, the one that he played on various occasions and always carried with him, this flute was meant only for special occasions. He had spent many months carving this delicate flute. His fingers traced the wood. Then there was a knock on the door. He was surprised to see it was Nuka. He stood there with his hands deep in his jeans pockets.

"Hi, what can I do for you?"

"Have you got a few minutes?"

"Yeah."

"Don't you want to know what for?" The boy looked at him, squinted, and bounced from one foot to the other.

"Well, if you're here to convince me to do something illegal, I'd have to—"

Nuka hastily shook his head, then spotted the flute in Woodwind's hand. "Did you make that yourself?"

"I did, but it's never been played."

The teen put out his hand, and Woodwind laid the instrument in it. With a look of amazement on his face, Nuka beheld its carved pattern and traced his finger over the small paw print of a bear that had been carved into the wood, just below the mouthpiece. "Will you ever play it?"

"When I find a woman I wish to give my heart to, then I will play her melody on it and after that, the flute will be broken in two."

Nuka handed back the instrument, but avoided Woodwind's eyes. "I'm sorry about what I said in the barn at Willow Ranch about flute playing," he mumbled, almost inaudibly.

"I accept your apology. Would you like to come in?"

"Could we go for a walk instead?"

"Sure. I'll just get my jacket."

A little while later, they set off through the desolate streets of the reserve. Woodwind kept glancing at Nuka, who was walking beside him with his shoulders pulled up to his ears and the hood of his sweatshirt covering his head. It didn't seem like he was close to saying anything. The cold March wind blew the snowflakes that had started to fall. They eventually arrived at the only diner located on the reserve.

Woodwind nudged Nuka with his elbow. "Should we go in?"

"I don't have any money."

"But I do." He spontaneously took hold of the boy's sleeve and pulled him through the door. They sat down at one of the only five tables.

"It's self-serve," a voice called out. An older Cree woman sat on a stool behind the register.

"What looks good to you?"

Nuka examined a basket of muffins and then glanced at Woodwind. "Just coffee."

Woodwind bought two muffins and two cups of coffee, and placed the tray on the table.

"Thanks." A smile crossed Nuka's face as he peeled the the cling wrap off the muffin.

"My pleasure." Woodwind took a sip of coffee.

"I talked to Una," Nuka said after he had gotten about halfway through the muffin. "She told me that you and Rabbit stood up for me."

"It was your brother's idea to start a program for you guys at Willow Ranch."

"I know, I spoke to him too. It's become clear to me that he hasn't had an easy life with our father." Nuka emptied two packs of sugar into his coffee. "My foster family was good to me. It's just that it wasn't easy being an indigenous kid living in a white family."

Woodwind nodded. "You must've felt very alone."

The young man shrugged as he took a sip of his coffee. "Some of the kids in my class were okay, but whenever they asked me anything about the Cree people, I didn't have anything to say. I didn't know what it meant to be a native."

"Do you know it now?"

"Yeah, I think so. And I have you to thank for that, so thanks."

Woodwind looked at the boy's face, his high cheekbones, dark round eyes, tan skin. "Are you letting your hair grow out?"

With an embarrassed grin, Nuka ran his hands through his messy, black hair that reached past his ears and neck. "It'll be a long time until it's as long as yours."

Woodwind smiled. "It happens faster than you think." He noticed the teen quickly grow serious again.

"Do you think my father ever loved me?"

The question came so unexpectedly that Woodwind had to first think about how to answer. He didn't want to placate him off with a lame, *of course he does*. "Your father didn't give you up because he didn't love you, but because he does."

"I don't understand that."

"After your mother's death, he didn't feel like he could be a good father to you. Rabbit was almost out of the house, but your dad knew that you needed parents to take care of you and a home. A foster family seemed to him to be the best option for you."

Nuka pressed his lips together and knit his brow. "I've never looked at it that way before," he said after a while. "But I'm still going to move in with Una whenever she finds a house for us."

"That's a good decision. You should be thankful to have a sister like Una."

The little bell above the door chimed and three girls came into the diner, giggling. Nuka slyly attempted to watch them. One of the girls nodded at him, and he raised his hand in greeting, then he hastily turned away and stared at his coffee cup.

"She's cute," said Woodwind. "You know each other?"

"A little bit," he mumbled. "I gotta go. Thanks for the coffee and the muffin." He stiffly got up, threw the girl a sideways glance, and stumbled out the door.

Woodwind watched the boy go, bought himself another muffin, and soon also left the diner.

April

Rosie took the brush and began cleaning Raweno. The stallion had since gotten over the trauma from the fire, but his ongoing attempts to get Sky's attention indicated that he missed Lori. Damn. She missed the old mare too.

Today was the day that the report from the fire investigator arrived in the mail, but the letter sat still unopened on the kitchen table. If it had been a short in the outdated electrical wiring that had caused the fire, she would never forgive herself. But she wanted to wait before opening the letter, because she had made a decision that would break her heart, but she knew was the right path moving forward.

She looked up at the sound of a car motor. A luxurious SUV came up the driveway. Rosie gulped and gave Raweno an apple, then left the pasture to meet her guest.

"Hello, Mr. Dunn," she greeted Calvin's father.

"Rosie, it's nice to see you again. And thank you for calling me." The man gazed over at the pasture as he walked up to the fence. "He is the spitting image of his father," he said. "Have you given him a name?"

"Yes, his name is Raweno. It means 'great leader' and also 'great voice.'"

As if on command, the stallion neighed loudly and trotted over to the fence with a snort. Mr. Dunn held out his hand, but the horse took a step back. "He's a shy one."

"His mother was lost in the fire, which has made him apprehensive," Rosie said. She climbed over the enclosure fence and stroked Raweno's neck. The stallion put his head against her shoulder. "It's okay," she repeated softly before turning back to Mr. Dunn. "What do you plan to do with him?"

"A few weeks ago, I would've said that I wanted to sell him for as much as I could possibly get for him."

"And now?"

He smiled briefly, but then turned serious again. "But now, my relationship with my son is more important, and I want Raweno to have a good home."

"Did Calvin get in touch with you?"

"Yes, and we've talked it out." He ran his hand over his mustache. "And for as funny as it may sound, I can even understand his motive. The two of us are both stubborn, and I have treated him like a teenager all these years, or even worse, like one of my employees."

Rosie was astonished at his honest admission, and Mr. Dunn must have noticed her surprise because a smile appeared on his face again. "The figurative kick in the pants it took me to realize my mistake came from Calvin's girlfriend. Andrea is a force to be reckoned with."

Rosie nodded and now also smiled. But then Raweno neighed again, reminding her of why Calvin's father was here. "What is going to happen to him now?"

Mr. Dunn looked around. His attention seemed to snag on the charred roof pillars, the only thing that remained of the barn. Eric had hired a company to come and take away the rest of the debris. "Calvin told me how attached you are to Raweno, and I know how much you loved Lori. But this isn't the place for a growing stallion." He looked at Sky, who was grazing on the other side of the enclosure. "More importantly, he can't be kept near a mare. Oh, by the way, Calvin gave me a letter that officially names you as her owner."

"Thank you," was all Rosie could say. She had a plan for Sky, but he didn't need to know about it.

"Calvin also told me that your former co-worker is now running the Tanner Ranch," the man continued.

"He mentioned Nick Flint?"

"I know that ranch, and I think it would be the perfect place for Raweno. He could begin a career as a breeding stallion and pass on his father's genes. What do you think about that?"

Rosie's thoughts spun wildly. "I don't know whether Nick has room for another horse, or if he even takes such young stallions. Are you thinking of selling Raweno to him?"

He shook his head. "Calvin and I have discussed it, and we decided that you ought to be Raweno's owner. If I were to sell him, it would only be a source of conflict between me and my son, and I don't want that."

Rosie stared at the man. She could hardly believe her ears. Was she dreaming? Her knees started to buckle, and she grabbed onto the fence for balance.

"I can see this is all coming as a great surprise to you." He laid his hand on Rosie's. "Now, I've spoken to Mr. Flint about it, and he is prepared to take Raweno. There's just one condition that I'd like to have in writing."

Rosie swallowed and gathered her thoughts. Of course, there was a catch. "And what would that be?" she asked pessimistically.

"I'd like for two of my mares to be the first ones to be inseminated as soon as Raweno is old enough to be used for breeding. And I would like twenty percent of the studding fee for each mare after that." Mr. Dunn winked at her and then looked at the young stallion. Raweno was standing closely behind Rosie, and it almost looked as though he was following the conversation.

He blew air down the back of her neck and, she couldn't stifle a giggle. Mr. Dunn offered her his hand. "Have we got a deal, Rosie?"

"Raweno and I agree to your conditions. Thank you very, very much."

She shook his hand, and he nodded with a satisfied expression. Rosie couldn't remember ever having seen Calvin's father so relaxed before. She accompanied him back to his SUV with a grin. He opened the passenger door and pulled out a briefcase.

"May I offer you anything? A cup of coffee maybe?" she suggested, but he waved it off.

"I need to get back." He pulled some papers out of the case. "Here is the letter stating that Sky belongs to you."

Rosie took the papers. He pulled out a second document and held it out in front of her along with a pen. "And this is the agreement to inseminate my mares when the little guy is full-grown, along with my share of the studding fees."

Rosie took the time to read through the document and then signed her name on the dotted line with a shaky hand. Mr. Dunn signed his name next to hers and gave her a signed copy of the contract. Then he pulled an envelope out of his briefcase and handed it to her. "Then it's official. Here is the deed of possession for Raweno."

Rosie took the envelope, pressed it to her chest, and tried to hold back the tears that had gathered in her eyes. Spontaneously, she hugged Calvin's father.

The man returned her hug, but then quickly pulled away, clearing his throat.

"Well, I won't take up any more of your time," he said. "Take care. And don't be angry at Calvin for not getting in touch. He is currently very busy with his plans for the future."

"It's perfectly okay. Tell him I said hello."

Just before Mr. Dunn was about to get into his car, he paused, and bent over the passenger seat. When he stood back up again, he was holding something that looked like a black blanket. Facing Rosie, he unfolded the velvet material, and she realized what it was. She ran two of her fingers over its red edges in awe. Mr. Dunn turned the blanket around and revealed the emblem: an embroidered red dragon's head.

"That was the insignia used to distinguish the bloodline of Raweno's father, Dragon," he explained. "If you'd like, your stallion may also wear the colors of his forefathers and be a dragon." He laid the blanket in Rosie's hands.

"It would be an honor to continue this tradition," she said, the feel of the velvet giving her goosebumps. Mr. Dunn nodded, climbed into his SUV, and waved out of the window as he drove away and out of Rosie's sight. She needed to call Nick right away.

Half an hour later, she laid her phone on the coffee table and sat down next to Hazel who was stretched out, snoring on the couch. She had to smirk as she recalled Nick's enthusiasm to take Raweno on at the Tanner Ranch. The way he tripped over himself as he talked gave her a warm, pleasant feeling. "Dragon's insignia is even internationally recognized," Nick had swooned. "Raweno will carry on his father's lineage with pride."

He had immediately agreed when she asked for his help with something else. She was grateful to him for not prodding her with questions, but had only said: "If you need me, I'll be there." She briefly closed her eyes and imagined what it would be like to be held in his arms.

A knock at the door interrupted her daydream. Hazel barked and jumped off the sofa. Rosie followed her to the door, and holding the dog by the collar, opened it. She was surprised to see a police officer standing there.

"Hello, ma'am," he said, "are you Rosie Laforge?"

"Yes. Has something happened?"

"I'm here about the fire you had in your horse stable. May I come in for a moment?"

"Of course." She stepped to one side.

He looked down at Hazel, who never let him out of her sight. Rosie pulled the dog closer. "She's harmless."

The officer came inside, took off his hat, and held it under his arm. "As you know, the investigation has determined that your fire is an arson case."

Her eyes flew wide open, and she shook her head. "No, I haven't opened the letter yet from the inspectors."

"It is important that you report this information to your insurance company," the man said, then cleared his throat. "We interviewed each of the firefighters who was here putting out the flames and one of them said that you had mentioned a man named Doug who was here on the day of the fire. Is that correct?"

Rosie's thoughts screamed at her like a gaggle of frightened chickens. She forced herself to keep calm. "Yes, Doug Fry was here. He tried to keep me from running into the stable."

"And where was he when the fire brigade arrived?"

"I've no idea. He simply disappeared."

"Have you heard from him since then? Has he contacted you?"

Rosie shook her head, although she almost blurted out that she had completely forgotten that he had even been here on that terrible day.

"Doug Fry has a record. He is suspected of having set other fires."

"But he's a firefighter himself?" Rosie couldn't believe what she was hearing.

"He was let go a few months ago. Shortly after that, he allegedly set his first fire. This was after his longtime girlfriend broke up with him. He presumably set fire to her barn in an attempt to win her back by making it look like he had come to save her. She pressed charges against him, but wasn't able to provide any proof."

Rosie gulped. "Do you have any proof that he caused the fire here?"

The officer nodded. "We found his truck along with a gas canister, but there's no sign of him. We suspect that he might have crossed the border into the United States and may have escaped to Mexico. I just wanted to come by and let you know."

"Thank you," Rosie mumbled. She could hardly comprehend that Doug was responsible for Lori's death and for putting her other horses' lives in danger. What an asshole.

The officer put his hat back on, adjusting it as he nodded at her. "Be careful, ma'am," he pointed to the letter from the fire inspector, "and you should call your insurance company right away. They typically pay out in such cases." He put two fingers to the edge of his hat and left the house.

Rosie fell to the sofa, her knees weak. The relief that the fire hadn't been caused by a short in the old electric wiring was diluted by her rage at Doug. If only she had listened to Samantha, who hadn't liked him from the very beginning.

Woodwind straightened up his house and felt ready for the plan he intended to implement. Late in the afternoon, he went to the community center and logged into the program course. Although he had missed the exam date, he could perhaps come up with an alternative solution with the course director. At the same time, he left a message with the office in charge that he would be handing in his certificate late and would indeed start working with the youth again as of June.

That was all he could do. He hadn't kept to the schedule, but accepting the situation as it had turned out was also not an option. He sent an email to the course director and hoped that she would answer him soon. He also explained the situation to Lee and Naira, and Naira had promised to speak to Mrs. Rultie and see what she could do for him.

With the little stuffed wolf finally freed from the glovebox of his car, he went the next day to Bull's house and rang the doorbell. A moment later, Bull opened the door, looking tired and a lot less threatening than during their last encounter. "What do you want?" he asked.

"I want to ask Ayita if she and Wynono will come and live with me."

Deep lines appeared across Bull's forehead, then he shrugged. "Yeah, well, looks like you're too late. They aren't here anymore."

"Oh, come on." Woodwind stepped up onto the porch. "Ayita," he called into the house, but no one answered. To his surprise, Bull stepped aside and allowed him to freely search the house.

"Go ahead, search any room you want. But Ayita and the boy aren't here."

"What happened? Where are they?"

"I've no idea where she is. She left in the middle of the night. She even took my old scrap bucket of a car, that bitch."

Woodwind shook his head. That didn't make any sense. "You let her go? Didn't you try to find her? At least to get your car back?"

Bull waved dismissively. "That car is just as much of a wreck as that woman is. She's done for. Let her go."

"What did you do to her, Bull? I swear if anything happened to her then—"

"I didn't do anything to her. Rabbit came storming in yesterday evening with all sorts of accusations against me. Completely out of his mind." Bull's lips stretched into a thin smile. "Who would've thought he had so much anger in him?"

"What did you guys fight about?"

"That's none of your goddamn business." He coughed and waved his hand again. "Ayita heard everything and immediately got on my case. So, then I told her where she could go. After that she left." He burst out in a short, scratchy laugh.

Woodwind searched his face for the truth. What he saw was disappointment, pain and resignation. "Why did you even start anything with Ayita in the first place?"

"It was payback. You turned my sons against me and filled Una's head with all sorts of garbage. I saw how important Ayita was to you."

Woodwind's eyes rested on the man, but he wouldn't look him in the eye. "You never treated Una like she was your daughter, but rather your slave. Yeah, you loaned her money, but that doesn't give you the right to tell her how to live her life. And your shitty relationship with your sons is your own doing."

The man looked at him briefly.

"But that's the whole truth, is it?" Woodwind lowered his arms and showed his palms. It was an invitation.

Bull dug his hand into his pants pocket and pulled out a pack of cigarettes. With practiced movements he lit one and took a few long drags. "Well, shit, if you ask me, Ayita owes me. I wanted to keep her for myself. I would have been a good match for her, we got along well."

"Except that you treat women as if they were your property," Woodwind blurted out. He was sick of hearing anymore of Bull's pathetic blathering. "What do you think Ayita owes you?"

"She never told you what happened back then?"

"Yes, that her boyfriend at the time was violent and had beaten her half to death," Woodwind replied.

"And she never tried to stop him; she even defended him and had attached herself to him like a leech. He went on and raped and brutally murdered my fiancée."

Woodwind's eyes grew as wide as saucers, and he inhaled sharply. So that was the connection. The young woman that Ayita's ex had murdered back then had been Bull's girlfriend. But something still didn't quite fit. Ayita had told him that she had tried to get help. Bull took another drag and blew the smoke into Woodwind's face. "Ayita wanted to make you think that she was the victim, eh? But there are always two sides to a story."

Woodwind waved the smoke out of his face with one hand. "You still didn't have the right to use her like this. She's a mother and an alcoholic who needs help."

"Blah, blah, blah," Bull cut him off. "I only took her in because you and Lyla wanted to take her son away from her. Is it too much to expect a little affection and kindness from her in return? Am I not a man who also deserves to be loved? Shit." He took a final drag, tossed the cigarette on the ground, and rubbed it out with his shoe.

"How can you expect to receive love if you can't give any?" Woodwind had heard enough. He turned around when he heard footsteps behind him.

Nuka was coming up the stairs. His eyes darted between the two men.

"Where were you?" Bull asked.

"What do you care? I'll be moving out soon anyway," Nuka replied and turned to address Woodwind. "My carving skills have improved a lot. It'll be cool to be back at Willow Ranch with you. You'll be there again this summer, right?"

"I'm working on it."

"Cool." Nuka smiled at him, lowered his head, and pushed past his father into the house.

"That boy could be a little bit more grateful that I let him live here," Bull griped.

"Then be a better father to him." Woodwind turned around. He needed to start looking for Ayita and Wynono.

"You have no idea what it means to be a father. All you do is run your mouth." Bull hocked a loogie and shot it onto the step next to Woodwind's shoe.

"Think what you want. Or be a man and admit your mistakes instead of hiding behind your sorrows. You're not the only one who's lost the love of his life. But no one's ever said that you're only allowed to love one person during your lifetime." Woodwind watched as Bull's stern expression turned into silent bitterness. The man's shoulders hung loosely as he propped one hand against the door jamb, as though he needed to support himself.

"Maybe I lack the strength to be a real man. Either way, I won't get in your way anymore. I can forget my aspirations of becoming chief. My children have turned against me, and I am scared of being alone. Now you know." With these words, Bull turned and slowly closed the door from the inside.

What was left behind was Bull's bitterness hanging in the air like the stench of a dead animal.

Rosie was sitting next to Nick in his truck. The vehicle slowly bounced over the uneven gravel road with the horse trailer behind it.

"Thanks for taking Raweno to the Tanner Ranch. I'm sure it sounds a little silly, but I once had a dream about this."

"What?"

"That my stallion would one day find a new home with you and that we—," she broke off as she suddenly realized what she had been about to say.

He threw her a quick look. "Was it a nice dream at least?"

She didn't trust her voice to hold out, so she only nodded.

"Well then, we ought to make the best of it." He reached out and stroked her cheek.

Rosie smiled and pointed at the narrow road ahead of them to the right. "See if you can back in there. It's not far from there to North Raven Creek and the clearing that Lyla spoke of."

"No problem." Nick drove past the turn, put it in reverse, and maneuvered the long, eight-horse trailer between the rows of trees. After about five hundred yards, he stopped. "I think that ought to be okay, don't you?"

She nodded, got out, and held open the rear door for Hazel to get out. The bloodhound jumped out of the truck and immediately began frantically sniffing the area. Rosie pulled out the long leash and hooked it to Hazel's collar. "Sorry, but today, you have to stay close." She held the leash out to Nick, and he took it.

"Well, let's get started," he said.

Rosie opened the door to the trailer. "Hi, Sky, do you know where you are?" She continued to speak softly as she stepped into the front of the trailer, pushing open the gate and placing her hand on the mare's rump. Sky turned her head, snorted, and scraped her hoof along the floor. The drive over had made her nervous, and Rosie hoped she'd be able to walk around with her for a bit on the lead once she was out of the trailer. Rosie began to loosen the knot, but then paused. Was she doing the right thing? What if the other wild horses didn't accept Sky into their herd? A horse out here in the wilderness alone was unlikely to survive.

Nick stepped into the trailer and joined her. "I have Hazel tied up outside," he said, standing next to her. "Are you having doubts now about setting her free?"

Rosie looked at him. The tears swelled in her eyes, and she swallowed. "A little. I want to set Sky free and give her her freedom, but ..."

"Mares always find a new herd. If you were setting a gelding free, then it could be the end of him."

Rosie nodded. "I know, you're right. And I'm sure Sky will quickly find her place in the wild. It is her home after all."

"I watched all the videos of the work you did with her. You gave her the opportunity to be part of a team with you, but she never really gave herself over to the idea. It would be the same with any other trainer, not just you, unless they were out to break her spirit. Granting her her freedom is the best way to protect her from a fate such as that." Nick laid a hand on her arm and smiled at her, then he led the way out of the trailer, and she followed him with Sky. The animal made a small jump coming down out of the trailer, and Rosie's fingers tightened around her rope.

She walked down the path with Sky, closely followed by Nick and Hazel. After fifteen minutes, Sky suddenly stopped in her tracks, lifted her head, and perked her ears. Rosie looked at Nick, but he could only shrug. Sky let out a heart- wrenching whinny. Shortly thereafter came the answer. Nick raised his arm and pointed to the right. Sky pulled on the lead. Rosie started walking again, but she couldn't keep a good hold on the mare's rope.

"You'd better let her go before she runs off with you dragging behind her," Nick called to her.

The area around her heart constricted. She'd spent so many hours with this brown mare. Sky jerked her head to the right and tried to bolt with Rosie still holding on.

"Whoa." Rosie dug her boots into the soft forest floor and hurried to remove Sky's halter. The horse stood still for a moment like a statue, as though she couldn't believe she was being set free. Then she threw up her head, whinnied, and sprinted off through the trees with her mane bouncing behind her.

"Goodbye, girl," Rosie mumbled, trying not to give into her disappointment that Sky wanted to get away so quickly. Hazel walked past her, sniffing, and a moment later, Nick was standing next to her.

"You did the right thing," he said. "I admire your courage to let her go, Rosie Laforge."

"Thank you." She swallowed back a sob.

"Did Lyla ever tell you that I helped her set Shining free?"

"No, wow, I didn't know that."

"It feels like an eternity ago. Lyla had just returned from Germany with Lee to take care of her terminally ill father."

Rosie looked at the cowboy and tried to read from his face whether he still had feelings for Lyla or not. And once again, it was like he could read her thoughts.

"That's all in the past now," he said, taking a step closer. "I know that you're a fighter and that you live your life the way you want. You don't need my help."

He now stood facing her, smelling of leather and sandalwood. Her skin, her entire body was electrified. She melted under his gaze and couldn't get out a single word. He grinned at first, but then became serious. "But I would really like to be part of your life. More than just a former co-worker and friend."

Rosie felt as though the ground below her feet had started to shake, and she grabbed onto his jacket. She pressed her lips against his before he could say another word. His arms wrapped around her, and he picked her up and held her tightly. Rosie was overcome with emotions: her grief over losing Lori and setting Sky free, the uncertainty of staying in her Uncle Eric's cottage. It all burst out of her at once and tears rolled down her cheeks.

Nick didn't say anything; he only held her tightly. He kissed her forehead and her hair while she pressed herself against him, sobbing. For the first time in her life, she was sure that this man wasn't going to use her vulnerability for his own purposes nor see it as a weakness. After a while, she pulled away from him. He used his thumbs to wipe away the last tears from her face. "I sent your training videos to Gordsteen by the way. They don't have any openings for the next training program, but he's looking to hire someone to help out and wants to get to know you."

Rosie stared at him. "I think I love you."

Once he had returned to his car, Woodwind called Lyla, who picked up after the second ring. He briefly filled her in on what Bull had said and explained that he was going to start looking for Ayita and Wynono.

"Where are you going to look? She could be on her way back to the Yukon."

"I don't think she is. She held out here long enough that I don't think she would up and leave just yet. Any idea of where you think her desperation might have sent her?"

"Perhaps to the rescue center, to see the wolf."

"That's a good guess, but Kachina escaped a few weeks ago, and we haven't been able to find her since then, but I'll still stop by there and see. If she's not there, then I'll drive west into the mountains."

"Lonefeather and I will also go out looking. Perhaps she's somewhere near the wild horses."

"Okay, we'll keep in touch. Oh, I'll try asking Rabbit."

Woodwind could hear a soft skip in Lyla's breathing.

"We'll find the two of them, Lyla," he said.

"I just feel so guilty that it's come to this."

"That doesn't help us now. We have to keep looking ahead."

"Good luck, Woodwind."

"You, too," he answered before hanging up. Then he dialed Naira's number. The more people looking for Ayita the better. Naira promised him that she and Lee and Samantha would set off within the next half hour.

Woodwind pulled into the center's parking lot. He sat there for a moment as he tried to reach Rabbit. No luck. Then he went inside and ran into Maja in the small kitchen.

"Oh, hello. Are you looking to move back in here again?" she asked, setting down the knife she had been using to cut apples.

"No, don't worry. I'm only here to see whether Ayita has been by."

Maja tilted her head. "Have you guys had a fight?"

"Um, no, it's a little more complicated than that, unfortunately. Was she here?"

"Yes. She was even here before I arrived and wanted to see the wolf. She was shocked and worried when I told her that she had escaped."

"What do you mean?"

"Well, she asked me whether I thought the wolf would survive and if she'd be accepted into a new pack."

Woodwind sighed. He knew he should've told Ayita about Kachina's disappearance when it happened. "What did you tell her?"

"What else was there to tell her apart from that we had tried to look for her but didn't have any luck. And that all we can do now is hope that she'll make it in the wild."

He nodded. "Thanks, Maja. Listen, we are really worried about Ayita and her son. If she happens to show up again, call me immediately, okay?"

Maja nodded. "Yeah, no problem. Oh, wait. Ayita also asked if I knew anything about those wolf hunters that were supposedly roaming around here last summer."

Woodwind stiffened. Was that the reason for the fight between Rabbit and his father? Was Bull really behind the wolf hunters? "And what you know about them?"

"Only that the forest rangers had received a tip and were following up on the information."

"Yeah, that's what I heard as well. It's all very vague."

Where to now? Woodwind wondered as he drove away from the rescue station. There was still the chance that Ayita might be at the small clearing near North Raven Creek, since she had also felt the area's special energy when he had taken them there. At the end of the street, he headed west along the gravel road. It was worth a try. Before he had lost cell phone reception, he called Lyla to tell her where he was going.

"That's a good idea. I'll give Cody a call, so that he can tell Emma and Sonja. I am meeting Naira and Lee in fifteen minutes."

Woodwind wiped his sweaty hands on his jeans and tried to suppress the worry that was starting to take over.

"Brother," he suddenly heard Lonefeather's calm, deep voice over the telephone. "We will find them."

The certainty with which he uttered these words calmed Woodwind. "I hope so."

Cody stared at the bouquet of flowers he had bought in town. The joy of seeing Emma again was making him fidgety, and he didn't want to lose any time. After their last call had cut out, they continued to text each other a few times. She and Sonja had been in an area with little to no cell phone reception. Two days from now, the two friends would be flying back to Germany. The prospect of never seeing Emma again was unbearable.

He turned off the highway onto the gravel road that led to the guest house. His mother had given him a box of homemade cookies for Emma, both as an apology and an invitation for another visit. That is, if the farm still belonged to them by then. Cody still had a lot to discuss with his father, but most importantly, he was on the mend.

Cody pushed away these thoughts. He didn't have time to think about that now; he needed to focus on winning Emma back. When he turned down the driveway, he wondered where the yellow Jeep was. He had sent Emma a text reminding her that they planned to see each other again one last time before her flight, but he had wanted to surprise her today with his visit. The two women would be spending their final hours packing, at least that's what he thought. But as he got out and peeked through the window, he didn't see anyone.

He walked around to the goat enclosure. It was also empty and, from the looks of it, had been for a while. What the hell was going on here? Where were Emma and her friend? Had he mixed up the dates and they had already left? He pulled out his cell phone and checked the calendar. No, their flight was still the day after tomorrow. He walked once more around the house and saw from one of the other windows that their suitcases were standing in the small hallway between the bedroom and the bathroom. There were clothes and other things strewn around the room. He wondered whether Una was still living here. He dialed Emma's number, but it went straight to voicemail. Strange. He was returning to his truck when his phone rang.

"Emma?" he asked, relieved.

"No, it's me, Lyla."

"Oh, hey. Sorry, I'm over at the guest house, but there's no trace of Sonja or Emma."

"Ugh, who else is going to go missing today?"

"What do you mean by that?"

"We're out searching for Ayita and Wynono. I just wanted to call you to see if you could also keep an eye out for them."

"Um, sure. Looks like I'll just have to wait anyway until later this evening when Emma and Sonja come back from God knows where. Where should I be looking?"

He listened carefully as Lyla told him where to go.

"Okay. We'll be in touch."

He hastily wrote down a note on a piece of paper and placed it in front of the door along with the flowers. Just in case Emma's battery had run out again. Then he headed west to the agreed meeting point to coordinate with the others. He was reminded of their search last year after Samantha had gone missing. Thankfully then, everything had turned out fine, and Cody was optimistic that Lyla's aunt and her son would also be found.

A few miles before reaching their meeting point, Cody saw a dip next to the gravel road with a path leading away from it. He glanced to the left as he drove past and then slammed on the brakes. Was that a yellow Jeep parked there? He put it into reverse and turned onto the road. He slowly drove along until he reached the vehicle and got out. The Jeep was parked at the end of the path, but there was no sign of Emma and Sonja. Why would the two of them come way out here in the middle of nowhere? And where the hell were they? He listened attentively, but didn't hear any voices. But suddenly, the sound of a wolf howling broke the silence.

Woodwind pulled onto the gravel road. He had almost missed the three wild horses that had suddenly emerged from the edge of the thick forest. He slammed on the brakes and came to a stop. Led by a majestic black stallion with a spiral blaze, the three horses nonchalantly crossed the road only a few yards in front of his car. It was Shining, Lyla, Ayita, and Wynono's family horse. His brother had told him about the stallion and the story of the shadow horse. Shining had even saved Lonefeather's life last year. There was no way it was a coincidence that that horse appeared again right now in front of him.

Before the stallion disappeared into the trees on the other side of the road, it turned around again. The animal stomped his foot against the ground and shook his head. His long mane tumbled down his neck to his muscular shoulders like a wave. Then the wild horses were swallowed up by the pine trees. Woodwind faltered. Had the stallion just tried to tell him something? Was Ayita here somewhere? Where was the car that she had taken from Bull?

He slowly started to drive on, making a mental note of the exact spot where Shining had just vanished. A few moments later, the road curved sharply to the right, and he slammed on the brakes once more. There it was. Bull's battered-up old car! It was in the ditch. Woodwind pulled off to the side, jumped out of his car, and rushed over. He cupped his hands around his mouth and shouted, "Ayita," a few times, but there was no answer. He went around the other side of Bull's car and searched for footprints. Then he spotted the imprint of a shoe in the gravel. It was headed in the direction he had just come from. With his eyes fixed in that direction, he slowly followed the footprints, but they stopped after only a few steps.

He looked more closely and saw what looked like hoof marks where Shining had scratched at the ground at this spot. Woodwind took a few steps further toward the forest and froze. A child's shoe lay before him. Wynono. Lyla had bought him those shoes so that he could keep up with Mud. He glanced around and found a small path snaking between the trees, barely noticeable and no more than a deer trail. Woodwind strode quickly back to his car and got out a rope. Then he marked the spot and hoped the others would see it when they came down the road. With that, he followed this path deeper into the woods.

After jogging along the path for a little while, he stopped. Was that a wolf in the distance? He quickened his pace. He didn't imagine the animal would pose a threat to Ayita, but what if Wynono and his mother had become separated? A small child would be the perfect prey for a pack of wolves. The sun was starting to set, and the forest grew increasingly darker.

Woodwind tried to get his bearings. North Raven Creek must be located to the west of him. The path that he was on wasn't very far from the path that led to the clearing where he had performed his last ceremony. Had Ayita deliberately chosen this path? Ten minutes later, the path turned sharply to the left, and Woodwind followed it, crossing over a narrow point of North Raven Creek. He was now sure that he was headed directly for the clearing.

A few minutes later, Woodwind recognized the spot where he had experienced his vision quest. He heard the howling again, this time somewhat closer. The hairs on the back of his neck stood straight up.

Was that someone sitting in the middle of the clearing? Woodwind drew closer and stood at the edge of the trees. Ayita was kneeling in the grass, while Wynono sat next to her at an arm's-length away. She was wearing the suede dress that she had made for herself, just like she had that time at Willow Ranch when he had explained the tobacco ceremony to the youth. Her black hair was loose down her back. Her hands rested on her thighs with her palms up. She seemed to be in her own world. He couldn't tell what Wynono was playing with, but the little boy kept glancing toward the trees in front of them, as though he was waiting for something.

It took all his strength to not run over to the two of them. On the opposite side of the clearing, he suddenly saw two figures approaching. In the faint light, he recognized Emma and Sonja. He waved at them so that they would see him and gave them a sign not to come closer. The women nodded and stayed back in the shadows of the trees.

A sound behind him made him turn around. Cody came up next to him. "Did you hear the wolves howling? I—"

Before he could finish, Woodwind placed a finger over his lips, and Cody fell silent. Woodwind pointed to Ayita and Wynono, then he raised his arm so that Emma and Sonja could see him.

"How did the two of them get over here?" Cody whispered

Woodwind could only shrug.

"I'm going to sneak over to them."

"Okay, but stay behind the trees."

Cody nodded and disappeared.

Woodwind watched Ayita pull something out of the bag over her shoulder. It was a tobacco offering. The sound of a stick cracking to his left caught his attention, and he saw two more people approaching in the dim light. It was Lyla and Lonefeather with Mud trotting silently behind them. He also gave them a sign to stay still and pointed to the clearing.

Lyla came up close next to him. "What are they doing there?"

"A tobacco offering ceremony."

"Is she okay? How long have you all been here?"

"Maybe twenty minutes. Cody, Emma and Sonja are on the other side of the clearing." Woodwind raised his arm and pointed to the three figures who were barely recognizable through the trees. "How did the two of you find your way here? Did you see the spot I marked with the rope?"

Lyla shook her head. "We saw your car on the side of the road, so we parked and got out there. Then Mud disappeared into the trees, and we followed him along the path."

"He must've been able to track Wynono's scent." A wolf's loud howl caught their attention. It sounded like it was very close by. Ayita, too, raised her head.

"That sounded pretty damn close," Lonefeather said.

"They won't do anything to you, brother. Didn't you guys plan to meet up with Lee and Naira?" Woodwind never took his eyes off of Ayita.

"We did, but they wanted to head further west, to the valley where the wild horses usually are."

Woodwind nudged Lyla with his elbow, and she fell silent. "Shit, look at that!" he mumbled.

Ayita all of a sudden had a bottle in her hand. He inhaled sharply. It sure looked like a vodka bottle. *Don't drink it*, he wanted to call out to her, but his throat constricted instead. Lyla's hand gripped his forearm, and he heard her desperately pleading to herself quietly. Ayita raised up the bottle and poured the contents into the grass. Woodwind and Lyla simultaneously let out a sigh of relief, and her grip on his arm relaxed. He looked at her and saw the tears glinting on her cheeks. Lonefeather had placed his hand on Lyla's shoulder, and the two men nodded to one another. Ayita was finally saving herself.

Woodwind was filled with an emotion that he couldn't immediately describe. Yes, he loved this woman, but it was more than that. He watched as she took out a small pouch and scattered something over the ground in front of her. More tobacco, Woodwind thought, to show her gratitude to Mother Earth. And, just like that, he knew what he was feeling. It was pride. He was unbelievably proud of her. Movement in the bushes in front of Ayita caught his attention. He glanced at Lyla and Lonefeather, who were also staring in the same direction.

An animal appeared from out of the forest. In the moonlight bathing the clearing in a creamy white light the animal's gray-brown fur shimmered. It was a wolf. No, it wasn't just any wolf.

From the markings on her face, Woodwind knew it was Kachina. The wolf kept her eyes fixed on Ayita and Wynono. Then he saw other sets of eyes shining in the darkness between the trees. A pack. Kachina had found a family.

Ayita nodded at the animal and reached out her hand to her son. Woodwind recalled the many times in the past that the little boy had ignored this gesture from his mother. Every time, he had noted the pained look on her face, underscored by weary indifference. But this time, with the eyes of the she-wolf and her new family on them, Wynono placed his hand in his mother's. Ayita pulled her son close, and he nestled into her embrace.

Woodwind heard Lyla next to him softly sobbing; even he had a lump in his throat. A loud noise behind him made him jump. The wolf perked her ears, turned around, and disappeared with her pack into the darkness of the night. Woodwind turned around and saw Naira and Lee coming toward them. He raised his finger to his lips, and the two silently stood next to Lonefeather. Lyla suddenly gently nudged him in the side with her elbow. His eyes followed her arm as it stretched out to indicate a spot ahead of Ayita on the right side. He could only make out faint silhouettes between the trees. He squinted to see better.

A cloud in the sky floated on, allowing more moonlight to fill the clearing. He saw one of the shapes step into the clearing. It was a wild horse, and others remained in the shadows. Shining approached Ayita. She raised her head, but continued speaking to Wynono, who was sitting on her lap. The two got up and went slowly, hand-in-hand, toward the stallion.

"Shining is welcoming Ayita back," Lyla whispered. "As our family's shadow horse, he will now watch over the two of them once more."

Ayita reached out her hand and laid it on the horse's muscular shoulder. Shining lowered his head, and his long, wavy mane brushed the ground. Wynono rubbed the stallion's blaze. The animal nudged the boy in the stomach, and the child turned to look at his mother. And for the first time since Woodwind had met him, Wynono had a smile on his face. Ayita stroked his hair with one hand and Shining's mane with the other. Woodwind tapped Lyla on the shoulder. "You should go to them. They are your family. The rest of us can all go now. We'll leave a vehicle for you so that you can drive home."

Lyla nodded and stepped out onto the clearing. Shining raised his head and let out a rumbling whinny. Woodwind gave Lee, Naira and Lonefeather the sign to head back to the gravel road. He turned back one last time toward the clearing. Lyla and Ayita stood there with Wynono between them. The three of them were holding hands, and each of the women had her other hand on Shining's shoulders, forming a circle, a family. This time, Woodwind acknowledged the longing he felt. Smiling, he turned back to follow the others.

Cody watched Lyla slowly enter the clearing. In the moonlight, he saw that Woodwind and the others were retreating. Emma grabbed his hand. "Let's go, too," she whispered.

"Yeah, I'm really starting to get cold." Sonja had her arms crossed around her body and was jogging in place. The three of them made their way back to the yellow Jeep together.

"We can drop you off at your truck," Emma offered.

"Sounds good," Cody replied, grabbing her colorful scarf and tugging it gently. She smiled, and he stroked her cheek with one hand. "You guys will be returning to Germany the day after tomorrow, eh?"

Emma shook her head. "Only Sonja. That's what I had wanted to talk to you about the last time on the phone. I was able to extend my visa."

His relief washed over him like a warm rain shower. She looked at him, full of hope. "Is everything okay at your parents' farm? Our last conversation got cut off."

"My dad is recovering from a fall off a tractor and exhaust fume inhalation."

Emma's eyes instantly widened. "How did that happen?"

"It's a long story. Now that you'll be here for a while, I'll explain it to you when things quiet down."

"One of our greatest downfalls as humans is that we assume time is eternal," Sonja interjected as she got into the backseat of the Jeep.

"She's right about that," said Emma. "Do you want to come over to our place? I'm sure we could all use a drink after what we just experienced there on the clearing."

"And something to eat," Cody added. "If you take me to my truck, I'll run into town and pick up some pizza and meet you back at the house."

An hour later, Sonja, Emma, and Cody were sitting at the small dining table with an empty pizza box in front of them.

"Boy, I didn't even know how hungry I was," Sonja said as she stood up. "Anyone want more wine?"

"Just half a glass for me please. I still have to drive," Cody answered. Sonja filled his glass and then her own. "I'm going to head off to bed. Good night, you two."

"Sleep well. And don't forget that we still have to take food for the goats over to Andrea's early tomorrow morning." Emma took a sip of her wine.

"I'll set my alarm." Sonja picked up her glass and disappeared into her room.

Cody and Emma moved over to the couch and made themselves comfortable.

"Did Mary sell the goats?"

"Yes. I would have continued to look after them, but Andrea made her an offer and the animals are really happy at her farm."

"How long can you stay here then?"

"We'll see." Emma smiled. "Maybe forever. I applied for a student work visa."

"Ah, is it as easy as that? I thought for that you needed a guaranteed job offer. How did you manage to apply for a work visa?"

"I got a job offer." Emma's soft voice sounded almost apologetic.

He looked at her in surprise. "What? From where?"

She set her wine glass on the coffee table, pulled up her legs, and turned to look at him. "I'm going to be the new manager at Mary's Diner."

Cody choked on his wine and carefully set his glass on the table as he coughed. "Well, that's a surprise," he squeezed out. "I thought Sarah was going to take over the diner. And what about your studies?"

"She will continue to work there at least until I have learned the ropes. And we'll also be getting Una on board. With her degree in culinary arts, she'll bring some new life into the diner. Sarah is looking to enjoy her life as a mother, and Mary wants to retire."

"That sounds like pretty solid plans. I would've thought you'd just ask Mary for a regular job."

"Well, I did. Ever since my first visit last year, I've thought the diner was a great place. Sonja convinced me to invite my parents over to discuss the idea, and they promptly got on the plane to Toronto. At first, my father tried to convince me to come back to Germany, but he quickly realized that he wasn't going to change my mind. In the end, I had to promise him that I would finish my MBA here so that his daughter would at least have a diploma to fall back on." Emma imitated her father's deep voice and then giggled.

"Well, I am completely bowled over. What great news!" Cody leaned back against the soft couch. His attempt to smile failed. She had taken her future in Canada into her own hands without any thought of him.

"You're disappointed, aren't you?"

"No, I mean why should I be disappointed? I'm happy for you."

She laid her hand on his thigh. "Because I want to stay here in Canada, but not move in with you at your parents' farm."

"I never expected you to. I didn't know myself for a long time whether I even wanted to take over the farm."

"Why didn't you ever talk to me about it?"

He took a sip of wine. "We had such a wonderful time in the mountains, and you had raved about my life as a cowboy so many times that I thought you wouldn't still love me if I became a farmer instead."

Emma smiled and slowly shook her head. "Oh, Cody, I love you, not the work that you do."

"But neither life as a cowboy nor as a farmer is just a job," he responded. "They are two very different lifestyles. And I don't know if I can make you happy as a dairy farmer."

"That's ridiculous. I thought you also wanted to make a few changes at the farm, don't you?

He nodded and laid his hand over hers on top of his leg. "That's true, and I admit that I have dreamed of building up the farm into something new with you at my side."

"Then let's use this time to get to know one another better. We can still do that with me running the diner and you at the farm. I want to make a life for myself here in Canada, but I can't solely base it on the hope that things will work out between the two of us."

Cody curled his fingers around her hand and pulled her closer. She cuddled into his arms, and he kissed her on the forehead. "Yeah, we'll figure it out. I love you, Emma Michaelis."

She raised her head. "I love you too, Cody Tippet. Please stay for the night."

He took her face in his hands, leaned forward, and answered her with a kiss.

May

Woodwind and Lonefeather sat on the porch at Willow Ranch. From inside, they heard the voices of the guests chatting and the food being prepared. He had asked his brother if he could talk to him, and they went out on the porch to escape the noise.

As the May sun warmed their faces, the last bits of snow were disappearing with every passing day. Woodwind picked up the box in his lap and held it out to Lonefeather. "This is a gift from Chinook. He asked me to give it to you once I was at peace with myself."

"And are you?" Lonefeather took the small box.

A yes dangled from the tip of his tongue, but then he hesitated. "Is anyone? I mean fully at peace with themselves?"

"Only very few of us are ever granted that much. The rest of us have to work at it daily, constantly reminding ourselves that the dark and the light, the good and evil, equally reside inside us all."

Woodwind nodded and made a gesture, encouraging Lonefeather to open the box. His brother pulled out a leather cord as well as a necklace with colorful beads and feathers. Chinook had often worn these pieces of jewelry. There was a note attached to the necklace. Lonefeather read it and chuckled.

"What does it say?"

"That I'm supposed to make a dreamcatcher out of these things when the time has come."

"For who? Come on, spit it out."

Lonefeather grinned. "Looks like you still need to work on your patience."

"I promise. Now spit it out."

"The dreamcatcher is meant to be for my child."

"Lyla's—?" Before he could say the word, Lonefeather raised his hand to stop him, shaking his head with a smile. "That's not all that's in there. There's also something here that belongs to you." Lonefeather handed him a leather pouch.

Woodwind looked at him in awe. It was a medicine pouch, very similar to the one the shaman had used.

"Chinook sees the wise man in you, brother," Lonefeather said.

"His eyes weren't great for years," Woodwind joked, but his finger repeatedly stroked the soft, colorfully embroidered deerskin bag.

"I can feel the magic awakening in you as well as your melody, flute player. Time will tell If you will choose the path to become a shaman."

Woodwind looked at his brother. "Perhaps you'll also follow this path."

Lonefeather tilted his head and smiled. "Then we bear brothers would be embarking on that path together. Let's get inside. I'm in the mood to celebrate."

Woodwind remained in his chair for another moment, grateful, but also a little surprised at the trust that Chinook had placed in him. His cell phone beeped, and he pulled it out. With a smile, he looked at the photo the librarian from the reserve had sent him. It was a picture of him on the day of his exam last week wearing a shirt, a tie, and a dark gray blazer. Even though it had only been an online exam, he had still wanted to look professional to make a good impression during the video conference with the three exam officials. He had given it all he had the past few weeks and studied hard. Once he had completed the written portion of the exam, he needed to then pass the question-and-answer session. Woodwind was sure that he had never sweated so much before in his whole life. But after four hours, he got word that he had passed and had immediately printed out his certificate with pride.

After the brief photo session, a small group of people was waiting for him outside the library to applaud and cheer when he came out. Among them was Una, Nuka, Mina, and some of the other teenagers. They had prepared a celebratory meal for him. *This is what it feels like to have arrived and be at home*, he had thought during the meal, especially because Ayita and Wynono were also present.

Woodwind raised his eyes and blinked into the sun. "Thank you, wise man, for everything," he mumbled. Then he stuck the medicinal pouch into the inside pocket of his leather vest and followed his brother.

The dinner table was overflowing with side dishes, plates, platters, and the smells of roasted meat, freshly baked bread, and herbs filled the house. Woodwind joined Lee's conversation with Cody and Chuck off in the corner. The men were talking about the wolf hunters.

"The four hunters have been identified," Chuck said. "They've been slapped with a hefty fine."

"Is it true then that this Jeremy Bull was behind it all?" Lee asked.

"At least, that's what they claim. They paid him for information on the pack's whereabouts. Bull wanted to use this money to secure his chances of becoming chief. A few of the Council members are said to be bribable and are okay with being persuaded to sell their votes for chief." Chuck took a sip from his beer bottle.

"That means Rabbit was spot on with his suspicion." Woodwind looked at the others. "But how could Bull know precisely where the pack was at any given time?"

"The Cree are allowed to hunt in this area anytime they want," Eric responded. "It was once their land, which makes the regulation is justified, but Bull abused this right by having spies from the reserve work for him. These individuals are allowed to be in the protected area without notifying the forestry office and therefore, they were always the first to know about the wolves' migratory movements."

"Is there any way to prove Bull's involvement?" Woodwind asked.

"I don't think so, though he can forget about becoming chief," Chuck answered as he smiled at someone standing behind Woodwind. "My dad skills are being called upon. Gotta go." Chuck went around the group to join Sarah, who was bounding baby John on one arm.

"I'm going to go have a look at what Emma is conjuring up in the kitchen," said Cody.

"Two happy men, they are," Lee remarked.

"Three," Eric corrected him, raising his beer bottle. "I'll also sneak into the kitchen and see if I can get a taste of something from Jeanne." He walked away grinning.

"By the way, Naira and I are very happy that you were still able to get permission from the authorities to be a youth counselor."

"And I'm just happy to have the exam over and done with," Woodwind added.

A hand appeared on his shoulder, and he turned his head.

Naira smiled at him. "You should be very proud of yourself." She slowly pulled her hand away.

He caught sight of something sparkling and looked her in the eye. "Let me see," he said.

She grinned as she held out her hand to him. He marveled at the finely crafted ring on her finger.

"I barely leave the two of you alone for a second and come back to find you filling your heads with crazy ideas," he joked.

"It's true. We were unsupervised." Lee grinned as he took Naira's hand.

"And naked," she added. "But we want to keep it under wraps for a little while still."

He motioned turning a key over his lips. "You won't hear anything out of me," he mumbled.

She giggled. "Let's go get ourselves some beers. You want one too?"

"No, I'm sticking to my soda." He nodded at Lee and Naira and sat down at the table next to Ayita. "Where's Wynono?" he asked.

She pointed to the sunroom. Samantha was sitting on the floor playing with Ayita's son. The boy seemed to be explaining something to her, and his words rang out like a melody to Woodwind's ears. Wynono had started speaking. It was a miracle. He laid his hand on Ayita. "How are you doing?"

"I haven't had a drink for the past three weeks. It isn't easy, but I plan to hang on."

"You can do it. You have all of us to help you."

One by one, the guests took their seats around the table. Lee raised his glass. "Thank you all for coming. Today is a day of celebration to honor Naira's grandfather Chinook. We also want to welcome Ayita and her son into our community. Let's raise a toast to spring, to new beginnings, to family and friendship."

"Hear, hear," Nick called out, leaning over to Rosie sitting next to him and kissing her. "And to love."

The guests raised their glasses, laughing and smiling as they clinked them. The food was served and a joyous atmosphere filled the room. Woodwind couldn't help wondering at the number of couples in love around the table, especially Eric and Jeanne, who were like teenagers again. He smiled and laid his silverware across his plate once he was finished eating. He felt the pouch under his shirt pressing against his chest. He glanced at Ayita, who was also finished eating. "Shall we go outside for a little bit?"

"Gladly. Wynono's in good hands with Sam."

They descended the porch stairs and followed the path between the willow trees. Their hands found one another, and their fingers intertwined as they silently enjoyed being together. When they returned, a campfire was burning in the backyard of the ranch house. They sat down somewhat apart from the others. Woodwind pulled out the medicinal pouch. Being near Ayita gave him courage, and he slowly opened it. Inside was tobacco, sage, a grizzly bear claw, birch bark, and a small clipping of both white and black wolf fur. He swallowed audibly and allowed himself to feel his grief over the shaman's death. Ayita placed her hand on his back, gently making circular movements until his sobs died away.

"You will make a wise shaman," she said.

"Will," he repeated. "If this really is my path. I still have so much to learn."

"And you will." She took his hand. "I still owe you my gratitude."

He looked up. The orange glint of the flames reflected in her dark eyes.

"You saw light in me when I could only see shadows. You awoke in me the hope of a future that I was afraid of at first. And when I thought that loneliness was my fate, you believed in me and showed me that I never needed to feel lonely alone again." She placed her hand on his. "And I want to thank you for convincing me to speak to some of the elders who had experienced firsthand all the drama that had happened years ago between Marc and me."

"What exactly did you talk about? Will you tell me please?"

A single tear rolled down her cheek. "One of them was a former officer of the reserve police force. He was able to confirm that I had sought to get help back then. Because Mark was white, I had first turned to the RCMP for help after he had become violent the first time. But they refused to believe me, a young Cree woman. They ridiculed me, saying that I probably had it coming and could count myself lucky that a white man was even interested in me."

Woodwind inhaled sharply, but he knew that she was telling the truth, and let her continue.

"And when I was living with Mark on the reserve and had asked for help, no one there had wanted to get involved. It was my own fault for getting involved with a white man, after all." She shuddered with a sob.

Woodwind pulled her into his arms and hugged her tightly until she had stopped crying, then he held her at arm's length and looked at her. "We need to let go of our pasts, the pain, and the shadows to make room for light and joy. I, too, had to learn that recently, and you gave me the strength to do it."

Ayita smiled and nodded. "The elders have apologized to me and officially welcomed me into the reserve. I can leave the darkness behind me and finally focus on building a future." She leaned over to him and kissed him gently but determinedly.

Woodwind felt this kiss in every fiber of his being, and it felt as though all the shards inside him had been pieced back together. He reached into his vest pocket and pulled out his small, hand-carved flute. He ran his tongue over his lips; they still reverberated from her touch. Playing the flute opened up his heart all the way to the very back corners. The melody, soft and penetrating, was picked up by the evening wind. He saw from her eyes that the notes had pierced her soul and that she understood all the words he didn't have the courage to say. When the melody was finished, he took the flute in both hands and broke it in two.

The End

Acknowledgments

Is anyone still reading this? I think so ... well, maybe one or two.

When we think about a movie production, everyone knows that it's Teamwork, and we can read all the names of the people involved rolling over the screen, after we have watched the movie.

With a book, it is not so clearly stated and many readers might still live with the impression, an author is a one-person team.

We are, when we are in our writing process of the rough draft ... well I am. But once I come out of my writing-hole, I thank all the people around me, who had my back, carried away my sorrows and worries while I was writing, and my partner, who did chores on my ranch and brought me food ... THANK YOU, GREGORY!

I simply will use this page to say thank you to everyone that knows me. Okay, maybe that's a little bit too broad. A special thanks and big hug goes out to my campfire-community, you are my VIPs.

Thanks to the editor and wonderful translator of this story from German into English.

The Canadian crime author Louise Penny wrote at the end of her first novel, that her greatest joy is not the fact that she published her first book, but indeed her joy is that she is able to thank so many people.

I second her words ... although I am incredibly happy to have published this fourth book.

author Natascha Birovljev im-
rated from Germany to Cana-
n 2005. She made her home
ranch in Alberta and lives
e with her horses and dogs. Her
ks show her fascination with
beauty of the Rocky Mountain
erness and her love for the peo-
she encounters in her chosen
e country.

natascha-birovljev.com/en

The books of the Willow Ranch set in the beautiful wilderness of the Rocky Mountains, tell stories about the lives of Canadian ranchers, cowboys and First Nation Communities. Adventures in the mountains and indigenous legends are intertwined with the longing for love, family and friendships. The stories around the Willow Ranch, the untouched nature and wildlife invite the reader to dream beside a crackling campfire.

natascha-birovljev.com

Manufactured by Amazon.ca
Bolton, ON

45993622R00203